The Ace of Diamonds

Vogue

Crown Jewelz Publishing

For the determined and the faithful

The Ace of Diamonds
Copyright ©2013 Vogue

ISBN-13: 978-0-9888004-0-3
ISBN-10: 0988800403
E-book: 978-0-9888004-1-0

Cover Design by Vogue

Quote on Front Cover by Edmund Burke

Website: www.simplyvogue.net
Email: blaq_pearls@yahoo.com; crownjewelzpub@gmail.com
Facebook: www.thefacebook.com/SimplyVogue (Author April Blanding)
Twitter: @SimplyVogue_B
Instagram: marilyn_monRHO1922

Part I:

Setting The Stage

Chapter One

"Sir, can I help you?"

Jay's eyes traveled around the main lobby of Davenport Realty as he took in the space. It was tastefully decorated by illustrations of luxury home floor plans and commercial real estate properties. In addition, there were several framed portraits that lined the wooden walls. Jay's attention was more focused on the single portrait of Lotus Pagua, which hung above the receptionist's desk, than the receptionist in front of him. He was staring at the portrait when her voice sounded once again in his ears. This time, she had a slight attitude.

"Sir, do you have an appointment? Who are you here to see?" she asked.

Jay raised his brow, hearing the harshness in her tone. He looked down at her desk and saw an enormous amount of paperwork. He figured she had other things to do so he decided to stop stalling. "Lotus," he told her.

The woman looked at him quizzically, and it was then Jay realized his mistake. Most people were unaware that the owner of the real estate company was born Lotus Pagua. "Harold Davenport, I need to see Harold Davenport," he told her, and then held up his briefcase as a sign he had come on business. The woman didn't seem to recognize him, a factor that could potentially work in his favor.

"You know, Harold Davenport retired. You chose the right day to come because he is actually in a meeting with the new CEO of the company. You'll have to wait until the meeting is over, though. Why don't you take a seat over there," she suggested, as she stood up from her desk and pointed to a row of chairs in the waiting area. "Would you like some coffee?"

Jay ignored her question, and headed to the row of empty seats. He sat his briefcase in the seat next to him before giving the lobby another once-over. The building that housed Davenport Realty was far more upscale than the premier office in Brookstone. Jay assumed the Texas location was more profitable.

"Yeah, yeah, yeah," a male voice burgeoned. "Don't make me have to come back up here. I retired for a reason."

Jay plastered a smile on his face as he saw Lotus walking into the reception area. He appeared to be in a dismal mood from the signs of stress on his face. It made Jay think twice about approaching him; however, he was determined that his visit to Dallas was not going to be in vain. He rose to his feet quickly and stepped into Lotus' path.

"Uh…" Lotus uttered as he blinked his eyes twice to make sure he was seeing right. Certain he was, he looked Jay over from head to toe. Lotus hadn't spoken or seen Jay in years. Jay lived in New York, so Lotus knew he had intentionally come to Texas and sought him out for a specific reason.

"Do you have a moment for Hector's son?" Jay asked him with a smile. He followed Lotus' gaze, which was fixed on his briefcase. He then looked back at him only to see his facial expression had turned to one of nervousness.

"Sure, I was headed out," Lotus told him, nodding his head. "Come with me."

Jay quickly grabbed his briefcase and followed Lotus out of the building. A black limousine awaited them directly in front of Davenport Realty. Jay made no hesitation in getting inside although his own limo was across the street in the parking deck. Before turning to address Lotus, he sat his briefcase in between them and buckled his seatbelt.

"Why are you here?" Lotus asked. "You're the last person I'd expect to see in Dallas."

Jay chuckled, because it was obvious Lotus was suspicious of his presence. He couldn't blame him, either. It had been a long time since they had held a conversation, besides; Lotus wasn't exactly his biggest fan. "Our paths are always bound to cross. I'm Hector's son, remember? He was your best friend. I also have two kids by your daughter, Carmen, and not to mention a little princess on the way. Your grandkids are a good enough reason for us to talk."

"Are you counting Rakim as your son?"

Jay looked over at Lotus hoping he could read his facial expression. Instead of answering his question, he opened up his briefcase. He pulled out a white envelope and handed it to him.

"As you can see," he said as Lotus opened the envelope, "I do believe Rakim is my son. If you want me to be honest, I always believed he was. I just didn't push the issue as much as I should have. Now that Carmen has broken up with me, I am going to push the issue. Rakim is still very young, but he needs to know I'm his father. By the time I get back to Brookstone, Carmen will have a copy of these court papers."

Lotus looked at Jay as he took the papers out of the envelope. He read the documents quickly before placing the papers back inside. "Is this how you intend to get her back?" Lotus chuckled in disbelief. "You take her to court for a DNA test, and then sue her for paternity fraud? Rakim is almost a year old. If you really thought he was your son then you would have did this a long time ago. Why bring it up now?"

The question Lotus posed was a good one. Jay was unsure of how to answer other than to explain it took him a while to make sense of it all. "Carmen told me her husband couldn't have kids. I believed her, but I got confused when Kane came with his paternity test. I thought maybe a miracle had happened. You know, maybe he was Rakim's father after all. Then, I used my common sense and remembered Kane had never produced a child naturally. The only child who is biologically his is Kristian and they used in vitro to conceive her. I know Rakim is my son. Since Carmen doesn't want to admit it, I have to take matters into my own hands."

Lotus gave the envelope back to him. "Okay, so what do you want from me?"

Jay focused the conversation on the real reason he had come to Dallas. He had recently linked up with one of his old comrades who had helped him put millions into a new investment, one he wanted Lotus to help him out with. His plan was to use their connection to his advantage.

"I figured since I'm Hector's son you would help me."

Lotus was taken aback. "Help you? Help you with what?"

Jay knew what he said next was going to send Lotus into a fury. "I need a warehouse," he told him, quickly.

"Oh hell no," Lotus said, taking off his seatbelt. "Stop the car, Arnold. Pull over."

Jay unbuckled his seatbelt as well. He grabbed Lotus' shoulder, in an attempt to calm him down. "Lotus, come on, listen to me. I know you helped me with this before, but I need another one. I mean, you sold me the building for Blue Magic. I'm making honest of the restaurant, aren't I? I promise you, I will—" Jay was interrupted as Lotus screamed in his ear.

"Are you out of your damn mind? What kind of shit are you getting into now?"

"I can't go to anybody with this project. I don't need a lot of ears or eyes on this. I trust you, Lotus. I know you won't publicize this sale like you do the others. I know you will take the warehouse out of your company's listings way before the sale is even complete."

Lotus shook his head, nervously. If Jay was asking for a warehouse then there was probably some illegal operation about to go down inside of it.

The last time he had sold him one, he ended up using the space to house illegal drugs and weapons. Now, he wanted one again. Certain Jay was still running a drug cartel, Lotus didn't want anything to do with it. His days of working alongside a criminal enterprise were long gone.

"Sir, should I still pull over?" his driver asked.

Jay looked at Lotus, waiting for him to respond. He smiled when he told Arnold no. It was a clear sign Lotus probably wanted to know more. If he did, Jay could potentially be leaving Dallas with a place to house his newest project.

"Jay," Lotus began. "Do you really think I'm going to risk my real estate business for your criminal enterprise? You know what, don't answer that. Arnold, head back to the parking deck so we can drop Mr. Santiago off."

Jay became uneasy as the conversation took an unexpected turn. He knew now he had to pull out all of the stops if he wanted Lotus to comply. "I'm begging you. You were my father's best friend, his right-hand man. I know our relationship hasn't always been good, but I'm asking you to put our differences aside. I'm not trying to get you in any trouble. I want to keep everything that is done between us discrete."

Lotus closed his eyes briefly as he thought of Jay's father. Everything Jay was saying was true. He had been Hector's best friend. In addition, he was also legally Jay's godfather. It was a secret he had never made known. Part of the reason was because his main concern had always been in establishing a new identity. He didn't want anything to do with Hector's criminal enterprise, which was why he had broken away in the first place. Even now, he didn't want to take part in Jay's project. Lotus felt if he gave Jay what he wanted, he wouldn't be working in his best interest. Instead he could be aiding him in getting another seventeen year stint in prison.

As the limo eased into the median, Lotus knew he was pressed for time. He still had to break the news to Jay that he wasn't going to help him and reveal his secret. If he gave Jay a heartfelt explanation of why he wouldn't help him, he would accept it. Besides, it was time for him to let a skeleton out of the closet.

"When you were first born," he revealed, "I signed court documents to be your godfather. Hector wanted me to watch over you in case anything ever happened. I hate to admit that I failed in that department, but I did. Even when we reconnected, I didn't play the part I was supposed to. But, today is a new day." Lotus turned towards Jay so he was staring into his eyes. "I don't want to see you back in prison. I don't want to see you following in your father's footsteps either. I know you're still running the cartel. Right now, I'm looking out for your best interest. My daughter is having a baby by you that is due this month. You need to be around to see that child grow. I don't believe you intend to use this warehouse legally and because of that, I won't help you. That doesn't mean I hate you or I'm trying to be spiteful. It means I want to look out for your best interest."

Jay looked out the window as the driver parked the limo directly across from his own. The bomb Lotus had dropped had made him speechless. He never thought in a million years that Lotus Pagua could be his godfather. Lotus was right when he said he hadn't played the part. He had been absent from his life for many years. While his secret helped Jay to better understand Lotus' stance, he still wanted his warehouse. Deep down, Jay knew Lotus wouldn't let up. Therefore, without bothering to respond, Jay got out of the vehicle.

Lotus took a deep breath as Jay's lofty frame disappeared into a white limo. He wasn't quite sure how to take Jay's reaction. In addition, he was very curious about his godson's newest venture. *What are you up to now? You're too much like your father, always working on something.* Lotus sighed at the comparison. He got ready to direct Arnold towards his house until he noticed a black velvet bag on the seat opposite of him. He had never seen Jay place it there but he figured his godson had pulled a fast one on him. Lotus picked the bag up, loosened the strings, and glanced down into it. A slight snicker escaped his lips as he saw the bag was full of diamonds.

***

Silence is golden, was the first thought in Carmen's mind when the door to the conference room finally closed. After three hours of being hemmed up in a meeting over the future of her company, she was glad to get some relief. The meeting had lasted longer than usual because it was the last one she would attend before her maternity leave.

Carmen was nervous about the break although she wanted and needed it. She trusted her team with the company, but what she didn't trust was the competition that was on the rise. Everyone at Flame, Inc. was aware of Mantra Designs, a California-based company that was making headlines in the fashion world. The numbers that company was putting up were too close to the numbers Flame was putting up. There were a slew of things she wanted to do to give Flame an edge. The timing wasn't right. Carmen believed that her ideas would have to be put on hold until the New Year.

She walked to the back of the conference area, hearing the sound of someone joining her in the room. She had expected more time to herself, but obviously, she wasn't going to get it.

"Mrs. Kane?" the person asked.

The voice behind her was male, professional sounding, and not recognizable. The latter prompted Carmen to turn around. She stared at the man in front of her, questioning in her mind why he was in her conference room. He looked to be of Hispanic descent and wasn't one of her employees. "Yes, I am Mrs. Kane," she told him. "Can I help you?" she asked, holding out her hand. He didn't shake it, choosing to place a large manila envelope inside of her palm.

"I'm here to drop off a letter from the law offices of Stern & Gomez."

Carmen bit her lip. She was very aware of the law firm and knew that Gomez was Jay's lawyer. For some reason, her mind was telling her that Jay was suing her. To find out why, she ripped the envelope open. "What is this?" she asked the process server as she pulled the papers out. He ignored her, leaving the room. "What is it not," she muttered as she glanced over the papers. "Mr. Santiago *is* suing me."

Carmen threw the papers down onto the conference table as she tried to control her anger. The lawsuit had come out of nowhere. She had spoken to Jay on numerous occasions, and he had never hinted that he was suing her. He also had never questioned Rakim's paternity aside from when Kane had first presented his test results. Now that he had placed a lawsuit in her hands, Carmen knew Jay was up to something. She thought to call him, but she needed to calm down first. If she didn't, she would only feed him a mouthful of expletives. He may have deserved it, but she didn't need anyone hearing a screaming match.

Carmen picked up the court papers and went back into her office where she hid them in her drawer. Only minutes away from five o'clock, she grabbed her purse and headed out of Flame. Traffic was always busy at the five o'clock hour, but somehow her driver, Donnie, had managed to be on time. His presence told her that she was only minutes away from being in the comfort of her home. Though she was upset over the lawsuit, she gave him a slight smile.

When her cell phone sounded in her coat pocket, Carmen knew her drive home may be delayed. She held up her right hand, signaling to Donnie that she was going to be a minute. She would have taken the call in the car, but there wasn't a limo partition. She never liked to discuss anything too personal around Donnie although he was her regular driver. Therefore, when she noticed that it was her father calling, she decided to answer while he waited in the car.

"Daddy," she greeted, taking a quick look up at the sky. "It's a little gloomy here," she told him. "How's the weather in Texas?"

Carmen expected to hear a response. Instead, all she got was silence. She was about to say his name once again until he finally spoke. His voice sounded troubled, which caught her attention more than the words he was saying.

"I would've called you earlier," he began, "but I had to get my mind together. You won't believe who paid me a visit yesterday." He didn't give her a chance to reply before he continued. "It was a Puerto Rican gentleman by the name of Jay Santiago. He was even carrying a briefcase."

Carmen felt her anger escalate to new heights. She had learned that Jay was suing her and now her father was telling her that he had paid him a visit. More than ever, she knew that Jay had something up his sleeve. Her father lived all the way in Texas, which meant that Jay had made a special trip. "You know," she replied, "that doesn't surprise me. It would have if he hadn't sent a process server. Did he tell you during his visit that he's suing me?"

Lotus' eyes closed when he heard his daughter's words. If Carmen knew about the lawsuit then it was possible that Kane did as well. He instantly became worried that the case would be another wound in their marriage. "I won't lie to you, Peaches," he told her. "He did mention it. He also mentioned that he wanted a warehouse. Now, I know you co-own Blue Magic. Are you two working on something else together?"

Carmen rolled her eyes in agitation. She didn't have one single clue as to why Jay would want a warehouse. He didn't need it for Blue Magic or his other businesses. Jay was embarking on something new that he hadn't shared with anyone. "Daddy, I'm being honest," she said, trying not to let her frustration show. "Jay and I aren't on the best of terms because of the break-up. If we do talk, then it's about Blue Magic and our kids. I don't know what he has going on."

"Well, I guess we're in the same boat," he replied with a sigh. "What about Rakim's paternity? What are you going to do about that?"

Carmen grunted as she turned to face Flame. She stared up at the high-rise building, planting her eyes on her office window where she had stashed the court papers. "I'm going to let this one play out in court. Jay will do his test, and Kane will do his. If it comes out in Jay's favor then I'm going to do what's right. I will make sure that Jay has a relationship with his son. I will also change Rakim's name."

Carmen took her eyes off the window, staring back into the street. It was then that she noticed the white limousine slowly pulling up behind her own. She could hear her father speaking to her on the other end, but the car had taken her attention away from the conversation. Once the back window of the limo rolled down, she interrupted her father and said, "Well, well, well, Jay has decided to pay me a visit, too. Daddy, let me call you back. I need to see what this bastard wants." Carmen hung up the phone without bothering to wait for her father to say goodbye. Now that she had the chance, she was going to unleash her frustration on its source.

She walked towards Jay's limo and waved his driver away when he tried to open the door for her. She opened it for herself, pushing her way inside. "So you know we need to talk," she blurted, nearly sitting on Jay as she got into the limo.

Jay sat back in his seat as he caught Carmen's tone. For her to have an attitude, he knew that the process server had gotten in contact with her. He didn't want an argument, but he did want Carmen to know that he was serious. From the way she was looking at him, he knew they were about to have it out. "You first," he told her.

At that moment, Carmen wished that she had the papers with her. If she did, she would have torn them up right in his face. Instead, she ranted, "You are one sick motherfucker, you know that? Out of all the meetings we've had, the checkups you've come to, you never said one word about Rakim's paternity. Now, you want to file a lawsuit. Did you read about Mantra Designs and said, 'Hey, let me find another way to fuck up Carmen's day?' Tell me, Jay, what is really going on?"

Jay's reply would have been filled with curse words, too, if Carmen's anger wasn't a turn-on. He smiled evilly at her as she continued to fuss.

"Then, my father calls me from Texas to tell me that you visited him. He said you asked him for a warehouse. Now, if *I* remember correctly, and it was like twenty fuckin' years ago, you asked him for a warehouse before. Is it for the same purpose?"

Jay's eyes narrowed as he realized how much Lotus had revealed. He never expected him to tell Carmen about the warehouse. Not wanting her to know yet, he decided to change the conversation back to Rakim. "Number one," he said, sternly, "if I remember correctly, your husband can't have kids. If he hasn't produced a child in twenty years then I'm certain that one night of fuckin' isn't going to make a difference. I let it slide for a long time because I thought that maybe a miracle had happened, but I'm not anymore. God knows and I know that I'm Rakim's father. Number two," he continued, "I did ask your father for a warehouse, and no was his final answer so we don't have to discuss it any further."

Carmen hated the tone he was using. It was firm yet he wasn't displaying the same anger that she was giving. "I have a very strong feeling that you're doing this because I broke up with you. If you felt like Rakim was yours then you should have done a test after Kane presented his. Wouldn't you want your child?"

Jay agreed with her. He should have done the test a long time ago. If he had, he wouldn't have missed some of Rakim's milestones. Now, after they went to court, he would have to play catch up. "I do want my child, which is why I'm going to let this play out in court. Do you agree?"

"I most definitely agree!" Carmen shouted. She set her purse down in between them, readjusting herself. Their unborn child, Nyla, was starting to kick, making her position rather uncomfortable. "If you win, you'll get what you rightfully deserve. If you lose, oh, I suggest you run back to that damn island. I got enough shit written about me on the blogs already."

Jay snickered as he reached his hand out to touch her stomach. She pushed it away, but he still reached out once more. This time, she allowed him to feel Nyla's kicks. "Speaking of winning, I want to discuss another business proposition. We both know that I can't do this drug shit forever. It caught up with me once before and I want to bow out before it does again. I've been conjuring a new idea."

Carmen pushed his hands away in disbelief. There he was admitting that he was suing her and in the same breath, he was asking her to team up with him. The last thing she wanted to do was go into business with him. It was bad enough that her name was on Blue Magic. "Have you been getting high? Why would I go into business with you if you have a fuckin' lawsuit hanging over my head?"

"I realized," Jay began, ignoring her question, "that you were the greatest asset that the cartel had. We never had a girl in the crew or at least it wasn't known. The whole time I thought it was my best friend, Carlos, who was stacking paper, but it was you. I see now that we work well together, be it legal or illegal. Your father turned down my offer, but he didn't have anything to lose or gain. As for you, if you help me, I'll drop the lawsuit."

Carmen's eyes narrowed in anger as she realized Jay's game. He wanted her hand in his business in exchange for a lawsuit. The thought of it all made her chuckle. Jay was definitely pulling out all of the stops. It made her wonder what it was that he was working on. "Drop the lawsuit? Well, it's obvious that Rakim's paternity isn't as important to you as getting my signature on your new project. That was a little low for even you to stoop."

Although Carmen made it seem as if she had him figured out, Jay knew that she didn't. If she had fully read the court papers then she would have known that she wasn't the only person he was suing. He had named her husband as well. "Don't get it twisted, Carm. I'm doing the paternity test. I won't take *you* to court, though. I'll still sue your husband. Right now, though, I want to get back to my proposal. If you really think about it, you've always been my Bonnie. Blue Magic was my idea, but without you, it wouldn't exist. We work well together. Our restaurant is evidence of that. Our kids are, too."

Carmen shook her head at how Jay continued to look past her anger. He kept trying to coax her as if she hadn't been handed a lawsuit. A large part of her wanted to slap him for his insensitivity, but she didn't. She decided to remove herself from the situation. She couldn't sit there any longer and listen to anything else he had to say. He had turned her entire day upside down and it was getting worse the longer she stayed in his presence. Before she gave him her reply, she got out of the limo. "My answer is no," she told him, leaning back inside. "Not just no, but hell fuckin' no." Not bothering to wait for his reaction, she walked back to her limousine, got inside, and directed Donnie to take her home.

Meanwhile, Jay grabbed his seat belt, putting it back on. He watched patiently as Carmen's limo merged in with the rest of the traffic. He then ordered his driver, Gus, to do the same. As he started to think things over, he realized that Carmen was the last lifeline he had when it came to his project. Other than her father, he didn't see himself collaborating with anyone else. He had no choice but to convince Carmen to help him. He had done it before with Blue Magic so he was certain that he could do it again.

Carmen would never admit it to him, but he knew she loved diamonds even more than he did. If she hadn't left so abruptly, he would have told her more about his plans. He knew now that he had to meet up with her again. The question of where was stuck in his mind. If he asked her to dinner, he knew she would say no. It also wasn't the best option to approach her at work. Still, he needed to do something to show Carmen that he was serious.

He decided to go with his next thought, which was to give her a bag of diamonds. If he did that, he knew the tables would turn. Carmen would become curious about his project and possibly want to know more. The sooner she had the diamonds, the better. He made a mental note to put together her gift as soon as he got home. Once that was settled, his mind could move on to other things. The first being the meeting at Blue Magic he was having in the morning.

Chapter Two

Blue Magic was housed in downtown Brookstone about three blocks away from Flame. It sat on the corner of 34th and Pendleton in a building that favored a brownstone rather than the traditional restaurant. The building spanned three stories—the restaurant was housed on the ground floor while the second floor was completely vacant. The third floor, however, had been constructed to be a large conference room, which served as the meeting space for the newly rebuilt Santiago cartel. The entrance to the room was guarded by Costa, one of the cartel's newest additions. A former bouncer, he served more as a bodyguard than a drug dealer. No one gained entrance to the conference room or better yet the third floor without going through him. Search and seizures were a common practice before any meeting took place because Jay believed it would help eliminate any narcs.

Jay signaled to Costa to close the door so the meeting could start. "In less than two years," he began, "we have taken over the drug trade of ten major states. Our west coast market is slowly booming, but in due time it will be where we need it. With more states, comes the need for more men. We all know about the situation with my son, King. He has already gotten a lesser sentence thanks to his defense team, and the judge getting a nice check. Still, he won't be home until next year and with him being gone things are going to get complicated. As you know, I have a little princess on the way and so does Malik. What all of that means is this: you will be seeing less of us, but more of someone else. We are looking for someone who can step up and keep things going while we take a hiatus."

Jay paused, catching his breath. "It's a lot of work, a lot of blood will be on your hands, but we won't lead you into this blind. Some of you have already shown immense potential."

When Jay paused for a second time, a loud knock sounded at the door. He glanced toward it as he told Costa to see who it was. When the door opened, Rico walked in casually. One of King's best friends, Rico had proven himself to be a reincarnation of Malik's twin brother, Rakim. He was extremely loyal and trustworthy, which made him stand out from the rest of the men. It was because of his persona that Jay excused his tardiness. "I hope you brought something green with you."

"Bank rolls are in the trunk," Rico replied. He took his usual seat beside his cousin, Jerome. A plate of food was immediately brought in for him along with a set of silverware. "May I request an update?" he asked.

Jay quickly began to sum up what he had said. "Malik and I are taking a break. King won't be coming home until next year and we need someone to keep an eye on things. We would like to give one of y'all the chance to step up." Jay made sure to look straight at Rico. He had been watching him for a long time. Though it was always his original plan to hand things over to King, his son was busy paying his debt to society. In his absence, he had no choice but to go to his next pick. He hoped that Rico accepted the position.

Rico picked up the peppershaker, beginning to season his scrambled eggs. Though his mind was partially on his food, he did want to share his latest find. "I think we need to discuss the market in the South. I got a phone call today from one of my friends in Bankhead. Word on the street is that the man in charge took over North Carolina. He already has four states on lock and he's slowly coming this way. The way I see it, we might be neck to neck. Personally, I feel that it's better to have him as an ally than an enemy. Maybe, we should bring him in."

Jay's forehead became wrinkled right after Rico's announcement. His focus hadn't been on the South though he knew the area had some heavy hitters. None of them were on his level so he never felt that they were a threat. Obviously, the thought had crossed Rico's mind. Jay was unsure of how to tackle the issue so he was glad when Malik asked for the man's name.

"Shawn Blumington," Rico answered. "But he goes by the name of Blu. He owns two clubs and a restaurant in Copperton City. Soulshock, that's the restaurant and then he has The Kingdom and the Sphinx Club. He is obviously putting his dirty money to good use."

"We need to take over the South," Jerome added, picking up his glass. "We can extend our market."

Jay could tell that the boys were set on the monetary gain and neither of them was thinking of the problems that could arise by bringing in an out of towner. Everyone that currently worked for him had a connection to him or his son. It was never his intention to bring in anyone new. "You are proposing that we hand the knowledge of our affairs to a complete stranger. That could be a bad idea. Besides, what makes you think that he is willing to cooperate?"

"Come on, who wouldn't want a spot in the Santiago cartel?" Rico replied with a chuckle.

"If he's moving like he is, he may not. Am I scared to go head to head with him? No," Jay said, sternly. "However, the last thing I want is to spend seventeen more years in prison as a result of a turf war. I'm also not so keen on the idea of bringing in someone new. This meeting isn't about that. It's about picking one of y'all to watch things while Malik and I are gone. I would need to scope out this dude first before I even thought about dealing with him."

Rico's eyes lit up, realizing that he had a challenge placed in front of him. He could see himself linking up the two kingpins to create an even stronger organization. He didn't know much about Blu, but from what he had heard, he definitely knew how to make money. "I can set it up, if you give me permission to."

Jay wasn't quick to answer. The whole scope of the meeting had taken a very different direction than he had intended. He wasn't ready to give his final decision so he told the men to finish eating as he excused himself. Before he left, he tapped Malik's shoulder so that he'd follow him out of the room.

When they were both standing in the hallway, Jay said, "I went from trying to hand this thing over to someone in that room to one of them trying to give it to someone else. I am interested in meeting Blu, but I'm not trying to bring him into our organization." Jay stared into Malik's face, looking for a sign that his underboss was thinking the same thing.

"Blu may acquire us a larger market," Malik began, "but we don't know anything about him. If you let him into our circle then someone who was playing the front could potentially be dropped down to an errand boy. Imagine if that was you. Would you step down from your organization to go work for someone else? Or what about this, will he clash with us?"

"We won't know until we meet him," Jay answered. He folded his arms across his chest as he thought the matter over. "Right now, let's set up a meeting with him. We'll feel him out for a couple of days. I'll put him up in a nice hotel and give him a nice Brookstone welcome. We'll also have Rico watch him for a few weeks to see how he is."

Malik knew that the plan sounded good yet he was still apprehensive about the whole thing. He wasn't set on bringing anybody new in, especially when they were trying to take a break. He understood why Jay wanted to meet Blu, but he didn't think that it should even go that far. "If he is running things like he is in the South, imagine how big his head would get when his name becomes attached to ours. He's going to want to be in charge. He's also not going to be pleased if he has to answer to somebody. We could potentially have an internal war on our hands."

Jay knew that Malik was right. Yet, something told him that he needed to see who Blu was. The man was claiming to have control of the drug trade in four states. If he was as ambitious as he was described then he was definitely someone that Jay needed to keep a close eye on. In a short amount of time, Blu could potentially run one of the largest cartels in

America. Jay wasn't threatened by it especially since he was considering breaking out. However, while he was still in the game, he wanted to keep his reign intact.

"I've made a decision," Jay said. "I'm going to have Rico set up a meeting with him. We'll feel him out for a few weeks and see where this goes. I'm not letting him in on any information regarding our operation. We need to get to know him as a person. After that, we'll discuss it again."

Malik let out a loud sigh once he heard Jay's decision. It wasn't what he wanted to hear, but he had already voiced his opinion. If Jay stuck to his word then they could potentially get out of the situation unscathed. If he didn't, they both could be fighting a battle that neither of them wanted. He gave Jay a simple head nod before following him back into the conference room. It was there that Jay made the announcement to the rest of the group. He then gave Rico the task of locating Blu. Once he found him, the man would be on his way to Brookstone, New York.

***

While Jay was busy planning the future of his cartel, Kane, was busy searching for his next case. He hadn't gotten far when Sanders ran into his office unannounced. His partner had a huge grin on his face, which let Kane know he had come to boast. Sanders had shown immense growth as a detective, which was proven with the slew of cases he had been handed. Kane assumed that he had been given another one with the way he was looking at him. The excitement that read on his face was clearer than a glass ceiling. "Do you have a new assignment?" Kane asked him, glancing back at his computer screen.

Sanders plopped down into one of the chairs that were in front of Kane's desk. He could barely contain his enthusiasm, which was shown when he stood right back up. He paced the floor as he started to tell Kane his news. "I got assigned one of the biggest cases to hit this department. It didn't even reach the desks at Triad."

Quite naturally, Kane snickered at his comment. Everything Sanders was handed, he deemed as being the biggest case to hit the Narcotics department. He put the label on every single one when in reality the cases were only mediocre. "If it's a really big case," he told him, "then the Triad would've gotten it first." Kane expected his words to dampen Sanders' spirit, but a smile was still plastered on his face. The sight of it made him exhale as he turned his attention back to the Triad's Most Wanted list on his computer screen.

Sanders' enthusiasm was slowly starting to fade as he realized that Kane didn't think his new case would be that promising. But Kane hadn't heard the details. Once he did, his whole attitude would change. "Three businesses in less than two years," he replied, plainly. He watched as Kane turned back to face him and continued, "I'm talking about your wife's ex-fiancé. Can you please explain how Jay Santiago acquired three businesses after seventeen years in prison?"

Kane minimized the browser window on his computer. Sanders had officially caught his attention. He had actually been given a case that should've been handled by a Triad agent. Kane didn't want him to know that he was slightly jealous, so he decided to play with his emotions. "I can explain," he replied. "First off, he had the help of Malik Washington. Then, he had the help of my wife, Carmen. He also put the businesses in King's name. We all know he received a nice chunk of change from his trust fund when he turned eighteen."

"So they all have some money wrapped up in his businesses?"

Kane swallowed, knowing he couldn't give Sanders a definite answer. He could only go off assumptions. "I don't know if they do. I know that they are all partners in the whole thing. Maybe they did kick out some money or something. Blue Magic was one of the buildings that were in Davenport Realty's listings. Carmen had major pull in that arena because her father was the CEO."

Sanders sat back down in his seat as he felt his excitement decreasing. He no longer had the same enthusiasm as when the lieutenant first handed him the assignment. Most if it was because of Kane's demeanor. He was being too nonchalant. Sanders tried to overlook it and continued to verbalize his thoughts. "Even if he had help from his friends and family, he still had to work with other people. He's a convicted murderer, Kane. Who in their right mind would grant him a business loan?"

Kane shrugged his shoulders in response to the question. He didn't know all of the people that Jay had business dealings with, but he did know three of them. If Sanders had been given the job of investigating Jay then he had to go after his wife as well. In addition, Malik and King would both be considered as accomplices. That part of the case didn't sit too well with him. "What's the bottom line?" he asked him.

Sanders smiled briefly. "He wants me to finish what you started. He wants to investigate Jay. Now more than ever, there are more drugs sweeping through this city. Lieutenant Harris believes that Jay is the source. If I can prove that, it may be my ticket to joining the Triad."

Kane felt as if the inevitable had been spoken. He was already thinking it and now it had been confirmed. Harris chose Sanders over him to investigate Jay. The whole idea made him want to explode. However, he couldn't blame the lieutenant. He had let Harris down once again when he admitted to having an affair with Tricia DeGonzaza, the mother of his two adopted children and Jay's ex-girlfriend. The lieutenant had no choice but to believe that he couldn't solve a case without falling for a woman involved. Kane knew that he had to change the lieutenant's opinion about him. To do so, he had to slide the case out from under Sanders. If he took down Jay, Lieutenant Harris would know that he still had his fire.

In addition, he could make sure that everyone he cared about stayed protected. Jay would be the only one to go down. If Jay were locked up, it would finally prevent Carmen from having any romantic dealings with him.

"Sanders, you're a good cop, we both know that. You even have the skills of the average Triad agent, but we both know that anything involving Jay should be put into my hands. I know more about him than any agent walking this earth. I wrote his file."

Sanders' facial expression turned to one of confusion. Kane wasn't sure what he was thinking, but he hoped that he had made him feel unsure of himself in some way. He wanted Sanders to think that he wasn't capable of solving the case. Once that happened, he would either give the case to him or ask for his help. Kane knew he would do the latter; though either way it went it would be beneficial.

"Look," Kane continued. "If the lieutenant wants to investigate Jay, that's fine, let's do it. Let's keep it real, you need me. You can't get close to Santiago without me."

Sanders knew that Kane's words were the truth. His ties to Jay were the strongest in the whole department. He also was their in-house Triad agent. He could only get so far on his own, but with Kane's help, he could bring home a win. "You're right," he agreed. "I do need your help. Are you going to help me?"

Kane knew when Sanders first started spilling the details that he would work night and day to make sure that Jay was locked up. "I am going to help you," he answered. "Let's get started." Kane held out his hand. As they shook on it, Kane smiled until an image of his wife appeared in his mind. Carmen wouldn't be pleased to learn about his new case. If things worked in his favor, by the time she found out, Jay would already be behind bars.

Immediately starting the investigation, their first stop was Blue Magic. From where they were parked across the street, Kane could see that business was in full swing. The crowdedness would help to ensure that their stakeout remained discrete while their unmarked car would blend in with the others around the restaurant. Not yet seeing anything suspicious, Kane hadn't taken any photos. Sanders, on the other hand, had been snapping pictures left and right. They were both looking at the same thing, but Sanders was ready to make everyone a suspect. Kane didn't become suspicious until about ten men walked out of the main entrance. They were dressed in designer suits and stood out from the rest of the restaurant's customers. The sight of them made Kane grab his camera.

He zoomed in and snapped a few photos as he recognized two of the men. Rico and Jerome McFadden were his stepson's best friends. He saw them on a regular basis for four straight years back when they were arrested for fighting, truancy, or selling dope. What he was seeing now was very different from the roughnecks they used to be. In fact, they both looked like executives who were ready for Wall Street. He wasn't quite sure what Rico and Jerome were up to, but he had a feeling that it had something to do with Jay.

"Look at them, they all look top dollar," Sanders muttered as he snapped a few more pictures. "So you think Blue Magic is where they conduct their meetings?"

Kane glanced over at Sanders before looking back at the restaurant. "That's a possibility," he responded. "The building spans three floors. Only one of them is used for dining. If the other two are vacant then it would be the perfect spot." Kane dropped his camera back into his lap when he realized that he was taking photos of the same subjects. He planned to scan the photos into the department's database to see if there was a possible match with anyone who had been booked. It would help him at least identify the other eight people. He stared at the men as they retreated to the restaurant's parking lot. Minutes later, a trail of luxury vehicles emerged.

Sanders snapped photos faster than he had been doing before. "Those boys must be stacking real well. They didn't even have cars two years ago. Now, they're pushing Benz's. I know something illegal is up in that. I can easily see a couple of grams or a kilo being hidden in one of those cars. With all the new compartments they're making, you can hide a whole family in your ride."

Kane agreed with him. He knew that Rico and Jerome didn't get those cars by any legal terms. His hunch deepened when he saw Jay and Malik walk out of the restaurant. They were dressed similar to the men who had come out before them. He grabbed his camera and snapped Jay's photo until he disappeared inside of a white limousine. Malik didn't join him, but had walked behind the building to the parking lot. "I think we've seen all we need to see," Kane stated. "If you ask me, there had to be some kind of meeting going on. They are all dressed alike and came out within minutes of each other. I say we create a list of who these men are and scope 'em out."

Kane started the car, pulling away from the restaurant. With ten potential suspects, he was certain that at least one of them could become an informant. At this point, anything could be a potential lead. He even drove into Flame's parking lot to see if a white limousine was in the vicinity. He circled the area twice, but the car wasn't in sight. Since it wasn't, he continued on to the police station.

***

Kane's presence outside of Flame was unbeknownst to Carmen though her husband was on her mind. She knew that Kane didn't know about the lawsuit, but it was hurting her that she hadn't disclosed it. With the clock now reading two-thirty, the guilt was steadily pounding her chest. Every time she thought to tell him, the words wouldn't come out. Now, she ran the risk of him finding out on his own. She feared that happening so she made a promise that she would tell him in the morning. She prayed that he didn't find out before then. If he did, she knew he would confront her about it.

Carmen decided to roll with that idea as her phone rung. The number calling her was listed as unavailable, but she picked up anyway. With fashion connects around the world, anyone could have been on the other line. "Carmen Davenport-Kane speaking," she greeted.

The voice on the other end didn't give a similar greeting, but simply said, "I miss you."

Carmen immediately hung up the phone. She could recognize Jay's voice from a mile away. She knew now more than ever that he was playing a game with her. He hadn't made comments like that since their breakup. His new project obviously had prompted his change in behavior.

When her phone rung a second time; she didn't answer it. Not that it mattered to Jay. He called her for a third time before leaving a voicemail message. For fifteen minutes, Carmen went back and forth about whether or not to listen to it. When she finally decided to, she braced herself for whatever he might say.

"It's obvious, Peaches," he said on the recording, "that you're still upset with me. I understand why, but I still want to talk. The only reason I called is because I want you to know that I'm sending you a package. You should get it tomorrow. We spoke about my project, but I never went into detail about it. All I'm asking is that you hear me out before you say no. Give me a call whenever you get it."

Carmen rolled her eyes as she pressed the button to delete the message. Jay could send his package all he wanted, but her answer was still no. She didn't care what was in it. She wanted him to leave her alone until they went to court. *Shoot*, she thought, *as if I'm not worried about enough. Now, I got him back on my ass! Instead of worrying about him, I need to be focused on my work. For the rest of the day, I am going to concentrate on this Peaches campaign and leave the personal problems alone.*

Her plan worked well and by the time six-thirty hit, Carmen was in the clear of all thoughts related to Jay. She left her office five minutes later, and slid into her limo as Donnie whisked her back home. On the way there, she made a quick phone call to her maid, Fiona, to get the heads up on dinner. The lady had a better memory than her, reminding Carmen that dinner was at Blue Magic. After thanking her for the reminder, she told Donnie to make his way back downtown. When she got to the restaurant, she spotted her husband's Jeep as well as their daughter's car in the parking lot.

"I know, I know," she said as soon as she was at their regular booth. "I forgot," she announced. She gave Rakim a quick kiss on the cheek before moving on to her husband's lips. Kane was sitting at the end of the booth next to Rakim's high chair while their other kids were in the middle. They were harder to reach so Carmen told herself that she would love on them later. At this point, she needed to play catch up. "Okay, so what did I miss?" she asked as she took her seat on the opposite end.

Kristian, who was sitting to the left of her, was the first to speak. She was in the first semester of her senior year at Brookstone High along with her adopted sister, Akaila. They both were set on leaving New York, having applied to the same college in Georgia. Carmen wasn't too thrilled with the idea of them being miles away, but she was more pleased that they were seeking higher education than anything. Malachi, on the other hand, was a freshman and had transitioned to high school fairly well.

"So, we checked the mail again today," Kristian announced. "Nothing yet from Copperfield," she continued. "My friends already know where they're going. Coco has already gotten her acceptance letter back from Howard. Dijuan is set for Duke."

Carmen sucked her teeth, playfully. She had told them both to apply to more than one school, but they hadn't listened. Now, they were sitting there with long faces like their future was doomed. "Sometimes, these things take time. There could be three thousand other high school seniors trying to get in. Keep your head up. Besides, if they don't accept you, you can always go to Brookstone. It's right up the street."

"No one wants to go to BU," Akaila interjected. "Almost everyone in our senior class is going there. We want to get out of New York."

Carmen mumbled a few words under her breath before sneaking a peek at Kane. He gave her a shy smile as if he had read her mind. He knew that she wanted the girls to stay close. She asked him with her eyes to help her out, but it was obvious that he wanted to stay out of the conversation. Malachi didn't bother to comment either. Carmen noticed a disgruntled expression on his face though she didn't ask about it. She had gotten to know him better over the years and knew when to leave well enough alone. She turned back towards her husband, watching him as he started to feed Rakim.

"This little boy can eat," he said, changing the subject. "What is Fiona feeding him?"

Carmen chuckled as the waiter approached the table. Since everyone else had ordered, she quickly placed hers before replying to Kane's statement. "The doctor says he's growing normally, but I beg to differ. I think he's bigger than most kids his age. Before you know it, he'll be eating your meals." Carmen watched as Kane parted his lips as if he wanted to say something but his phone rang. She thought he was going to ignore it until he answered. When she heard him say the name Sanders, and he left the table, she knew for sure he was on a new assignment. She tried not to let it bother her as she focused her attention on Rakim. It took a while for Kane to return, and when he did, she decided not to question him about the call. In due time, Kane would tell her about his case. Besides, she needed to be worrying about how she was going to break the news of Jay's lawsuit.

Chapter Three

Carmen's eyes naturally fluttered open when she recognized the sound coming from Kane's beside dresser. It was followed by his hand slapping the alarm clock and then sudden silence. She thought he had set the alarm back to snooze until she felt his movements in the bed. She would have preferred another fifteen minutes of sleep, but it was obvious she wasn't going to get it.

"Good morning, baby," Kane whispered, amiably. His hands rubbed alongside her lower back before landing on her bottom. He then planted a single kiss on her forehead, repeating his words again.

Carmen couldn't help but to smile inside. This morning was a perfect example of how she loved to wake up. Unfortunately, the grin she wanted to wear on the outside wouldn't come to fruition. She had promised herself that today she would tell Kane about the lawsuit. If she didn't, she ran the risk of him finding out on his own, which would cause unnecessary discord between them.

She opened her eyes only to see Kane staring directly into her face. His hands were still on her bottom, which he gave a slight smack. She giggled, the sound prompting him to kiss her lips. As much as she was enjoying his affection, she knew she needed to share her news. She couldn't let him stay in the dark although it was a terrible way to continue the morning. Carmen broke away from him as he sat up in the bed.

"It's a little after six-thirty," he told her, pushing the comforter off him. "I'm not sure what time you're going in, but I need to be at the precinct by eight. I'm not going to have time for breakfast so maybe we can meet up for lunch. What do you say?"

Carmen pursed her lips when he mentioned the precinct because it made her recall his behavior at dinner. She had let it go then, but now she wanted to ask him about it. "Eight is a little early for you. Most of the time, you're not there until ten. What are you working on?"

His eyes narrowed down at her as he grabbed his bathrobe. He put it on before giving her a sly grin which made Carmen even more suspicious. Kane could've pulled a fast one despite the many promises he had made to never go back undercover.

"Carmen, my main focus is the Brookstone PD. You know that. What I'm working on has nothing to do with the Triad. No worries."

Carmen couldn't help but to yearn for his words to be true. The minute he had said, no worries, her mind had begun racing back to the court papers. She told herself that the comment was a cue to start the discussion on Rakim's paternity. "We need to talk about something," she began. Kane was right in front of the bedroom door as if he was getting ready to go wake the kids. He looked at her inquisitively, and she continued. "You know that my relationship with Jay is not a good one. There was still some animosity because of the breakup. Lately, he has been contacting me. He has expressed some concerns over Rakim's paternity."

Carmen could already see the rage building inside of Kane; she knew once he hit his climax, he would unleash all of his anger on her. He dropped his arms down at his sides and furrowed his forehead.

"What did he say, Carm? What did he tell you?" he yelled.

Carmen stood on her feet so that they were at eye level. She folded her arms across her chest as she moved closer to him. "He filed court papers against us. He wants a DNA test to be done on Rakim. He is also suing us for paternity fraud."

Kane's eyes bulged out of his head. "I haven't received any fuckin' paperwork, Carm! When did you find out about this?"

"Tuesday," Carmen muttered. She sat back down on the bed as silence filled the room. She could hear doors opening in the hallway, but she prayed that their discussion didn't disturb the kids. "Look, Kane, I don't know how all of this is going to go. I—"

Kane interrupted her. "What the fuck does that mean?" he screamed. "You don't know how all of this is going to go?" He moved closer to her until he was only an inch or two away. He made sure to invade her body space so she could feel his wrath firsthand. "Rakim is my fuckin' son! Do you think I'm lying to you? Is that what you meant?"

Carmen held her hands up in defense. "I wasn't saying that, Kane. I'm…shit; I don't know what I'm trying to say! Jay has a pretty good argument to make. We haven't had a biological child together since Kristian. With her, we used in vitro. We all know that you have a problem when it comes to making kids. It's no secret around here."

Kane dropped to his knees so that he could stare Carmen in the face. He made sure that they were eye to eye before his next statement. "Ask me to my face if I lied."

Carmen didn't want to reply out of fear of the answer. She wanted to trust that her husband didn't yet the chance of Rakim being Jay's was great. Kane may have produced a test, but there was a small probability that an error was made. The thought made Carmen tremble and she grabbed her husband's hands. "I would be lying if I said I didn't have any reservations. I want to be honest with you, though. I also want you to be honest with me. Do you think that anything could have happened to alter your results?"

Carmen nearly cried at the expression on Kane's face. She knew he would have given her an earful if there wasn't a loud knock on their bedroom door. He didn't say anything to her as he rose up off of his knees. He walked to the door and opened it. When she saw that it was Kristian, she knew that the discussion was over.

"Is everything okay?" her daughter asked. "It was getting kind of loud in here."

Carmen stared at her husband, but she knew his answer to Kristian's question was no. He proved it when he mouthed the words fuck you before leaving the room. His harsh reaction was a clear sign that he was hurt. Yet, Carmen was hurt that he had never given her an answer.

"Mama, what's going on?" Kristian asked. She hadn't caught the full conversation, but her mother's tears said it all.

Carmen quickly wiped her face, rising from the bed. She moved closer to Kristian, rubbing her shoulders. "We had a disagreement," she summed up. "Go ahead and finish getting ready for school. Make sure Malachi is up."

Carmen knew that Kristian didn't believe her words. Still, she left the room, allowing her to be by herself. Although she needed to get a move on, she retreated back to her bed. She waited for Kane to return, but he didn't. Eventually, she gave up, going to work without speaking another word to him.

***

After his brief argument with Carmen, Kane had gone to one of the guestrooms. He stayed there for a good hour as he tried to get his thoughts together. A part of him was hurt by Carmen's question while most of him was hurt that she had reminded him that he couldn't have kids. In a way, his wife had told him that she believed he wasn't the father. He could understand her thinking, but he thought he had proven to her that he was. He had showed her a test that said Rakim was his. It was a certified medical document. Still, Carmen believed that he had lied.

Her questioning him had angered him to the point that he didn't want to see her. He waited until she left for work before he went back inside of their bedroom. It was then that he showered and dressed before heading downtown to meet Sanders. Signs of stress were on his face, but he hoped that Sanders wouldn't pry. If anything, they needed to be focused on gathering enough information to indict Jay.

As soon as he arrived, he called Sanders who informed him that he was on the rooftop of an abandoned building across from Blue Magic. His partner explained that it was beneficial for them to change locations ever so often in case someone picked up on their presence. Kane agreed and walked onto the rooftop as Sanders started snapping photos.

"Good morning," Sanders greeted, lowering the camera from his face. "I brought the finished list for you. It has the names of all the men we saw at Blue Magic yesterday. I know it was hard to hear in the restaurant last night."

"Thanks," Kane replied, holding out his hand. Once he had the list, he gave it a quick scan. There were only three names that he recognized while the others he knew belonged to men of Hispanic descent. Though it did aid them in knowing more about Jay's operation, Kane didn't care about Jay's workers. His main focus at this point was to simply take down Jay. He showed his new stance on the case by tearing the list in half before ripping it into tiny pieces.

"What are you doing?" Sanders yelled, attempting to grab the paper from him. It was pointless as it became scattered across the rooftop. "That was my only copy!"

Kane looked over at Sanders with a nonchalant expression. "What are they without their leader? The only person I want is Jay. He should be the focus."

Sanders stared into Kane's face, knowing that he had changed overnight. He went from being concerned about all the men to not caring about them. It was obvious that something had happened to change his focus and perspective about the case. "We needed those names to get closer to Jay. If we get one of them then we get an informant. You threw away our golden ticket. Now we're back to square one."

Kane shrugged his shoulders. Jay Santiago was his only target. If he got him back in prison then he wouldn't have to worry about him anymore. His life had been golden when Jay was serving out his seventeen years. After he was released, Jay had started his daily task of making his life pure hell. "Right now," Kane replied, "I don't give a fuck about them. I want Jay and that's it. If you want a new list, get it. I'm not working on taking any of them down. I'm making it clear to you now that I only want Jay."

Sanders inhaled as Kane stated his new direction on the case. He knew that his partner's drastic change was coming from somewhere personal. Not wanting to interfere, he saw that he didn't have a choice. As Kane's partner, his name would be attached to almost anything that he did. "What happened last night? When you were at Blue Magic, you wanted this. You begged me to finish the list. Now, it's nothing to you?"

Kane peered over at the restaurant as he realized his error. He didn't want Sanders to question him, but his actions and words led him to do it. Now, Sanders was looking for an answer. Kane knew that he deserved one, too. To get out of answering, he quickly mumbled he was leaving. He wasn't headed anywhere in particular, he simply needed to drive around the city until he cleared his head.

***

The day was continuing to be rocky, not only for Kane, but also for Carmen. It didn't surprise her one bit that it had started raining. She was already sulking and felt the weather was nothing but a manifestation of what she was feeling inside. Normally when she felt like this, she would throw herself into her work. At the moment, it was nearly impossible although she had plenty to do. Carmen was almost certain that she would get nothing done today. Most of the morning she had spent sulking and now she was on the phone with her lawyer, Clement, conferring about the details of Jay's lawsuit.

Clement had been tying up the loose ends of almost all of her business affairs for the past ten years. Then he went on to be the main person to tie up the loose ends of her oldest son's criminal charges. Carmen swore to herself that she paid the man more money to handle King's affairs than her own. Whatever he did for them, he always got the job done even if the outcome was jail time. Now that she needed him again, Carmen wondered what kind of strings Clement could pull. From the way their conversation was going, Clement didn't seem so sure of himself this time around.

The first words out of his mouth were, "The last thing you want is for this thing to get messy. The reason I'm saying this is because you told me that Jay saw Kane's paternity test. For some reason, Jay doesn't believe that test is legit. Now, I'm going to ask you this and you need to be honest with me, yourself, and your husband. Do you think Kane's test is legit?"

Carmen didn't answer right off and she knew her moment of silence answered for her. In her heart, Carmen wanted to believe that Kane's test was legit. For some reason, though, she did doubt it. She knew the doubt was coming from the fact that she had spent the majority of her marriage believing that her husband couldn't father a child. She had lost faith in him and even in the idea of conceiving naturally.

"Look, Carmen," Clement said, realizing that his client wasn't going to answer. "From the papers you've faxed to me, Jay is not only requesting that he and Kane take a DNA test; he's also claiming that Kane lied about the results. He's asking for a lot of money, which I know he will get if Kane's test is shitty. I'll be honest with you. You have a fifty-fifty chance of winning this thing. Kane can do the test and the results can come out in his favor. He also can do the test and have the results come out in Jay's favor. Now you're all good if Kane is truly the father. If the test says that Jay is the father, we might as well be up shit creek without a paddle. The only way I can get you out of possibly paying millions to this man is if we find the doctor who analyzed Kane's results. If the doctor made an error then we can sue him. Hopefully, Jay will drop that part of his lawsuit since nothing was done intentionally."

Carmen exhaled deeply after hearing Clement's response. Her concern wasn't in paying Jay a million or two. She could easily toss him the cash. Her concern was about her marriage.

"Okay, so you're still not saying anything," Clement said, interrupting her thoughts. "Have you talked to Kane about this? Has he been served?"

Carmen closed the blinds, and walked away from her office window. She sat down at her desk, knowing that she needed to be open with Clement. "I tried to talk to him this morning. As of yet, he hasn't been served."

"I see," Clement replied. "Well, maybe, I should wait until he is. He's going to need me, too."

Carmen nodded her head in agreement although Clement couldn't see. She had hoped that he would have said more, but it was obvious that their conversation was coming to an end. In addition, her receptionist, Cathy, had walked into her office unannounced with a FedEx box in her hands. "Clement, let me call you back," she said quickly, hanging up the phone. "What in the world…"

"FedEx came through." Cathy sat the large box on Carmen's desk before pointing at the mailing label. "It's for you."

"I figured," Carmen muttered, grabbing a box cutter out of one of her drawers. She sat it on her desk wanting to shake the box around to see if she could hear the contents.

"It's definitely not fabric," Cathy joked, hearing the rustling sound.

Carmen shook her head no, setting the box back down onto her desk. She twisted her mouth trying to figure out what it was. There wasn't even a return address on the mailing label. She started to drum her fingers on her desk until she remembered Jay's message. He was supposed to be sending her something regarding his project. Carmen knew that this was it.

However, she wasn't going to open the box with Cathy in her office. "Um, can you give me a minute?" she asked her. Carmen smiled at Cathy's reaction. The woman's ice blue eyes told her that she wanted to stay and be nosy. "Don't look at me like that. I need some privacy."

"Yeah, yeah, yeah," Cathy responded, giggling. "You're lucky you're the boss."

Carmen smiled as Cathy made her way back to her desk. The second her door was closed, she grabbed the box cutter, slashing the tape straight down the middle. Her hands immediately dived inside once both flaps on the box were opened. "Huh?"

Carmen frowned as she pulled out the thick wad of paper. Her fingers worked double time trying to unfold it as quickly as possible. The paper almost covered her whole entire desk and she understood why when she realized that she was staring at a floor plan of Flame. Carmen looked back inside of the box, spotting a black velvet bag in the upper right-hand corner. She grabbed it and loosened the strings, already having an idea of what was inside. A slight croaking sound emerged from her lips as she stared down at the vast array of diamonds.

More than a million dollars was right there on her desk. While the diamonds brought a smile to her face, it was one in particular that made Carmen gasp. The black diamond was the only one of its kind inside of the entire bag. She picked it up, and held it in the light. The stone was a rarity and the sight of it made her put all the diamonds back into the bag. She then proceeded to dial Jay's number. He answered within seconds, but she didn't give him a chance to speak. She told him to meet her at the Brookstone City Park in five minutes.

***

Jay's mouth had formed into a smile when he hung up from Carmen's phone call. He knew that when she saw what was inside the box she would come running. It made him think that he should have told her about the diamonds earlier. If he had, he would've already had a place to house his jewels. Now, he was waiting for Carmen to give the okay. When she did, he would start the construction of turning her basement into his own production facility.

After the call, he immediately headed to the Brookstone City Park. Once he got there it was a matter of seconds before he heard her calling his name. "So you got my proposal?" he asked her as soon as she got within earshot. "I knew that would do the trick. So," he continued, noticing that she hadn't replied. "What do you think?"

"I don't think you get it," Carmen snapped. "I think that you're willing to pull out all of the stops for whatever you want. The diamonds were nice, but you forgot one thing. To be honest, you almost made me forget. I know how you get your diamonds. You steal them. You hire professional thieves who rob the rich of their private collections. Now, you want me in on it, too. Since you forgot, let me remind you, I like my freedom."

Jay grumbled when he realized that she had fooled him. Carmen still wasn't going to cooperate not even after receiving a shitload of diamonds. If that didn't impress her, he didn't know what would. "I have stolen before. I would never lie to you about that. The diamonds that I gave you are not stolen. The stones are from an actual diamond mine. I bought them." Jay made sure that his eyes stayed on Carmen's as he spoke. He wanted her to see that he was telling the truth, but her expression said otherwise. He could tell that she thought he was lying. "On the real, Peaches, I can't do this drug shit anymore. I know I can't. I want to get out of it, but I got to slowly back out. I've got a lot of men on payroll right now. I got to set up something for them."

"So you break out of the drug game to enter the diamond trade? What does that have to do with me? What does it have to do with my father? I mean, you sent me a floor plan of Flame."

Jay started to walk away because he needed time to put his words together. Carmen was already on the verge of saying no, so he had to say the right thing to change her mind. "I need a place where I can house them. In addition, I have employed a slew of jewelers to turn the stones into some exquisite pieces for my new store, Iceland. My employees need a place to work."

Carmen narrowed her eyes as she heard his request. He wanted to use her building to stash his jewels. About to say no again, he didn't give her the chance. He started speaking at a fast pace like he was almost begging.

"I figured I could put them on your basement floor. We will fix the elevators so that the basement is only accessible by using a special code or combination. My packages are coming from overseas. They will be picked up by my FedEx connects on the border and then personally delivered to your basement for safekeeping. If you let me do this, I'll share some of the diamonds with you. It'll be like my rental fee. I know you enjoyed the first ones I gave you."

Carmen couldn't help but smile at his persistence. Still, she couldn't help him, no matter how much she enjoyed seeing the diamonds. There were too many people coming in and out of her company for him to run the kind of operation that he wanted. Even though he told her that the diamonds were acquired legally, Carmen didn't believe him. "The diamonds were beautiful, I will admit, but this whole thing isn't going to work. I know it won't."

"It will," Jay corrected. "You have FedEx men in and out of your building all day long. Anyone can see that. If we make the basement only accessible to the people that need to get to it then we won't have any problems. I will pay for anything that needs to be constructed. I need you to say yes."

Carmen exhaled as she went over his proposal in her mind. Jay made it sound so easy, but she knew it was because he wanted to use her space. She realized now why he needed the warehouse. She also knew why he contacted her father instead of another realtor. "Does anyone else know about this?" she asked him.

"No one, but you," he responded. "Your father got the diamonds, but he didn't know what I wanted the warehouse for."

Carmen shook her head as she heard the word no ringing loud in her ears. Diamonds had gotten her in trouble before and she was leery of having millions of them in Flame. "Jay, you are asking for a lot and at the wrong time. I don't have a choice, but to say no to you. For one, you are ruining my marriage with this lawsuit. Two, I don't believe that these diamonds were acquired legally. You say otherwise, but I need more proof than what you've given me." Exasperated with the whole conversation, Carmen said, "To be honest, I think we're done here. My answer is no and I bid you good day."

Jay kept a straight face as Carmen walked away from him. She was his last lifeline and he needed her help. He was being upfront with her on everything though she couldn't see it. It was the main reason why he stopped her. He grabbed her arm, turned her around so that she was facing him, and then gave her stomach a slight caress. "When I let this drug shit go, the money won't be the same. These diamonds are going to secure a future for our kids. You have money now, but we all know that Mantra is on the rise. Pretty soon, they'll be number one."

Carmen pushed his hands away from her. She was offended by the comment and she knew it showed on her face. "I'm not looking for some 'get rich quick' scheme. I've already set up a future for my kids, all six of them to be exact. It's the reason I work as hard as I do."

Jay could tell that he had hit a nerve. She was getting heated and so was he since she had declined his offer. "All of this," he replied, "is a surprise. I knew that when you got that stash that you were going to say yes. I swore on my father's grave that diamonds were the one thing that you loved more than me. I knew that when you saw those stones that you were going to get in on this."

Carmen was taken aback. She loved diamonds, but she loved her family more. She couldn't make decisions on a whim anymore. Everything she did affected someone else. "I do love diamonds," she admitted. "I also love my freedom. Believe it or not, you may make me mad, but I still love you. I definitely love you more than some damn stones."

Jay placed his hands back on her stomach. The second he touched her, he felt Nyla move inside. It put a smile on his face that his baby girl could tell that he was near. He looked at Carmen, and told her two simple words: "Prove it."

Carmen knew that Jay was testing her. He was using his charm to coax her, which was partially working. Nonetheless, she knew she had to stand her ground. "I can't do it. I'm sorry."

Jay rolled his eyes, realizing that it was going take more work than he expected. She may have said no, but that didn't mean he had to give up. He had to keep pushing her until he got what he needed. As he watched her retreat to her limo, he told himself to give her some more time. He would stop pressuring her for a few days to let the proposal sink in. Then, he would make another move.

Chapter Four

It was without question that the paternity suit had set the tone for the day. It stopped Kane from being able to focus on the Santiago case and kept Carmen from working on her fashion line. It was also one of the roadblocks that kept Jay from convincing Carmen to let him use her basement.

Not the only ones affected, Kristian was well aware that there was tension in the household. After her parents' spat that morning, she went to Akaila's room to ask her if she heard it. Her sister claimed she didn't before reminding her that her room was at the far end of the hall. Kristian hated to be the gossiper, but she told her all of the details of the argument. The quarrel had stayed on her mind for most of the day and even now, she was thinking about it.

"Did you check the mail?" Akaila asked, interrupting her thoughts.

They were sitting at the dining room table, both working on their homework while their brother, Malachi, pretended to be doing his. Kristian shook her head as the front door opened. Her father walked into the house, not bothering to speak. He walked up the steps like he was mad at the world. *Great*, Kristian thought, *now dinner is going to be even more awkward.*

"We should be checking every day," Akaila continued as she flipped through her notebook. "I should have done it before we came in."

Kristian listened as Malachi asked Akaila what she was looking for. Since the conversation had caught his attention, she decided to reply. "We're looking for our acceptance letters. We talked about it at dinner last night." Kristian looked at Malachi as he rolled his eyes. Seconds later, he flipped open his textbook like he was actually going to read one of the assigned chapters. "Um, is there a problem with Copperfield?" she asked him.

"Why do y'all want to go down South?" he shot back. "Why can't you stay here?"

Kristian chuckled at his tone before running through the list of reasons why Copperfield was at the top of their list. "For one, it's close to Atlanta. Second, Copperfield is known for their Theater program and I want to be an actress."

Malachi slammed his textbook closed. He didn't get up from the table, but his annoyance could be clearly seen and heard. "That's what all the models say. Do something new for a change."

Kristian met eyes with Akaila as her sister shrugged her shoulders. "Whatever, I'm going to go check the mail." Kristian left the dining room, heading outside. She was starting to think that the change in Malachi's behavior came from the fact that Akaila was going to be far away. They had lost their mother and with Akaila in Georgia, she could understand him feeling as if he was losing her as well. Still, she wanted him to lose his attitude.

When she reached the mailbox, she opened it only to reveal the large stack of envelopes, circulars, and magazines. She pulled everything out including two large white envelopes with Copperfield's logo. Both envelopes were the same size, telling her that she and Akaila both had the same fate. They had either gotten in or they hadn't. Without hesitation, she ran back into the house and dropped the excess mail down onto the floor in the foyer. "Akaila," she screamed, staring into the dining room as she held up the envelopes. "One is yours! Open it!"

"Did y'all get something?" Malachi yelled. He got up from the table as well, following his sister into the foyer.

"This is the news we've been waiting for." Akaila shrieked. She grabbed her envelope from Kristian's hand, starting to tear into it. Her sister was doing the same and before long, the torn envelopes were on the marble floor. Akaila ignored the letter on top, opening up the portfolio, which furthered advertised the college's amenities. "We're in!" she screamed.

"Congratulations on your acceptance to Copperfield University," Kristian began to read. "We commend your decision to seek higher education..." Kristian's voice trailed off as the excitement set in. "We've got to start shopping for college stuff!"

Malachi picked up the letter that Akaila had thrown down. "They accepted y'all?" he asked as he scanned it. When he saw that the college had, he dropped the paper back down onto the floor. "Man, that school will probably accept anybody. Y'all names are probably what got y'all in!"

"Shut up, Malachi," Kristian retorted. "We have excellent grades. Besides, one day you will be in the same boat."

"Hell no, I'm going to be hustling with King."

Kristian held the papers at her side. Based off Malachi's statement, she knew he hadn't taken King's situation seriously. If he had, he wouldn't want to be like him. "Hustling, Malachi? King is not a hustler. That was something he was. Right now, he's a businessman, one that happens to be in jail. You should learn from his mistakes."

"Man, fuck y'all!" Malachi yelled. He ran back into the dining room and grabbed his things before returning to the foyer. Without saying another word, he went up the steps, two at a time, as Kane was coming down. His footsteps were loud yet the slamming of his bedroom door was even louder. The sound of it made Kane pause on the steps as he looked up the steps.

Kristian could see on her father's face what he was thinking. He knew he had missed an argument and wanted to know what it was about. Though instead of asking her, he continued down the steps to the front door.

"I can smell dinner cooking," he said, not mentioning Malachi's behavior. "Tell Fiona not to save me any. I have some work in the field to do." Kane grabbed the doorknob, opened the door, and as he was about to step out, glanced back and said, "Tell your mother I probably won't be in tonight, too."

Kristian watched as her father stepped out of the house. First, Malachi was throwing a tantrum and now her father wasn't coming home. Not to mention, she hadn't even told him about the acceptance letters. Kristian looked over at Akaila wondering if both of their faces wore the same expression. Seeing that they were, she looked back at the steps not knowing which issue to tackle first, Malachi or her father's. Somewhat irritated, she decided to let Malachi be while she relayed her father's message to her mother.

***

The time on the bedside clock now read 1:06. At the sight of it, Carmen rose from her bed, flipping off the light switch. Though Kristian had warned her that Kane wasn't coming home, Carmen thought that he would change his mind. She knew there was tension between them; however, he was taking it too far. Every time he avoided her, he was making the situation worse instead of better.

Unable to take the distance any longer, she grabbed her cell phone from off her bedside dresser. She quickly composed a text message, which was their usual form of communication when they weren't close. *I miss you,* she wrote, *I know that things are awkward because of this morning, but we need to talk. We can work through this. You know we can. We've been through so much already. Be safe. I love you.* Now, all she hoped for was a response. Well aware that she couldn't be up all night, Carmen turned the ringer on. She set the phone on the dresser before pulling the covers up to her chin. Naturally, she tried to stay awake and catch his call. After about fifteen minutes, the phone hadn't rung and she dozed off to sleep.

***

Kane stuck his cell phone into his pocket after reading Carmen's message. It made a part of him feel guilty for not coming home, but he told himself he would make up for it. At the moment, he had to put his personal issues aside. For about five minutes, he had been parked outside of Jay's club, Sapphire, looking for any sign of Malik. While he had first come to tell his friend of Jay's lawsuit, he now wanted to warn him of the investigation. By giving Malik a heads up, he was now officially playing a dirty game. If Malik knew what was good for him, he would break his ties to Jay before the Brookstone PD got close. If not, he would be taken down in the crossfire.

From where he was sitting, Kane could tell that the club was only half full. It was Thursday and Sapphire wasn't a packed house until the weekend. He figured Malik would have time for a visit. As for himself, he needed to get a move on in case Sanders had decided to scope out the place, too. The last thing he needed was his partner finding him there. If he did, he would instantly become suspicious and might even report him to the lieutenant.

It was the main reason Kane checked the scene for a second time when he exited his vehicle. A few bouncers were outside smoking while three partygoers were walking towards the parking lot. A doorman and another bouncer were at the door letting two young females inside. Kane approached them first, thinking that they would know where Malik was. "Hey," he greeted, catching their attention. "Malik Washington, is he in?"

The doorman looked at him rather oddly before glancing over at the bouncer. He knew they were trying to figure out who he was so he decided to speed up the process and took out his badge. Before holding it up in front of the men, he said, "Agent Kane, I'm with the Triad. Malik is a good friend of mine. Can you tell him that I'm out here? I want five or maybe ten minutes of his time."

The bouncer nodded his head before disappearing into the club. A minute or so later, he returned with Malik who was holding a Kamikaze in his hand. He could tell that Malik was surprised to see him, but it didn't stop him from following him into the parking lot. Once they were at his Jeep, his plan was to discuss the news of the week; however, Malik stopped him before he could speak.

"I don't see you around these parts much. You're usually not out this late on a Thursday night. I suppose there are problems in the Kane household," Malik joked.

Kane wasn't ready to jump into a discussion on the paternity suit so he bypassed it. His mind went back to the real reason he had showed up at Sapphire. "The Brookstone PD has their eyes on Jay," he told him. "If they take him, you want your nose to be clean. You don't want your name on anything. I'm talking Sapphire, Blue Magic, nothing."

Malik chuckled as if he didn't take the news seriously. It was either that or he had too much to drink. Kane assumed it was the latter when Malik set his glass down onto the hood of his car. "They're not going to find anything," Malik told him, straightening his grin. "Everything we got is legit. We got books to prove that. They can meet up with our accountants and our investors. Matter of fact, one of them lives with you."

Kane knew that Malik didn't believe him when he laughed in his face. Although he offered up a good excuse for why the police wouldn't find anything, he also didn't mention the cartel. Jay could work wonders paperwork-wise with his businesses, but he couldn't hide kilos of cocaine. "If any types of drugs are found anywhere on Jay's property, the police and the Triad are going to believe that he funded his businesses illegally. No piece of paper, no accountant, no lawyer, and definitely not my wife will be able to prove otherwise. The man has established three businesses in a very small amount of time. I suggest you cover your tracks."

Malik grabbed his drink, taking a long swallow. He finished it before slamming the glass back down on the hood of the Jeep. His anger reached new heights and his volume changed right along with it. "What do these motherfuckers want, Kane? Jay hasn't been out that long. What is going on that makes them want to take him back down? If they want him that bad then they shouldn't have let him out!"

Kane wasn't the least bit surprised to see Malik's change in reaction. His friend was very instrumental in helping Jay rebuild his empire. "Drugs, Malik, it's always been about the drugs. Y'all aren't selling narcotics, are you?"

"What do you think?" Malik's tone was harsh. He walked up on Kane until only an inch or two of space was between them. "You steer those Girl Scouts away. I know you don't want to see your wife in prison. If Jay goes down, he takes Carmen with him."

Kane shook his head in agreement. He didn't want to see Carmen in prison. Nevertheless, he couldn't persuade her to take her name off of Jay's businesses. Carmen was in love with Blue Magic and had done much more than hand over her name. For that reason she would be harder for him to work off while Malik would let it go out of fear of losing his freedom.

"Who are we looking for?" Malik asked, interrupting Kane's thoughts. "Who is the lead detective on this thing?"

Kane rubbed his head in nervousness. Sanders' name was on the tip of his tongue, but he thought twice about saying it. Instead, he decided to tell on himself. "This motherfucker has a million-dollar lawsuit hanging over my head. He's trying to take the one thing that I have. He has a son of his own, but he won't let me have mine."

For three solid seconds, Malik couldn't move. He stared into Kane's eyes, hearing the man's revelation. Twenty years ago, Kane had made a name for himself by taking down Jay. Now, he wanted to do it again. Malik didn't know that Jay was suing him, but now he was aware of Kane's motive. He knew that without a doubt he had to warn Jay. There was no question about it. He also had no choice, but to cut his ties with Kane. With him working to take Jay down, he could potentially be arrested as well before the birth of his first child. The idea of it made him shake his head in disbelief. "Jay will always be a threat to you. Throwing him in prison is not going to change one damn thing about the past. That book has already been written. Stop taking your anger out on him because he can make a baby."

Kane's temper rose although his body language didn't exhibit it. He stared blankly ahead. His whole body was numb as Malik's words plunged like a knife into his heart, cutting him to the core. His friend had reminded him of the power that Jay would always have over him. As much as he tried to forget it, he couldn't. Not when he had spent nine months watching Jay's seed grow inside of his wife.

"We're done here," Malik whispered. "I know you want me to stay out here and talk to you all night, but I can't. I have a business to run and a very important meeting tomorrow morning. Personally, I believe that you should leave as well. It's not safe anymore."

Kane didn't need Malik's suggestion, as he was already retrieving his keys. He knew he had outstayed his welcome when Malik reminded him that Jay could make a baby. Those words alone made him want to leave, which he did once Malik had walked back inside.

Chapter Five

After he got back inside of Sapphire, Malik decided to keep the news of the investigation to himself. Jay was only a few feet away but Malik decided to tell him about it after the meeting with Blu.

The very next morning, Malik was the first to arrive at Blue Magic. He stood in a corner of the third floor conference room, watching as one of the waiters set four place settings. Only one table had been decorated, with a pure white tablecloth, for the occasion. Three place settings were on one side of the table and one on the opposite side, indicating where Blu was expected to sit.

With time drawing closer to the start of the meeting, Malik watched as the door to the conference room opened. Jay walked in while Rico was not too far behind him. "Is he here?" Malik asked, taking another peek into the hallway.

"Getting checked in," Jay replied, sitting at the place setting in the middle. "Costa is waxing him down real good. He travels light."

Malik looked back at the doorway, but no one was near it except for Rico. He knew that Blu and Costa couldn't be far because they kept business away from the dining area. "So, have you talked to him? What does he look like?"

Jay narrowed his eyes at Malik's second question. The man's looks were of no importance considering what they were going to be discussing. Nevertheless, to tell the truth, Blu's appearance had surprised even him. Jay grinned a little before answering, "A skinny ogre." He would've said more, but he could hear footsteps steadily approaching. He looked behind him to see Rico and Costa appearing in the doorway. After Rico came in, Costa gave a nod that Blu was ready to make his entrance.

When their guest entered, Malik was taken aback. Blu wasn't necessarily ugly, but he had distinctive features. He was extremely tall, approximately six-seven, and had a butterscotch complexion. His large nose was crooked and had been offset by deep, sunken, brown eyes.

"Shawn Blumington," Costa introduced. "Where can I direct him?"

Malik pointed at the place setting where he was standing. Blu came forward, prompting him to move. He retreated to his own seat as their waiter stepped into the room with pitchers of orange juice and ice water. Another one followed behind him with a thermal carafe of coffee. Malik watched the waiters as they presented Blu with the selections. After he selected a glass of orange juice, Blu looked at him.

"It's a pleasure to meet all of you," Blu began, taking his eyes off of Malik. "All of this was really on short notice. I had a feeling for a minute there that I had ran up in the wrong territory. I'm glad to see that this trip is on good terms." He took a large gulp of his orange juice before grabbing a cloth napkin to remove the residue from his lips. "After Rico located me, I told myself I had to school myself on you, Santiago. You come from a very powerful empire. Your father ran a cartel and was a politician? Damn, I know you got racks of money somewhere."

Malik shifted his body as he thought about how Blu had obviously done his research. He was unsure if Jay had done his since he personally didn't know anything about the man.

"So you've done your homework," Jay replied. "I guess that's a good sign. You don't want to walk into a meeting unprepared. Speaking of territories, though, let's go back to that. I've learned that you have four states on lock. I also know that you work—" Blu interrupted him.

"I'm getting started. I'm nowhere near being on your level, though. I'm dedicated, though. I know how to play the game."

Jay was offended at the interruption. Blu had done his homework though not too well. He'd shown his first sign of disrespect, which Jay wasn't use to. He decided to let it slide as he noticed one of the waiters returning. The waiter held a tray filled with four bowls of fresh mixed fruit, which he sat in front of each of the men. Blu was the first to grab his fork, but Jay stopped him. He slid his hand over his so he couldn't raise it to his mouth. "We haven't blessed the food."

Out of respect to God, Blu dropped his fork.

Malik took it upon himself to pray since it was obvious that Blu was hungry. Once he was finished, Blu dug into his food before resuming the conversation.

"Word on the block, Santiago, is that you're holding about ten. Your name is popping up all over the west coast. You got some people mad. Now you want to run the South. Haters are going to hate, though. I obviously was doing something right if I caught your eye. So, what was it, the fact that I took Tennessee or my businesses?"

Malik looked over at Jay, anticipating his response. The expression on his face let him know that Jay wasn't impressed. Blu had a cocky attitude which would be a terrible match for their organization. He needed to be broken in before he could even be considered for their team. When Jay grabbed his fork, Malik was unsure if he was even going to answer.

"Why do you think you're here?" Jay asked, chewing. "You obviously dropped everything at the last minute to make this trip."

Blu stuck his fork back inside of his bowl after eating a few blueberries. He wore a serious expression on his face as he saw where the conversation was going. "I know what kind of legacy you have and I respect it. I also know you brought me here for a reason. Obviously, I was making some sort of move that caught your attention. Now, if you want me to be honest, I think you're in need of my services. Right now, I'm in collaboration with a very powerful drug family in Colombia. If you want me to join your cartel, I would have to end things amicably with them."

Jay chuckled at Blu's expectation. He had no desire to have him in his cartel. For one, he was trying to break out of it and it wouldn't be beneficial. The person who he wanted to run things had to be in-house. Two, he was too arrogant. He already believed that he was at the top and wanted to be treated as such. It was obvious when he snapped his fingers for one of the waiters. The main entrée hadn't been brought in, but he wanted to make a special request. "Mr. Blumington, I don't want to waste your time. Right now, I'm not looking for any new employees. You did catch my attention, which is why I wanted to meet you. It's better to have allies than enemies. Now, for the remainder of your stay in Brookstone, Rico will accompany you. He can make sure that you're well taken care of. Everything has been exceptional, right?"

Blu shook his head yes as a waiter set a silver platter down in front of him. He immediately took off the lid, displaying a plate of grits, scrambled eggs, turkey links, and a large buttermilk biscuit. He dove right in before replying with, "It has." He spoke in between chews, continuing to show his gratitude. "Everything has been nice. So," he said, meeting eyes once again with Jay. "Since you're not looking for anyone new, what do you want with me?"

Jay dropped his napkin down onto the table as he stood on his feet. "I wanted to meet you. I wanted to get a feel for your personality and I did. I don't like your cockiness. You said that you thought I was in need of your services. I don't need anything from you, Mr. Blumington. Now, if you want to stay for a few more days, feel free. The trip's expenses have all been paid. Enjoy the city."

Blu stood on his feet as well, holding out both of his hands in an apologetic manner. "I didn't mean to offend you, Mr. Santiago. I apologize. I find it to be an honor to be here with you. Let's see if we can come to some kind of agreement," he said with a chuckle. "Let me work for you for a couple of months and I promise you, the paper will be longer and greener."

Jay looked over at Malik, and then back to Blu. "I have money, Blu. More of it is always better, but it brings a shitload of problems. Right now, you need to enjoy your time in Brookstone. Also, do your research on how I roll. Interrupting me while I'm speaking isn't going to help you get in this cartel."

Blu seemed satisfied with his answer, and he sat back in his seat. He resumed eating, but Jay wasn't finished with him yet. "Can you handle yourself around pussy?" The question seemed to have come out of nowhere, but it needed to be asked. Jay watched as a large grin formed on Blu's face as the man started to think that he was offering him a girl. The idea was far from Jay's intent. In fact, he wanted to warn him of one. "Carmen Davenport is one of the richest black women in this country. I highly suggest if you ever see her in this city that you don't even look at her. She's off limits."

"Oh, someone has a crush," Blu joked.

"She's mine," Jay corrected, "only mine. It would be in your best interest to look away. I promise you." Jay hoped that his words hadn't gone in one ear and out the other. Blu would find out the hard way if he hadn't paid attention. "I'm going to step out for a minute," he announced. Jay pushed his chair in, leaving the table. He had barely touched his food, but he no longer had an appetite. Based on what transpired, he honestly felt like he had wasted his time.

"I know what you're thinking," Malik began, having followed Jay into the hallway, "but we have something else to talk about." He posted himself up against the wall, draping his arms at his sides. "Kane paid me a visit last night. He came by Sapphire while you were in VIP. Apparently, he has teamed back up with the Brookstone PD to take you down. It doesn't look so good that you've acquired three businesses since your release."

Jay rolled his eyes at the news. He would've been surprised if it was another agent on the case. He had filed court papers against Kane and now he wanted to send him back to prison. Kane had forgotten the biggest piece of the puzzle. His wife's name was on Blue Magic. "If he takes me down, he takes down Carmen, too. He's not going to do that. Since he's not, the investigation shouldn't be a concern."

Malik disagreed. He knew how Kane was when it came to solving a case. He would keep at it until he solved it. That was how he had got Jay in the first place. "You can have a cool shoulder about all of this, but I suggest we tighten up. Before that, though, what are you going to do about that cocky motherfucker in there?"

Jay scratched his chin as he thought of an answer. He knew what he wanted to do, but he also wanted to see if Blu could redeem himself. He drummed his fingers furiously on the wall until he came to a decision. "I'm going to let him enjoy the city. Rico can be his personal tour guide."

"I can tell already that he wants to roll with us. Your name is powerful, Jay. You're Hector Santiago's son. You're a mystery to a lot of people," Malik expressed. "He's ready to get his hands in on this. Say, you let him go and he refuses? What are you going to do?"

"I dare him to step out of line; one wrong move and chop-chop." Jay illustrated with his hands to further prove his point. Pushing himself off the wall, he headed back into the conference room to dismiss the meeting. Rico and Blu remained there eating, while he and Malik went their separate ways.

***

It was unbeknownst to Jay that when he left Blue Magic Kane and Sanders were across the street. They were standing on the rooftop of the same abandoned building from the day before. Unlike their previous stakeouts, Sanders hadn't taken any pictures. From what they had seen thus far, there wasn't any major action at Blue Magic. It made Kane believe that they needed to move their stakeout to Sapphire. Friday nights were the most popular and something told him that all of Jay's men would be in attendance. It would be the perfect time for them to get footage of them at another one of Jay's businesses.

"I've worked with you long enough to know when you have something on your mind," Sanders disclosed.

Kane looked in Sanders' direction, but he didn't give him a reply. He had been in deep thought about a lot of things that morning that he needed to get off his chest. Normally he would talk to Malik, but he needed to confide in someone who wasn't connected to Jay. From the way things were looking, Sanders was the only one he had in his corner. Since he trusted the man with his life, he figured he could trust him with his personal affairs, too. "Jay is trying to convince Carmen that Rakim is his son," he explained. "He's suing us both for paternity fraud."

Sanders exhaled loudly in aggravation. He knew he should have listened to his gut. Kane didn't sign on to the case because he wanted to rid the city of drugs. He signed on because he wanted to get Jay away from his wife. Once again, Kane couldn't separate his personal from his professional life. Now, he had to be on the same page or neither one of them would get any work done. "Did you do it?" he asked him, bluntly.

"Did I do what?" Kane replied. He tried to figure out what Sanders was getting at until it clicked. "Are you asking me if I lied about my son's paternity?"

Sanders knew it was a difficult question to voice, but he had done it without hesitation. In his opinion, if Kane's test was legit then he didn't have anything to be worried about. However, Kane was looking extremely concerned. "I am asking you that," Sanders admitted. "I'm asking you because this thing is weighing more on your mind then it should. If Rakim is truly your son then you don't have anything to worry about. Chill out, Jay is going to lose his case. Besides, you need to be contacting your wife. You're doing exactly what Jay wants you to do. He wants this lawsuit to break y'all up. If it does, you know where Carmen is going. She will be going one way, and that's straight back to Jay."

Kane knew that Sanders was right. He stood there for a few minutes to allow his partner's words to sink in. Rakim was his son and he had nothing to lose. The only thing that was going down the drain at the moment was his relationship with Carmen. However, he could fix that. Carmen was willing to talk it out and deep down, he was, too. He was about to share his thought until he was interrupted by the sound of Sanders snapping photos. "What's wrong?" he asked as he looked across the street. He fixed his eyes on the front entrance of Blue Magic. A tall man was emerging through the doors with Rico at his side. They both were dressed in business suits and were being picked up by a limousine.

"Well, back to the station we go," Sanders muttered, having gotten the shot. He grabbed his binoculars, taking a step forward. "Once we scan this photo we can find out who the cartel's latest addition is. Now, can you work or should I get a new partner?"

Kane smiled as he snatched Sanders' camera from his hands. "I can work," he told him. His mind was a little clearer, but he still wasn't one hundred percent focused. He wouldn't be until he cleared things up with Carmen.

As they headed back to the precinct, he made the decision to call his wife. If he didn't, the tension would only continue to build. That was the last thing he wanted to happen, so he told himself that it was time to make amends.

***

Since her business meeting hadn't gotten underway, Carmen found herself checking her phone for any last minute messages. She saw only a few emails, which she read before glancing back up at Tiara. Though she regularly led the meetings, Tiara had asked for a couple of minutes to discuss an email she had received. Carmen had obliged and now the front cover of Mantra Designs' e-newsletter appeared on the projector screen. A T strap dress sandal was advertised on the front as the company's newest venture. The sight of it made Carmen nervous, but she told herself not to let it show. If she did, the whole room would become hysterical. Then, they would start to press her for a new collection right before her maternity leave.

"As all of you have heard," Tiara began, "Mantra has made headlines because of their tremendous increase in sales. Now, after barely a week, they are announcing a new venture." Tiara clicked the mouse, allowing the other pages of the newsletter to be shown. On each page, there was a new shoe even more exquisite than the last. "The first shoe I showed you, the T strap dress sandal is supposed to be debuting next month. There are also rumors that they may be opening up a store in Paris. Mantra is trying to go international."

Carmen's body shifted in her seat. Flame was known as one of the most prestigious fashion companies in America, but she had never opened a store overseas. All of their international sales came through online orders. It made her almost question her success.

"Mantra is about to be a cash cow," Jerry said, loudly. "We need a shoe line."

Carmen knew that out of all the executives in the room, Jerry would be the first to voice his opinion. He had been the senior marketing director of Flame for several years and was always two words from a pink slip. Jerry was someone that Carmen considered to be her frienemy. While they worked well together, they also butted heads. "Flame does not follow," she told him. "How does that look? Mantra premieres a shoe line and then we make the announcement that we're doing the same thing?"

"Look at these designs, Carm," Tiara replied, "They are right up there with Jimmy Choo and Louboutin. They're going to make a killing off of this." Tiara went back through the pages of the newsletter, giving everyone a second look. "We talked about doing something new in our last meeting. Then again, we did agree that the time wasn't right because of Carmen's maternity leave and mine. But now, I think that we need to make a move. The last collection we debuted was *Peaches* and that was nearly three years ago. Since then we've been adding pieces to the other collections. Flame needs something new that can keep its name on the blogs, in the magazines, *and* on the runway."

"A shoe line," Jerry suggested.

Carmen gave him a side eye before looking back at Tiara. Her best friend shrugged her shoulders like she was trying to persuade her to at least consider the idea. Carmen parted her lips to say no, but she was interrupted by the sound of a door opening, followed by an all too familiar voice. Cathy was standing closely on her right side with a cordless phone in her hand.

"Carmen, it's your husband," her receptionist whispered in her ear.

Carmen rolled her eyes at Kane's timing. She had been waiting on his phone call for several hours, and then he called right when her team was about to start pressuring her into doing a shoe line. "Excuse me," she said quietly as she grabbed the cordless phone. She stood up from her seat, giving Tiara an expression that was more of a warning. She may have been stepping out of the meeting, but it didn't mean that the team could push forward on a shoe line for Flame. It meant that they needed to discuss something else until she returned.

After following Cathy out of the room, Carmen waited until her receptionist was back at her desk before speaking. "Hey," she said, softly. Carmen didn't hear any background noise, which made her think that Kane was either at home or the precinct. Wherever he was, Carmen knew he was alone.

"Hey, baby," he greeted. "How are you?"

Carmen chuckled, "Hmm…wouldn't you like to know? Let's see, I'm an emotional wreck. It's been awhile since I've had a pleasant conversation with my husband."

"I know," he replied. "I'm well aware that we need to talk."

The phone went silent for a few seconds before Kane's voice returned. This time, he said a whole lot that Carmen desperately needed to hear.

"I wanted to apologize for what happened yesterday. I was upset and I took it out on you. I know you're confused about all of this and so am I. I want you to know that I was wrong and I shouldn't have said what I said." More silence filled the line as he paused. "I love you and we're going to work through this like we've done everything else. Twenty more years, right? Wasn't that our agreement?"

"Twenty plus," Carmen corrected. She couldn't help but to smile that she and Kane had officially made up. She knew she couldn't spend another night in bed without him and now, she didn't have to. "We do need to talk, but it's going to have to wait until later. I'm in a meeting."

"We can talk later, that's not a problem. I knew you were probably busy, but this was like a now or never thing. I, um, I wanted us to go to dinner, too. Let's give Fiona the night off and have a family dinner at Mancini's. I have a taste for Italian. Then, I was thinking that we could have some alone time to reconnect and talk through this bullshit. What do you say?"

"I'm down," Carmen agreed. Kane replied with a quick I love you before hanging up. With a grin on her face, Carmen hung up as well, placing the phone back down on Cathy's desk. Her receptionist was on her own call and gave her a head nod before continuing her conversation. Carmen returned to the conference room and found that the board was into a heavy conversation, which stopped when she walked into the room. "Okay," she said, slowly, noticing the change. "Give me the update." Carmen returned to her seat, but the room was still quiet. She glanced at Tiara whose expression said that she was worried. "Don't stare at me," she chuckled. "What happened?" When Tiara didn't answer right off, she knew to expect the worse.

"We want to do a vote for a shoe line. We've been talking and we think it is something new and fresh for Flame."

The happiness that Carmen was feeling was quickly diminishing. From the way Tiara had broken the news, it was like the board had already agreed to do the line. It seemed that they only wanted to do a vote so that they could say they won the argument fair and square. Carmen tried not to jump to conclusions, but she couldn't help it. "So, you want to do this vote when?"

"Well, our next meeting will possibly be on Wednesday. We can do it after we review the new commercial for the *King* collection."

Carmen's body shifted double time. The board wasn't giving her that long to change their minds. Matter of fact, she knew that they didn't want her to. Even if she came in the room cursing and screaming, their minds were so set on Flame coming out with shoes that they wouldn't hear anything she said. "I think that we all need to remind ourselves of why Flame is here. We're not followers, we're leaders. Coming behind Mantra should not be an option."

"Let's think about the money," Jerry added.

Carmen didn't bother to look at him. She didn't agree with their decision yet she was one voice against many. It told her that she had to work day and night to come up with something that would change their minds. She hated having to prove herself, but she would never be a follower. She put her life on it.

Chapter Six

Back at the precinct, Kane had been staring at a copy of Shawn Blumington's driver's license. From what he gathered, the man was a resident of Copperton City, Georgia. It was the exact same city where his daughters had applied for college. That bothered him, but his nerves settled when he reviewed the other information he had printed. From what he had collected, Blumington didn't have any criminal charges. A few speeding and parking tickets was the only thing he found in the man's name.

As he stuck the papers in the folder he had been creating, he heard the sound of his door opening. He knew it was Sanders before his partner even spoke. "He has a restaurant called Soulshock. It's like a down South version of Blue Magic," Sanders disclosed. "Then there is The Sphinx Club and The Kingdom, which are two dance clubs. Nothing wild has happened there, cops never had to come out, all of their paperwork is legit." Kane watched as Sanders placed the papers onto his desk. He looked at if briefly before handing his partner his own set of documents.

"I don't have anything either. He's not a criminal or at least there aren't any charges to say that he is. I say we keep our eye on Jay." Kane stood up from his desk as he noticed it was nearing five-thirty. He needed to get a move on if he wanted to be on time for dinner at Mancini's.

"So, you think we should forget about him? I personally think that someone needs to keep an eye on him. He may seem innocent, but we've only seen the surface."

Kane grabbed his keys and cell phone as he thought the issue over. Shawn Blumington didn't seem like a threat or at least not yet. For the most part, Kane wanted to keep the focus on Jay. He didn't see anything wrong with Sanders going after Blumington, but he didn't want him to forget who they were truly after. "If you want to look more into him, do it, but my focus is Jay. Right now, I need to get out of here. We'll catch up later." Kane hated to leave so abruptly yet time was of the essence. He had initiated the dinner at Mancini's and wasn't about to let anyone down. Besides, it was time for work to come second to family.

***

If work was coming second to family, Kristian didn't see any signs of it. It was going on almost six and the family dinner that had been planned at Mancini's seemed to be almost nonexistent. So far, she was the only one in attendance. Akaila and Malachi were both at the house with their mother while she was stuck at the restaurant waiting for everyone to show.

She turned to look at the hostess stand to see Rico heading towards the restaurant's exit. A tall man followed behind him almost on his heel. She stared in their direction as they walked until she saw Rico turn to look behind him. Not wanting to be noticed, she grabbed one of the dinner menus, using it to shield her face. She thought the disguise had worked until she realized she was no longer at the table alone. She dropped the menu in front of her as Rico and his associate slid into the booth.

"It's been awhile," Rico said, forming his lips into a smile.

Kristian rolled her eyes, pretending to be annoyed. Her act didn't play out for long as she noticed Rico's attire. He was clad in an all-black suit, which had been accentuated with a topaz-colored tie and handkerchief. "It has," she replied, sneaking a peek at his friend.

Kristian's disappointment in the man's appearance read on her face. He wasn't bad looking from far away, but up close, he was atrocious. His chestnut brown eyes seemed to be locked onto hers with a look of admiration, which forced her to turn her gaze.

"This is Blu. He's new to the area," Rico said, pointing at the guy next to him.

Kristian nodded her head, but didn't bother to return the gesture. From the way Blu looked, the last thing she wanted was for him to know her name. "Welcome to Brookstone," was all that she managed to squeeze out.

"It's Shawn Blumington to be exact," the man replied, sticking out his hand. "Who are you, beautiful?"

Kristian didn't reply nor did she shake his hand. Something in the pit of her stomach told her that Blu wasn't someone that she wanted to know. However, she had a feeling that Rico was going to make sure that they were on a first name basis.

"Kristian is Carmen Davenport's daughter. Her mother's name is on Blue Magic. It was where we ate this morning," Rico said, doing the exact thing that Kristian had expected.

"Carmen Davenport?" Blu questioned. "I think I've heard that name."

Kristian gave Blu a shy smile, but decided not to feed into his statement. The way he was looking at her told her that he was up to no good. His eyes were piercing through hers like he was ready to devour her. A hidden agenda seemed to be motivating his gaze.

"Look, we have some things to take care of," Rico announced, tapping Blu's shoulder. "Maybe I'll see you around again."

"Maybe," Kristian replied, grabbing her menu. She smiled at Rico before glancing back over at Blu. His mouth was shaped into a grin and it wasn't long before he draped his right hand over hers.

"It was a pleasure meeting you, Kristian. I have a feeling this won't be the last time we'll cross paths. Maybe, we could get up again in private."

Kristian chose to remain mum as she was trying her best to ignore Blu's presence. He wasn't ignoring her which he proved when he spoke again.

"I'll see you later, beautiful. Thanks for the welcoming spirit."

Kristian glanced up at him and followed him with her eyes as he left the restaurant. Certain that this was their last encounter, she told herself to forget about him. It would have been easier to do if her family was arriving. Since they appeared to be running late, Kristian focused more on Blu than she wanted. Nevertheless, her appetizer did the trick the moment it hit the table. She dove right in while all thoughts of Blu left her mind.

***

It surprised Carmen that she and Kane were both running late for dinner. When she had arrived with the kids, Kristian was the only one at the table. Shortly after, Kane walked in, apologizing for his tardiness. Once he was seated, Akaila announced that she and Kristian had been accepted to Copperfield. Though she knew they were going to get in, the news wasn't exactly what Carmen wanted to hear. She wanted her daughters to stay closer to New York. Now, they were officially moving to Georgia. It was one of the things that she and Kane had discussed after dinner was over. While the kids had returned home, they had taken a stroll in the park.

They made small talk for the first couple of minutes until Carmen turned the tables. She had to know if there was anything that could have happened to alter his test results. She didn't want to ask him yet she found the courage to do so. Carmen could tell that the question disturbed him from his reply. In a stern tone, he told her that he was the only one who could be Rakim's father. As his wife, Carmen wanted to believe him. A part of her did while she still had some doubt. However, she promised to never ask the question again. In fact, she told him that they needed to work together to build a paternity case that would assure them a win.

Once that was resolved, they returned to the house and Kane retreated to the bathroom. He closed the door which he generally didn't do to shower. Carmen took that as a sign that something was bothering him. Forty-five minutes later, she heard the shower finally come on. She was now certain Kane had been stalling. Bundled up in the covers, Carmen decided to stop timing him. She wasn't sure how much longer he had been in the bathroom but when he finally emerged, she was already half asleep.

When he climbed in the bed, Carmen made sure that she didn't budge. She continued to drift off until Kane's arms wrapped around her. He started to fondle her breasts affectionately like he was trying to get her in the mood for sex. Instead of responding in kind, she adjusted her position just as his hands started to massage her stomach. "It's almost that time," she heard him whisper. Carmen nodded her head, but didn't respond verbally. His comment was sincere although she knew deep down that he was hurt. They might have renewed their vows, but she still was about to give birth to Jay's baby. "Are you happy?" he asked.

Carmen sat up slowly, allowing his hands to fall down from her stomach. She turned over so that she was facing him. "Am I happy?"

"Yeah, are you happy?" he repeated.

Carmen stared into his eyes, trying to read him. She felt like, he should have known that she was happy. She had always wanted more children. Although the way she conceived them was not right, she wouldn't trade it for the world. "I am happy," she told him, giving him a smile. "I'm very happy. I can't wait until Nyla comes." Carmen studied his face, smiling broadly when she saw a grin emerge. Then, as quickly as it had come, it disappeared.

"You should be," he told her, firmly. His face now wore a solemn expression. "This is what you wanted for a long time." He paused for a couple of seconds before speaking again. "We both wanted it," he corrected. "I wish that I could've given it to you."

Carmen swallowed as she took notice of his tone. Nervously, she watched as he got up out of the bed, grabbed a pair of jeans and a t-shirt, and dressed. Knowing that he was getting ready to leave, she asked, "Where are you going?"

Before responding, Kane stuck both of his feet into his Timberland boots without bothering to lace them up. He didn't know where he was going, but he knew he needed a chance to clear his head. He glanced at her before answering, "Out."

Chapter Seven

Carmen stared out the window as Kane's Jeep backed out of the driveway. She wanted to call him to come back, but she knew that he wouldn't. While they had cleared the air on one issue, another one had surfaced. This one, though, she couldn't fix. She was nine months pregnant and Nyla was coming regardless of how Kane felt. He might not have liked the idea, but he knew when they renewed their vows that she was pregnant. He seemed okay with it then, but obviously the whole thing was an act.

When his car disappeared out of the gates, Carmen began to think that her marriage wasn't going to survive. If Kane was running out now then she knew it would be worse when Nyla came. Jay would be around more than ever and she would be forced to communicate with him. There might even be times when he had to come to the house. The distance between her and Kane would only grow.

Carmen pulled the curtains closed as she made her way back to the bed. She sat down, and tried to fight back her tears. She and Kane had been fine until Jay's lawsuit, which sent them spiraling back into a place that neither one of them wanted to be. Carmen wanted to come up with an answer to fix everything, but she couldn't. Softly crying, she did the only thing she knew how; she prayed to God for guidance and strength. She told herself that this would be the last time she would allow Kane to leave. After tonight, she would put her foot down. If she wanted to save her marriage, she had to act like it, now or never.

***

Kane knew that things were getting worse and not better. While he had given Carmen an answer regarding Rakim's paternity, her question still bothered him. Instead of replying, he felt like he should have questioned her trust. If she trusted him then she wouldn't have asked the question a second time. For her to do so, he knew that she had doubts about him being Rakim's father. Even with a test to prove it, she still didn't want to believe him. Her lack of trust along with her pregnancy was enough to make him leave.

While he thought he would drive around Brookstone all night, he ended up parked outside of Jay's high rise. He wasn't there to start a fight, but he did want to confront Jay. Since it was a Friday night, he knew that he would be getting in late. Sapphire was the hot spot on the weekend and it didn't close until two in the morning. When the clock hit three, Kane knew he was bound to see him. Surprisingly, he never did and Kane ended up falling asleep while he waited.

When he finally awoke, Kane knew he had missed him. It was going on eight o'clock and the city was in full throttle. He quickly wiped the sleep from his eyes and stared across the street at the apartment complex. From what he could see, there wasn't much action going on. He took his eyes off the scene in front of him and looked down to check his phone. Before he could, a screeching sound made him peer up. A taxicab was now parked outside the complex. An older gentleman was emerging from the car, tossing a few bills at the driver.

He was dressed in a grey trench coat and hat, which he took off when he approached the security guard. Kane recognized the man to be his father-in-law. *What in the world is Lotus doing? Why isn't he in Texas?* Kane grabbed his cell phone, quickly calling him, but Lotus didn't answer. His instinct was to follow him yet he knew he wouldn't get in the building. Security was tight and even with his Triad pull; he would have to have a warrant before they would allow him inside. His best bet at the moment was to simply wait for Lotus to come out. Once he did, Kane planned on questioning him.

***

Jay looked behind him before he hit the button for the elevator. Ever since he had moved into his apartment complex, he had been gaining entry through the basement. He knew what kind of press his name brought and he wanted to keep his residency a secret. The second people learned that he was one of the tenants; he would have paparazzi constantly trailing him.

Luckily, the elevator car came quickly and as expected no one was on it. He was able to make it onto his floor without even being seen. When he reached his door, he quickly opened it and was surprised to see Lotus inside. The sight of Carmen's father made him scratch his head as he wondered how he'd gotten in. He looked back at the door and noticed that it was still intact. He then closed it, and put on all of the locks.

"Oh, come on, Jay, you know I'm good with buildings," Lotus joked. "I got inside without a problem. The security guard didn't even question me. He let me right in."

Jay turned back to him and saw the lock pick he had used in his hand. "I didn't expect to see you. Not after our last visit," he told him, joining him on the couch. Jay looked him over as Lotus stood up to take off his coat. He laid it on the arm of the loveseat before sitting back down. "I went out for breakfast. I would've invited you if I knew you were here. Did you come alone? How's Patricia?" he asked him, inquiring about Carmen's mother.

Lotus snickered. Patricia didn't even know that he had left the state. When he returned, he knew that she would have a slew of questions for him. "No, she's still in Texas," he replied. "She doesn't even know I'm here. Let's talk about our last visit, though. I got your package. I'm guessing that the diamonds are somehow tied to your new operation. My decision hasn't changed, but I do want to say thank you for the gift. I also want to let you know that your stones are safely locked away." Lotus paused for a few seconds only to give Jay the chance to reply. When his godson didn't speak, he chose to disclose the real reason he was in Brookstone. "I'm sick," he told him.

Jay gave him another once-over. He could see something different in his eyes; similar to what he had seen when he was in Dallas. He had felt like something was wrong then. "You caught cancer or some shit? Is that the reason you stepped down from being CEO?"

"No, Jay, I have diabetes. I've known for years. Patricia and I didn't publicize it. However, I passed out yesterday. My blood sugar dropped. Patricia took me to the doctor and well, things aren't looking too good. Of course, they gave me some insulin and other medicine. For many years, I haven't been taking care of myself in terms of what I eat. I was physically in shape, but now that I'm older, I haven't been as active as I once was."

Jay's face was expressionless as he took in his words. From the way Lotus was talking; his case must have been serious. Especially, if he had flown from Texas to New York for a day trip. Lotus hadn't even come to see his daughter. It made him wonder if Carmen even knew that her father was in Brookstone. "She doesn't know anything, does she?"

Lotus took a deep breath before he responded. His daughter was more in the dark than anyone. For all she knew, he was in his prime. "I never could find the time to tell her. After we moved to Texas, it was something that Patricia and I kept to ourselves. Then, I figured I would wait until Nyla was born. I would tell everyone then." Lotus covered his mouth as he thought of how Carmen would react. The image of her upset made him regret not having another child. Carmen needed someone that could help her bare some of the burden. Although Jay was secretly her godbrother, they weren't exactly on good terms. In fact, they were in the same boat. "Hector Santiago only had one child."

Jay looked at Lotus oddly when he changed the subject.

"I only had one child," Lotus continued. As he spoke, he felt himself reliving some of his past. "He had a son. I had a daughter. We used to joke about you two getting married," Lotus said, laughing. "Then I found you in Carmen's bedroom." Lotus let out a deep breath. "I know we've had our share of troubles, Jay. Lord knows I wanted to butcher you when you beat up my daughter. I swore on your father's grave that I was going to. However, the Lord gave me a forgiving spirit and I forgave you. You've changed a lot."

A slight smile appeared on Jay's face. He knew he had changed. Many people saw it in his clothes, but he saw it in the way that he handled situations. For all the things that Kane had done, Jay knew he would've killed him by now. By allowing him to live, he had proven to himself that murder wasn't always the way to go. "Seventeen years in prison will do that to you," he said, firmly. "However, we don't need to be discussing me right now; our focus needs to be on you. We can fight this thing. I know the American Diabetes Association has the latest research. Once I get in contact with the right people, we can find you a doctor."

Lotus waved his right hand, indicating that he didn't want to talk about medical treatment. There was more that he needed to tell Jay and his flight back to Texas was in less than two hours. "You were six years old when Carmen was born. Do you really think that the first time you laid eyes on her was at that diner in West Brookstone?"

Jay shrugged his shoulders. He knew that Lotus and his father were best friends, but it had never crossed his mind that he could have met Carmen years before. The only thing he had ever questioned was whether his mother was friends with Patricia. He was certain that his mother had to have met the woman before Lotus had broken out of the biz. "To be honest, I never thought about it," he answered. "I assumed that our first meeting was at that diner. I was twenty-seven then. Six years older than she was."

"You were infatuated with her even then."

"When I first met her?" Jay was confused. Lotus was nowhere near West Brookstone when he and Carmen had first met. The only people that were there were Malik, his twin brother, Rakim, Carlos, and Tiara. They were the only people who knew how he felt when he saw her. Lotus might have seen it down the line, but it wasn't that day.

"No, Jay." Lotus chuckled, "I'm talking about when you were six. I had brought Carmen to the house one day so Hector could see her. You were playing and you came into the parlor where we were. You asked to hold her. I let you and it was like pulling teeth to get her back. It was then that Hector and I made the joke about setting up an arranged marriage between you two. It would be beneficial to Hector because he wanted to continue his legacy. As the father of a little girl, I wanted to die knowing that I left her in the hands of a man who could take care of her. Judging from the way you held her, I got the impression that it could be you. Sad to say, I never brought Carmen back to the house. You didn't see her again until she was twenty-one."

It all clicked in Jay's head as he heard Lotus' spiel. He knew now why he had come to visit him. He wanted him to look after Carmen. However, when he mentioned the word marriage, he had gone into an arena that neither of them had control over. "I know what you're trying to tell me, but there is a brick wall in between—"

Lotus interrupted him when he understood where Jay was going. "I'm not telling you to ruin her marriage. I would never tell you to do that. What I'm trying to say is this. You and Carmen have a daughter that is due any day now. Things are going to be different. You two are going to have to communicate way more than what you do now. Nyla is your first shot at being a father from the womb. You didn't have that with King and you're barely having it with Rakim. I think that this baby is going to bring you and Carmen closer together. If it does, you have my blessing."

Jay smiled at him, but was reluctant to admit that he was still trying to win Carmen back. Even if he wanted to, Lotus wasn't going to give him the chance. His godfather was now standing on his feet like he was preparing to leave.

"I wish I was there more for you than what I was. I can picture the type of relationship that Hector wanted us to have." Lotus took a deep breath. "You are like your father, but remember his fate. The last thing you want is to let this cartel consume you. You have a strong business mind that can take you far. Remember who you're here for, your family."

Lotus did expect a response, but he knew he had put a lot on Jay's shoulder. Instead of prolonging his visit, he grabbed his hat and placed it on top of his head. He then put on his coat as he prepared himself for his flight back to Dallas. Without another word, he gave Jay a head nod before leaving the apartment.

***

Kane waited impatiently for Lotus to walk out of the complex. His hand was already gripped around the door handle ready for the moment Lotus appeared. Almost thirty minutes had passed since his father-in-law had went in, which made him believe that this was more than a friendly visit. Lotus and Jay were obviously discussing something important.

Impatiently waiting, Kane opened his door. He stepped out of his Jeep and sprinted across the street. When he made it to the security guard, he saw Lotus as he walked out of the building. His father-in-law didn't see him at first until he cut off his step. It was then that Lotus gave him a deadly expression that told Kane that he wasn't fond of having him approach him. "Good morning," he greeted. "Carmen didn't tell me that you were coming into town." Lotus didn't reply, simply stepping to the side. He headed towards the sidewalk as he waved down a cab. Kane made sure to follow him so Lotus would know that he wasn't getting off easy. "So you're not speaking to me?" Kane asked.

"Not when you're doing your little detective work," Lotus shot back. "What are you doing here?"

Kane let out a snicker. "What am I doing here? I live in Brookstone. I've spent the last twenty years of my life in this city. Before that, I was in Manhattan. Now, the question is, what are you doing here? You've spent the last twenty or so years of your life in Dallas. Did Patricia come with you? Did y'all fly in early to be here for the birth?"

Lotus didn't answer any of his questions. He knew Kane was suspicious of him, which wasn't a shock. For the longest, he had displayed disdain towards Jay. Even Carmen would be surprised if she knew he had flown to New York to see him. Still, Lotus wasn't going to give in to Kane's interrogation. "I have a flight to catch," he finally said. "By the way, don't tell Carmen I was here."

Kane opened his mouth to respond, but Lotus didn't give him the chance before he got inside the cab, and closed the door. As the cab drove off, Kane watched it blend into traffic before walking back to his own vehicle. He had tons of questions in his head, but no one to answer them. Though he had confirmation that Jay was at home, he decided to leave well enough alone. At this point, he needed to be getting to his own house.

Chapter Eight

The last thing that Carmen could say she got was a pleasant night's sleep. Aside from how she was feeling emotionally, Nyla had been a busybody, keeping her up for most of the night. Since sleep was no longer an option, there she was, wide awake at six am. Naturally, the first thing she did was check the driveway. Only two cars were there, her old car that Kristian drove, and her Lexus SUV, which hardly got driven at all. It was all she needed to see to know that Kane hadn't returned home. She didn't know where he had stayed, but she was certain it wasn't at Malik's house. If he was there, Tiara would've called to tell her.

Carmen closed the curtains back and grabbed her bathrobe. She slid it on only to return to her bed. She lay there for another two hours until she decided to cook breakfast. Fiona was normally off on the weekends, leaving her to do much of the household duties and chores. Carmen didn't mind, which was why she grabbed the baby monitor and went to check up on Rakim. Most mornings, she found him wide awake, but this morning was different. He was still asleep and she decided to let him be.

By the time she was downstairs, the front door was opening. She knew it was Kane before she even laid eyes on him. When he did come in, she stared at him, nervously. Carmen was unsure of what to say and the feeling was mutual. The silence made the moment awkward as if they were preparing themselves to offer apologies again. However, Carmen felt as if she was owed an apology first.

She decided to break the ice, telling him, "I'm going to go fix breakfast." Carmen walked past him and headed into the kitchen. She grabbed a loaf of whole wheat bread from the bread box as Kane came in a few seconds later.

"This isn't easy for me," he said, finally speaking as he sat on one of the bar stools. "I'm trying to hold it together, but it's not working. This Rakim situation then Nyla, it's getting crazy around here. I hate to take it out on you so I leave, but nothing is getting solved. We wind up saying sorry and going on about our day. I want to fix this, I just don't know how."

Carmen stopped what she was doing. With her back to him, she said, "What do you exactly want to fix? I'm having this baby. It's too late to turn that around now. Not that I would even want to."

Kane stood up from the bar stool. He walked around the island until he was right at the counter where his wife was standing. He didn't want her to think that Nyla was the problem because she wasn't. "I want to get him out of our lives. Do you remember what it was like without him? Everything was perfect. We were happy, Carm. We went to church together every Sunday and Wednesday, we were the ideal family. The only problems we had were with King and the Triad. He was always in handcuffs and you were scared that I would go back undercover. When Jay came, all hell broke loose."

Carmen chuckled more so out of frustration than humor. Jay was a problem that neither one of them could fix. He was always going to be around because she had ties to him. He was both King and Nyla's father. The last thing she would do is deny him time to spend with his children. "You can't fix Jay," she replied. "You have to learn how to tolerate him. For one, you don't have anything to be worried about. I made a decision to remarry you and that's what I did. You should trust me." Carmen opened up one of the cabinets, taking out a casserole dish. She sprayed it down with canola oil before ripping the edges off of six slices of bread.

"I trusted you for six months. I came back home and you were pregnant."

Carmen caught the hint he was trying to throw. Instead of ignoring it, she went straight for the punch. "What do you want, Kane? Since it is obvious you don't trust me. What is it that you want? Do you want to separate? I'll tell you now that I don't want that. What I want is for you to tell me that we're going to fight through this lawsuit and stick it out. I asked you about your results and you promised me that your results are one hundred percent accurate. I'm going to trust you on that. Now, I'm asking for the same. If you can't give it to me, then you need to make a decision on what you want to do."

Kane felt as if he was being put on the spot. Carmen wanted him to make a decision like he was ready to give up on their marriage. Though he had some reservations about how things were going to be down the line, he wasn't ready to separate. He wanted her to know that he had some doubts. "I'm not leaving you," he stated. "The thought never crossed my mind. Leaving you is letting Jay win. That's what he wants, anyway. He wants you, bottom line."

"Jay knows how far to go," Carmen shot back. "Believe me, he does." She tossed the edges of the bread into the trash before crumbling the leftovers into tiny pieces into the dish. "You two are going to have to learn how to get along. Put the past behind you."

Kane wanted to laugh at the comment, but he knew not to. He couldn't put the past behind him when he was trying to recreate it. He took Jay down twenty years ago and wanted to do it again. All he needed was a little more time and a little more evidence. After he got both, he would have the privilege of seeing Jay back in prison. Until then, he had to deal with him. "I'm going to try. I want you to be patient with me."

Carmen nodded her head, but she didn't give him a verbal response. He didn't seem to need one either. He simply kissed her cheek, whispered, I love you, before disappearing from the kitchen. She assumed that their conversation was over though there was more she wanted to talk about. For example, she wanted to know where he had gone when he had left. Certain that she wouldn't get the answer that morning, Carmen finished preparing the casserole she was making. When she slid it into the oven, Rakim's cries could be heard loud and clear from the baby monitor. Her son was obviously awake and upset so she grabbed it and headed out of the kitchen. About to climb the steps, she paused when she heard Kane's baritone.

The mere sound of his voice gave her an idea. She usually didn't work on Saturdays, but she was pressed for time. She needed a new collection to present to the board that would sway them from voting yes for a line of shoes. If she went to work for a couple of hours, Kane could watch Rakim. It would give them some bonding time and she could start work on a new collection. Unsure of what Kane's plans were, she was anxious to find out. She continued up the steps to find him in Rakim's room holding their son close to his chest. His back was to her yet Carmen couldn't bear to make her presence known. The moment they were sharing was one she couldn't interrupt. Slowly, she backed out of the room without saying a word. Once Kane came down for breakfast, she would ask him then. For now, he needed to have his time with Rakim.

Chapter Nine

It didn't take much coaxing for Kane to agree to stick around the house. He seemed happy to do it and even joked that he had a full day planned for him and Rakim. With things working in her favor, Carmen was able to make it to the office by eleven o'clock. So far, she had spent the past hour or so flipping through several fashion magazines to find inspiration. While a collection of purses was a good idea, she was not very enthusiastic about drawing the product. Fifteen minutes into her first design, she lost focus when heavy footsteps sounded. Certain that there wasn't a security guard on duty; she grabbed a letter opener off of her desk to use as a makeshift weapon. She stood up as the door to her office opened. When Jay walked in, she felt a mixture of relief and anxiety.

"Who told you I was here?" she asked him shocked. She dropped the letter opener onto her desk, sitting back down. "Shit, what are you doing here?"

Jay took a seat on her sofa, knowing that his presence was a surprise. He was in route to Blue Magic when he saw her Lexus parked in front of Flame. He became suspicious since it was a rarity for her to drive herself around town. Lucky for him, he still had the security badge Carmen had given him when they were working on their restaurant. He never returned it, which allowed him to use it to his advantage. "I wanted to see you," he told her, plainly. "Your car gave you away."

Carmen rolled her eyes and wondered if Jay was coming to talk more about his diamonds. If he was then she obviously hadn't gotten through to him. Though he hadn't said anything about it yet, Carmen waited impatiently for him to do so. "Are you going to tell me what you want?" she asked him, watching as he admired one of the mannequins in her office. "Do you like the suit? I guess I need to offer it before it makes its debut. That is my duty as your stylist, right?"

Jay turned around to face her. While he did like the suit, it had nothing do to with his visit. After receiving Lotus' blessing, his main intention was to get closer to her. "Why don't you remind me?"

Carmen didn't hesitate to approach him. From the moment he had walked in the room, she had noticed his crooked necktie. It was starting to aggravate her to the point that she could rip it apart. "You're forty-seven years old and you still can't get this shit right," she said, straightening it. Carmen giggled to herself as she pulled it tighter around his neck. "See? What would you do without me?" She took a step back, giving him the once-over. Very much pleased, she folded her arms across the top of her stomach. "Well, since you're all dressed up, you obviously have something big planned today. What's on your agenda?"

Jay didn't respond verbally, but gave her a look that said she was his agenda. To stress it even more, he moved closer to her. It was then that Carmen picked up on his intent. Despite the nervousness that she was showing, Jay still reached out and embraced her. After a few seconds, she attempted to pull away, but he didn't let her. "Jay," he heard her whisper, "I think I'm wet." Jay smiled at her words, allowing her to slide out of his arms.

"Perfect timing," he replied, "because I came over here to get you wet."

Carmen backed away when she realized his mind was in the gutter. "No, Jay, I'm serious. My water broke. I think I'm about to go to into labor."

Jay's eyes bulged out of his head. He glanced down at Carmen's stomach as if the baby was going to drop out. "She's coming? Like right now? Maybe it's a false alarm. Don't women have those? I mean, she is due soon, but right now?"

Carmen scratched her head as she started to walk back to her desk. "It's not a false alarm," she said with a slight chuckle. "I've given birth three times and I definitely know when my water has broken." She picked up a notepad and ink pen, beginning to write a small to-do list. Jay was shooting questions at her left and right, making it hard for her to think, while she tried to focus on what needed to be done.

"Do you feel pressure?" Jay asked, steadily pacing the floor. "Are you still leaking?"

"Not yet," Carmen told him, answering his first question. "Don't start freaking out yet, papi, this is the easy part." Carmen looked away from her notepad to take a peek at him. She could tell that his nerves were going haywire by the way he was walking around her office. "Chill out. I'm the one that's going to be doing all the work." Carmen gave him a quick smile before grabbing her purse. She tossed the notepad inside of it and motioned for him to head to the door. As much as she wanted to soothe his nerves, she knew it was pointless. In less than twenty-four hours, they would welcome their daughter along with a new set of problems. If they weren't ready, they both would be in for a rude awakening.

Chapter Ten

Jay stared down at Carmen's hands as her fingers moved rapidly across the keypad of her Blackberry. Despite being confined to her bed and an IV in her left arm, she hadn't missed a beat. She had spent the last hour or so trying to make sure that her home and business were in order before Nyla's birth. Jay had done the same, but he had taken the easy way out. He put everything on Malik's shoulder, giving his right-hand man full control of the Santiago cartel and his businesses. Once Tiara gave birth then the cartel would fall into the hands of Rico and Costa.

"My parents boarded their plane," Carmen announced, setting her phone down beside her in the bed. "Hopefully, they'll be here by this evening. I don't think they have any stops."

Jay picked up her phone, setting it on the meal counter. Although he had heard her statement regarding her parents, he didn't comment on it. His mind was more centered on her Blackberry than Lotus and Patricia. In his opinion, the phone had only been a distraction. "You need a break from that thing," he told her. "I don't want to see you touch it anymore."

"You sound bossy," Carmen joked, rearranging herself in the bed. "I thought I was supposed to be the one with the attitude. I hope that tone will clear up before my parents come. Are you excited to see them?"

Jay shrugged his shoulders. "Maybe," he replied, thinking of Lotus' visit that morning. "Is Kane on his way?"

"He's supposed to be," Carmen told him, looking up at him.

She said the words as the door to her room opened. *Speak of the devil,* Jay thought, when Kane walked in with Rakim. Kristian followed behind him along with Akaila and Malachi.

"You see all of this stuff," Kristian yelled, showing off Rakim's baby bag. "You would think he was the one being born!" She flung the bag down onto the floor before hurrying to her mother's side. Akaila joined her there as well, bringing over a handful of balloons.

"We've been secretly collecting stuff for months!" Akaila squealed. "I can't wait for you to see it! Some of it is custom-made. Are you having contractions?"

"Some," Carmen admitted. "Like one or two every hour. Nyla probably won't be here until the morning. As you can see, I haven't started cursing yet." Carmen gave her a small smile and took a peek at the balloons in her hand. She mouthed ooh when she noticed that Nyla's name had been decorated on a few of them.

"Do we have to be here all night?" Malachi asked, catching her attention.

Carmen looked at her son who was standing behind Akaila. She knew he wasn't as excited as everyone else, but she didn't expect to see him looking so disappointed. "You don't have to be here all night. You don't want to see Nyla come? She is your little sister, you know."

"I don't know," he mumbled. "It's not like I have a choice. I can't drive myself home." Malachi plopped down in a chair, allowing his bags to fall onto the floor. He had spent most of the pregnancy mum about his feelings, but now he was putting his displeasure on full display. He hoped that his parents saw it. Then, they would realize that he was feeling sort of left out. In fact he'd been feeling that way since Rakim was born.

Although Carmen did notice, she didn't have the energy to address the situation. She was starting to feel another contraction, which was more painful than her previous ones. She took that as a sign that she was drawing closer to giving birth. The pain showed on her face and it wasn't long before Kane crept up to her side. He placed his hand inside of hers before leaning down to give her a kiss on the lips. Carmen returned it and simultaneously had another contraction. The kiss ended as a knock sounded at her door. Carmen assumed that it was one of the nurses until an unknown man stepped into the room. A large envelope was in his hands and he didn't speak to anyone as he entered. When he headed for Kane, Carmen instantly thought the worse.

Out of all the places that Jay could send the process server, he had to pick the hospital. The only thing that made the situation less uncomfortable was that Kane already knew about the lawsuit. Since he did, Carmen didn't expect an over the top reaction. She simply expected for him to push the papers aside. For some reason, that wasn't what happened. As Kane read the documents his face changed from content to one of rage. His expression was followed by him ripping the papers apart.

"So what do you think this lawsuit is going to do?" Kane shouted, handing Rakim over to Akaila. "I've already done a paternity test. Rakim belongs to me."

"Please don't start," Carmen begged. She sat up straight in the bed, her eyes focused directly on Kane. "Not here, not now." She looked to the left of her where Jay was sitting and asked him with her eyes to do the same. He seemed to comply because he remained quiet, but Kane continued to mouth off.

"This wasn't a surprise," he said, continuing to speak loudly. "Carmen already told me about it. I was waiting to be served. You wanted to do it here because my wife is about to have your baby. It makes the perfect scene, huh?"

Jay stood up as if he was going to feed into Kane's tirade. Carmen automatically extended her arm to hold him back from making any sudden moves. "Please," she whispered, "don't do this." She turned back to Kane, asking him again, "This is a very uncomfortable situation, but can you let it go? As soon as the news hits that I'm in labor, the paparazzi will be everywhere. We don't need to give them anything to talk about."

"You should've told him that before he filed the papers!"

Carmen let out a deep sigh. She was about to speak again until Akaila walked out of the room. She took Rakim with her and Carmen knew it was because she didn't want him to be a witness to the arguing. A few seconds later, Kristian and Malachi announced that they were going to wait in the lobby. Although she didn't necessarily want to continue the conversation, she felt more comfortable doing so without the presence of her kids. "Can we all sit down?" she asked looking back and forth between the two men. The room became silent for a few short seconds while the tension pulsed.

"Fuck it," Kane muttered, pulling his car keys out of his pocket. "It is what it is. I know this shit was planned, including this pregnancy."

"Kane, we can talk—" Carmen began but wasn't given the chance to finish.

"Congratulations. You deserve it."

The words that came out of Kane's mouth were cold and stern. His tone was fierce and it didn't surprise Carmen when her husband headed for the door. He slammed it closed behind him, a direct reflection of his anger. Drowned in worry and confusion, Carmen turned on her side. Jay hadn't spoken a single word during the fiasco and she hoped it stayed that way. All she needed was silence.

In the meantime, Kane left the hospital without even acknowledging his kids; although he passed them in the lobby. It wasn't until he was walking into the parking lot that he noticed Kristian was following him. He wanted to tell her to go back inside, but he knew she had followed him for a reason. Either she wanted to know what had happened or she was going to try and convince him to stay. If it was the latter, Kane would tell her to save her breath.

"What now?" Kristian asked once they were standing outside of his Jeep.

Kane slowly exhaled. "I'm getting out of here," he told her. "I don't need to be around this bullshit. I'm going to head to my parents' house in Manhattan. I might be there for a few days. Who knows?"

"Maybe—" Kristian didn't bother to finish her statement. Her father clearly needed space and the trip might have been the perfect solution. Manhattan wasn't far from Brookstone yet it was enough of a distance to give him what he was looking for. "Maybe this will be good for you," she told him. "I knew that you and Mama were arguing over Rakim, but I never knew why. Jay is suing you?"

Kane was not mentally or emotionally prepared to deal with Kristian's question. He knew that if he answered it, she would only ask more. Therefore, he simply mumbled yes and kissed her forehead. "I don't want to talk about this. Tell your mother where I went." He gave her a quick hug and then proceeded to get into his car. He immediately started up the engine, and pulled out of the parking lot. He didn't even wait for her to go inside. At that point, the only thing on his mind was getting away from the hospital and to his next destination: Manhattan.

***

When the wall clock read one a.m., Jay counted the number of hours that Carmen had been in labor. He knew that it had been close to ten, but he wasn't certain. After the incident with Kane, it seemed as if time was moving slower than usual. The atmosphere in the room also hadn't changed. Part of the reason was because Kristian had informed them that Kane had left for Manhattan. Though he was pleased with the news, he knew that Carmen was hurt. She wore her pain on her face though she tried to hide it when Tiara and Malik arrived. She carried on a decent conversation with them and did it all over again when her parents came an hour later. Now that they were alone, she was back to being quiet.

"It's one," he heard Carmen say, finally breaking her silence.

Jay's eyes traveled back to the clock as he nodded his head in agreement. For Carmen to have been in labor for as long as she had, Jay had to admit that she was being a trooper. He hadn't heard her complain although he knew that she was uncomfortable.

"You want to check up on my parents?"

Jay shook his head no, knowing that they probably were asleep. When they had first arrived, they had simply come in, said hello, and then went to the cafeteria for a bite to eat. He hadn't seen them since then so he figured they were watching television or asleep in the lobby.

"You want to stay with me, huh? You're not going to miss anything."

Jay blinked his eyes a few times, wondering if he heard right. "Why wouldn't I want to stay with you? This is where I should be. Nyla is my daughter."

Carmen shrugged her shoulders. "I don't know. I know this is new for you." She looked over at him, noticing the solemn expression on his face. "Thank you for not stooping to Kane's level. I appreciated your silence."

"I didn't do it for you," Jay replied, honestly. "I did it because I don't have anything to fight over. I know Rakim is my son. As soon as we go to court, you and Kane will know, too. If I were you, I wouldn't take my kindness for weakness."

Carmen wasn't quite sure how to respond and was saved from saying anything when she felt another contraction. It wasn't until it passed that she realized Jay had grabbed her hand. Typically, she tried not to look into his eyes, but this time, she stared right into them. "Your daughter is ready to meet you. Can you gather everyone together? The kids are still here. They can at least stand outside the door while she comes."

Jay didn't want to leave her side, but he left to do as she requested. Not expecting to see the lobby packed, his eyes traveled around the room as he searched for familiar faces. Everyone appeared to be asleep except for Kristian. She was wide awake with a magazine in her hands. "Nyla's coming," he announced. He walked over to Lotus, shaking his shoulder as he repeated his words. He did the same to Patricia and Malik until everyone eventually stirred. "Come on, y'all. The baby is coming." Jay stood there for a minute or two until everyone got situated. When he finally returned to the room, he could hear the doctor telling Carmen that she couldn't have an epidural. From the way she was positioned, it appeared that she was literally only minutes away from giving birth.

"This baby is coming too fast, Mrs. Kane," the doctor said. "For some reason, you dilated quicker than I expected. I'm sorry, but Miss Nyla decided that she is ready now and she doesn't want to wait another second."

Carmen quivered when she heard the doctor's words. The last thing she wanted was another natural childbirth. It seemed she didn't have a choice. Jay was busy putting on scrubs and her mother was the only other person in the room aside from two nurses. Their presence was a reminder that Nyla was indeed on the way.

"Well, here we go for round four," Patricia joked. "You seem to be ready for this."

Carmen tried to ease out a small smile, but the pain from the contractions stopped her. She knew it showed on her face because her mother grabbed her hand.

"Don't squeeze too hard," her mother told her. "I still have to draw with that thing."

Carmen would have laughed if the pain wasn't so severe. Not to mention, the doctor was starting to direct the birth. He asked her to push and when she complied, it seemed as if time started to move slower than usual. While only two minutes had passed, it seemed like almost ten.

"Mr. Santiago, can you come over here?" the doctor asked. "I need a really good push this time, Mrs. Kane," the doctor continued. "I promise you, Nyla is ready for the world, but you have to help her. Mr. Santiago is my witness."

Jay stared in between Carmen's legs as she pushed. When he saw Nyla's head emerging, he nearly vomited on the floor.

"Mr. Santiago, are you okay?" the doctor asked, hearing the gurgling sound.

"Yeah," Jay replied, covering his mouth. "I am." He swallowed, watching as the doctor instructed for Carmen to push again. It was then that the man grabbed Nyla's head starting to slowly pull it out.

"Do you want to do the honor? I'll lead you through it. No worries, you can't go wrong."

Jay looked down at his daughter's head and bit his lip. The chances of him witnessing another birth was slim to none so he shook his head yes. He positioned his hands around Nyla's head at the doctor's instruction and when Carmen started to push, he slowly pulled Nyla's head out. Tears wailed up in his eyes as he pulled her towards him, revealing her legs and feet. He then placed her down on a blanket as the nurses rushed to his side. Almost automatically, the room erupted into hand claps and yells. Even with the commotion, Jay never took his eyes off of his daughter. Not even when Carmen announced that the baby's full name was Nyla Jaslene Santiago. However, it wasn't until he cut the umbilical cord that he noticed the color of her hair. Soft curls dangled around her face in a medium auburn hue.

"What's wrong, Jay?"

He heard Carmen as she called to him, but he didn't answer right off. He waited until Nyla was in his arms before he spoke. "Her hair is red." Jay brought the baby over to her, laying her down onto Carmen's pillow. "Look at her, Peaches. She has red hair."

Carmen stared down at her daughter for the first time, admiring everything about her. From her light butterscotch complexion to her tiny fingers that were naturally curled into a ball. "She looks like you," she told Jay, seeing the resemblance. "She's all Santiago."

Jay looked down at Nyla, staring into his daughter's brown eyes. Her skin was almost the exact color of his and he could already tell that she was going to have his nose. As much as he wanted to be alone with her to dissect all her features, it wasn't possible. The noise in the room escalated dramatically and before long, Nyla was pulled away from him.

"Dang, she looks like Jay," Tiara blurted as she carried the baby over to Malik. "Look at this little girl, baby. It's like he spit her out."

Jay sat down on Carmen's bed, staring impatiently as Tiara and Malik took their time with Nyla. The rest of Carmen's family were now in the room and had gathered around them to see the new addition. A part of him became slightly selfish as he began to want his daughter to himself. The feeling slowly went away when he turned to look beside him. He could tell that Carmen was worn out though she wore a small smile on her face. Not thinking, he neared his face to hers and softly kissed her lips. After he pulled away, he realized she had succumbed to him. He knew he could never get her to admit it, but he was certain that Carmen still had feelings for him.

In actuality, Carmen did, though guilt was starting to plague her heart. She knew that Jay had gotten caught up in the moment, and that she shouldn't have let him kiss her. By doing so, she was entangling both of them in a web of lies and danger. Luckily, her family was too enthralled with Nyla to have noticed the kiss. Since they hadn't, Carmen told herself to forget that the smooch had happened. It was hard for her to do until Nyla was placed back into her arms. At that time, she erased the kiss from her memory.

***

The news of Nyla's birth never reached Kane's ears. With every intention to go to Manhattan, he'd changed his mind when he got on the interstate. It was then that he remembered Sanders telling him that all Jay wanted was to bring strife into his marriage. Sanders advised that if he allowed that to happen then it would be like he was letting Jay win. By leaving the hospital, Kane had taken a loss. The only way to fix it was to take the first exit back to Brookstone. He went straight to the hospital where he was currently sitting in the parking lot. No one knew he was there, which is what he wanted. Already aware that Carmen was starting to believe that their marriage was crumbling, he wanted to change her thoughts. He needed her to believe that they still had a chance.

Kane picked up his phone and dialed the direct number for the hospital. When the receptionist answered, he asked to be connected to his wife's room. Carmen picked up in no time, but he didn't allow her to speak. He had a lot to say to her and the first thing was an apology. He knew he was wrong for how he had acted. His emotions had simply gotten the best of him. Any man walking the earth wouldn't be pleased to see the woman they love carrying another man's child. It was even harder for Kane because he had struggled to give his wife a baby. Jay, however, had easily done the job.

Kane repeatedly asked her to bear with him. He knew that she would be bringing Nyla home and he did want to have a relationship with her daughter. He also was going to have to accept Jay. He would be coming around more often and he wouldn't have a choice, but to deal with him.

Now that they had cleared the air, Kane felt comfortable returning to the house. He was the only one there, which he decided to use to his advantage. He prayed, meditated, and did whatever he could to prepare for Nyla's arrival. He knew the road ahead was a long one, but he braced himself for whatever was to come.

Part Two:
Flashing Lights

Chapter Eleven

January

Both of Kane's fists were clenched tightly. It was a sign that his nerves were still on edge. For the past thirty minutes, he and Carmen both had been hemmed up in the airport. Now, he was watching a plane as it took off for Puerto Rico with his wife and stepdaughter onboard. Kane knew that a day like this would come, but he didn't think so soon. In his opinion, Jay's spur of the moment trip to San Juan was nothing short of a trick. Instead of taking the baby with him when he left, Jay had called Carmen's cell, demanding that she bring Nyla to the island. Since Carmen was all about making sure that Jay had a relationship with his daughter, she had quickly obliged. He had tried to talk her out of it and even reminded her of the pending lawsuit.

Unfortunately, it was an argument that he had lost. Carmen ended up booking a flight, promising him that she would call whenever the plane landed. Still, that wasn't enough. Kane wouldn't have been satisfied unless he was on the flight with her. If the trip hadn't of been so sudden, he would've been able to go. Nonetheless, work was screaming his name. Now that Lieutenant Harris had picked up on his involvement in the Santiago case, he demanded more evidence than Kane could provide. It kept him and Sanders both in the field trying to gather as much as they could. After nearly two months on the case, both of them were coming up short. The only thing they knew for sure was that Shawn Blumington had become a permanent resident of Brookstone.

Kane knew that he had thought Sanders up when he felt his phone vibrating. With Carmen on an airplane, Sanders was the only one he could think of who would be dialing his number. Seconds later, he learned that he was right. "Yeah," he answered.

"I need you to get downtown," Sanders was saying. "A bunch of Jay's men are walking into Blue Magic as we speak. Shawn Blumington is here, too. These little meetings are sporadic. If you ask me, we need to get one of these guys to be an informant. If we get one, we get Harris off our back."

Kane knew that he needed to get to the restaurant. He quickly told Sanders that he was on his way and hung up the phone. Feeling like the stakeout could be their lucky break and give them enough evidence to indict Jay, Kane hurried to his car.

***

The third floor of Blue Magic currently held the major players of the Santiago cartel. Initially Malik was the only one absent, but that soon changed. He had run into the restaurant not knowing that Sanders and Kane were looking down on him from an abandoned building across the street. Already late, he didn't hesitate to knock on the door of the conference room. When it finally opened, he raised his arms, allowing Costa to check him. Once he was finished, he took his usual seat at the head table. For some strange reason, the mood in the room didn't feel right. He looked to his left, seeing Blu seated next to him. The man was sitting in the same seat that used to be occupied by Jay. He was also leading a discussion.

"No one in America can touch us now," Blu was saying. "You should reward yourself for how quickly you have added on to our repertoire. We control nearly half of the United States. I see how many of you are reaping the benefits of our feat. Y'all are looking good out there. However, with every dollar spent, there should be a dollar saved or invested. Don't get caught up in the lifestyle, many of y'all are pushing whips and sitting up in expensive houses. You can't put that shit in West Brookstone. The poor man sees it as his treasure. Cover the shit up. Take some of that money and get a degree."

Malik ignored the bowl of broccoli and cheese soup that was placed in front of him. His mind was more focused on the fact that Blu was in the room. Not only that, the man was speaking as if he was in charge. Malik knew that somewhere along the line, a pair of wires had been crossed incorrectly. Right before Nyla's birth, Jay had immediately put the cartel into his hands. Shortly after, Rico had started to vouch for Blu. He wanted him to assist them in the next re-up. Blu had showed a change in attitude, but Jay had refused to let him become a part of the operation. Somehow, Blu had done the job on his own.

"As we all are aware," Blu continued, "King will be coming home soon. We all need to tighten up so that he can see the progress that we've been making. I don't want him to have to come home and clean shit up. I want us to be rock solid. I expect all of you to respect his position like you've been respecting me. The last thing I want is to hear that someone has been questioning his authority. Let's remember his bloodline." Blu paused before turning to Malik. "Is there anything you would like to add?" he asked.

Malik narrowed his eyes in anger. Blu asked the question like he was his sidekick. It was a thought that Malik hoped would disappear from Blu's mind. He chose not to show his temper right off, deciding to speak. "As most of you are aware, Jay is still on hiatus. While I was handling most of the affairs of the cartel, I am now moving the responsibility over to Costa and Rico. Two days ago, my wife gave birth to a baby girl who will now be my focus. If you need anything, Rico and Costa are your go-to men, no one else."

"Does everyone understand?" Blu asked, looking around the room. He watched as the men slowly nodded their heads. "Great, finish your meal."

With the meeting coming to a close, Malik grabbed the steak knife that was on the table. His mind was telling him that Blu had fucked them over while his heart was telling him to talk the problem out. Malik knew that when Jay brought Blu up from Georgia that it wasn't to put him in the cartel. In a month or so, Blu had started his reign. The idea of it made Malik want to thrust the knife in his chest. He changed his mind when he thought of his newborn daughter, Robin.

"I want in," Blu whispered, placing his hand on Malik's shoulder.

Malik looked at him dumbfounded. "You want in on what?"

Blu let out a small chuckle. "Come on, Malik. I've had a lot of time to myself. I had a limo at my disposal, Rico as my tour guide. Did you really think I was enjoying the city? Hell no, I was doing my homework. See, I know all about Santiago's little FedEx scam. Shit, you can fool your workers, but you can't fool me. I know the real meeting starts after this one. You and Jay plan a lot of shit behind closed doors."

Malik's grip tightened on the steak knife that was in his hand. Blu was speaking on a topic that he knew nothing about. It made him wonder how much Jay really had going on. He thought his best friend told him everything, but it was obvious that he didn't. "Believe me when I say this, I don't know what the fuck you're talking about. I don't know shit about FedEx."

"Come on, Mr. Washington." Blu laughed. "You're a better liar than that. Tell me about Carmen. Isn't she in on the scam? Word is that she and Jay both have a love for the brighter things in life."

Malik dropped the steak knife onto the table. If he had kept it in his hand, it would've ended up in the side of Blu's neck. By putting it down, he kept himself from getting a murder charge. "I don't know shit about a FedEx scam. Who were you listening to? I know for sure that I wasn't in on that conversation. For your own personal safety, I would suggest that you forget that a woman named Carmen exists. Jay warned you about her. Whatever you think you know, you need to forget."

Blu may have heard Malik loud and clear, still he wasn't going to let up. He knew his information was factual whether Malik was informed about it or not. "Damn, I thought Santiago had more respect for you than that. He didn't let you in on this?" Blu stood up, placing his cloth napkin onto the table. "I guess not," he assumed.

Malik rose to his feet as well, blocking Blu from leaving. He wasn't quite finished with the conversation. Blu had information that he wasn't supposed to have. It had to come from somewhere and Malik was adamant about finding out the details. "How long have you been eavesdropping on Jay's conversations? Who told you about FedEx?"

The evil smile returned to Blu's face. He could tell that Malik took him for a snitch, which he wasn't. He would never tell where the news had come from. "I may get the info, but that doesn't mean I did the dirt. I bid you good day, Mr. Washington."

Malik watched as Blu walked past him. When he left the room, his temper flared. Without a doubt, Malik knew that he had to get word to Jay. Blu was on to something and it bothered him that he didn't know what it was. Once he was in private, he had to get Jay on the phone so he could get the answers he needed and wanted.

***

San Juan, Puerto Rico

Jay peered over at the pool chair as he heard his phone ring for the fourth time. He chose to ignore it once again and planted his eyes back on Carmen and Nyla. Their attention was focused on the water until his phone rung for the fifth time. Then, they both looked at him. He almost felt like they were asking him to answer it. When the phone rang a sixth time, Jay mumbled a few curse words under his breath. He gave Nyla another quick glance before picking up his phone. There were six missed phone calls and all of them were from Malik. That only told Jay one thing: something was wrong.

Not wanting to deal with the issue, Jay set his phone back down onto the pool chair. He knew it wasn't fair to leave Malik to handle whatever was brewing, but Jay planned on doing that. His plans to spend quality time with his daughter were not about to be ruined by the drama back in Brookstone.

"I thought you were taking a break," he heard Carmen say.

Jay looked down at the indoor pool as he watched Carmen carry Nyla up the pool's steps. She was dripping wet so he grabbed a few towels, beginning to wrap one of them around her. "I am," he replied, "I didn't answer my phone."

"Yeah, but someone was calling you like crazy. Maybe you should check it out."

Jay tightened the towel around her. "Maybe you should mind your business." He glanced down at her, noticing the disapproving look she was giving him. He knew she didn't mean anything by her comment, but he didn't need her prying in his affairs. If she was going to focus her mind on anything then it needed to be his proposal. He still didn't have a place to house his jewels, which meant that there was a delay in the product line for Iceland.

"Speaking of business," Carmen replied after a few seconds of silence. "I'm going back to work tomorrow. Tiara is officially on leave so it's time for me to get back. I want you to know that for most of the week, it'll be you and Nyla. I know you're excited about her being here, but I would like it if you came back to Brookstone on maybe Tuesday or Wednesday. I can't be away from her that long." A smile appeared on Carmen's face as she thought of her next set of words. "Besides, I am her food supply."

Jay's eyes glanced downward at Carmen's chest. His mind fell into the gutter, but he told himself to control his urges. He couldn't put too much pressure on her or she would go running back to Brookstone. Though she had a flight scheduled for later that evening, he was hoping he could get her to change her mind. He had already scored by getting her to join him and Nyla in the pool. Jay grabbed a towel to dry off with only to hear his phone ring for the seventh time. Once again, it was Malik.

"Take it," Carmen ordered. "Go ahead. Obviously, you've got business to handle."

Jay grabbed his phone, but he didn't answer it. He held it up so Carmen could see who was calling. When he was certain that she had caught the name, he hit ignore. "Family comes first. Malik should know that better than anybody. His wife just had a baby," he said, sternly.

"You may want me to believe that," Carmen responded, jokingly, "the truth of the matter is this; you don't want me in your business." Carmen poked him in the chest. Her right index finger was right on top of his heart where he had the face of a lion tattooed. "So, I'm going to take our daughter up for a bath while you return Malik's phone call. How does a little privacy sound?"

Jay cracked a smile. He decided to let his actions speak for him. He dialed Malik's number and put the phone to his ear. His plan seemed to work as Carmen started to walk away. Meanwhile, Malik answered right when the door closed to the pool area. Jay wanted to give his friend a mouthful, but he told himself to let Malik speak. If he was calling him back to back then he probably had good enough reason.

"I was running late to the meeting this afternoon," Malik told him. "I walked inside and guess who was leading it."

Jay felt the word you about to slide off the tip of his tongue. He stopped realizing that if Malik was asking him to guess then his friend wasn't the one leading the meeting. The only two people who could've been leading a discussion were Rico and Costa. However, they weren't supposed to find out that they were in charge until that day.

"Since you can't say it," Malik continued. "I'll tell you. It was Blu. You brought him into this city and in two months, he earned the respect of every man in that room. This motherfucker was sitting at the head table in your seat. He had the fuckin' nerve to ask me if there was something that I wanted to add. He looked at me like I was his fuckin' sidekick. Rico says that they're supposed to be heading to Continental tonight. You know that's where we keep our stash. I bet Blu is going to be in on that. You see this shit, Jay? This is what I warned you about. You didn't want to listen. You wanted to test him. Here's your test. Now, what are you going to do?"

Jay chuckled. His friend was talking to him like he had a situation on his hands that he couldn't handle. Jay was upset, but he wasn't about to show his wrath yet. It wouldn't have been beneficial since he was in San Juan. Jay reasoned that it would be better if he saved his anger for when he returned to Brookstone. For now, all he could tell Malik was that he would handle everything in due time. He didn't even give him a chance to respond, hanging up the phone. Carmen had said that she wanted him back in Brookstone by Tuesday. With Blu trying to run his cartel, Jay was certain that he would be back in time.

***

Brookstone, New York

Jay's men were still inside of Blue Magic, which meant that Kane and Sanders hadn't left their post. There was also a black Bentley parallel parked in front of the restaurant. Kane was certain that the car belonged to Shawn Blumington. With Jay in Puerto Rico, the car definitely wasn't for him. Besides, Malik had pulled up in his own vehicle. "I don't get it, Sanders, I don't," Kane admitted. "All of these men right here in New York and Jay employs an out of towner to handle his shit. You don't see any of Jay's men being chauffeured around. Malik doesn't even have a chauffeur."

Sanders joined Kane at his side, looking down at the restaurant. Two women were coming out of its doors, which prompted him to look away. "He must have some kind of rank," he assumed. "Based off our finds, he's the only man besides Malik and King that actually owns something. All of those other guys are associates. They don't have anything going for them."

"Like that one," Kane stated, pointing across the street. A young Hispanic boy had walked up to the restaurant's entrance. He didn't go inside, but was standing out front like he was waiting for someone. When Shawn Blumington emerged, Kane knew that the boy was waiting on him. "Who is he?" Kane inquired, looking over at Sanders.

Sanders could see the boy from where he was standing, but he needed a closer look. He grabbed his binoculars and zoomed in on the boy that was joining Blumington in the Bentley. "That's Jarrod Luis," he told him, removing the binoculars. "He wasn't on the list. He's been at the precinct a few times for some fights. He lives with his uncle and his grandma. From what I've noticed, the young dudes are hardly ever in the meetings. It is mostly the older guys. If you ask me, Jarrod probably works a corner or something."

Kane kept his eyes on the car as it slowly moved away from the restaurant. Although he had no intention of following it, he knew someone valuable was inside of it. Jarrod was probably regarded as being one of the lowest people on the cartel's totem pole. If anything, he probably only brought in two thousand a week in hustles. "That's him," Kane said, taking a step back from the edge of the roof. "He's the one we need to go after."

"Jarrod Luis? You want him?" Sanders probed.

Kane nodded his head yes. "He's nobody to the cartel. Shit, look at him. I bet he knows as much as anyone that is actually sitting in those meetings. He's the one we need. He's our informant. Who else have you seen Blumington with?"

"No one, but Rico and Jerome," Sanders replied. "So he's our pick? Let's get on it."

Kane took a final glance at the restaurant as he waited for Sanders to gather his things. Not quite sure where Blumington's car was headed, he wasn't going to let that stop him from getting close to Jarrod. All he needed was his address and everything else would fall into place. They would watch him for a few days before scooping him up for a field trip to the precinct. If they found Jarrod with a few dime bags on him, it would be enough to threaten him with a charge. That way, he would have a reason to tell everything he knew about the cartel. With an informant, they would be one step closer to arresting Jay.

Chapter Twelve

San Juan, Puerto Rico

If she didn't get a move on, Carmen knew she would end up missing her flight. The original plan was to simply drop Nyla off then head straight back to New York. Somehow, Jay had talked her into getting in the pool with him. That took almost two hours of her time and then Nyla's bath was another twenty minutes. Now that the baby was asleep, Carmen was able to steal away for a few minutes to shower. Jay's butler, Silvas, had offered to peek in on Nyla which made her feel a little bit more comfortable about leaving her. She hadn't seen Jay since she left the pool area, which meant that his attention was elsewhere. From the way Malik had been calling him, she figured something was wrong. Jay wouldn't tell her until the last possible minute. It was one of the things that irritated her about him, but she had learned to deal with it.

As she stepped out of the shower, she grabbed a body towel. She quickly wrapped it around herself, hearing a set of heavy footsteps. With Silvas being a small-framed man, Carmen automatically knew that Jay was in the guestroom. She put her guard up, knowing she would have to face him. At that exact moment, she recalled her husband saying, I told you so. When they were at the airport, he argued with her that Jay only wanted her to come to San Juan for one reason: sex. Kane believed that the trip was a ploy to get her in bed while Carmen argued differently. Now, she knew his words were more than likely true.

She opened the door of the bathroom to find Jay standing next to the bed. He was still shirtless, wearing only his black swimming trunks. The sight of him was tempting, but Carmen knew she couldn't give in to him. She had already given him a freebie when she allowed him to kiss her at the hospital. She couldn't let it happen again. "Can you excuse me for a minute?" she asked him. "I need to get dressed."

Jay stared at her for a few seconds before looking down at the bed. Her clothes were nicely folded on top of it and a pair of shoes was on the floor. "I got a disturbing phone call from Malik," he told her, ignoring her request. "I was going to talk to you about it, but there are other things we need to be discussing." Jay held her gaze and asked, "Did you really come all the way here to bring Nyla?" He knew the answer she would give was yes whereas her subconscious would give a different one. Carmen would never admit that the sight of him made her vulnerable. She would continue her façade only because she liked to be in control. By letting her guard down, she would be giving in to him.

For Carmen, yes was the safest answer. If she said no, he would know that he didn't have anything but space and opportunity. He would make his move and they would be right where they had left off. Not wanting to feed into his mind game, she made her way closer to the bed. She reached for her clothes only for him to grab them before she could.

"Answer the question," he ordered.

Jay didn't want to force the discussion on her, but he did want to tell her how he felt. "I don't have to beat around the bush with you, Carmen. I've dealt with you for too long to have to resort to that. You know the underlying reason why I asked you to come. Less than a year ago, we were planning our wedding. You broke up with me and before I knew it, you were married again. You didn't even give me a chance to try and make it right."

"This isn't what I came here to talk about," she told him, finally replying. "I'm married, Jay. I want to be faithful to my husband. I know we have this connection, yet our relationship never seems to work. We try, something always goes wrong." Carmen stopped speaking when the disappointment showed on his face. It was obvious that she hadn't given the answer that he wanted.

"What went wrong, Peaches? I told you, if Kane didn't find the diamond in three days then I got you. It meant that I didn't want it back. I—"

"I don't need you to explain," she yelled, interrupting him. She took a step back, not expecting for her voice to be as thunderous as it was. "We tried, okay? It didn't work. Maybe…maybe, you should move on." Carmen grabbed her clothes from him, clutching them to her chest. She suddenly became uncomfortable as the silence mounted in the room. If that wasn't enough, Jay was now wearing a look of hurt and resentment. He then told her to get out before walking out of the room.

Now that he was leaving, Carmen dressed quickly before heading to Nyla's room to say goodbye. Jay was inside with their daughter, but she didn't utter one word to him. She simply kissed Nyla and left the house.

As for Jay, his temple was throbbing even harder than before. While Malik's news had upset him, it was Carmen who had almost sent him over the edge. He was open with her about how he felt only for her to reject him. Jay didn't want to believe for one second that Carmen didn't want to be with him. He could see in her eyes that she did. Yet, she was fighting it.

Jay knew that there would never be another woman that could handle him like her. She was the only girlfriend he had who went the extra mile to get close to him. He had told Carmen things about his past that he had kept buried for years. Sometimes, he felt like she was the only one who understood him.

"Love is tricky, eh?"

Jay looked up, as he heard his butler's voice from the doorway. Nyla's bedroom door was still open, which was where Silvas was standing. He didn't respond to him, but he knew Silvas didn't need a reply. He had been his family's butler since he was four or five and knew him like the back of his hand. Silvas always knew what he was thinking before he even said it.

"You solve one problem with another," Silvas continued. "Remember that."

Jay didn't know what his butler meant right off. As time passed, and he thought about it more, he knew what Silvas meant. All he needed was the results of his paternity test. It would give him back Rakim and in the process, Carmen would come back as well. Though he hated to wait, he told himself to be patient. It would be only a matter of days before Carmen would learn the truth. Then, she would come rushing back.

***

Brookstone, New York

Jay was not the only person stressing over Carmen. Kane was worried about his wife as well yet his anxiety eased when she told him she had landed back in New York. The news had cleared his mind enough for him to continue working on the Santiago case. After leaving Blue Magic, he and Sanders had returned to the precinct. They located Jarrod's address and had spent several hours on a stakeout outside of his home. Kane believed that their time was wasted until Jarrod pulled up driving an exterminator's van. He thought nothing of it until Jarrod emerged later that night. He got back in the van and they started to trail him to several different houses. One of them even belonged to Jerome McFadden. Jarrod picked up four or five men before heading downtown. His final stop was Continental, a brokerage firm, about four or five blocks away from Blue Magic.

It was then that Kane believed they had found their golden ticket. The men began unloading several boxes and carrying them into the back of the firm. They did so for a straight fifteen minutes. "I timed them," he announced to Sanders. "They are very punctual and efficient. They get in and out." Kane peered up from his watch and noticed that the men were getting back into the van. The brake lights came on and the van started to move again.

"Do you want to follow them or should we see what's in those boxes?" Sanders asked.

Kane wanted to do both, but he knew that he couldn't. For one, they needed to get a warrant to search Continental, unless they broke in. Sanders certainly wouldn't go for that idea. "We need to get a warrant," he told him. "We get that then we can see what's in those boxes. I have a feeling this is Santiago's stash house, but I want to make sure before we go to Harris."

Sanders chuckled as he realized they had stumbled upon their biggest find yet. "The last place anyone would think to stash some damn bricks is in a white-owned brokerage firm. I wonder how he inked this deal. Either the owner is getting a nice chunk of cash or a decent supply of coke."

Kane agreed though he didn't comment on the matter. He was becoming more concerned that they didn't have more of a visual. Though he knew Jay's men were carrying boxes into Continental, he didn't know where they were storing them. Until they got the warrant, it would remain a mystery. "The warrant," he said, speaking his thoughts. "If we get it tomorrow morning then we can put some cameras in the building. That way, if they come back, we can see exactly where they're headed. Then, we can find out what's in those boxes."

Sanders looked directly in front of him at Continental. He believed wholeheartedly that Jay was stashing drugs in the building. With Kane's plan, they could have ocular proof in a matter of hours. "So let's do it, which judge do you want to call?"

Kane looked over at Sanders, giving him a quick smile. "We'll contact one tomorrow. I'm calling it a night. Wifey is back." With those words, Kane started up the car. He pulled away from Continental, heading back to the precinct.

***

Without opening her eyes, Carmen knew that it was Kane who was wrapping his arms around her. She didn't respond to his affection, knowing that in less than five hours, she had to be awake. Though Tiara had kept her up to date on Flame's activities, Carmen knew what the week would bring. The board had agreed to table the vote on the shoe line, but it wouldn't be tabled much longer. Now that her leave was over, she knew they would want to vote this week. Unfortunately, she still hadn't come up with a collection to sway their minds.

The thought of it all made it hard for her to sleep. She was slightly groggy in the morning though she tried to appear cheerful. She and Kane both seemed to be in a rush, which didn't leave them much time to talk.

They simply said good morning and gave each other a few kisses before going on with their day. He headed off to the precinct while by eight-thirty she was walking onto Flame's executive floor. The office was already abuzz with activity and Cathy was talking a mile a minute on the phone.

Carmen felt out of the loop given that she had been on leave since late November. Nevertheless, it would only take an hour or so before she would be back in the swing of things. To start her off, Cathy came strolling in her office with a notepad.

"Well," Cathy began, "let me first say that it's good to have you back. Thankfully, we didn't ruin things while you were gone," she joked. "First thing first, *Seventeen* wants to do a feature on Kristian. They faxed over this letter to our publicist."

Carmen wandered to Cathy's side, and took the sheet of paper out of her hands. She quickly scanned the letter to learn the details of the cover shoot. "See, this is the kind of news that I need to hear. I know sales are picking up for Mantra, but this will definitely generate some attention our way. It might make the board concentrate more on the *Peaches* collection. I need anything I can use to take their minds off of a shoe line."

"*Seventeen* wants to do the shoot on Saturday," Cathy continued, reading from her notepad. "Um, you need to keep this afternoon open. Jerry is going to be interviewing some potential interns so you might want to sit in on that. The board meeting is scheduled for Wednesday, but I've already made a note to cancel it. I know you're going to be in court so I will postpone it till next week." Cathy gave her pad a final look to make sure she had covered everything. "Last, but not least, what was it like having a month or so off?"

Carmen picked up her cell phone, preparing to text Kristian about the *Seventeen* cover. "Fun," she answered, coyly. "I got a lot of rest with two babies. I'm glad to be back at work though. Nyla is in San Juan, but as soon as she's back, she'll be right here, watching mama work." Carmen looked up and met eyes with Cathy as her receptionist gave a small wave before returning to her desk. In the meantime, Carmen let out an anxious sigh. She had more on her plate than she thought. Ads from the *King* collection were strewn about her desk, but she'd have to deal with them later. First thing first, she had to tell Kristian about *Seventeen*.

Chapter Thirteen

Only ten minutes was left in the school day, but Kristian was itching to get out of her seat. Her cell phone had been buzzing since nine o'clock yet she hadn't been able to get her hands on it. When the final bell rung, she made a beeline for the door and headed toward Akaila's classroom. By the time her sister emerged, Kristian was able to see that she had twenty unread emails and two text messages. One of them was even from her mother.

"What's the news of the day?" Akaila asked her when she noticed that Kristian was checking her messages. "Did Mama do okay back at work?"

Kristian wasn't quick to answer as they started to make their way out of the main academic building. She was still trying to read her mother's text and maneuver around her peers at the same time. It wasn't until they were outside that she got the news of a lifetime. In a split second, she had gone from content to ecstatic. "I got a *Seventeen* cover!" she yelled. She showed the text to Akaila before running towards Coco and Dijuan. They were standing around on the ramp like they had been waiting for her and Akaila to arrive. "I—" Kristian's face turned to a frown when she saw the way Coco was looking. "Well, I was about to share good news," she mumbled. "What happened?" Kristian quickly glanced back and forth between the two of them. From what she could see, neither one of them wanted to spill any details.

"We just saw Malachi," Coco disclosed. "He got into some trouble today."

Kristian looked behind her at her sister. Akaila was still reading the text message, which meant she hadn't heard. "What trouble?" Kristian probed. "It can't be that big of a deal, I mean, my mom didn't have to come up here."

"He cursed at his Science teacher. He got a referral and detention. You'll have to come back and get him."

Kristian rolled her eyes, angrily. The last thing she wanted to do was make another trip to the school. "Okay, okay," she said, trying to figure something out. "Detention is over at like what, five or six?" Kristian watched as both of her friends shrugged their shoulders. "You know what? I'll get my dad to scoop him. He has to drive by here from the police department. It's no biggie." Kristian tried to ease out a slight smile though she knew her friends weren't buying it. If Malachi was getting detention then in a few weeks, it would turn into in-school suspension. In a month, it would be expulsion. Kristian had seen the same pattern with King. However, he had gone from detention to straight jail. She didn't want Malachi to follow in their brother's footsteps, but he could potentially be headed there.

"So are you going to do the honor?" Dijuan asked. "Someone has to tell her."

Kristian looked beside her, seeing that Akaila had reached them. She needed to break the news, but she wasn't ready. She decided instead to change the subject to her Seventeen cover. The conversation kept them occupied for a good ten minutes until Dijuan had to leave for basketball practice. It was then that they headed into the student parking lot. Kristian still hadn't dispelled the news regarding Malachi, but she knew she would have to soon. If he wasn't with his usual set of friends, Akaila would become worried. Then, the questions would start.

"Whose parents bought them a Benz?" Coco asked, interrupting her thoughts.

Kristian paused in her step as she noticed the pearl white SL500. The car was decked out in platinum rims and even had a set of tinted windows. Kristian couldn't think of anybody whose parents could afford a vehicle like that except her own. Nonetheless, she got her answer when the back window rolled down, revealing no one other than Blu. Something in the pit of her stomach told her that he was there to see her. She pretended that he wasn't and walked around the car.

"Oh, don't play me out like that," Blu yelled behind her. "What's the rush, beautiful?"

Kristian ignored him as she made her way to her car. She quickly unlocked the doors, telling Coco and Akaila to get in. Before she could do the same, Blu was at her side.

Kristian stared up at him in disgust. She could tell from the first time she met him that he was attracted to her. Yet, his attraction seemed almost dangerous. "What do you want?" she asked him, sitting down in the driver's seat. "I don't even know you."

Blu took a long drag of his cigar as he admired Kristian's face. She was a miniature version of her mother, which made him realize why Jay was so caught up. Both of them had chocolate complexions that had been paired with curvaceous frames. "I'm a guest in this city. You should get to know me. Do what Rico did; show me the finer parts of Brookstone. A man like me would love to have a pretty girl like you on his arm."

Kristian wanted to vomit in repulsion. Blu looked like a deformed monster. The last thing she wanted to be was his tour guide. She wanted to run away from him therefore she grabbed her door to close it, but he wouldn't let her. It was obvious he wasn't done with her.

"Why you got to leave so fast?" he asked with a chuckle. "Damn, Kris, can't I get some time? We haven't seen each other in months. I've been busy, you've been busy. You know I'm running the Santiago cartel, right? Jay and Malik had to take a little hiatus. I'm the one bringing in the money. Rico didn't tell you? Shoot, he was the one who told me where you went to school. See—" Blu paused as a red Cadillac pulled up in front of Kristian's car. It caught his attention as he studied the style of the vehicle. From looking at it, he figured the driver had to be male. "Do you know him?"

"Do you?" Kristian asked, smartly. She stared up at Blu, sensing that he might be growing nervous. The red Cadillac belonged to Nicholas Powers, otherwise known as Lil' Noc. He was a former fling of hers and her older brother's number one enemy. With Nicholas parked beside him, she knew that Blu wasn't going to bother her anymore. Six seconds hadn't even passed and Blu had moved away from her car. He got back into the Benz and left the parking lot. Almost immediately, Coco and Akaila started to scream questions at her. She ignored them for the time being, sneaking a peek over at Nicholas. She wanted to say something to him, but he drove off before she could even get out the car. She was disappointed though she tried not to let it show. She started up the engine, and told her sister and Coco that she would explain everything on the ride home.

***

Not only had the day taken a turn for the worse for Kristian, it had done the same for Kane. For most of the morning, he had been calling judge after judge in an attempt to get a warrant to search Continental. His request was denied by two judges and he couldn't get a hold of three others. The last one he spoke to had given him the runaround before finally giving the okay. The judge had argued that he didn't believe the brokerage firm was a stash house. Kane knew it was hard to believe so he kept coaxing the judge. In the end, he got what he needed. With the warrant in place, Kane headed straight for Sanders's desk.

On his way there, he passed the lieutenant's office. Harris' door was open so Kane took a peek inside. Good thing he did because he saw that Sanders was sitting at the man's desk. Without bothering to knock, Kane walked into the room.

"He's good, this man right here is good," Harris was saying, clapping his hands together. "So you found out where Santiago is keeping his stash?"

Kane looked over at Sanders not knowing that he had been discussing their find. He thought that there was a non-verbal agreement in place that it would remain a secret. "We have our suspicions," Kane said, swallowing, "but we don't have any photographic evidence."

"Not yet," Harris replied, pointing his right index finger at Kane. "Sanders came in here this morning with the idea of putting a camera system in the building. I agreed. We put the cameras on every floor, including the basement. I got some men right now looking at footage."

Kane clenched his jaw as he was learning secondhand that Sanders had gone behind his back. They were supposed to be working together, but his partner was already one step ahead of him. Kane was working on the warrant so that they could search the firm by foot first. Then, the cameras were going to come. From the way Sanders had handled things, they were working backwards.

"We need to take action, Kane. Y'all have been on this thing for two months already. We'll get a lot funding if we take down Santiago. His businesses will go down, too. I still don't get how he has so much. Seventeen years in prison and he should be working a nine to five."

Kane tried to keep his composure as Harris mentioned Jay's businesses. While he did want to take Jay down, he had his reservations. Carmen's name was on Blue Magic, which made the case delicate. He had to be careful when it came to her. One wrong move and his wife would be arrested right along with Jay. Not to mention, Malik could be behind bars as well. "Harris, you know I want to take Jay down," he expressed, "but there are some issues with this case. My wife's name is on Blue Magic."

"So we're going to get two for one?"

Kane's anger escalated to the point of him losing control. He didn't realize that he had charged at the lieutenant until Sanders was pulling him out of the room. His temper had already been ignited from the situation with the judges and then Harris' question pushed him over the edge.

"See, see," Sanders yelled as he pushed him down the hall. "This case is too fuckin' personal for you! You flipped back there!"

Kane balled up his fists as he tried to walk off his steam. He thought he'd cooled down some, but realized he hadn't as he answered his vibrating phone with a loud and gruff, "What!" He hadn't looked to see who was calling but when he heard Kristian's soft voice he calmed down. He wasn't composed for long as she was quick to tell him that Malachi had gotten detention and would need a ride home. Before Kane could tell her to pick him up, she was already stating that she couldn't. If it wasn't Carmen's first day back at work, he would've told Kristian to call her mother. However, he knew that Carmen was swamped. Kane finally agreed to pick him up and ended the call.

"Look," he said, pointing his finger at Sanders. "I got to handle something. Don't put one foot into Continental until I get back. Don't even look at the cameras. You've done enough damage already."

Sanders rambled off in his defense, but Kane didn't stick around to listen. He walked away from him, heading towards the closest exit. He could feel himself becoming antsy and he told himself not to take all of his anger out on Malachi. He wasn't quite sure what his son had done, but he told himself he would deal with the issue later. His mind was too wrapped in the case to even begin to deal with why Malachi was in trouble. When he did reach the school, Malachi was standing out front like he knew he was coming. His face already showed signs of nervousness. Kane didn't ask him any questions neither did he ask how his day was. He simply told Malachi to buckle up and that they were going back to the precinct.

"Call your mother when you get in my office," he said. "I got work to do and I'm not driving back to the house to drop you off. She can come get you on her way home. Work on your homework while you're waiting. Don't touch anything; don't even try to look at anything. Shit, don't even talk to anyone."

Kane didn't look at Malachi as he spoke. He kept his eyes on the road as he drove back to the precinct. As for Malachi, all he said was a simple okay in reply. In Kane's opinion, it was all he needed to hear. Once they were back at the precinct, he let Malachi into his office before heading over to Sanders' desk. Though he was still angry, they needed to be getting over to Continental. While Harris had other officers watching the firm's day to day activities, Kane now had a warrant. They could get inside of the building; get the evidence they needed, which would result in an arrest. Unfortunately, their plans were halted again, when Kane looked inside one of the precinct's interrogation rooms. Lieutenant Harris and Jarrod were seated inside, two people that Kane hadn't expected to see. The sight of them made him grab Sanders' shoulders in anger. "Did you tell him about Jarrod, too?"

Kane saw Sanders' lips move, but the only sounds coming out were mumbles. It was enough for Kane to know that his partner had. Instead of cursing him, he grabbed the doorknob, and entered the room. "What's going on?" he asked, loudly.

Harris looked stunned at his presence. "We brought him in for questioning."

Kane looked over at Jarrod who had a nonchalant expression on his face. He could tell that Harris wasn't getting much out of him, which prompted Kane to sit at the table. "What did you find on him? Is he clean?"

"Shit," Jarrod muttered. "Clean as Lever 2000. I told y'all, I don't know shit."

Kane watched as Jarrod slumped down further in his seat. It was then that he noticed that he was wearing handcuffs. He was about to question the arrest when Harris interrupted him.

"We saw you at Blue Magic. There are photos of you getting inside of an exterminator's van. It's the same van that was at Continental last night. You were dropping off something. We know you work for Santiago," the lieutenant argued.

Jarrod laughed in Harris' face. "Man, get out of here. You saw me at Blue Magic because I like the food. I was driving that van because my uncle owns an extermination business. Shit, I needed a few extra bucks so I took a few bombs to the firm. I haven't even gotten paid for it."

Kane began looking for any chance that he could step in. He knew he could get Jarrod to talk. Unlike Harris, he knew that arguing wasn't going to earn Jarrod's trust. Kane felt that if Jarrod saw what he was up against that he would tell them what they wanted to know.

"Look, Jarrod." Harris grunted. "We got a lot of stuff that we can make stick. We know you work for Santiago. Now—"

"Man, fuck that shit. You don't have anything on me. What did y'all find? It definitely wasn't any dope. I'm clean as fuck. You come to my block, scooping me up like I stole something. I haven't done shit."

Kane could feel the tension rising in the room. If it continued to increase then they wouldn't get anything out of Jarrod. They would be forced to let him go since there wasn't any physical evidence that said he was bringing drugs into Continental. "What is the real reason you were at the brokerage firm?" he asked. Jarrod looked his way, but didn't respond. Instead, he shifted his gaze to an officer who was stepping into the room.

"Harris," the officer said upon entry. "The cameras were destroyed. We no longer have any footage. Every single screen is out."

Kane looked behind him, staring into the officer's face. He cursed under his breath before he looked up at Sanders who was standing up against the wall. He didn't need any proof to know that Jay's men had located the cameras. How they found something that had the size and look of a quarter, he didn't know. He looked back at Jarrod as Harris left to handle the issue. In the meantime, Sanders joined them at the table. "Okay," Kane whispered. "I'm going to try and work with you, but you have to work with me. The lieutenant is going to stick you with every charge he can unless you cooperate."

"Cooperate?" Jarrod said, pointing at the door. "He doesn't know who he's fuckin' with. But *you*," he said, pointing at Kane, "man, you're about to sign your own death certificate."

Kane took note of Jarrod's words. Without even knowing it, Jarrod had said a mouthful. "So you know my connection to Santiago. What else do you know about me? Do you know my stepson, King?"

Jarrod chuckled as he slumped down in his seat. "Man, selling dope ain't my thing, homes. You got the wrong man. I don't know anything."

Kane looked over at Sanders, knowing he had to go to Plan B. "Get the photos. Maybe if Jarrod sees himself, he'll talk. We know and he knows that he was at Continental last night. We have the proof. All we need him to say is whether or not that is Santiago's stash house."

"Shit," Jarrod replied. "That isn't me in those pictures."

Sanders left the room to get the photos, but Kane stayed behind to interrogate. At this point, it was on him to get Jarrod to talk. "What do you think Santiago is going to do when he finds out that you've been here? Maybe, I should post those photos of you up in Blue Magic where they put the business cards. Then, he can see who's been slipping." A different expression formed on Jarrod's face. "See, that doesn't sound too good, does it? You're not the only worker in that picture. We got a lot of evidence that can bring down a lot of people. Now, if you talk, you can walk out of here with police protection. If you don't, Harris is going to charge you with a lot. Drug charges are different than your little school fights."

Jarrod squirmed in his chair as if he was weighing out his options. He didn't say anything right off, but a few minutes later, he did. For two hours straight, he told everything he knew.

Chapter Fourteen

The cameras in Continental had been destroyed by Jay's men, but it had been done without his knowledge. He wasn't aware of the latest drama surrounding his cartel since he had arrived in Brookstone only minutes ago. At the moment, he was walking into his apartment, trying to balance Nyla as well as her numerous baby bags. With the baby asleep in his arms, he tried not to wake her as he headed into her room. He placed her on the changing table only to deal with her fussiness as her sleep became interrupted. "I know, Princess, I know," he told her, pulling off her skirt and onesie. "You need a bath, but at least I am compromising." He quickly changed her into a pink pajamas set and placed her in her crib. Back to sleep in no time, Jay smiled at how quickly she had calmed down. He watched her for a minute or so before grabbing a baby monitor and heading into his bathroom.

Upon entering, he immediately stripped himself of his shirt. Well aware that he had a long night ahead of him, he splashed cold water onto his face. Not only did he have to deal with the situation that was brewing with Blu, he also needed an update on the last re-up. Rico and Costa may have been dealing with the day to day affairs, but he still had to keep up with everything that was going on.

When he finally did pull out his phone, he was able to see he had ten missed calls from Costa. To Jay, it was a clear sign that something else had gone down. Without hesitation, he dialed his number. "What the fuck happened now?" he yelled once Costa said hello. Jay could tell from the sounds coming from the phone that Costa wasn't at home. In fact, he heard several voices around him. "Talk to me," he ordered. "What happened?"

Costa exhaled loudly before he spoke. "The Brookstone PD is on our trail. We found these cameras down here in the basement. They are small, look something like a coin, and they were up on the ceiling and the walls. I don't know how long the cameras have been down here, but they probably got footage of everything. We confiscated them, but I know there has to be more. We wouldn't have even known about the cameras if Blu hadn't told us to do a walkthrough."

Jay's eyes blinked several times. Not only had Costa admitted that he had followed an order from Blu, but he was also telling him that Kane was closer than he had originally thought. Jay let out a deep growl, realizing that he had never slipped like he was. Still, he gave the same message to Costa that he had given to Malik. "Everything will be handled. Get everything out of the brokerage firm. Place it back in the exterminator's van and hide it in a chop shop. Make sure you contact every single man attached to this cartel. I want them in the basement of Iceland at six o'clock in the morning. Blu doesn't need to make an appearance. Get the word out. If anyone is missing, best believe that come nightfall, they honestly will be."

***

The basement of Iceland wouldn't have been as hot if it wasn't for all of the people gathered in the room. Despite the heat, Jay walked in fully dressed without one button undone. "It's 6:00," he announced, turning towards Costa. "Lock the door." Jay didn't look at anyone as he took off his suit jacket. He laid it down onto a wooden table, which was the only piece of furniture in the basement. He then started to work on the sleeves of his dress shirt. "What happened during the re-up?" he inquired, calmly. "Sunday night, some of you were at Continental without even thinking of a camera. Now, y'all are concerned. What happened?" The room remained quiet as if everyone was scared to speak. "No one knows?" he asked, taking his eyes off his left sleeve. He looked around the room attempting to eye each man that worked for him. Some of them he couldn't see, but it didn't bother him.

Jay knew they were being silent out of fear. Therefore, he decided to give them another chance. He undid the buttons on his right sleeve as he waited for someone to respond. Once it was loose, his fingertips touched his collar. "What happened during the re-up?" he asked again, starting to unbutton his dress shirt. No one said anything, but by this time he was expecting to hear a response. "Costa, can you please explain? I pay a bunch of deaf motherfuckers."

Costa cleared his throat as he draped his Uzi at his side. He hated having to be the voice, but it was him and Rico that Jay had left in charge. "The re-up went as planned. There were no errors. We made time. The walkthrough that Blu requested was where our problem occurred. We found three cameras installed in the basement. All of them pointed towards our safe."

"Three fuckin' cameras," Jay began, "inside of my stash spot. Can at least one of you motherfuckers tell me how the fuckin' Brookstone PD got inside of my shit?" Jay watched as the men shifted their feet. No one spoke so he looked at Malik. "Can you explain?"

All eyes fell upon Malik. While he knew the answer to Jay's question, his nervousness kept him from saying it. He knew what was about to go down whenever Jay started to undress. It may have confused some only because they weren't used to seeing that side of him. As much as Malik wanted to prevent the inevitable, Jay was already on a roll. "We have a snake in the grass," he finally responded.

"You hear that?" Jay shouted. He waited to hear a response, but the only thing that came were two loud knocks at the basement door. Immediately he looked over at Costa who already had his Uzi pointed in the door's direction as if he was preparing to shoot. "Don't," Jay ordered. "See who it is first." Jay watched as Costa did as he asked, opening the door for a young male. Jay recognized the late arrival as Jarrod, a high school-aged boy from West Brookstone. Unsure of why he was late, he allowed Costa to check him before he continued. "There has to be a snake in the grass," he griped. "Unless someone is slipping, the Brookstone PD doesn't have a single reason to search Continental. I take a little break and come home to three fuckin' cameras in my spot," he spat. "No one knows shit, though. I see, I see, I guess everyone gets it then."

"I know what happened," a voice said in the room.

Jay focused his eyes in on Jarrod. His lack of punctuality already had him heated and now his confession made him wary. The boy didn't know that he was about to start walking on thin ice.

"They were on my block yesterday," Jarrod started to explain. "They arrested me on some bogus charge saying I had some dope on me. I was clean as shit, man. They took me in, talking about how they had pictures of me outside of Blue Magic. Matter of fact, they said they had pictures of everyone. If you ask me, they are probably out there now. All they want is an informant. They don't have me, though. I know how to keep my mouth shut. I called my grandmother and posted bail this morning."

Jay continued to unbutton his dress shirt not showing any type of reaction to Jarrod's statement. He waited until he was down to his undershirt before he spoke. "Do you remember who took you in? What was the officer's name?"

"It was the lieutenant at first," Jarrod replied, "but then Michael Kane came in. He had a white guy with him. His name was Sanders or some shit. I know about your history with him so I knew not to talk. I was going to call Blu the minute I got out. I heard about the meeting when I got back on the block and came straight here."

Jarrod's words were reassurance that Blu was indeed acting as if he was in charge. Even Jarrod who was at the bottom of the barrel thought proper protocol was to seek out Blu. Still, Jay decided not to tackle the issue. "This happened last night? You posted bail this morning?"

Jarrod nodded his head, which made Jay believe that he was fuckin' with him on purpose. It was getting harder for him to maintain his composure as Jarrod lied to his face. "I know from experience and from dealing with my own son's troubles that you didn't get arrested last night and was able to secure a bond hearing this morning. I don't see that happening, especially not on some damn drug charge. It's six o'clock in the morning. The judge probably doesn't even know about this case." He stared into Jarrod's face, hoping he was catching the hints. "They seem to have told you a lot. You knew they were outside of Blue Magic. How did they get to Continental?"

Jarrod's feet shifted and he started to pace the room. Jay could tell that he was trying to cover his tracks. When he saw his lips move, he hoped that Jarrod had chosen his words wisely.

"Um, they saw the van," Jarrod muttered. "They saw me getting in the van. They were following us. They must've followed us to Continental on Sunday."

"You didn't notice that shit!" Rico yelled. He snatched Jarrod up by his shirt as he screamed in his face. "You're a part of the fuckin' lookout. That was your shit to handle!"

Jay grabbed the back of Rico's collar, pulling him away. The battle Rico wanted to fight was his own. In due time, he would handle Jarrod. He wanted to give him some time to come clean. Once Rico appeared calm, Jay took his hands off the back of his collar. He then walked up to Jarrod, allowing him to read his facial expression. Well aware that he was caught in a lie, tears started to form in Jarrod's eyes. His words became incoherent, but it didn't faze Jay. All he could think about was how his future with his family was being severely threatened.

Without speaking to Jarrod, he turned to face the table. His hand found its way underneath it and he grabbed a silver pistol. Jay didn't hesitate to fire a round of bullets into Jarrod's face. Mayhem filled the room as his men began to scatter, heading for the nearest exit. Unfortunately, there was only one. Costa immediately cocked his Uzi, blocking the doorway. It was a sign to the men that they were going to be forced to watch.

Some of them were covering their mouths in disgust while others were wiping blood off their clothes. Their behavior was exactly what Jay wanted it to be. "This should be a reminder of who I am. You can fuck with me if you want to." He turned back towards Costa giving him permission to open the door. In a split second, the men started to flee the room. When Rico passed him, Jay grabbed him by the arm, pushing him back. It was his way of telling him that he wasn't finished. He didn't speak to him, but waited until there were only two other men left in the room, Malik and Costa. "Who put Blu in charge of the re-up?" he asked him, angrily. "You thought I wasn't going to say anything, huh?"

"N-n-no," Rico began to stutter, not having a sensible answer.

"Who put Blu in charge of any of my shit?" Jay yelled. "I put you in charge and I end up with this shit on my plate? Fuck you, Rico!" Jay fired a bullet into the boy's leg.

Rico staggered to the floor, grabbing at his wound. Well aware of Jay's intention, he quickly began to ask for forgiveness. "I'm sorry! He knew what to do," he muttered. "He had a plan. If it wasn't for him, we wouldn't have found the cameras!"

Jay shook his head angrily before turning to look at Costa. "You know better," he told him. "You, of all people, you know better." Jay fired a shot at his arms, allowing the Uzi to fall to the ground. The bullet only managed to graze Costa's wrist. "You should've known better," he repeated. "You broke my heart." Jay paced the room, trying to gather his thoughts. There was one dead body in the room, but he wondered if there should have been three. He thought to get a second opinion and looked at Malik. It was then that he noticed the vomit on his friend's clothes.

"Jay, don't—" Malik was too late. He watched as Jay pulled the trigger, sending Rico into a deep sleep. He covered his mouth, watching as the boy's brain matter began leaking onto the basement floor. He turned away only to hear the sound of another fatality.

"Oh, this esé is trying to live."

Malik gazed over at Costa. He watched the man as he clutched his chest in an attempt to control the bleeding. Although he hoped that Jay would let him be, he knew he wouldn't. It was proven when he fired another shot. This time, Costa didn't move. Malik looked over at Jay seeing the evil smile that was on his face.

"I told you I would handle it," he told him. "You shouldn't have doubted me." Jay paused for a split second to look at the three dead bodies in the room. "Today is a new day, Malik. I'm making the call right now. It's done. There will never be another re-up. Lucky for you, you invested your money well. Now, for the others, we might need to start issuing some severance packages. First, though, we need to clean up our mess." Jay took out his cell phone and made a quick phone call to his connects at Jimenez Funeral Home. He quickly informed the owners that he had three good bodies for them to pick up.

∗∗∗

Jarrod Luis had been the first thought in Kane's mind since he had opened his eyes. After taping his conversation with him, Kane knew enough about Jay's operation to go after the physical evidence. The current plan was for him and Sanders to meet up with Jarrod at Continental. From what Jarrod had told them, the drugs were kept in a safe in the firm's basement. Though Jarrod didn't know the code, he had all morning to get it. Once he had it, he was supposed to meet them at Continental.

From what Kane could see when he pulled up, Jarrod hadn't arrived. Sanders hadn't either. Instead of leaving, Kane remained parked across from the firm. He hadn't found the link between Jay and the owner, but he knew he would. Right now, he was itching to get inside.

"Have you seen him?" a voice asked.

Kane looked to the right of him where Sanders was standing on the sidewalk. Without saying hello or good morning, Sanders got into his Jeep, continuing to talk.

"We can't get the evidence if we can't get in the safe."

"If he doesn't show, we'll break it open," Kane retorted, leaning his head back. "Let's wait it out. Jarrod knows he has a lot weighing on him. The kid is only seventeen." Kane closed his eyes, telling himself that he wasn't going to wait much longer. If Jarrod didn't show in the next hour, he was going inside of Continental. He would find the CEO and take matters into his own hands.

Chapter Fifteen

Kane's presence at Continental was unbeknownst to Jay. Since he had killed Jarrod without getting the major details of the interrogation, he was unsure of how much Kane actually knew. Until he was arrested or word came from the Westside, he would remain in the dark.

With the corpses now headed to Jimenez Funeral Home, Jay returned to his apartment to clean himself up. Once he had changed, he headed over to Blue Magic where one of the hostesses, Naomi, was babysitting Nyla. He would've preferred dropping his daughter off with her mother, but Carmen would question why he was returning her at five o'clock in the morning. It also didn't help that he was still angry with her for turning him down in San Juan. On the other hand, Jay knew that Carmen was not his only problem. He knew that when Rico's murder reached King's ears their relationship would become strained. He hoped that it remained a secret until he found a way to tell him.

"Here she is," Naomi called out, interrupting his thoughts. She handed Nyla back over to him along with her baby bag. Surprisingly, his daughter was wide-awake.

Jay grabbed her into his arms, kissing both of her cheeks. He hated that he had to leave her with a complete stranger, but he didn't have a choice. "I really appreciated this," he told Naomi. "She wasn't any trouble, was she?" Jay opened up his wallet, taking out two hundred dollar bills. He handed them over to the hostess, which she took kindly.

"Oh no, Mr. Santiago, she was a doll. She slept most of the morning until she got a little hungry. She drunk the last bottle you had in there. I could tell that she wanted more, but I didn't know what formula she took. Other than that, she was fine. I can tell she's glad to see you."

"Yeah, I know she missed Daddy. I'm glad to hear she wasn't any trouble," he replied. "Thanks again." Not wasting any time, he headed for the exit. He knew now that he had to take Nyla back to Carmen. He had never given his daughter formula and wasn't about to start. Though he wasn't ready to see his ex, he knew that was his next stop.

As he drew closer to the restaurant's exit, he stopped in his tracks when he noticed Jerome and another one of his workers, Phase. Since Rico was his cousin, Jay prepared himself to deal with the forthcoming drama. Even with Nyla in his arms, he planned on taking care of business. He went straight up to them, knowing that they came to Blue Magic to see him. It was obvious when they started walking towards him. Not allowing Jerome to speak, he told him exactly what was on his mind. "If you need two seconds to think about what you're getting ready to do then take it. It is the exact length of time you'll have before you end up like your cousin." Jerome looked over at Phase. Jay could tell that the coward inside of him was slowly starting to reveal itself. If Jerome didn't make a move then he knew that Phase wouldn't either. He had only brought the man as his muscle.

"Rico didn't mean any harm," Jerome whispered. "Blu is very intimidating. He has more knowledge than Rico or Costa. Back in December, he started begging Rico to let him be in on the next re-up. Malik was around, but not like he should have been. If he was there when we were handling things, then Blu wouldn't have learned as much as he did. Rico felt that putting things in Blu's hands would ensure that there weren't any errors. He never expected anything to happen. The cameras weren't his fault. We all know who was responsible for that. Jarrod led the police right into our trap."

A simple shrug of his shoulders was all Jay gave as a reply. He knew his action was heartless, but he didn't have any remorse. With the way things had been handled, he was now looking at more time in prison if Kane found what he was looking for.

"I know you killed Rico," Jerome continued. "We waited for him and Costa to come out, but they never did. We saw the undertakers." Jerome paused as his emotions started to get the best of him. He tried to keep himself together though it was getting harder to do. "What am I supposed to tell his mother?" he asked. "Can we at least get his body? Let us give him a proper burial."

Jay could see the tears starting to well-up up in Jerome's eyes. He understood why he was upset, but Jerome would never see the bigger picture. Their freedom was now threatened and it was partially a result of his cousin. Jay was prepared to voice that yet their conversation was starting to attract attention. "I suggest we take this outside," Jay whispered through gritted teeth. He looked over at Phase so that he could know that his words applied to him as well. When they headed for the door, Jay followed behind them until they were next to his limousine.

"You will understand if I told you I had to bow out," Jerome continued. "I don't see how this could work considering what happened this morning. I would appreciate it if we called it even. I know I owe you money, hopefully, you'll forgive the debt."

Jay couldn't have cared less about Jerome calling it quits. However, he wasn't going to lose money. "As far as you bowing out, that's fine. Our mutual understanding will be this; you will pay me what you owe me. I suggest you contact Malik about settling your debt. Do that and there won't be any problems." Jay opened up the back door, sitting Nyla inside of her car seat. He didn't buckle her in, placing her baby bag in the car as well.

"So it's done. I'll contact Malik. Send King my regards."

Jay was taken aback at the mention of his son's name. Jerome walked off as if his comment was a reminder of what he would have to deal with when King came home. Deep down, Jay knew that Rico's murder wasn't going to go over too well. Nevertheless, once he explained the situation, he hoped King would understand. He had simply eliminated a snake that could have cost them more than their cartel.

Jay believed that the conversation was over so he turned to Nyla, buckling her in her car seat. He was getting ready to get inside as well when a voice spoke behind him.

"We don't know what he told those cops. We don't even know how long those cameras have been down there. Shit, there could be more."

Jay peered behind him, and stood up straight to see that Phase had stayed behind. It was obvious that he wasn't cutting his ties. Jerome hadn't left yet either. He was standing several feet away in the parking lot, watching them converse. He appeared to mutter a few words under his breath before continuing to his car. Once he was gone, Jay looked back at Phase, "You came with him for a reason. Were you going to step to me, too?"

Phase didn't utter a reply, but Jay knew that one wasn't needed. If Phase was still down for him, he would show it by accepting his test. "If you really think that there are more cameras in that basement, maybe you should do another walkthrough. Matter of fact, leave it alone. They want us to go back in the building," Jay said, thinking of a new idea. "The cable company, downtown, has vans. I know we got some pull somewhere in there. See if we can scoop one today. I got a few Mexican friends in there. Have them do the walkthrough. They can pretend to be installing something. Do it in broad daylight."

Phase replied with a nod. "I'll make sure we get all the cameras this time."

"Y'all don't have a choice. Jarrod was the beginning."

Jay slid inside of his limousine indicating that their discussion had ended. Phase took the hint and even closed his door. When his driver, Gus, turned around to face him, Jay instructed him to take him to Flame. Unsure if Carmen was in a meeting, he pulled out his phone and called Cathy's direct number. Once she answered, he told her he was coming and to make sure that Carmen was available. With the visit set, Jay set his phone down and stared over at Nyla who was already sleeping peacefully.

"This is going to have to hold us, Princess," he whispered, touching her recently pierced earlobe. "I can't afford to spend another seventeen in prison. I will kill myself before I let that happen. Your daddy is changing careers. I promise you."

Breaking away from the cartel was a plan that was always in Jay's mind. He never thought that he would do it so soon. In fact, the initial plan was to hand it over to King. With Jarrod snitching on him, he had to let go of the whole thing. All of the men who had been eating off of him were now officially unemployed. He could only keep a couple as a part of his team. As for the rest, he hoped they had saved well.

"We're here," Gus yelled from the front seat. "You want me to carry the baby in?"

Jay mumbled a quick no before grabbing Nyla's car seat. He made his way out of the limousine and inside of Flame. Normally, he would interact with her employees whenever he visited, but this time he went straight to Carmen's office. The second he stepped inside, his phone started to vibrate. He ignored it for the time being, setting Nyla's car seat onto Carmen's desk.

"Good morning," Carmen greeted. She peered up from her sketchpad where she had been drawing a set of designs inspired by her youngest son, Rakim. The sketches were for a new collection she planned on naming, *Fresh Prince*. Despite the last conversation they had shared, Carmen's intention was to remain cordial. "Cathy told me you were stopping by. She said I needed to keep the next hour or so free. Did you have something planned?"

"She ran out of milk," Jay explained, pulling his cell phone from his pocket. He quickly learned that the vibration was from a text message sent by Blu. In a short amount of time, one of his men had already snitched about the incident at Iceland. Now, Blu wanted to meet with him to discuss all of the details. While it wasn't originally in his plans for the day, Jay knew that he needed to put eyes on Blu. It was time for the man to get his walking papers.

"Is that all?" Carmen asked, looking down at their daughter. "I guess things between us haven't changed." She looked back at Jay who was sliding his cell phone back into his pocket. He looked rather uninterested, which told her that his mind was elsewhere. "Look, Jay, I know we're dealing with a lot. We go to court tomorrow and it's only going to make things worse between us. We still have to communicate when it comes to Nyla and I want—"

"I need to go," Jay interrupted, backing away from her desk. "You can keep her for a few days and I'll pick her up at the end of the week. Is that cool?"

When Carmen said yes, it came out as a stutter. Unsure of what was going on, Carmen could only stare at him as he walked out of her office. Eventually, she told herself to let it go. Until Jay came around, she would be in the dark. For now, she had to focus on what was important, her new collection, and the court hearing.

Chapter Sixteen

It was never Jay's intent to leave Flame the way that he had. He knew his actions surprised Carmen, but he couldn't give her an explanation for his behavior. With less than twenty-four hours until the court hearing, he needed his actions that morning to stay under wraps. If Carmen learned that he had murdered three people she would only use it against him. He would lose custody of Rakim before he even got it. Not to mention, Blu's text had put the itch back in his finger. Unsure if he would give him the same treatment, he debated the issue in his mind as Gus drove him to Sapphire.

His uncertainty came from the fact that Blu had never forced his control on anyone. Rico and Costa had merely handed him a position of leadership that Jay now had to take back. While he expected to have made the decision prior to walking into his club, the truth of the matter was that he hadn't. Since he was still unsure, he decided to play the meeting by ear.

As he waited for Blu to arrive, Jay pulled two glasses from the mini-bar. He filled both glasses to the brim with cognac.

"Me and you?" he heard a voice ask.

Jay looked straight ahead at the doorway where Blu was standing. He held up a glass to him, prompting him to walk into the office. A crooked smile was already plastered on Blu's face, which Jay tried his best to ignore. "Take a seat," he ordered.

"Damn, Santiago, it's been awhile," Blu said with a chuckle. He sat down across from him, but didn't bother to touch his drink. "You were dodging us left and right. Back in November, Malik was telling everyone that he was in charge. Everything had to go through him. Come on, Jay, you know Malik doesn't know how to run this thing. I had to come in and fix all his shit. I made us plenty of money."

Jay realized that Blu was saying a whole lot for a man who was walking on death row. He still had the same narcissistic spirit that had kept him out of the cartel in the first place. "This lifestyle doesn't last forever," Jay told him. "When it's all over, it's over. When I took my hiatus, I put the cartel into the hands of men I trusted. Or so I thought," Jay said, sitting down. "Obviously, I picked the wrong ones. You can't trust anyone in this game. Everyone wants what you have and will do anything to get it."

Blu raised his glass to his lips, but decided not to take a sip. He set it back down on the desk that separated him and Jay. "Nah, you can't trust people," he said, straightening his legs. "People come in and mess up all your shit. If you ask me, you can't trust the people closest to you. Malik trusts you, but you don't care enough about him to let him in on your FedEx deal. He didn't know shit about it when I questioned him. What's up with that?"

Jay felt his face tighten. If Blu was mentioning anything about FedEx then it was a clear sign that he had dug his nose in the right place. He thought that he had kept everything with his diamonds on the hush. Somehow, Blu had gotten the information and had told Malik in the process. What bothered him though was that Malik had never mentioned it. He only told him that Blu was acting as if he was in control.

"Ahh, don't worry, Santiago," Blu muttered, pulling a cigar out of his jacket pocket. "We don't have to harp on it. Let's talk about this morning. See, you done went and killed two of your best men. Rico was a dude with heart. He was loyal. Costa, he had the street smarts and the gunplay. Since they're gone, I'm the one that's next in line. What do you say? Let me run this thing." Blu lit his cigar and took a long drag.

"You were never the one," Jay said, sternly. "I made it clear when we met that you weren't joining the cartel. You tricked yourself into thinking your time here was a test."

Blu laughed as if he took Jay's words to be a joke. "A test?" he questioned. "I didn't have to pass anything. I already had mines. I was trying to help you out. Your own son couldn't run this cartel like I did. Did you even look at the money that came in within the last month? I made it greener and longer. Now, it's time to pay up."

Jay pulled his nine out of his waistband and set it on the table. He watched as Blu looked at the gun and smiled. A flash of fear never even went across his face, but that didn't matter to Jay. He still picked up the gun, cocked it, and pointed it at Blu so that he clearly understood that whatever he chose to say could get his head blown off. "I made the call this morning to end this drug shit. I'm not going back to prison because of some damn snitch. I'm going legit. I suggest you pack your bags and get out of Brookstone. Checkout at the Trump is tomorrow morning at nine o'clock."

Blu's chest began to heave up and down. He looked at the glass of cognac and although he needed it, he didn't take it. Everything that he once had aside from his businesses was gone. He had ended things with his connection in Colombia because he was set on taking over the Santiago cartel. Now, he was learning that it wasn't even going to exist. He had put in work for nothing. "This is how you do it?" he asked, angrily. "You have to come more correct than this, Santiago. You done killed your men and got the whole cartel scared sick. What are your men going to do about money now? They ain't got shit, but some expensive cars and houses. Some of that shit isn't even paid for. Who's going to take care of their kids? Shit, you're probably saying fuck 'em. You got yours."

Jay fired a shot, intending to miss. However, he got what he wanted, a flash of fear appeared in Blu's eyes. He even turned around to stare at the bullet hole in the center of the wall. "You catch on quickly," Jay told him when he saw Blu stand on his feet. They stared each other down for a few seconds before Blu walked backwards out of the office. Jay didn't move an inch until he could no longer hear Blu's footsteps on the stairwell. It was only then that he turned towards the camera system. Blu was getting inside of a black Bentley that was parked outside of the club. Once it was out of the parking lot, he picked up his phone, dialing Malik's number. When he didn't get an answer, he questioned Malik's whereabouts. From the way he had acted in Iceland, Jay feared that Malik had skipped town. He hoped that wasn't the case as he grabbed his glass of cognac. In one huge gulp, he swallowed it.

***

Malik's mind had been running ragged since the incident at Iceland. He didn't know where to turn after learning that Jarrod had snitched on them. At one point, he was even parked outside of the Brookstone PD to try to convince Kane to drop the case. When he discovered that he wasn't there, he went home. The sight of his wife and baby girl only made him more nervous. Tiara could tell that something was on his mind, but he wouldn't open up to her. He left shortly after, going to the county jail where King was serving out his sentence. He hadn't spoken to his godson in a couple of weeks and he had to warn him. A lot of heat was coming their way and he needed to be aware.

"Three gallons of milk expired today," he told him when King picked up the telephone in the visitation room.

King's eyes narrowed as he took in Malik's words. Certain that there wasn't any beef with the other cartels; he asked Malik if Jay had tossed the milk in the trash. When his godfather responded with a single head nod, King felt a grumbling in his spirit. The last thing he wanted to hear was that his father had resorted back to killing. Even if it was necessary, the murders would only put them further under the microscope with the police. "I didn't buy it, did I?"

Malik shook his head yes. "One came from Publix, one came from Bi-Lo, and the other one is from Wal-Mart." Malik paused for only a few seconds. "They all were sour. Right now, it actually works in our favor that you're in these walls. If we get more sour milk, you can be the one to go to the store. Jay will supply the paper, but you have to write the list. You know what items we need. If someone gets the wrong thing, you can go back and get the right one."

King chuckled to keep from expressing his real thoughts. Whereas he had been trying to make the best of his day, it was now ruined by Malik's visit. "So that's the plan?" he asked him. "Everything will be put on me. Tell me, Malik, how deep is this mess, for real?"

Malik knew that the story was going to get worse. King wouldn't be too thrilled to know that the problem existed between his two fathers. "Candy *Kane* deep," he replied.

King shook his head frantically. Malik's news left him speechless. He knew that if he was back in Brookstone none of this would be going on. He also believed there was more to the story then what Malik was telling him. If he wasn't behind steel bars, he knew his godfather would've revealed everything. He would've told him who snitched. Regardless of the real issue, King knew one thing. He had been chosen as the clean-up man. It wasn't a responsibility he wanted, but he didn't have a choice. Until the investigation blew over, all of their freedoms were threatened.

***

The pending investigation wasn't only a major concern for King and Malik. Having spent two hours outside of Continental, Kane, and Sanders didn't have anything to show for it. Jarrod never showed and they started to assume that the boy had skipped town. While Sanders suggested that they search the firm without him, Kane had another idea. He wanted to search West Brookstone. Kane knew that it would take more than physical evidence to indict Jay. Physical evidence plus an informant would give them a leg up on the case, and possibly, a win. Kane believed that they didn't have a choice but to find Jarrod.

After explaining his reasoning to Sanders, his partner agreed to scope out the area. They spent most of the afternoon driving around the Westside and even checked Allen's Field, a common place where dead bodies were found. When Jarrod didn't show up, they started calling funeral homes and hospitals. With no luck, they strolled into the precinct at a quarter till midnight. Carmen had called Kane six times and he'd sent each call to voicemail. He knew she was worried, but he couldn't talk to her. Too much was on his mind for him to consider going home. If he didn't have an answer in regards to Jarrod by eight o'clock the following morning, he would be in hot water.

"You don't see that, do you?" Sanders asked him.

Kane looked at him inquisitively until he saw where Sanders was pointing. A slew of papers were on his desk that hadn't been there before. Kane quickly scanned the documents, as his worst fears became a reality. The lieutenant was already aware of everything and he had left the documents out for Kane to see. "It doesn't make sense," Kane stammered, throwing the papers down onto his desk. "Jarrod only spent one night in jail. When we let him out, he should've gone straight home. Obviously, he didn't because we now have a missing persons' report on our desk. His grandmother filed it late this evening."

"Jay has to be responsible for this," Sanders argued. "That kid didn't go ghost. He's dead, Kane. We both know it. Go ahead and put it on the books."

Kane didn't reply as he read another paper that was on his desk. It wasn't a report, but a note from the lieutenant. "Harris had some men at Continental," he announced, skimming the paper. "Word is that the firm was putting up some plasma televisions in the lobby. They even had a cable company down there installing new wiring," he disclosed. He set the papers back down onto his desk. "All of the men doing the job were Hispanic. The officer got their names, checked them out, they all work for the same cable company. If you ask me, Jay knows we're on to him. He had those men looking for more cameras."

Sanders balled his hand into a fist, striking the table. He didn't curse though it was on the tip of his tongue. "You got to talk to him, Kane. Come on, your wife has a baby by him. You and Jay have to meet up at some point. Doesn't he come by the house? Can't you question him?"

Kane looked at his office phone as an image of Carmen entered into his mind. "To be honest, we'll actually be in the same room in a few short hours. It's the reason my wife keeps calling me. She needs me at home." Kane closed his eyes at the thought before reopening them. He wanted to be back on the hunt for Jarrod, but he had to deal with his own issues. "Look, let me get through this court thing and we'll get back on Jarrod. For now, let's call it a night." Kane grabbed his car keys off his desk and followed Sanders outside of the office. With a quick goodnight, they went their separate ways, heading for the nearest exit.

Chapter Seventeen

Both parties rose early the morning of the court hearing. While Carmen and Kane spent the first hours of the morning in conference with Clement, Jay was eating breakfast at Old Town Bistro. In consideration of the events of the day before, he had three main issues that needed to be discussed with Malik. One was the FedEx scam, the second was Blu, and then there was Carmen. With only three hours to go before the hearing, Jay was hoping he could get through it all before meeting with his own lawyer.

He was busy seasoning his grits when Malik came to the table. He didn't start the discussion right off, giving Malik the chance to order. Once the waitress left the table, he started in on him. "When I was in San Juan and you called me, you left out a lot. Why didn't you tell me that Blu knew about FedEx?"

Malik was taken aback by the topic of conversation. About to pour a cup of coffee, he sat back and didn't even touch his mug. "I didn't know the full scope of everything. It's not like you told me about it. Shit, your business is your business. If you want to partner back up with Carmen, do it. It's your heart and your money."

Jay dropped his fork as he took offense to Malik's tone. Either his friend was upset that he wasn't in on it or he was upset that Blu knew about it before him. "As my right-hand, you need to tell me everything. If Blu comes to you with shit you don't know about then you call me. Your name is on all of my shit. If I go down then you go down, too. You won't have anywhere to hide."

"I won't have anywhere to hide?" Malik spat. "You should be thanking God that I hid when they took you down. If I didn't, you wouldn't have the shit you do have. I know you're on edge because of the trial, but don't take it out on me. I didn't fuck you. That was Carmen's ass. If you remember, I was the one who spent seventeen years trying to keep your shit afloat. I kept an eye on your kid. I made sure that you kept your house."

"Now I am going to fuck with you," Jay snapped. He held his fork up to Malik, putting it only an inch or two away from his face. "Don't sit up here and bitch about the shit you did for me. We've done shit for each other. I was the one that put you and Rakim on. Y'all were damn near close to being in foster care when your parents died. I gave you a job. I didn't do it because I wanted something in return; I did it because I had a heart. We both didn't have parents. I—"

"What is this really about Jay? You called me up here at seven in the fuckin' morning, for what? You want to talk about the murders? You want to talk about Blu? What is it? You want to sit and mumble about how Carmen broke your heart? What is it this time?"

"I want to talk about all of it," Jay answered, honestly. "As for the murders, you were vomiting like an anorexic bitch. I've never seen that side of you. You were always the one ready for war. I guess little Miss Robin made you soft. That baby hasn't been here for a week and she has you on edge. If Jarrod had of lived, he would've continued snitching and we both would've ended up with life sentences. As for Blu, I told him to take his ass home. He checked out of the Trump this morning. Phase made sure that his ass got back on a plane to Georgia. So long and farewell," Jay spieled.

"Thank you and you're welcome," Malik shot back. "His ass wasn't supposed to be here in the first place. I warned you about him and you didn't listen," Malik said as he picked up his mug. He poured himself a cup of coffee and stared at Jay who was giving him a piercing look. Malik knew Jay was heated, but so was he. It was obvious that it wasn't a good morning for either one of them.

"You're absolutely right. You did warn me about him. However, I left the cartel in your hands first. Rico and Costa weren't the only ones not keeping an eye on him. According to Jerome, you weren't where you were supposed to be. Blu slid in without a problem."

"Like you were there, too?" Malik replied. "You weren't the only one who chose your family over the cartel. I did the exact same thing. That's why I took a hiatus."

Jay was starting to see that blame could be placed on both sides. "All I'm saying is that I left you with a responsibility. You didn't do what you were supposed to, which left Rico and Costa wide open to let Blu get in their heads. To be honest, I shouldn't even be focusing on this. What is important is this shit with FedEx. That's what Blu is after."

Malik chuckled at Jay's words. "Blu thinks that Carmen is a part of the scam. Are you on some Bonnie and Clyde shit with her? Is that what this FedEx shit is about? You chose her as your partner so you can get back in her panties? How many years does it take for you to realize that she isn't going to marry you? Why do you even do this to yourself?"

Jay dropped his fork onto his plate as he stared at his half-eaten breakfast. He was fed up with their conversation and wanted Malik to know it. He pulled out his wallet, dropping a twenty onto the table. "The reason you don't understand is because you've never loved her. Your relationship with Carmen has always been platonic. Kane is just as crazy over her as I am.

Your brother, Rakim, was, too. Even Carlos wanted a taste of her and he was the one who hated her. Shit, he got a taste of her."

Malik watched as his friend gathered his things. His relationship with Carmen had always been platonic, but that didn't mean he never had feelings or thoughts. In fact he had acted on them a little over a year ago only to be rejected. It was before his marriage to Tiara and a secret that he would take to the grave. Though nothing had happened, Carmen knew that he was secretly attracted to her. "What would you do if I told you that I had slept with Carmen?"

Jay's eyes quickly became bloodshot red as he imagined Carmen and Malik having sex. "At some point today, you should think about what I would do. Once you figure it out, don't worry about sharing. You'll be wrong until you multiply it by one hundred."

Malik's eyes widened as he pictured the nightmare. He knew where Jay's mind had gone and he had to let him know that it had never happened. "I would never do that to you, Jay. You know that." He made sure to meet eyes with him as he spoke, but Jay didn't respond. He simply left the booth. Malik resented himself for asking the question, but he couldn't take it back. He prayed that Jay believed him.

Meanwhile, Jay retreated to his limousine. As he walked, he replayed the conversation with Malik in his mind. They hardly ever argued, but that morning, something had come over them. Now that he was making his way to his lawyer's office, his mindset had to change. Gomez wouldn't want to hear about anything that didn't have to do with the paternity suit. He had put in countless hours trying to guarantee them a win. News of a pending investigation would only dampen his spirits. Well aware that he had to tell him about it, Jay decided not to do so that morning. Once he had his son back, he could concentrate on everything else. For now, all of the issues with the cartel had to take a backseat.

***

The entire courtroom was filled to capacity with more spectators than supporters. The only person in the audience who was there to offer support to both parties was Tiara. Although she was sitting on the side of the defense, she supported Jay wholeheartedly. Malik, on the other hand, would've been on Jay's side to show his support. He was currently at home with Robin, allowing Tiara to be there for Carmen. Though it wasn't necessarily where he wanted to be, he knew that one of them had to stay home with their newborn.

As for the defense, Carmen had been studying Clement's face ever since Gomez had started his opening argument. Her lawyer looked nervous almost as if he had already failed. His strained expression came from the fact that Kane could not conjure up the name of the doctor who analyzed his original results. Without a name, Clement had nothing that could aid him in arguing the legitimacy of Kane's test. They had to pray that the new test results showed that Kane was the father.

Her husband had barely said anything to her all day aside from praying with her before they went into the courtroom. Carmen knew that he was worried that things wouldn't work in their favor. He had never said it verbally, but it read on his face. If they lost their case Carmen wouldn't accuse her husband of lying. Kane had produced a certified medical document shortly after Rakim was born so she believed there wasn't anything erroneous done on his part. Still, Gomez would try and convince the judge otherwise. Currently, he was questioning the doctor who had analyzed Jay and Kane's present test results. There was tons of paperwork in front of him, which he had finished explaining.

"Based on these DNA results," the doctor began, "it is evident that the only man who could be the father of Rakim Antonio Kane is Jay Santiago."

Carmen's eyes started to tear up and she could feel someone rubbing her shoulders. She didn't dare to look at her husband or Jay. One part of the case may have been settled, but there was still another half that had to be worked through. Her real emotions would show when Gomez started his argument of how Kane had purposely lied about Rakim's paternity. Not knowing what he was going to say had her worried.

Although she was crying, Carmen saw Clement out the corner of her eye as he leaned closer to her. "Right now," he whispered, "The best route to go with Jay is to settle. We can still argue on the civil fraud, but after the doctor's explanation of the results, it would be pointless. Rakim doesn't have any part of Kane anywhere." Carmen nodded her head in response. "What do you want me to do?" he asked.

Carmen looked at her husband, seeing him with his head in his hands. Clement should've been talking to Kane; however, if anyone was going to be paying Jay then it was going to be her. The amount of money that Jay was requesting definitely couldn't come from Kane's pockets. She decided to answer and quietly nodded her head as an indication that she agreed to settle. Understanding what he needed to do, Clement requested a brief recess. Carmen knew that he was going to use the time to talk to Jay and Gomez. When the judge granted it, Carmen decided to take a break herself.

"Carmen," a deep voice beside her said.

She turned to face her husband. More tears stained her face as she decided to ask him one last time about his test. "What happened?" she asked him before he spoke. "I asked you if there was anything that could have possibly altered your results. You said no. You promised me that Rakim was your son."

"Carm, we—" Kane began.

"Don't beat around the bush," Carmen interrupted. "Whatever you won't say, Gomez and Jay will say for you. Believe me. They are going to paint a horrible picture of you as soon as this trial reconvenes. It's better if you tell me now."

Kane stared at his wife as his spirit began to fill with guilt. Hurting her was the last thing on his agenda, but he knew now it was inevitable. He looked over his shoulder, watching as Clement conversed with Gomez. He couldn't hear what the two men were saying, but he knew that they were trying to reach some sort of compromise. He turned back to Carmen, saying, "I'm sorry," before heading out of the courtroom.

A part of Carmen wanted to follow him, but Tiara encouraged her not to. She took her friend's advice and ended up in the ladies' room with several tissues in her hand blotting her face. Kane's apology made her believe now more than ever that he was withholding a secret. She didn't express the thought to Tiara who was busy keeping up with the time.

"Are you ready?" Tiara asked her, seeing that the recess was almost over.

"Do I have a choice?" Carmen cried. Still sniffling, she dumped her tissues into the wastebasket. "This shit is crazy, Tee. Kane told me that his test was legit. He even said it to Clement. I promise you, Tee. I will choke him in that courtroom if Gomez has solid proof that Kane altered his test. I promise you."

Tiara closed her eyes, knowing that Carmen was good for it. From having read her diary years ago, Tiara knew that Carmen had murdered a man named Enosis with her bare hands. She honestly believed that if the right words were said in the courtroom, Carmen would try and do it again. "We're going to keep praying, okay?"

Carmen met her friend's gaze, but didn't respond. She had been praying ever since she had been served. She wasn't going to stop although her faith was slowly diminishing. "Yeah, Tee," she replied, "we're going to keep praying." Tiara gave her a smile in return before opening up the door. She followed Carmen out of the bathroom and into the hall.

The courtroom was further down the hallway and Carmen dreaded walking to it. She figured that they had an hour or two left before the whole thing would be over. Then, she would have to start the process of changing Rakim's name and getting him more accustomed to Jay. It would be a lot of work, but she knew that it had to be done. As they approached the door to the courtroom, Carmen inhaled. When Tiara opened it, Carmen didn't step inside, instead she moved away from the door, and leaned up against the wall.

"Come on, Carm. Let's get it over with."

"Easier said than done," Carmen replied. She shifted her feet, watching as Jay returned to the courtroom with his lawyer. They were in heavy conversation and she could tell that whatever they were discussing was angering Jay. She also knew that she was going to get some of his wrath when he stopped in front of her. His expression was cold, but his tone was even colder.

"You know how to play a dirty game, Bonnie. So you think I only deserve a mill? You give my son to this lying motherfucker and you only want to pay me a million dollars? Man, that's some dirty shit, Carm. How did you come up with that number? Did Kane do it for you?"

The last thing that Carmen wanted was to give him the pleasure of starting an argument. She tried to bypass the whole conversation by heading into the courtroom, but Jay didn't let her. He grabbed her arm and yelled, "Nah, don't run!" He pulled her towards him as they stared each other down. "You know that shit is foul. I deserve a whole lot more than a million dollars."

Carmen jerked her arm away. "You say that shit like I knew you were the father and intentionally made him Kane's son. I had the proof of a fuckin' paternity test in my face, what was I supposed to do? I slept with y'all back to back!"

Jay scrunched up his face, knowing that him and Carmen were about to go at it. "Do what a woman is supposed to do. A real woman would make both men get a fuckin' DNA test. You knew your husband couldn't have kids, but you were so quick to give him Rakim. Is it because he came out dark? He still has my eyes, Carmen! You heard that fuckin' doctor. Rakim is 99.9% all me. I dare you or your fuckin' husband to try and change that shit."

Carmen told herself to calm down before things got too heated. She tried her best to watch her tone as she gave Jay a piece of her mind. "You got what is rightfully yours. What do you need the money for? If your lawyer does his job and does it right, you might even get to see Kane behind bars for fraud. What do you really want?"

Jay cracked a smile, knowing that Carmen was going to use her manipulative spirit to turn everything around. He knew that the moment he told her what he wanted, she would be willing to give it. She would do anything to save Kane even when he was in the wrong. "You'll figure it out, Bonnie." Jay walked back into the courtroom with Gomez intentionally leaving a million thoughts running through Carmen's mind. He knew that when his lawyer brought in their next witness he would have her right where he wanted her. In no time, Carmen would be back in his arms and his diamonds in her basement.

Jay was partially right because when the next witness took the stand; Carmen was on pins and needles. Gomez had thrown her for a loop since she had never seen the lady before. It made her wonder about the direction that Jay was leading the case. "Do you know her?" Clement whispered in her ear. Carmen shook her head before tapping Kane's leg. She asked him with her eyes if he knew who she was, but he didn't respond. He simply looked away like he didn't have an answer. Carmen turned back towards the witness stand as the woman was sworn in. She took note of her physical appearance wanting to remember everything about her. From the blonde streaks in her hair to the mole that rested on the left corner of her mouth. She had a face Carmen knew she would never forget.

"Can you please state where you work?" Gomez asked.

The woman nodded her head as she begun to clear her throat. "I used to work for the International Triad Intelligence Agency. It's commonly known as the Triad. I was there for about six years," the woman replied. "Then they decided to let me go."

"So you know this man, then?" Gomez asked, pointing at Kane. "You've probably seen him before, right? Maybe you've seen him walking the halls at the agency."

The woman shifted in her seat showing her nervousness. "Yes, I know him. I know him very well. We worked together ever since I became employed with the agency."

Carmen slowly turned to her husband. "She knows you very well," she whispered to him. Kane looked at her, but he didn't answer. Carmen could tell that her husband was indeed hiding something. She would even bet money that the witness was holding one of his secrets.

"Kane and I did work together, but we were also friends. He confided in me about things. Like, one time, he told me that he was having problems at home. His wife had given birth to another man's son. He told me that he was desperate. They had separated, but he was still in love with her. He said that his daughter had convinced him to do paternity test on his wife's son. He did it, but the results had come back negative."

Carmen grabbed her chair out of anger.

"So you're saying that Kane knew that he wasn't the father?" Gomez inquired.

The woman wiped a tear from her face as she looked over at Carmen. "My position at the Triad was valuable to him. He needed someone to alter the test results and he knew that I could do it. I've analyzed tons of DNA at the Triad. My specialty is genetic research. In return, I asked him for half a million dollars. I, I—" the woman began to stammer. "I knew that what I was doing was wrong, but I needed the money. Everyone at the agency knew about my son's medical condition and how much his treatments cost. I was desperate. Kane had the money to give because he had gotten a large sum of money out of his divorce settlement. I took it and did what he needed me to do. Once the lawsuit appeared in the news, I knew everything would be traced back to me. I couldn't live with the guilt so I decided to say something. In the process, I lost my job. Now, I'm trying to live off my savings until I find something else."

It took only a split second for Carmen to turn into a raging bull. A bunch of hands tried to loosen the grip that she had on Kane's neck, but only one pair was successful at separating her from her husband. The judge's gavel was sounding loud and clear, but it meant nothing to her. "I swear I'm going to kill you," she cried. "I swear!" She repeated the words several times as she was ushered out of the courtroom. Being removed was the least of Carmen's worries. She had heard everything that she needed to. She even heard the judge when he announced another recess without stating when they would reconvene. With the secret out, Carmen didn't care about returning to the courtroom, her desire to argue had diminished.

Chapter Eighteen

The judge granted a recess after Carmen's tantrum, which was only followed by a request from Gomez that the rest of the case be settled out of court. Clement accepted on behalf of his clients since they both were preoccupied. Kane had spent several minutes trying to get his own emotions together while Carmen was being calmed down in the hallway. Kane expected to see his wife when he came out, but she was long gone. Even their limousine was gone from the courthouse's parking lot.

Kane knew then that their relationship was indeed on the rocks. It was the main reason he had returned to the house and started packing his things. His duffle bag was almost filled to capacity, but he was still piling items into it as if it was only half full. To him, the more stuff he got inside, the fewer trips he would have to make to the house. Not quite sure where he was headed, he figured that he would spend a couple of days at Malik's house. If that didn't work then he would go to Manhattan.

"How long are you going to be gone this time?"

Kane heard a faint voice coming from the hallway. He zipped his bag up before he peered at the doorway where Malachi was standing. "I don't know," he told him, honestly. "I don't know about anything anymore." Kane grabbed his duffle bag, and then slid the strap over his shoulder. "You need to be getting in bed, you have school tomorrow." Kane grabbed his suitcase, pushing his way past Malachi as he headed for the stairwell. He knew his son wanted him to stay, but it wasn't an option. If he did, Malachi would be a firsthand witness to the tension between him and Carmen. Not wanting any of the kids to see that, he knew it was best for him to leave.

"You don't have to go," he heard behind him.

Kane turned around once he reached the steps. "It's not going to work. All we're going to be doing—" Kane didn't finish his statement or at least he didn't finish it verbally. In fact, his thought process changed when he began to see the bigger picture. *If I leave, all I'm going to be doing is giving Jay what he wants*, he thought. *Jay wants me out of the house. It wasn't really about Rakim. He used the baby as a ploy to get Carmen. Now that he has won his case, he's going to go full throttle for her. I'm helping him by leaving.*

Kane's eyes focused in on Malachi. His son wasn't even seventeen, but had the maturity of a grown man. Carmen had never asked him to leave so he had no reason to walk out the door. If anything, he needed to be fighting for her. Quickly changing his mind, he told Malachi that he was right and headed back into his bedroom. He unpacked his things and prepared for bed. The only way Carmen could get him to leave was if she kicked him out. Until she did, he was there to stay.

***

The afternoon following her court appearance was more stressful than Carmen had imagined. Her first stop was home, which was where the kids had remained during the trial. After giving them an update on the case, she packed a bag for Rakim and Nyla. Her next stop was Jay's penthouse apartment where she stayed for several hours. Despite the tension between them, she had brought Rakim over so that the two could start building a father-son relationship. So far, it seemed that they were getting along perfectly.

"Yeah, I can tell I've worn you out already," she heard Jay say beside her. "Might as well let you sleep. Your sister already dozed off on us."

Carmen looked down at Rakim's baby bag, realizing she had gone through it several times to keep herself occupied. She decided to check it one more time as Jay disappeared into the hallway. She could hear him putting Rakim to bed through the baby monitor that was in the living room. To keep her mind at ease, she continued checking her son's bag until Jay returned to the room. Then she rose from the couch and grabbed her purse. "I guess I should be heading out," she told him. "Tomorrow is a busy day."

Jay gave her a simple head nod as she headed for the door. He needed to have a serious conversation with her, but he was waiting for the best possible moment. When he saw her open the door, he knew he had to stop stalling. "I'm dropping the civil fraud suit," he announced. "You were right. I got what I wanted so what do I need the money for? I have my son."

Carmen sighed. She did it because she knew that there was more to come. Jay was about to hit her with a new deal like he had done before when he planned to trade the lawsuit for her hand in his new project. Carmen thought he had accepted that she wasn't going to help him, but he still thought there was hope.

"I'm leaving the drug game," he continued. "I made the call yesterday. Right now, all of my money will be coming from my businesses. We need to set up something big for our kids. This project, Peaches, I promise you. It will have us set for life. I only need to use your space."

Perplexed, Carmen stared at him. "My answer didn't change because I learned that you were Rakim's father. It's still the same. On the other hand, I am glad to know that you're no longer a kingpin. At least I don't have to worry about you going to prison on drug charges." Carmen stepped outside of the apartment. She didn't bother to say goodbye or wait for a response. If

Jay was as persistent as he appeared to be, he would stay on her trail until the diamonds were in her basement. Certain of it, Carmen proceeded home.

She had left so abruptly after saying no that it made Jay speechless. He was certain that after he was named as Rakim's father she would come to her senses. From the way the evening had played out, it seemed that he needed to come to his. He had tried for the last few years to get Carmen to commit to him, but she wouldn't. Thus, moving on was his only option. Twenty years of his life was already down the drain and he couldn't waste any more time. If Carmen wasn't the one for him then he needed to go out there and find the woman who was. Time waited for no man and the clock was indeed ticking.

For Carmen, the idea of re-establishing her relationship with Jay was far from her mind. Her focus was more on the dissolution of her marriage. When she arrived to her house, the only thing she noticed was her bedroom light pouring out of the upstairs' window. It was a clear sign that Kane was home.

From what she could hear when she walked in, the house was quiet. The silence lingered even when she stood in front of her own bedroom door. Without hesitation, she opened it to see her husband underneath the covers. She let the door close quietly behind her before she spoke. "Look," she began, speaking above a whisper. "I know it's late so I'll compromise. For tonight, you can stay where you are. However, tomorrow you need to move into one of the guestrooms. By the end of the month, though, you should have your own place. I want to separate."

Carmen knew her words were shocking yet Kane didn't give any kind of a response. His eyes were focused straight ahead like he hadn't heard a single word she had said. She got ready to call his name until she saw his lips move.

"The shit is everywhere," Kane said. "I've gotten like a hundred Google Alerts already. Even the captain at the Triad called me. He said the second he heard the news, he had to let me go." Kane swallowed before turning to Carmen and saying, "I've lost my job, and now you tell me that I'm losing you, too."

Carmen set her purse on the nightstand before sitting down on the bed. She didn't like the idea that he had been fired, but she had seen it coming. If Jay's witness had lost her job then Kane should've known that he was going to lose his as well. What he had done was unethical and even dangerous. "You used your job to your advantage," she told him. "Now you've learned that actions have consequences. You were so quick to shelve out the dough to be Rakim's father, but did you think about the risks?"

"No one thinks of the risks when they're doing things to get what they want. The same goes for Jay when he was filing the lawsuit. He didn't care about Rakim's paternity, he wanted you. It looks like he might get you, too. "

Carmen didn't want to believe that he had responded like he had. He wanted to compare his situation with Jay's because they both were trying to win her heart. His comment, along with the outcome of the case had only fueled her anger, causing her to grab the bedside lamp. She threw it at his head only missing him by a few inches as it hit the bare wall. Carmen ignored the sound of breaking glass and headed into one of the guestrooms, slamming the door closed.

Chapter Nineteen

Kane could only stare at the broken glass that lay on the wooden floor. Completely shattered, the only part of the lamp that was still intact was the lampshade. He was too frustrated to sweep up the mess so he simply turned away from it. By the time morning came, the sunlight made the mess look ten times worse than it had the night before. He quickly cleaned up the broken glass before anyone could see it and then dressed.

Despite the ongoing problems in his personal life, he still had to report to the Brookstone PD. He and Sanders met in the parking lot of the precinct in an unmarked car to continue their investigation of Jay's illegal affairs. Since the news of the paternity case was now public, Kane didn't give Sanders a chance to question any of the details. He spoke first, making sure he kept them focused on the investigation. "So, where do you want to start with this whole Jarrod thing?" he asked. "You want to see what the streets know?"

"I want to go to the brokerage firm," Sanders responded as he studied Kane's face. Kane's voice may have appeared calm, but his face told a different story. Sanders questioned whether Kane should be working. "Are you up for this? I know things are difficult right now."

"Sitting at home isn't going to do anyone any good. It's better if I'm out here in the field. Shoot, I thought I had a motive before," he shared. "I really have one now."

Kane expected to get more of a response, but Sanders only started up the car. He drove them in silence to Continental so that they could look in the basement. With a warrant in their hands, Kane had every intention of finding something in the firm that they could use. Certain that the drugs weren't housed in an office, he and Sanders had went straight to the ground floor. The basement was completely bare and the sight of it made Kane curse underneath his breath. "We probably would've had better luck if we had of searched this place when we first found out about it. If Jay cleaned this place out, he had to do it when we weren't watching," he spat.

"We have to stay optimistic," Sanders suggested. "So the drugs aren't here, big deal, let's go back to where we started. We had a full list of men that we knew worked for Jay. Let's try and get one of them."

Kane responded with a firm no at the idea. Sanders didn't understand what they were up against. They only had one shot at an informant and they had picked Jarrod as their choice. If he was missing then there wasn't any other way that they could get another one of Jay's men to talk. If Jay had

Jarrod murdered then the rest of his men probably feared for their own lives. They wouldn't snitch no matter how much he and Sanders tried to coerce them.

Nevertheless, one name was now ringing loudly in Kane's mind. He had forgotten all about the gentleman once they had locked in on Jarrod. "Shawn Blumington." Kane looked over at Sanders, hoping he had remembered the name. "We never finished looking into him. We know he's associated with Jay."

Sanders shrugged his shoulders, figuring it was worth a shot. At this point, they needed whomever they could find. He didn't know where to start, but he figured that Kane had a plan. He learned what it was when they ended up across the street from Blue Magic. Kane was betting on Blumington showing up there. Sanders believed that they were more likely to see Jay; nonetheless, he went along with it. Regardless of who showed first, they would be there until one of them did.

***

Regardless of his personal turmoil, Kane found he was dealing with enough of a level head to continue working. The same couldn't be said for Carmen who had spent most of the morning staring out of her office window. If it wasn't for Cathy pestering her about the upcoming Seventeen shoot, Carmen would have never found the energy or focus to work. Thankfully, piecing together different looks for Kristian's spread had helped her snap out of the mood she was in. In no time, she had gone from wallowing in her troubles to shopping the racks at the Brookstone Mall.

By the time it hit four o'clock, Kristian, Akaila, and Seventeen's in-house stylist had joined her in Forever 21. By that time, Carmen was so full-fledged into her work that she didn't even notice when her daughters left the store after an hour.

Kristian and Akaila had headed to Club Monaco, which was about four stores down from where Carmen was. Since they were still relatively close, Kristian didn't feel as if they had run away. They were merely helping to put together one of her looks. She knew her mother was going towards a rock vibe so she headed straight to a rack of jackets. They had been sorting through the blazers for only a few minutes when she got an eerie feeling in the pit of her stomach. Not sure where it had come from, she took a few steps backwards. It was then that she noticed that Blu was standing directly in front of her, towering over the rack.

"Are you surprised to see me?" he bellowed. "You thought I was gone, huh? I intentionally missed my connector flight to Georgia. I like it here." Blu let out a round of evil laughter before he continued speaking. "Did your brother tell you about Jay shutting down the cartel? Ungrateful motherfucker," he snapped.

Kristian slowly backed away from him, but Blu only came around the rack so that it was no longer separating them. His gaze was still frozen on hers as if he was sexing her with his eyes. He was looking at her from head to toe in pure lust, which disgusted her even more than his monstrous appearance.

"The Cadillac," he questioned. "I can't find it. I've been looking all over East Brookstone for it. I'm talking about the red one that pulled up when we were at your school. I don't appreciate some hoodlum trying to get up in my business. Once I find out who it is, I'm putting twenty thousand on his head. He obviously doesn't know who he's fuckin' with." Blu started to say more, but their conversation was attracting an audience. People were looking at him as if they knew he shouldn't have been talking to Kristian. Since he was back in New York without Jay's knowledge, he knew he had to keep a low profile. "I got to run, but I'll see you around. You get out at three, right?" He didn't wait for her to answer as he started to walk away. "I know you do," he yelled back at her. "I'll find you."

Kristian stood there in shocked horror. As her encounters with Blu increased, she realized how serious the problem was. Blu barely knew her, but he had become obsessed with what he saw. Turning to look at Akaila, she didn't get a chance to speak because she saw her mother steadily approaching them. A slew of shopping bags were in her hands and a disgruntled expression was on her face. Aware that they were in trouble, Kristian waited for her to unleash. Thankfully, her mother didn't say much aside from shoving the bags into their hands.

"Look girls, I have to run. Jay wants to meet with me to talk about Rakim. I shouldn't be gone long. If you need me, call me," she told them. "The stylist is still in Forever 21 so make sure you hook back up with her. She has some more bags."

Carmen looked back and forth between her daughters when neither one of them responded. "Did y'all see a ghost or something? What's wrong?"

Kristian was still too stunned to answer. If it wasn't for Akaila rambling about paparazzi then they wouldn't have had a story to save their asses. Kristian knew that she needed to tell her parents about Blu, but her fear was that they would blame Jay and it would possibly create more drama. Well aware that they needed to know, she decided that she would tell them in due time; for now though she was keeping it away from them.

If Blu's presence at Brookstone Mall had been made known to Kane and Sanders, they wouldn't have spent the majority of their day outside of Blue Magic. Jolts of desperation were no longer flowing through Kane's veins as he became certain that Blumington wasn't going to show.

"Let's go back to Continental. Maybe, we can see something there."

It wasn't the first time that Sanders had tried to persuade him to change locations. It was probably the hundredth. Kane knew his partner meant well so he gave him the go ahead. They had merely wasted time scoping out the restaurant and hadn't gotten any closer to an indictment. Kane felt like they'd get the same outcome at the brokerage firm. Sanders circled the building until they were sure there wasn't any activity. They then made their way back to the precinct. Upon their arrival, he told Sanders that he was ready for the night to be over.

"We're not going to give up," Sanders expressed. "Blumington is around here somewhere. Even if we don't find him, we need to get someone. Anyone from that cartel will do. Let's go home and start fresh tomorrow. Staring at that restaurant all that time didn't do us any good, mentally or physically."

Kane agreed with him yet all he could muster in response was a simple head nod. That appeared to be enough for Sanders because he got out of the car without another word. As Kane readied himself to return to his own vehicle, he found that he couldn't. The realization that everything was falling apart made him numb. His marriage was ending, he had been terminated from the Triad, and there weren't any solid leads on his case. He hated to admit it, but he knew it was too much. Sanders had asked him that morning if he wanted a break, but Kane had declined. He now was aware that he needed one. He reasoned that if he took a few weeks off, he could get himself together and come back to the case, brighter and fresher.

Once his decision was made, Kane quickly dialed Sanders' number to tell him what he planned to do. His partner didn't answer so he left him a detailed voicemail informing him that he needed to take a break. He wasn't sure how long his break would be; albeit he needed enough time to get his personal life together before he could devote his full attention to the case. When he finally hung up the phone, Kane instantly felt a sense of relief. With the heavy weight lifted he was able to make the transition from the car into his own Jeep. He made the short trip home only to find his bedroom completely empty.

The room was completely black and when he flipped the light switch, he saw that the bed was still made. It was only going on nine o'clock and he questioned Carmen's whereabouts. The lack of her presence reminded him that she wanted him out of the room. Immediately, Kane started to gather his things. In the process, he heard a door open down the hall. A few seconds later, he heard footsteps drawing closer to him. He hoped that the person would let him be as he made the transition into the guestroom, but his wish wasn't granted. When he heard the faint hello behind him, he turned to find Kristian standing in the doorway. She was already in her pajamas and her hair had been swept up into a tight ponytail.

"Can I talk to you for a few minutes?" she asked him.

Kane shrugged his shoulders at first, but only because he didn't want to come out and say no. If Kristian wanted to talk about the court case, he didn't want to hear it. He also didn't want to discuss the separation. For now, he wanted to get his things out the room before Carmen showed. "Maybe another time, tonight isn't a good night," he told her, dropping his shirts into a bag. He headed over to the walk-in closet, opening the door. There were several shelves of jeans and pants, which he decided to start removing.

"I know you have a lot going on, but I needed someone to talk to," Kristian replied. "It won't take long, I promise. I've been having this issue with this guy." She followed her father into the closet, watching him grab a bunch of his things. When he pulled out a suitcase, she knew what he was doing. "Don't you think there needs to be some sort of family meeting?"

Kane glanced at her behind him but he didn't reply to her question, he simply continued to pack. When she spoke again, Kane knew how the rest of the evening was going to play out. He told himself to simply let her vent until she left the room.

"So, here we go again, huh? It's like it's the same 'ol shit, just a different day."

Kane hated to be standoffish, but he wasn't up to talking. It didn't take her long to catch the hint and soon she left the room. Kane didn't dwell on their short interaction, as he continued to pack up his things. By the time he was finished, Carmen still hadn't made it home. Kane tried not to let it bother him as he moved his things into one of the guestrooms at the end of the hall. For all he knew, there were many more nights like that one to come.

Chapter Twenty

Carmen had been sitting outside of Jay's penthouse apartment for about an hour. She hadn't yet told him that she was there though he could see her limousine if he happened to look out of his living room window. Shortly before she had arrived, her father had called her to tell that the news of her case had reached Texas. Once she confirmed the outcome and disclosed that she was on her way to Jay's apartment, her father had gone off on a tirade. Unsure of what had brought it on, she was still replaying his words in her mind.

"Peaches, I know you," was how he had begun his rant. "I know you better than your mother despite the fact that she carried you for nine months. I have a very strong feeling of what's about to happen. For one, it has happened before. Kane does something traumatic and you run back to Jay. Now, this might sound like a bit of a surprise coming from me, but I know you're looking for a rebound. You're upset and you are looking for a way to get back at Kane.

"Do you think this is a fuckin' game, Peaches?" he had continued. "This isn't halftime. You are playing with two delicate lives right now. You can't keep going back and forth between these two men. Don't you see that? You need to make a decision. I mean, today, right now. You need to decide on what you're going to do before you walk into that apartment."

Carmen was shocked by his tone then and still was now. She hadn't told her father about the separation yet he already saw it coming. She didn't voice it to him, letting him continue with what he had to say.

"I'm not trying to upset you, Peaches. Really, I'm not. I love you. I want you to be happy. I firmly believe that you need to make a solid decision. If you don't want to work things out with Kane then let him go. Don't string him along. Take a few minutes before you walk into Jay's apartment to think things over. Ask yourself, what do you really want? What do you need for your kids? Why don't you ask yourself the million dollar question, who do I really love? If you don't, you will end up making another mistake. I promise you."

Carmen was quiet the entire time she took in her father's words. All she was able to give him was a single okay before she hung up the phone. She knew he meant well, but she didn't quite understand where his tirade had come from. A small part of her wanted to assume that he had talked to Kane or Jay. If he had, then it would explain a lot. Even though she was confused, she took his advice. She used her time wisely and analyzed everything. While she might have started with her wants and needs, she definitely had ended with her heart.

Now that she was ready to see Jay, she made her way out of the limousine. She told Donnie to take a break and to return in about an hour. When she got to Jay's door, she knocked only once before he answered. Automatically, she started apologizing because she knew she was supposed to be there earlier. "I know it's late," she told him, stepping into the apartment. "I hope you don't have an early rise tomorrow." She placed her purse down onto the couch before giving the apartment the once-over. Numerous baby items were scattered around the room and there were two plates of uneaten food on the dining room table.

"What took you so long?" he shot back. "The food is cold now. I would've warmed it if I knew you would be running almost two hours late."

From what she saw on the table, Carmen understood why he was slightly upset. A surprise dinner wasn't what she had been expecting. From what he had said on the phone, he wanted her to come over so that they could discuss Rakim. Since the gesture was sweet, she tried to soften the tension by picking up one of the plates. She took it into the kitchen and placed it in the microwave to show her appreciation. When he did the same, she knew she had been forgiven.

"What happened?" he asked once she took the warmed food out.

Carmen walked to the table, taking a seat. About to dig in, she decided to reply first. "Well, my father called. He was practically jumping down my throat and I decided to take his words to heart. I've been meditating for the past hour or so."

"Share," he ordered.

Carmen looked up at him with a blank expression. She didn't want to jump into the discussion so quickly, but he was almost forcing her to. "My father thinks that I'm going to run back to you because of what happened with the case. He thinks that you're going to be my rebound and once we get into it, I'm going to go back to Kane. He said all that without knowing that Kane and I separated last night."

"Shit," Jay muttered. "You say that like y'all aren't going to get back together. I know this game, Peaches." Jay looked over at her before gazing back at the microwave. "Y'all are going to work it out." The timer went off right when he finished speaking. He took his food out of the microwave and joined Carmen at the table. After he blessed his food, he started to speak again. "Tell me one good reason why I should believe that you're going through with this separation. You better make it good, too."

Carmen stuck a spoonful of macaroni and cheese into her mouth to buy herself some time. Once she had chewed the food, she answered. "You and I, we have dealt with each other for more than twenty years. We've apologized, we've made up; we've done it all. Still, I want to do it again. I know I was wrong for what I did. Everything from Carlos to the pink diamond, I was wrong. You forgave me, you look passed it and even gave me another chance. I was devoted to making it work and then I hurt you again. The game that you and Kane played to win me, I let it break apart what we had built. I don't want to do that anymore. I want to give you what you deserve and what I feel we both need. I want to make it work with you."

Jay dropped his fork down onto his plate. He didn't want to appear agitated, but the feeling was coming quicker than he could control. "What the fuck are you trying to say? I told you, I know this game. If you want to fuck, get someone else. I'm not doing this shit anymore. I'm forty-seven now. I have three kids and I deserve more than a one night stand."

Carmen didn't blame Jay for reacting in the way that he was. She knew she had put him through a lot, which is why she didn't speak right off. She wanted to choose her words carefully. "I didn't come over here for sex," she replied. "I came over here because you said you wanted to talk about Rakim. However, the discussion I had with my father, made me think about things. He felt like me coming over would lead to something that I probably wouldn't be able to handle. If I hadn't of took the time to think things over, I would have made that mistake. Since I did take that time, I now know what I want. I can honestly say that I don't want to have sex with you. What I want to do is rebuild. I want us to work on being friends and parents. In terms of business, we can start with my basement."

"So now I can use your basement? What's the catch?"

Carmen slid her plate away from her, knowing she had his attention. "The catch is that you give me what I want. You put one hundred percent into creating a partnership with me that will last until death. You promise me that you will be the father that I need you to be to all of my kids. Also," she said with a smile, "you give me some of the diamonds."

"You're fuckin' with me," Jay spat. He went back to eating, knowing her words were too good to be true. She had spent two months declining his offer and now she wanted to help him. He knew it was because she wanted revenge. If his diamonds were in his basement, it would be the perfect comeback because Kane was working on taking him down.

"Do you think this was an easy decision for me? I'm taking a chance right now, Jay. I'm doing it because I took the time to analyze things in my life. I realized what I wanted and needed. One of those things is you. Yes, I fucked up many times before, but I'm asking you to trust me. I'm not saying let's go full throttle. Let's take it slow. Let's work on rebuilding."

Jay grabbed his plate from the table, emptying the contents into the trash can. He then tossed it in the sink having lost his appetite. "Stand in my shoes for one minute," he yelled. "Look at things from my fuckin' perspective. Why should I be so quick to say yes?"

"You shouldn't be," Carmen replied. She stood up from the table, joining him in the kitchen. "You should have reservations. That is why I'm not asking you to go into this headfirst. I'm asking you to give it a chance. I want you to tell me that you're going to trust me."

Jay rubbed his hands over his face, not knowing what to think. He hadn't even prepared himself for the conversation they were having. He was even skeptical about using her basement. Still, he was inclined to take her up on the offer. If he didn't get started on the product line for Iceland, the store would be ready without anything to sell in it. Nevertheless, he wasn't so quick to say yes concerning starting back up their relationship. He knew he loved her, but he didn't want to be rejected again. Despite his reservations, Jay couldn't see himself turning down that offer either. Getting Carmen back had always been his goal. Now, the opportunity was right in front of him. He had to step out on faith and take it.

"You need to divorce your husband if you don't have any intention of getting back with him. You also need to file for a legal separation. I want to see the paperwork, too."

"So does that mean we're in?" Carmen asked him. She looked into his eyes, but he wasn't staring in her direction anymore. In fact, he was looking past her. "Say something, Jay, does this mean that we're in?"

"Can you stand here for a second?"

His request confused her; still Carmen nodded as Jay walked past her. She saw him as he went into his room but after that, he was no longer visible. Not sure what he was getting, she listened as he came back out.

"Close your eyes," he told her.

Carmen looked at him, curiously, but did as he asked. When she felt his arms on hers, she got slightly nervous as he pushed her around the room. "Jay, what are you doing?" He didn't reply, but Carmen could feel him moving her hair away from her neck. Seconds later, a cold object touched her chest. "I'm opening my eyes," she told him. Carmen saw that she was standing in front of a glass mirror. Jay was standing directly behind her, but she couldn't focus her eyes on him. Instead, her eyes were planted on the diamond necklace around her neck. It contained one of the biggest white stones she had ever seen. She estimated it to have about seventy carats.

"Do you trust me?" she heard him ask. "You're wearing a twelve million dollar necklace around your neck. It was part of a private collection in Switzerland. My friend in Africa sent it to me."

Carmen blinked as she rubbed her fingertips along the stone. She knew she needed to answer, but she was almost speechless. The necklace was a representation of the items that would be in her basement. She took a deep breath and then turned to face him. "I trust you," she told him. She reached her hand around her neck, taking the necklace off. She handed it back to him as his face drew closer to hers. Typically, she would back away, but this time she didn't. In fact, she stepped closer to him, allowing their lips to meet. As much as she enjoyed the embrace, Carmen knew she couldn't get carried away. After a minute or two, she touched his chest to let him know that they had done enough. "So it's a deal? We're going to give this one more shot?"

Jay believed wholeheartedly that the question didn't need to be asked. The kiss they had shared was enough to say that the answer was yes. For some reason, Carmen wanted a verbal answer. "I'm all in, but I swear on my parents' grave that this is your last chance." He kept his tone stern so she would know that he was serious. "You fuck this up, I'm through with you."

Carmen nodded her head in agreement. "I won't. I promise." She planted another quick kiss on his lips before telling him that she needed to check on the kids. She looked in on them for a few minutes before returning to the living room. "I guess we don't need to discuss Rakim, huh?" she said with a smile. "Why don't you stop by Flame tomorrow so you can see the basement? You can at least see if the space will work for you."

After Jay told her that he would, she made her way out of the apartment. As she rode home, Carmen realized that she didn't have any reservations about her decision. Regardless of what he had put her through and vice versa, she knew she had made the right choice. Jay was her soul mate and it had taken her too many years to see it. Now that she was going in the right direction, she was determined not to look back.

Part Three:
Set It Off

Chapter Twenty-One

June

The parking lot was packed as families poured into Blue Magic. Due to Brookstone High's graduation, the restaurant was more crowded than usual. Luckily, Carmen was well prepared. She had reserved one of the restaurant's meeting rooms in advance for graduation day. Although she was still waiting for everyone to arrive, she was glad that she had left the ceremony early to get everything ready. Not to mention, it gave her time away from her father's side glances. From the way he looked at her, she could tell that he had noticed that her relationship with Kane was nonexistent. Though her husband still lived with her, she considered him a roommate. Once he closed on the purchase of his condominium, that status would change. In the meantime, she had begun meeting with Clement to file for divorce.

"Is everything situated?" a voice asked.

Carmen turned around to see her father coming into the room. He appeared to be alone, which meant that he had come to pry into her love life. She tried to keep the conversation on the occasion at hand by answering his question. "Everything is coming together," she told him. "No worries. Why don't you have a seat?" Carmen pulled out a chair for him, which he sat in. When he pulled out the one next to him, Carmen knew where he was headed. Instead of fighting it, she sat down as well.

"So," he began, giving her one of his famous looks. "It's been a long time since our discussion. We've talked since then, but there are a lot of things that you failed to mention."

A shy smile appeared on Carmen's face as she and her father met eyes. She knew he wanted her to be open with him, but a part of her was scared to. Her relationship with Jay was something that she held dear to heart and she didn't want him to judge her. Though she hadn't given herself to him sexually, she was still having an affair. Until her divorce was final with Kane, she was indeed a married woman. "I am almost finished preparing the divorce papers. Hopefully, everything will be complete soon and I can file them." Carmen didn't expect her father to be smiling, but he was.

"You and Jay can't hide that," he told her. "I don't know if your mother noticed, but I did. I saw it all during the ceremony. I saw the way y'all looked at each other. Get the papers before the world sees it, too."

Carmen squeezed his shoulder as she heard several voices entering the room. "I will," she quickly whispered to him. As a sign that the conversation was over, she stood up, heading to the doorway. Kristian and Akaila were both coming in with Coco close behind. Quickly seating the girls, she watched as the room became packed with their family as well as Coco's. Once everyone had arrived, she found her way back to her seat. Jay had chosen to sit directly across from her, which also put him across from her father. Thankfully, Kane had chosen to sit at the far end of the table.

Despite the occasion, she barely spoke two words to her husband. To her, it wasn't abnormal, considering the status of their relationship. Almost everyone around them knew that they were separated. Even when everyone had gone outside so that they could give Kristian her new car, Carmen didn't mutter a word to him. She simply let him present the gift. It worked to her benefit when Coco's mother approached her out of nowhere.

"You know we had a hard time with Coco this morning," Maya stated.

Carmen turned to face the editor-in chief of *XXL* magazine.

"She really wanted King to be here. It broke her heart when she heard the news. She didn't understand how they could push back his release date. I tried to explain it to her, but you know how girls are when it comes to their first love."

Carmen rolled her eyes, but only because she knew that Maya didn't want Coco with her son. If anything, Carmen was certain that the woman was secretly praising God that King was still locked up. Maya wasn't fond of him and often expressed her displeasure.

"I've learned to accept him, Carmen. I have. I mean, you know how your son is. You know his history. Sometimes, though, I believe she can do better."

Carmen jerked her head faster than a speeding bullet. "Excuse me?" she asked her. About to give the woman a mouthful, her attention was diverted by a Mercedes Benz entering the parking lot. The car was a newer model, a silver Cabriolet, with tinted windows and a set of rims that Carmen hadn't even gotten her hands on. Since it was graduation day, she wasn't surprised to see such an expensive vehicle. Yet, she couldn't help but wonder who it was for. Kristian had already received a new Lexus while Akaila was showered with jewelry and money since she still didn't have her license. The only other person who could receive such a lavish gift was Coco. While she knew her parents couldn't afford it, King could. He might not have been there, but he knew how to have a presence.

Carmen stared at the car as it came to a halt. Not letting it prolong her response anymore, she turned towards Maya, giving her a piece of her mind. "No one in this world is perfect. King has made mistakes and so have

I. And," she continued, "So have you. My son—" Carmen paused when Maya pointed her finger. She looked in the direction in which she was pointing, and automatically clutched at her heart as she saw King emerge from the car. He was clad in a tan seersucker suit and looked more like a young businessman than a twenty year-old male who had been released from the county jail. As much as Carmen wanted to grab her firstborn into her arms, she kept her distance. She stared in awe as he greeted Coco and the rest of the family.

***

King had been released a few hours ago, which didn't leave him much time to spread the news. The only person who he had called was Jay, and that was who he had put in charge of getting Coco's gift. Jay had promised to keep it a secret, which was obvious when he stepped out of the Benz. Everyone looked like they had seen a ghost. He may have come with a car, but he knew he was the real surprise. While he wanted to celebrate the graduation, he was being pulled into too many places. Coco wanted him all to herself while his mother wanted some private time as well. Then, there was Malachi who was demanding that they hang out and play video games. He also had a baby sister who he was meeting for the first time. Though he wanted to do it all, he couldn't. He had to prioritize things. The first on his list was getting an update on the cartel.

During the last several months, he had been left in the dark. When he did get visits from his father or Malik, they never could share any major details with him. Now that they could talk freely, King wanted an update on their operation. He waited until everyone had left before he sat down with Jay and Malik. "So, what's new?" he asked, starting in on his first meal since his release. He hadn't gotten the chance to eat earlier, too busy trying to catch up with his family. When no one answered, King looked at his father who was exchanging glances with Malik. He could tell that they were silently discussing something. He figured Malik had won because his father started talking.

"From what Malik has told me," Jay began, "you know about Kane's investigation. Since he's trying to send me to prison, I broke out the biz. I sold what we had left of our product. Everything in Continental is completely gone. The last shipment is on a van to California. We're selling it to a cartel out there. Once we get that money, all drug deals will be complete."

Jay looked over at Malik as he tried to decide about whether or not to tell King about Blu. With the expression his friend gave him, he knew that he should.

"Back in November," he continued, "I announced my hiatus and decided to put things in Malik's hands. However, I knew that when Robin was born that Malik was going to bow out. Therefore, we had to find someone that we could turn things over to. Around that time, Rico had heard about a guy named Shawn Blumington. He was pushing major weight in the South and Rico wanted to bring him in. I met with him, but that was about it. Somehow, he got involved in the re-up. I didn't authorize it, but it happened. He's gone now, but I thought that you should at least know about him."

King looked over at Malik and then back at his father. "Rico referred him?" Out of everything that his father had said, Blu was the main thing that had stood out. When King had first started working alongside his father, he was the one who brought in the men. Everyone that worked for him, he knew and trusted from grade school up. They had never had an out of towner in their inner circle. "He never mentioned Blu to me. Shit, now that I think about it, I haven't spoken to Rico in a hot ass minute." King was confused, but he tried not to take it personal. Since he was out, he figured that he had plenty of time to catch up with his friends. "So this Blu guy," he said, chewing. "When can I meet him?"

"He's not here anymore," Malik explained. "We sent him on a plane home. Phase made sure of it. We haven't heard shit from him and don't want to."

King chuckled as he dropped his fork onto his plate. "So you brought him up here, he ended up being schooled on our business, and then you sent him home? He still knows about all our shit. Y'all were talking about expired milk, you should have expired him. He's the one who is probably snitching. Get him on the phone. I want to meet him."

"He's not important, King," Jay stressed. "We haven't heard from Blu since January. He's gone." Jay stared directly into his son's eyes, hoping he believed his words. While King was focused on Blu, his son's mind should've been on their businesses. Money was going to be solely coming from there, which meant he couldn't be buying Benzes left and right for his girlfriend. If anything, he needed to start investing in other properties.

"I don't care, I want to meet him. Set it up."

Jay looked over at Malik. His friend shrugged his shoulders at him like he didn't know what to do either. Thinking that he knew best, Jay continued to try and get King's focus off of Blu. After fifteen minutes, he had lost the argument, and ended up texting Blu to tell him that they needed to meet. In a few short seconds, he got a response. "He asked when," Jay announced. "Y'all want to do this Monday morning? It'll give him enough time to get a flight." As he waited for one of them to reply, he felt his phone vibrate in his hand. It was Blu again. He read the message and narrowing his eyes, he said, "This motherfucker is still here."

King simply shook his head, knowing that his father had been fooled. Blu had outsmarted them, which was proven when he showed up at Blue Magic. King tried his best to keep his anger under wraps and watched in silence as his father checked Blu for weapons. When the man was finally permitted to walk into the room, King knew immediately that the man couldn't be trusted. Blu had a sinister look about him. He even sat down at the head of the table like he knew he was in charge.

"So as you can see," Blu said with a chuckle. "Rico was an excellent tour guide. I missed this place so much; I got on a plane and came back. Y'all did give me a nice little break, but I'm ready to work. So are we all clear with FedEx? Who's been working on that?"

King looked over at his father, as he had never mentioned anything about FedEx. He didn't know what Jay had planned, but it had to be something that was created while he was locked up. He glanced over at his father for a response as Blu continued speaking.

"I haven't been vacationing. I've been keeping an eye on things. For example, I've noticed several FedEx trucks dropping off deliveries at Flame. There is one, though, that stands out. Maybe, it's because it's always the same driver. It only comes once or twice a week. Now, Jay, you wanted to fire somebody, which you did, but you also shut down the cartel. All I'm asking is that you put me on this FedEx thing. Tell me what's in those boxes. I have a feeling I know what it is, but I want to hear it from the horse's mouth. I mean, you brought me up here for something. Rico took his time schooling me on your operation so use me. Why push me to the side?

"Why do you keep sticking your nose in places it doesn't belong?" Jay snapped.

Blu let out an evil chuckle. "You do the same with your dick."

Blu jumped out of his seat when he saw the steak knife swung in his direction. He knew Jay had come close when he saw the slash that had been made in his dress shirt. Even though it wasn't a laughing matter, he let out a slight snicker. "Ahh, come on now, man, we ain't got to resort to violence," he said, taunting him. "What was it, the comment about Carmen? I've seen you two together. Y'all do a lot in public to be having an affair."

Since he was weaponless, Blu slowly made his way to the door. It might have been closed, but there were numerous onlookers on the other side of it since they were on the first floor. He decided to use it to his advantage. He quickly opened it so that anyone could see inside of the room. Almost instantly, Jay tossed the knife back onto the table. "See, Jay, we could've gotten this money together. You were the one who didn't want to help a brother out." Blu stepped into the doorway as a .22 was pointed in his direction. "Like father, like son, eh?" Blu stared at the gun in King's hand unsure if he would shoot or not. Not ready to take the chance, he slowly backed out of the room. "I'm going to see y'all," he muttered, "believe that."

King tightened his grip on the trigger as he tried to coax himself out of killing Blu. He had been released that morning, but he wanted the man dead. When he saw him walk out the room, he ran to follow him, but Jay stopped him. He pulled him back into the room before slamming the door closed.

"This shit could've gone two ways," Jay stressed, pointing at the door. "We got a restaurant full of people and a man we need to dead right now. No more games with him, you hear me? I'm getting on his ass right now. I want to know where this motherfucker has been hiding. His ass has been here for six months and no one has said shit. Once I find out where he's living, I'm ripping him apart. If I get him before the party tonight, I'll put him in the basement of Iceland with Phase. I'll do it there and get the body cremated. Understood?"

"We should've waxed his ass now," King mumbled. "I got plenty of bullets."

"What good would that have done? You see all those people out there?" Jay shot back.

King knew that it was a close call, but they had taken a chance by allowing Blu to leave. "This isn't the end of it," he told his father. "You know he's going to come at us, right? If he says he's going to see us, he's going to see us. I suggest you get your security up at Sapphire tonight. Bullets will be spraying."

"We'll get on this shit right now," Jay expressed. "Since everyone will be at the party, I suggest we make appearances, too. We can have Phase and a few of the runners keep watch on the streets. If Blu pops up, they'll catch him. Agreed?"

Jay didn't have to wait for anyone to answer. He knew that whatever he said went. He gave himself until nightfall to find Blu. If he didn't lay hands or eyes on him then he knew to expect retaliation. He prayed that he was well prepared for whenever Blu came at him.

Chapter Twenty-Two

Most of the evening had been spent searching every nook, cranny, and crevice of Brookstone for Blu. At ten o'clock, Jay passed the assignment over to Phase while he headed to Sapphire. If the club wasn't hosting a party for the high school graduates, Jay would've continued the search on his own. Since Carmen expected him to be there, he had no choice but to make an appearance. If things worked in his favor, Phase would find Blu by eleven and he would have him dead by midnight.

So far, things weren't looking up. Jay was standing in King's office, which overlooked the dance floor when Phase sent a text saying that he hadn't had any luck. Jay encouraged him to continue the hunt and popped open a bottle of Hennessey to help calm his nerves. He was on his second glass when the door to the office opened. King walked in, holding a glass of his own although he was still underage. Jay overlooked the drink and without his son asking, shook his head no. He knew King was worried about Blu like he was. Until they found him, no one would be getting a decent night's sleep.

"It's been an hour," King stated, changing the subject. "The DJ has been announcing my release all night. I haven't seen Rico or Jerome. You got my boys on the hunt for Blu, too? Where the fuck is Costa? He isn't even working the door."

Jay shrugged his shoulders as he took another sip of his drink. He fixed his eyes back on the dance floor, spotting Carmen coming into the venue. Jay watched her carefully as she made her way over to one of the club's bouncers. When the security guard pointed in the direction of the office, Jay knew that she was looking for him.

"So, you don't know anything?" King asked as if he were desperate for an answer.

Jay looked in his son's direction as Carmen appeared in the doorway. She didn't come into the room as if being helmed up in an office wasn't in her plans. Clad in a strapless black mini-dress, she made him forget all about Blu or King's question. The dress fitted her to the T, but it was a number that Jay wished was for his eyes only. He could only imagine the thoughts that were going through the bouncer's mind when he saw her.

"You two obviously need some privacy," King muttered, leaving the room.

Jay smirked at how uncomfortable King had become. Carmen hardly ever wore revealing clothes and her dress left little to the imagination. Jay didn't comment on his son's reaction, instead he held up his glass and said,

"VIP?" Carmen placed both of her hands on her hips as if she was inviting him to VIP herself. Without another thought about Blu or King's friends, Jay grabbed Carmen's hand, leading her downstairs.

***

With the amount of heat that was pouring through Sapphire, it was obvious that the club was packed to capacity. Most people were on the dance floor including Kristian and Dijuan. Feeling as if she might be subject to a heatstroke, Kristian broke apart from him, motioning that she needed a break. Dijuan took the hint and they sauntered through the mobs of people heading in the direction of the bar. Akaila was already sitting there with two empty cups in front of her and one in her hand. "We're back," Kristian said to her, hopping on a stool. They exchanged smiles before her attention went back to the dance floor which was mostly occupied by her peers. In the process, Kristian spotted her mother and Jay walking through the crowd.

They weren't doing anything out of the ordinary, but her mother's dress was almost too much for her to handle. The dress was made entirely of black lace and had a bustier top. "Please tell me that was not my mother. Say it was some random woman." Kristian watched as her mother and Jay disappeared into the VIP area.

Dijuan laughed in reply though he was surprised himself. "She looks good to be in her forties," he said, honestly. "At least we know where Kristian gets her big titties from!"

Kristian playfully punched him in the shoulder. His comment and her mother's dress embarrassed her. She couldn't see inside the VIP room, but she wanted another look. Since her father wasn't at the party; she figured she needed to keep an eye on her mother. "I've never been more embarrassed in my life," Kristian admitted, turning to face Dijuan and Akaila. "She looks like a freakin' video girl! Did you see her before we left the house?"

Akaila shook her head no. She found her mother's dress to be a little out there, but it wasn't anything that she was about to make a scene over. After dealing with her father's suicide and her mother's drug overdose, there wasn't much that fazed her. Kristian didn't feel the same, which was obvious when she announced that she was going into VIP. Akaila knew her sister wanted to snoop, but she wasn't going to let her do it alone. She followed behind her and Dijuan as they headed for the VIP lounge. It was filled with swarms of people, but they easily spotted their mother and Jay at the bar. Several shot glasses were already in front of them while they each held one more. "Shit, they can throw it back," Akaila whispered. She stared in awe as both her mother and Jay downed more shots than she could imagine.

Kristian could tell that her mother was having a good time despite the tension at home. Initially she was glad to see a smile on her mother's face. The feeling changed when she saw Jay's face move closer to her mom's. In one swift move, he grabbed her, placing a firm kiss on her lips. Instead of her mother pushing him away, Kristian watched as her mother embraced the kiss. "What is she doing?" Kristian screamed, balling her hands into fists. "Look at her!" She ran into the room, but Dijuan caught her arm before she made it all the way inside. She tried to break away from him, but Akaila grabbed her other arm.

They pulled her from the room, maintaining their grip until they were outside of the club. Kristian felt the urge to run back into VIP, but she knew it was pointless. Her parents' relationship had been nonexistent for several months. While Kristian believed it was because of the outcome of the paternity suit, she now wanted to place the blame on her mother. Based on what she had seen, it was crystal clear that her mother was still in love with Jay. *If she's not then she wouldn't have kissed him*, Kristian thought.

"We definitely shouldn't have seen that," Dijuan said. "Your parents aren't even divorced, are they? We might need to call it a night. I'm going to go tell Coco where we're going. Hopefully, Malachi can catch a ride with her and King, wherever he is."

Kristian didn't mutter a reply. She stood there quietly in the parking lot as she tried to come to grips with her mother's tryst. Even when Akaila said she was going back inside, she didn't speak; she gave her a head nod before peering out into the parking lot. She contemplated confronting her mother, but she didn't know how. While she could tell her that she saw the kiss, her mother could flip it on her and blame it on the alcohol.

"Did you save me a dance?"

A hand caressed her backside, jerking Kristian's body to attention. She turned around only to find Blu standing behind her. As usual, he had the same evil smile plastered on his face. The mere sight of him made her show her wrath as she slapped him across the face. He used it to his advantage and pulled her closer to him. His hands caressed her backside once more as she tried to separate herself from him. She even attempted to slap him again yet the chance was lost when King rushed in between them. He had come out of nowhere so quickly that she didn't even notice the silver glock in his hand. King's gun collided with Blu's head, sending a streak of blood through the air. Kristian cried out in horror as she realized what King was about to do.

As for King, he knew he had the perfect opportunity in front of him. Blu had chosen the right time to show up at Sapphire. A bounty was on his head and King was about to make sure that it was carried out. "You don't know who you're fuckin' with, do you? I will have your brain all over this damn parking lot. You done fucked with the wrong family." King backed away from him, allowing Blu to stand on his feet. Once the man seemed stable, he pistol-whipped him again, sending him back down onto the trunk of a Camry.

Blu let out a slight chuckle as he ran his hand down the left side of his head. He brought his hand to eye level, noticing the smudges of blood in his palm. "Damn, King, it's like that?" Blu looked over at Kristian, but he knew the girl was no help to him. At this point, she would say anything to get his head blown off. "See—" Blu didn't finish his statement. The cold steel of King's gun was back at his temple. He told himself that if he made the right move he could get his own weapon. He had never intended to get into a gun battle, but Kristian had thrown him off. His urge to sex her had taken over, landing him in his current predicament. If he hadn't seen her, he would've been carrying out his original plan, which was coaxing Jay into giving him a position in the Santiago cartel.

When he heard the gun cock, Blu knew that time was winding down. It also didn't help that King was yelling for someone to get Jay. Blu knew that if the man saw him, he was as good as dead. "Let's talk about this shit, King," he said, calmly. "I was wrong, I'll admit that. Can you walk in my shoes for a minute?" Blu paused, hoping his words could buy himself some time. "When your father took his break, I was the one who did his job. If it wasn't for me, he wouldn't have known about the cameras in Continental. I orchestrated that shit. I was the one who had the area scoped out. All I want in return is a little appreciation."

"Motherfucker." King couldn't force his fingers to squeeze the trigger. He knew he needed to, but something was holding him back. A part of him wished that his father would hurry up so he could do the deed. For the first time in his life, King was starting to realize that he wasn't a killer. He had gotten into tons of fights, but none had resulted in a death.

"I promise you, King, after tonight, we're as good as gold. You won't ever see me again. I'll bow out like a man." Blu watched as King's eyes searched the parking lot. Certain that he was waiting on his father; he quickly said, "I swear, I'll leave New York. I'll be on the next flight out. You won't ever see me again."

The last thing that King wanted to do was let Blu go. However, his father wasn't showing up. People were starting to congregate around him and he saw two of the club's bouncers running toward him. He kept the gun at Blu's head as a familiar voice sounded in his ear. Coco was begging him to put the gun down. When Kristian joined in, King felt even more pressure to spare his life. After a back and forth debate with himself, King dropped the gun at his side.

"Good call," Blu mumbled, standing back up on his feet. He straightened his clothes as he studied all of the people who had gathered around. "Continue on as you were."

King watched in agony as Blu walked away from him. He watched him as he got inside a black car and once he was driven away, King knew that he had made a mistake. He paced the parking lot, cursing aloud to himself. There were a million eyes on him, but not one of them belonged to his father. Angered by his absence, King marched up to the club's entrance as Dijuan and Akaila were coming out. "Take them home!" King ordered, "No games, Dijuan, take them straight home." King knew Dijuan was confused, but he wasn't about to explain. He went back inside with Coco in tow. He headed to his office with the thought that Jay was there, but he wasn't. "I've only been home for one fuckin' day," he muttered, "and this is the shit I got to deal with?"

He faced Coco, knowing that it had been awhile since she had seen him that way. As much as he wanted to be open with her, he knew that he couldn't. She wouldn't understand even if he did explain.

"Are you going to go look for him?" Coco's voice was trembling with nervousness. "I swear, King, if I'm in this for the long haul, you can't go looking for him. I've already put in months visiting you in a damn jail. I'm not doing it anymore!"

King stared at her as tears began to stream down her face. "You saw what I saw, Coco," he told her. "I have to handle—" King was cut off at the sound of voices outside the office door. When Jay and Malik walked in, he knew that his conversation with Coco was over. Not to mention, his father said it. Unsure of what was about to happen, he encouraged Coco to go back downstairs. He knew she didn't want to, but he couldn't have her up there as they discussed Blu.

"I got Phase running his ass all around this damn city and he comes here!" Jay yelled once Coco had left. He overturned the desk sending glasses and paper flying everywhere. "You had him in your fuckin' hands! What the fuck were you thinking? You couldn't bring him up here?"

King looked at his father sideways. He didn't expect his anger to be directed at him, but it was. His father blamed him while King wanted to throw the stone right back. Blu would've been dead if Jay was there to do the job.

"You know what? I don't even have time to dig into your ass. He couldn't have gotten far. His ass is around here somewhere. You go to the

Westside where Phase is, Malik and I will take the East. Don't fuck up this time."

King stared at his father, angrily. He wanted to defend himself, but Jay was already walking out of the room. He looked over at Malik who only shook his head. "Whatever," he mumbled, taking his car keys out of his pocket. He followed Malik out of the room before they went their separate ways. Like Jay had instructed, Malik headed to the East while he took the West. They spent hours on end searching the streets for Blu only to come up empty. It wasn't until it hit four o'clock in the morning that Jay called off the search. While everyone else went home, King continued driving around West Brookstone.

He didn't have the desire for sleep; his insomnia, a direct result of the conflict with Blu. Added to that was the absence of Rico and Jerome. At this point, he needed them. He knew they would've been the ones with him driving through the Westside. They would've been by his side when he staked out the airport. Even when he searched hotels, they would've been right there with him. Now, he was completely alone, looking up at Rico's house.

At first, no one appeared to be home until he noticed that a light was on. He stared at the window until he saw a shadow move inside the house. It was all he needed to see to get out of the car. King was certain that his presence would be known before he even knocked on the door. Despite the reconstruction that the house had gone through, the front steps creaked terribly. Still, he struck the door twice before it opened. "Shit," he muttered seeing Rico's mother. The woman's appearance had thrown him off. He had always known Ms. Rosetta to be a smoker, but it was obvious that cigarettes were not her only downfall. "I know—" he was cut off as she grabbed him into her arms. King became confused when he realized he was hearing the sound of her sobbing. "I was going to say I know it's been awhile," he continued.

"Y-y-y-you—" Ms. Rosetta couldn't get her words out.

"It's okay, calm down," King whispered, breaking into a smile. "You must've thought I was never getting out. Rico didn't tell you that I was being good in there?" King chuckled, but he soon stopped. The woman was crying even harder than before. Perplexed, King looked up at the ceiling. *Three gallons of milk expired this morning.* King separated from her as he replayed Malik's words in his mind. He shook his head, refusing to believe that the inevitable had happened. To ease his worries, he stared into the woman's face, asking her one simple question. "Is Rico home?"

Ms. Rosetta covered her mouth as her head shook violently back and forth. "H-h-he's been missing for months now. Jerome said he got into some mess with a drug dealer. He told me not to go to the police. He said it was pointless." Ms. Rosetta slid her hand down her face, draping it at her side. "After that, Jerome moved down South. He didn't leave me with a number or an address. He said that he had gotten some work down there since y'all aren't slinging anymore. He did buy his parents a house in New Rochelle, though. They moved over there. He also gave me a little something to help with the bills. You know I had a baby last year."

King's jaw tightened at her words. Ms. Rosetta had confirmed that Jerome was still alive. Nevertheless, she didn't know about the whereabouts of her own son. Rico was the more down to earth one among him and Jerome. He didn't seem like the type that would get involved in any drama, especially not one with a drug dealer. The thought alone made him think that Blu might have something to do with Rico's disappearance. If he did, King believed that he might have found the right motive to kill him. Kristian was enough, but Blu taking his friend's life was even more. "N-n-no matter what," he stated, "I got you. You don't have to worry about anything. Whatever you need, I got it."

Ms. Rosetta shook her head at him before going back inside of the house. King hated to end things on that note, but he knew she was grieving. He was, too, which was why he didn't leave the property. He returned to his car, choosing to sit there and think instead of going home. As he thought things over, he became more confused. If anybody knew about Rico's disappearance it would have been Malik and Jay. They had been around the entire time while he was locked up. Jay tried to shrug off his question earlier, but King wouldn't allow him to do it a second time.

Ready to dial his father's number, King paused when he saw an image of Kane. If Rico was missing then he should've been the one he was contacting. His stepfather could look into the case personally and get the answers that he and Ms. Rosetta deserved. Without hesitation, he called Kane and woke him up out of his sleep. He quickly told him of his suspicions and how he thought Rico might be dead. His stepfather's voice was groggy, but he still promised to find him. King prayed that he kept his word. Not only for his sake, but for Ms. Rosetta's as well.

Chapter Twenty-Three

When King called Sunday morning, the last thing Kane expected to get was another missing person's report. If anything, he thought King was calling because he missed him. When he saw that wasn't the case, he hurried King off the phone in disappointment. He promised him that he would look into Rico, but he knew it would end up on the backburner. Monday marked his first day back at work since his break and all he wanted was an update on the Santiago case. From what he could see, Jay was still a free man. It meant that Sanders hadn't gotten very far without him. Kane was certain that this time around they would gather enough evidence to make an arrest. Nevertheless, he couldn't help but to form reservations when he ran into the lieutenant in the hallway. Harris appeared to be in a pleasant mood, but Kane still didn't want to deal with him.

"Did you enjoy your six month vacation?" Harris didn't give Kane an answer before going in on him. "I hope you kept in contact with Sanders. From the way you're looking at me, it seems that you haven't. You should be all smiles like me. Last night, your partner confiscated over a million dollars' worth of cocaine headed to California. Take a shot at who it belongs to." Harris paused, but only for a quick second. "It has Jay's stamp on it. Isn't that the best news to come back to?" He let out a slight chuckle before poking Kane in his shoulder. "Now that you're back, I expect a whole lot more out of you than what I've gotten. Sanders just graduated from his rookie status. If he takes down Santiago, he's going straight to the Triad."

Kane stared in frustration as Harris walked past him. If he hadn't of been a former Triad agent, the lieutenant's words wouldn't have bothered him. However, Harris' words stung tremendously. Giving in to his emotions, Kane rushed to Sanders' desk. He believed that a find like that was one that his partner should've called him on. It was enough evidence to send Jay straight back to prison. "Give me the damn police report!" he barked. He grabbed the papers that were in Sanders' hands, looking them over. "Where is it? Harris told me all about you and this damn coke! I know you raided Jay's shit!"

"Whoa, whoa, what are you doing?" Sanders asked, standing up. He grabbed the papers back from Kane only to have his partner jerk them back. Seeing how heated Kane was, he said, "Let me explain." He sat back down in his seat, saying, "I found the coke on that exterminator's van. It was headed to Cali. After you took your leave, I went back to the brokerage firm. I even staked out Blue Magic. Nothing was happening. There weren't even any meetings going on. Eventually, I went to West Brookstone with another officer and that's when I saw the van. I followed it, waited for it to make a stop and when it did, I made my move."

"So where are they?" Kane yelled. "Where are the men you took in? If you got the coke then I know you got us some informants. Those men are all we need to convince some jurors that Jay is a drug dealer. If they got something to lose, they'll snitch till there's no tomorrow."

Sanders took a deep breath. He knew Kane was going to be disappointed in what he had to say next. "I didn't take anyone in. When the man got out, I wired the car and took off back to New York. I left him there." Sanders stood again when Kane's temper flared. In one swift move, Kane had pushed everything off his desk onto the floor. "It's still Santiago's coke!" Sanders roared, "We still have it!"

"What kind of bullshit is that?" Kane spat. "You make an arrest to get informants. Informants help us build a case against Santiago so we can fry him. You don't even realize when you've fucked up. The lieutenant lets you slide because you brought in this large amount of coke when he needs to be slitting your throat. Do you know what information that man could have given us?" Kane pulled out a chair as he noticed that all eyes in the division were on him. Not wanting to attract Harris, he spoke in a calmer tone. "If that van had drugs on it, at some point in time, they had to get the drugs from the brokerage firm. We know that is Santiago's stash spot."

Sanders disagreed. He knew more than Kane did because he had never taken a leave from the case. "The brokerage firm is drug free. Jay went legit. He's not running a cartel anymore. That has to be the reason why the drugs were on their way to Cali. That's the word on the street. I paid thirty dollars to some crackhead for that information. As for Blu, most people in the Westside haven't seen him. Jarrod Luis never showed up either. You can say he's missing or that his murder is still unsolved. Pick whichever one you'd like."

Kane didn't want to hear anything else that Sanders had to say. The last thing that he wanted to know was that Jay was out of the drug game. He got up from his seat, leaving Sanders' desk. It was his first day back and he already needed a breath of fresh air. Unsure of where to turn next, he stared out into the parking lot. A slew of cars drove past him, but only one caught his attention. It was a white limousine with tinted windows. It could have been anyone, but something in the pit of his stomach told him it was Jay. He decided to follow the car and hurried to his vehicle. Once he had it started, he pulled into the street. Several cars were in between him and the limo, but it didn't matter. When the car turned into Flame, Kane made sure he was right behind it.

***

Drama may have been brewing on the outside of Flame, but it was nonexistent on the inside. After reviewing some of the designs for the Fresh Prince collection, Carmen was currently leaving out of Tiara's office. Once the hoopla surrounding her paternity fiasco had died down, she had presented the idea to the board. They agreed that the line was something new and unique for Flame and that it would give them an edge over Mantra. Though half of the collection was already approved, she still shared her ideas with Tiara prior to any board meeting. Since Tiara liked her preview, Carmen felt comfortable leaving the office early so that she could head over to Jay's apartment for a lunch date. She wanted to use the time to ask him some questions about King's brawl at Sapphire. She had already asked her son, but he chose to give her the runaround. Carmen refused to let up on getting an answer, which Jay would see in a few short minutes.

Upon returning to her office, Carmen grabbed her things and gave Cathy a few last minute reminders before running to the elevator. When she reached it, the door was already open and a man was standing in the far left corner. She had never seen him before, but it wasn't something that fazed her. She figured he was a guest of one of her employees or a potential intern. A temporary badge was around his neck, which meant that he had made it past security without a problem.

"Good afternoon," he greeted.

Carmen turned in his direction, giving him a small smile. "Good afternoon," she echoed. She then turned back to face the doors, which were closing. She inspected the controls and saw that the button for the first floor had already been pushed. She assumed that he was leaving for the day as well. A grin was on his face, which inclined Carmen to stare. The man had distinctive features that she couldn't help but study. Tall and caramel-complexioned, his nose stood out on his face because it was crooked. Her focus on his appearance wasn't distracted until he spoke to her.

"You're Carmen, right? Carmen Davenport," he questioned. "You got quite a company here. You're pulling in some major cake. My name is Shawn," he said, extending his hand, "Shawn Blumington. It's a pleasure to meet you."

Carmen didn't want to get too friendly, but decided to shake it. The moment she did, she wished that she hadn't. He raised her hand to his lips, giving it a kiss. "It's an honor," he told her. Carmen jerked her hand back in nervousness and quickly glanced at the controls, seeing that they were nearing the first floor. When the doors opened, she walked off swiftly, but the sound of the man's voice stopped her in her tracks.

"Mrs. Davenport," he called out.

Carmen turned around, giving him her attention once again.

"You and Tiara are doing good work around here," he said. "I see that you respect the ones that helped you. Some people don't do that. Never forget where you came from."

Carmen's face became tense, but she didn't comment. Instead, she watched as the man headed down the hall to a side exit. She waited until he left before she headed out the main entrance. Jay's limousine was parked out front and she got inside without noticing Kane's Jeep behind her. Before she was even in her seat good, Jay had kissed her lips and asked how her day was. "It was fine until now," she told him with a sigh. "There was this guy on the elevator and he said something that didn't sit right with me."

Jay slid his cell phone into his pocket as he took in Carmen's words. Her comment made him think about his psychiatrist. "Dr. Stuart makes me feel that way sometimes. She thinks she has all the answers to my life," he joked. "Tell me more about this guy, though."

Carmen had a feeling that Shawn Blumington was nothing short of a maniac. His appearance made her feel that way in addition to what he had said to her. "He said that Tiara and I were doing good work around Flame. He also said that he could tell that I respected those who helped me. I promise you; I have never seen this man a day in my life. How would he know anything about me or Tiara? He looks like a freakin' monster. It worries me that he has a badge, he's walking around freely."

Jay narrowed his eyes as his mind went into overdrive. With Carmen referring to the man's looks as monstrous, he knew that Blu was still in New York. The stakeout they had done at the airport was only a waste of their time. Not only was the man still in Brookstone, he had made his way into Flame. Jay knew that he needed to pull out all of the stops. He grabbed his briefcase, realizing that he had to give Carmen her gift earlier than expected. He opened it and pulled out a pink Cobra pistol. He handed it to her, but she didn't take it.

Carmen hadn't carried a weapon on her since her early twenties. Since her days as a hustler were over, she hadn't felt the need to. She also didn't travel with a bodyguard. The only security she had was on her property because she lived in a gated area. If Jay was giving her a gun then she knew it was because he wanted her to be cautious. "So this has to do with what? Is it the guy on the elevator or King's brawl? Carrying guns isn't my life anymore.

It may be yours, but it's not mine." Carmen didn't take the gun, but Jay still placed it in her lap.

"King's brawl was an effect of me breaking out of the drug game. Money isn't coming through like it used to. Some people are heated. One of them was brave enough to step to King. End of story. Now as far as this gun goes, I want you to keep it on you at all times. It has a full clip and whenever you think you need to use it; do so, don't hesitate."

Carmen stared down at the gun before looking back at Jay. She knew he was hiding something from her, but she wasn't quite sure what it was. She put the gun in her purse, which she sat on his kitchen counter once they had arrived at his apartment. Chinese takeout was already on the table and Carmen sat down to eat. She thought Jay was going to join her until she heard his phone ring. Five seconds into the conversation, she learned that he was talking to King. Though his tone was peaceful, Carmen knew the conversation was about to turn rocky.

"You're still not listening to me, Jayceon," he was saying, calling King by his birth name. "I made a decision to get out. I made a formal announcement. I gave a few dudes the chance to work on some businesses, but other than that, I let them all go. In terms of Rico and Jerome, I can't give you answers to things I don't know." Jay's volume seemed to increase dramatically after a few seconds of silence. "I don't know shit about Rico," he was yelling. "If Rosetta told you that shit then you need to go back to her. She's your source, not me. Okay, Jayceon, I see how we're playing this game today. You tend to forget who I am sometimes. I don't work for you. You work for me!"

Carmen bit her lip, knowing that it wasn't good for Jay and King to be on bad terms. Jay's words proved that their professional relationship had become more important than their personal one. It made her regret that she had even allowed King to become a part of Jay's businesses. She wanted to voice her opinion so she walked into the living room as he hung up the phone. "I was having a bite to eat," she told him. "I was hoping that you would join me."

Jay turned around, noticing that Carmen was standing next to him. The mere sight of her made him remember why she was there. He wouldn't have forgotten if King hadn't set his nerves ablaze. He decided to play innocent though he was guilty for having forgotten their lunch date.

Carmen waited for a reply, but she never got one. "Something is bothering you. You want to talk about it? It might help."

Jay shook his head no. It was pointless for him to even discuss. He was digging himself into an even deeper hole as the lies poured out. King had found out enough from Rosetta to assume that Rico was dead. All it took now was for one person to confirm it. When that happened, Jay knew that his relationship with his son would be over. Carmen wouldn't even be able to put them back together. She may even turn on him.

"I only heard a little bit,' Carmen admitted. "I'm a little hesitant about getting involved because I don't know everything that is going on. It would help if you remembered this, though. King may work for you, but before you are his boss, you are his father."

"And you're a wife."

Carmen froze in response to what he said. His comment was enough to let her know that he was taking his anger out on her. She decided not to feed into his tantrum and give him some time to calm down. "When you're ready to talk, let me know." He didn't reply, but Carmen didn't need him to. She knew Jay would come around when he was ready. It could be in the next hour or the next fifteen minutes. Whenever it happened, she would be there to listen.

***

While Carmen and Jay sat on the inside of his high rise apartment, Kane stood watch outside. From where he was, he couldn't see anything, but he could imagine. A jealous spirit had formed inside of him when he saw his wife step out of Jay's limousine. When she went inside the complex, it felt like a knife was lodged in his heart. Due to the outcome of the paternity case, he was certain that Jay had played on Carmen's weaknesses. It explained why he and Carmen were unable to make amends.

On the other hand, Kane also felt like his wife had him handcuffed to her. If she wanted to work on the marriage, she didn't show it. If she wanted a divorce, she didn't make him aware of that either. Then again, he hadn't helped the situation. He only spoke to her when it was absolutely necessarily. Since there wasn't a clear direction in where their relationship was going, Kane felt as if he was forced to go with the flow.

Not wanting to leave, he shifted his gaze towards the busy New York street. When he saw a squad car pass by him, he knew it was time to leave the area. It reminded him that he hadn't looked into the coke that Sanders had confiscated. The thought of the case led him to start up his car and head back to the precinct. Once there, he headed down to the ground floor, sliding his hand into the biometric reader. When the vault's locks started to turn, all he could think about was how a million dollars' worth of seized cocaine was inside. Immediately, he started to search for it. In the far left corner of the room, there was one box that looked similar to the ones that he and Sanders had seen during the re-up. He headed over to it, opening it up to reveal its contents. *Shit*, he thought, seeing the stamp, *he really did do it, one million dollars' worth of Santiago coke.*

Kane picked up one of the packages turning it over in his hands. "Didn't even get a fuckin' informant," he muttered. He shook his head at the thought before dropping the package back down inside of the box. Kane knew he could use the coke to his advantage. Sanders claimed that Jay had gone legit, but he felt the evidence proved otherwise. With the right legal team, he could convince twelve jurors that Jay was still one of America's biggest kingpins. Once he did, Jay would be out of his life forever.

Chapter Twenty-Four

Every so often, Jay would stare over at the dining room table. Carmen was still sitting there, but he wasn't ready to join her. There were too many things on his mind for him to even have a decent conversation. Blu had met up with her, King was getting closer to finding out about Rico, and he didn't have a handle on any of it. He couldn't even find Blu to kill him. If he stopped the man's heartbeat, it would at least eliminate one of his problems. It was a reminder that he needed to contact Phase. He had put him in charge of locating Blu, but he always came up empty. Phase would be in one part of town searching while Blu seemed to pop up in another. A cat and mouse game was in progress with the mouse in the lead.

Clenching his jaw, he continued to look at Carmen. Her phone was glued to her ear and he realized suddenly that she was talking to her mother. He had been so into his thoughts that he didn't realize what was happening in front of him. Carmen was on her feet, her eyes gazing around the room like she was in search of something.

"Mama, calm down, I can't understand you," she was saying, loudly. "You're screaming at me!" She moved away from the table, heading back into the kitchen where Jay followed her. "Is he stable? When did this happen?" Carmen grabbed her purse, but Jay didn't allow her to walk out of the kitchen. He stood in front of her, blocking her path. "Mama, you should have told me about this! Wait, tell 'em to hold on. We need to…okay, Mama, whatever, we'll talk in a few." Carmen hung up the phone, throwing it down inside of her purse. Her eyes met with his and he knew she could tell that he wanted an explanation. "My father fainted about an hour ago," she told him. "He has diabetes. My mother, the lovely Mrs. Patricia, decides to break the news now instead of when they were here for graduation. This is a wonderful time to find out, don't cha think?"

Jay listened as Carmen used her sarcasm to keep from showing her true emotions. It had been several months since Lotus had disclosed the secret to him, but he had never told her. He knew it wasn't his place. It was something that Lotus wanted to do yet Patricia had stolen the moment from him.

"I need to get home," Carmen said, pushing past him. "I need to get a few things together before I head to Texas. Can I bring Nyla and Rakim over here?"

Jay nodded his head, but it didn't seem to be enough. She marched up to him, staring him in the face until he said the word verbally. Trying to play nice, he gave her a quick kiss on the lips. Jay knew it was a bad day for the both of them so he didn't take her behavior personally. He stood there quietly as she left until his phone rung from the couch. When he saw it was Phase, he exhaled before he answered and said, "Talk to me."

"I received a phone call," Phase told him. "It's bad news, too. Diaz was too scared to contact you so he called me. He was the one transporting the bug killers to Cali. Word is that someone stole the extermination van. Diaz went into a convenience store, came back out and it was gone. He got on the Greyhound about an hour or two ago. He should be back in New York tomorrow."

Jay cursed loudly, overturning one of the end tables. When he finally replied, he only had one instruction for Phase. "Meet me at Iceland in thirty minutes. I'll get word to Malik and King. Someone else is fuckin' with us and it's not Blu. Make sure you contact Diaz, too. Tell him that if he wants his life, I better not see him." Jay waited until Phase stated understanding of his instructions before he hung up. He was about to leave when he remembered that Carmen would be on her way back. He didn't want to miss her, but he knew he had business to handle. He decided to take his chances and left the apartment.

Meanwhile, Carmen dropped her purse in her foyer as she ran up the staircase. When she hit the third step, she saw someone move out the corner of her eye. She thought the house was empty until she noticed Kane seated at the dining room table. She told herself to continue on, but she knew that she couldn't. Her father was in the ER and she felt that Kane needed to know.

"My mother called me," she told him. "My father passed out when they got home." Carmen swallowed as she hesitated, partly because she didn't want to believe it. "My father has diabetes," she continued. "He's at the emergency room right now. They haven't admitted him, though. I'm actually about to head to Texas."

"So your father had to pass out to get you to say something to me?" Kane shook his head in disbelief. "I definitely didn't think it would take a scare to get us to talk. Well, not after twenty years of marriage. I thought I meant more to you than that."

Carmen was taken aback, but she knew that she shouldn't have been. They hadn't spoken in a long time. Since she took care of the majority of the household, it was easy for them to do. Not to mention, she had been working nonstop on *Fresh Prince* while he had taken a leave from the Brookstone PD. While she was gone all day, he was at home doing whatever. "I wanted you to know," was all that she could muster in response.

"Well, I want you to know something, too," he voiced. "I saw you at Jay's apartment complex. Rakim and Nyla are both here with Fiona. You weren't dropping off a baby. You didn't have any bags so I knew you weren't styling him. Are y'all fuckin'?"

Carmen's eyes grew big. His tone was very harsh, but she knew it was because he suspected her of cheating. Though she was, she had yet to sleep with Jay. Not that it made the time she had been spending with him right. "So, you're stalking me now? Is that what you've been doing for six months?" she shot back.

"For six months I've been swimming in a shitload of depression," he screamed. "I've been watching you waltz around here like you're happy as hell while I'm living in misery! I lost my job, my wife, and my fuckin' sanity! I wasn't able to go back to work until today. What the fuck is this shit, Carm? I gave you twenty years of my fuckin' life and you treat me like this?"

Carmen opened her mouth and started to respond with the same amount of rage, but she heard the sound of a door slamming. The noise made her look behind her and there was Kristian standing in the foyer with a slew of shopping bags. A pair of sunglasses covered her face, but Carmen could still read her expression of disappointment. Certain that her daughter had heard them outside the front door; she didn't fault her for not speaking. Kristian went up the steps as if she didn't want to get involved.

Letting out a deep sigh, Carmen looked back at Kane. "I'm going to Texas. I want to be on the next flight out of New York. I'm taking the kids over to Jay's while I'm gone. This is also a good time for me to tell you that I'm about to file divorce papers. You'll have them soon enough." Carmen turned on her heel, not even waiting for a response. She headed up the steps, quickly packing before getting the kids ready. By the time she made it back down, Kane was gone from the dining room.

***

While Carmen was headed to Jay's apartment, he was busy pacing the floor of Iceland. His anger was clearly displayed, which kept anyone from saying anything to him. Malik, King, and Phase stood there quietly as they waited for Jay to speak.

"Shawn Blumington," Jay began. "We'll start there." He cleared his throat as he had a flashback of his conversation with Carmen. "He's still in Brookstone. Carmen had a run-in with him this afternoon, but lucky for us, she doesn't know anything about him. He said enough for her to be concerned, but words aren't my problem. My problem is that he has ties to Flame. He got inside somehow, which means that someone in that company knows him. Blu isn't afraid to test us. Now, if he's still here, he has to be living somewhere. Why can't we find him?" Jay glared at King. "All you had to do was hold him long enough for me to pull the trigger. Instead, you let him go. It would've eliminated all of this bullshit."

King felt like Jay was turning the tables on him once again. However, this time, he had a chance to defend himself. "I couldn't do it," he replied. "Murder ain't for me. I'll fight all day, but I can't do that shit. There ain't no coming back from death. Once you're gone, you're gone."

"Look," Malik said, speaking up, "we all had a chance to kill Blu. We didn't, though. What we need to be focusing on is what we're going to do. We've checked every hotel, motel, and every other got damn place in this city. He's not here. Now, we can start searching other places, but by the time we get there, he would have moved again."

"I say wait it out," Phase voiced. "Who's to say that his confrontation with Carmen wasn't a last shebang? He didn't physically touch her. Shit, he could be on a plane as we speak. Probably mumbling, 'fuck them' as he goes back to stacking his own paper. He has the same things that y'all have; a restaurant and clubs. He has to go home at some point."

Jay agreed with Phase. There wasn't much they could do if they didn't have an exact location on Blu. They would have to wait for another encounter to see where he was. If he didn't pop up soon then Jay could assume that he had gone back to Georgia. Still, he wasn't betting on that being the case. It was the reason he had went ahead and set up protection for his family when he was on his way to Iceland. If Blu ever wanted to retaliate, he would have something in motion to ensure the safety of his kids and Carmen. "If we wait it out, we've got to be prepared. I got two men from San Juan already headed this way to watch mine. They are on a plane right now."

"So you think it's that serious? You think Blu might try some sort of retaliation or something?" Malik asked. He looked over at King and Phase whose expressions asked the same question. "I should hire someone to keep an eye on Tiara and Robin?" Malik took a deep breath, knowing that he didn't want to resort to that kind of lifestyle. He wanted to protect his own, but without having to look over his shoulder.

Jay nodded his head. "I'm doing it for my family so you can decide if you want to do it for yours. Shit, we might need to do it for ourselves. We only have so many guns."

"Done," King replied, leaning up against one of the glass counters. "On to the next topic, what are we going to do about the missing keys? Diaz won't be back until tomorrow."

"Diaz isn't coming back," Phase said with a chuckle. "I gave him Jay's message."

Jay ignored Phase's comment. Diaz would be the last person on his mind unless he laid eyes on him again. He was more concerned about who took his coke. "I know for a fact that some hoodlums didn't steal that van. If it was some locals, they would have sent a message our way by now. They would want something in return. Whoever got Jarrod to snitch probably got the keys. More than likely, it's the police."

King stood up straight at the mention of Jarrod's name. He knew all about the boy's involvement in their operation, but he didn't know about him snitching. "Jarrod snitched on us?" He glanced over at Malik, but his godfather didn't say anything. "Shit, what else happened while I was locked up? Where is his ass now? Was he one of the milks that expired?"

Jay pulled out his cell phone as he felt it vibrate. Carmen was calling him. He knew he needed to get home and took a few steps forward. Before he could get far, King cut him off. He looked into his son's eyes and immediately knew where the conversation was about to go.

"You killed him, didn't you?" King asked. "He was sour. Who else got it? I mean, there are two others missing. Did you kill Rico and Costa, too? Is that why Jerome moved away?" King looked deep into his father's eyes until Jay pushed him to the side. He knew Jay was angered by his questions, but he wasn't ready to let up. He wanted answers and he knew he had to force them out of his father. "Say something, don't run. Be straight up with your shit," he yelled at him. He grabbed his arm, but Jay quickly had him off his feet, and was holding him down on one of the glass counters.

"Stop fuckin' with me," Jay whispered, sternly. He loosened his grip, moving away from King. As a sign that he was out, he held up his phone for everyone to see. "We're done here," he said and walked out of the store.

Chapter Twenty-Five

Carmen had to wait fifteen minutes before Jay showed at his apartment. If she wasn't in a rush to get to her father then she would've cursed him. Since she was, she simply shoved Rakim and Nyla into his arms and raced out of the complex. She kept her cell phone in her hand, which was beneficial when she walked into the airport. The second she heard it ringing, she pressed it to her ear, answering with a loud hello.

"Well, he's doing much better," her mother told her with a sigh. "They aren't admitting him. He checked out fine, but he needs to watch his diet a little more. He also needs to take his shots on a regular basis. That's what sent him into that fainting spell. On another note, your father thinks that you should stay in Brookstone. He doesn't want you coming all the way here. He also apologizes for the scare."

Carmen wrinkled her face at her mother's news. She had spent the last thirty minutes rushing for no apparent reason and had even squeezed in a brief argument with her husband. Carmen quickly grumbled, "Okay," to her mother. She would've said more, but her mother rushed her off the phone saying that her father needed her. Certain that her mother would call her back if there were any changes; Carmen quickly telephoned Donnie. He was still in the airport's parking lot and instructed for her to come back to the front.

Despite her mother's call, Carmen still debated about whether or not to take the flight. Even though Donnie was waiting on her, she knew she could tell him to leave. Her father's health was a major concern for her and she wanted to be there for him. Unsure of what she was going to do, Carmen didn't make a final decision until five minutes later. She ended up returning to her house where she found Kane's car still in the driveway. She knew he was going to be surprised to see her and she hoped her presence wouldn't prompt another argument.

When she went to unlock the door, she nearly ran into him. He appeared to be in a hurry as if he had an emergency of his own.

"The lieutenant called me," he said as if he had been reading her mind. "One of the officers got a phone call about a fight in West Brookstone. Come to find out, it involved Malachi. I don't know how he got over there, but he punched a kid. He messed up the boy's nose pretty bad, but his parents aren't pressing charges. I was going to take care of it, but I need to check up on my new place. Can you get him?"

Carmen's mouth formed an O, but she knew she should've seen it coming. Malachi had been acting rather odd for the last couple of months. She figured it was time for her to give him some one on one time. "Yeah, I'll do it," she told him as she took a step backwards. She turned around and headed back out the door as she tried to come to grips with Malachi's arrest.

Once she picked him up from the precinct, she took him over to Blue Magic for a bite to eat. So far, he hadn't said much. He repeatedly pushed and pulled his straw in and out of his glass of iced tea. Carmen knew he was doing it to keep from being open with her. After having to deal with King's problems, she thought it would be easier to deal with his. She was now learning that her thinking was warped. "Are you going to at least tell me what the boy said to you?" she asked him. "What were you two fighting about?" Carmen rested both of her arms on the table as she waited for his reply. "I haven't told Akaila about this," she began. "Do you want to speak to her?" Carmen watched him as he shook his head no. "Are you mad at her, too?"

Malachi stuck his straw all the way down into his iced tea and Carmen knew she had hit a nerve. She knew he wasn't happy about Akaila going to Georgia, but she wasn't sure if it was connected to the fight. "Maybe I'll stop with the questions," she whispered. Carmen took a deep breath and looked in the direction of the kitchen. A waitress was coming through the double doors with a large tray and Carmen prayed that she was headed for their table. With food in front of her, she could buy more time to think about how she was going to get Malachi to open up.

God answered her prayer.

As soon as the food hit the table, Carmen dove right in and so did Malachi. Busy with stuffing her face, Carmen was caught off guard when he started to talk. He only asked a simple question, but it spoke volumes.

"Are you going to have another baby?" he whispered.

Carmen dropped her fork as she suddenly became disturbed. "Where did that come from? I don't plan to have another baby. The six of y'all are enough. Besides, with Flame to deal with and your grandfather's diabetes scare, I have enough on my plate. Do you think I should have another baby?"

Malachi dug his fork into his coleslaw not answering. The Kanes had done so much for him that he felt awkward telling them that he felt abandoned. Every time a baby came, the attention would go to them. It was like they had forgotten he existed. He figured it would keep happening if he didn't speak up. Therefore, he shook his head no.

"I knew that would be your response." Carmen reached for her fork again, but she didn't pick it up. Instead, she pushed her cell phone over to him. "Why don't you call your best friend? Don't cha think you should be the one to tell King what happened? I mean, you don't want me to do it, do you?" Malachi whispered a low no before grabbing the phone. Once he had King on the line, Carmen went back to her food. She wasn't eating for long before their waitress returned to the table.

"I was told to pass this to you," the woman told her, setting a small folded note on the table. "It came from the gentleman in the booth over there. He said he knew you."

Carmen's sensors automatically went up as she turned to face the direction that the waitress was pointing. Not seeing anyone there, she glanced down at the note.

Therefore, whatever you want men to do to you, do also to them.

Carmen felt chills as she realized the message was parallel to Shawn Blumington's words in the elevator. Even without seeing him, she knew that he had sent the note. Not wanting Malachi to see, she slid it into her purse. Her son was still on the phone with King so he didn't even notice that something was bothering her. She tried to continue eating, but the note made her shiver and she subsequently lost her appetite. She even began to wonder if it was somehow connected to King's brawl. She knew the best thing to do was to talk to King, but she didn't want to interrupt Malachi's conversation. For now, it seemed the best thing to do was to push the note aside.

***

If King didn't have problems of his own, he would have devoted more time to his conversation with his little brother. When Malachi told him that he had been arrested, it crushed his entire spirit. King hoped that his recent stint in jail would've taught Malachi a lesson, but his brother was already following in his path. It let him know that he had to help his parents keep Malachi on the straight and narrow.

In fact, he was trying to stay on that same path himself. The only thing that was keeping him from pushing forward was his concerns about Blu and Rico. As long as Blu was breathing, King knew that he could never concentrate on anything but him. The feeling was the same when it came to Rico. In fact, his friend was the main reason that he was standing outside of his father's door. He wanted answers and refused to give up until he had them.

King knocked twice on his father's door, hearing his footsteps long before the door even opened. When he finally appeared in the doorway,

King gave him an expression to let him know that he had come to continue their conversation. Jay let him inside though he didn't utter one word. He simply retreated to the couch while King remained standing. "You can't speak?" King asked when he saw his father starting to type on his laptop. "I know our last conversation was heated, but damn. At least I came over to try and clear the air."

Jay closed his laptop as he tried to choose his words carefully. He knew they had unfinished business and if it wasn't settled, nothing with Blu would be solved. King would keep coming at him because he couldn't let bygones be bygones. "I don't babysit anyone in this camp," he said, finally speaking. "You gave me the upmost disrespect when you called me about Rico and Jerome. Like that wasn't enough, you came at me again in Iceland. You were interrogating me like I was the got damn informant. Jarrod was the snitch. He was the snake in the grass that had to be handled."

King chuckled out of agitation. "Well, I guess you're going to have to handle me, too."

Jay peered up at his son before rising to his feet. "Do you think I have something to do with Rico and Jerome not being here?"

King replied with a firm yes. "You know what happened. You run this shit. Everything comes to you first. I've handled enough in this cartel for you to be man enough to tell me what happened. Shit, if it wasn't for me, there wouldn't even be a cartel. You wouldn't even be where you are. I'm responsible for everything you have."

Jay studied his son's face, seeing a full display of anger. As much as he wanted to strangle him, he didn't. Instead, he told him his secret. "Rico deserved to die." Jay was taken off guard as King's hands wrapped tightly around his throat. Quick to get the upper hand, he broke his son's hold before throwing him down on the couch. King was fast, jumping back on his feet until he felt the cold steel of a machete at his neck. It was then that he froze.

Jay quickly patted him down, removing the guns that he found on him. He tossed the weapons over to the other side of the room, keeping the machete in place. "Maybe now you'll listen," he told him, pushing the blade further down onto his skin. "Do you want to know who's responsible for Blu? The answer is Rico. He put our cartel in this motherfucker's hands. I never did that shit. He betrayed us! See, King, even your closest friends can behave like your enemies."

"You should've let me handle it."

"Where would that have put us? You were locked up. Blu was too deep into our operation. He was controlling their minds. I left Rico in charge and he gave that motherfucker his own position. Costa didn't even try to stop him. I had to splatter 'em both."

King shook his head in disbelief as tears streamed down his face. Forty percent of him was betting that Rico was dead, but the other sixty hoped that it wasn't true. Now, he knew that his friend had been murdered and at the hands of his own father, nonetheless. "You are never going to be shit," he sobbed. "Nothing about you is going to change."

Jay didn't take King's comment to heart. "What you see is what you get," he replied. "Get the fuck out my house." He dropped the machete down onto the floor before backing away. He waited until King had collected his guns before he opened the door, allowing him to leave. His son moved slowly, wiping his tears as he went. Jay could see the grief on his son's face, but he tried to ignore it. He let him walk about a foot from the door before he gave him one quick reminder. "Remember this, if it wasn't for me, you wouldn't be where you are," then Jay slammed the door closed.

***

Drama in Brookstone was on the rise and it wasn't even dinnertime. Carmen wasn't aware of everything going on, which was a blessing in disguise. At the moment, her mind was wrapped around the note that had been given to her at Blue Magic. She had read it a total of eight times before she crumpled it up and tossed it into her wastebasket. She told herself to forget about it, but it was hard to do. If it wasn't for Fiona coming into her home office to tell her that King was in the foyer, she would've still been thinking about it.

"He doesn't look too good, Mrs. Kane. There's something wrong."

Carmen stood up from her desk as Fiona's statement made her put up a red flag of worry. Her concern worsened when she saw King for herself. His face was grave and solemn, a state she hadn't seen since his sentencing. When she asked him what was wrong, he didn't give a reply. He paced the floor like he was deep in thought. She let him have his moment until he started punching his fist into the wall. He managed to do it twice before she caught him. "Is breaking your hand going to make you feel better?" she yelled.

King jerked his arm out of her grasp, starting to pace the floor again. He tried to get himself together, but his adrenaline was still running high. After a few minutes, he could feel himself calming and he blurted, "Jay killed Rico. He killed Costa, too."

Carmen grabbed her chest almost unable to breathe. "H-h-he killed Rico?"

"This motherfucker is walking around so nonchalant about the whole thing. Lying in my face, pretending he didn't know shit. At this point, Mama, the worst mistake I made was allowing that bastard into my life. I fuckin' hate him. He isn't going to change. He is always going to be the same murderin' son of a bitch that he is. I want—" King was interrupted by the sound of his mother's cell phone. He wanted her to ignore it until she told him that it was his grandmother. She then explained why she needed to take the call.

"Long story short, your grandfather was rushed to the ER," Carmen told him, quickly. "Let me handle this and I'll fill you in on the details. Get a drink to cool off or something. I'll be in there in a minute." Carmen waited until King left the foyer before she answered.

"Well," her mother began with a sigh. "Your father wanted me to call you because he wants us to move back to Brookstone. He wants to be closer to you and the grandkids." Patricia paused, but it wasn't long enough for Carmen to respond. "Now, we don't have a place picked out or anything, but he figured that we could stay with you for a while. You know, maybe a month or so until we can close on a new house. How does that sound?"

Carmen knew she wasn't in her right state of mind when she yelled yes. If she was thinking clearly, she would've said no because of her nonexistent marriage and extramarital affair. The word came out impulsively but Carmen couldn't retract her statement, by now her mother was jumping for joy over her response. It was obvious that the move was what both of her parents wanted.

"Well, we're going to take care of things on our end, Peaches. Don't worry about a thing. We won't be in your hair for long. You won't even know we're there. I promise you."

Carmen couldn't even ease out a small smile. She simply told her mother okay before hanging up the phone. Upset by the agreement, she wasn't quick to rush back to King. She had to get herself together first. When she did finally enter into the kitchen, she made sure that she gave him her undivided attention. King told her a lot, but there still wasn't much she could do. The damage was already done. She could only promise him that she would talk to Jay. She didn't know how far that would get her but at least it was a start.

As King prepared to leave, Carmen noticed that he looked ten times better than when he first arrived. She wished that she could've said the same for herself. Lately, she had been feeling as if all of her problems had come one right after another. It started with her father's fainting spell and was followed by Malachi's arrest. Then, there was the note and King showing up at the house, announcing that Jay had murdered his best friend. She thought that was the end of her trials until Kane walked into the kitchen. He didn't speak to her, but his presence reminded her that she had to tell him about her parents moving in. Not ready to deal with his reaction, Carmen chose not to mention it. She simply walked King to the door and let him out. When she returned to the kitchen, Kane was gone.

Chapter Twenty-Six

The following morning could only be better than the day before. Or at least that was the plan. To ensure a peaceful start to her day, Carmen left the house fifteen minutes earlier than normal to head to Flame in order to avoid her husband. Kane, on the other hand, stayed in bed an hour later than usual. He arrived at the precinct to learn that the lieutenant had scheduled an impromptu meeting. Very much aware that he hadn't shown a positive attitude on his first day back, Kane knew he had to redeem himself. Once he showed Harris that he still had his spark, the lieutenant would stop singing Sanders' praises.

"I know you all were busy this morning with your assignments," the lieutenant began. "I want to have a quick discussion regarding the new focus of our department. As you all know, Detective Sanders and Michael Kane have been working the Santiago case. Right now, all we have on him is a million dollars' worth of coke. Now from the information that Sanders has received, Jay Santiago has decided to fly the coop on this drug shit. Still, we have a good enough start. I say, we go ahead and take him down."

Kane's eyes widened at the news. It was what he needed to hear especially after his wife had told him that she was filing for divorce. Smiling from ear to ear, he looked over at Sanders. Unlike him, his partner wasn't wearing the same expression. In fact, he looked like he was against it. When he raised his hand, Kane knew he was going to try to change Harris' mind.

Sanders stood and turned sideways so that he faced the lieutenant as well as the other officers in the room. "We do have the drugs in our possession. However, if Santiago has gone legit, why should we take him down for drug and money laundering charges? If we buy ourselves a little bit more time then we can find out if he's behind the disappearance of Jarrod Luis. He was the informant that we had secured. His grandmother has reported him as missing and we haven't been able to find his body."

Kane looked at Sanders, wondering what he was doing. He appeared to be trying to sway the lieutenant in a direction that wouldn't end with Jay being in prison. Apprehensive of his motive, Kane stood up as well, but the lieutenant interrupted him before he could speak.

"I've made my decision," Harris said, clearing his throat. "The Brookstone PD is going to take down Jay. I called you all in here because I want to form a tactical team for this operation. We can't go into this unprepared. Santiago is a brilliant man with ties all across the world. We need to know everything that he's involved in. That's the reason I want to start

tapping his phones. If we get on it after the meeting, we can be listening—"
Kane cut him off.

"I can do that, sir. I'm on it," Kane responded, eagerly. "I'll spearhead everything."

Lieutenant Harris knew that Kane was the best person for the job, but the agent had personal connections to the case that could interfere with their investigation. "Kane, I have no problem putting you in charge. However, I want Sanders to assist you. This case is too personal for you to do alone because of your wife. If we prove that Jay was using dirty money to fund Blue Magic then we have to bring her down as well. To be honest, we need an officer outside of Flame right now. We also need to tap her phones."

The raging bull that Kane usually kept hidden had been awakened once again. Everything had happened so fast, and the next thing he knew his hands were around Harris' neck causing him to struggle to breath. Kane felt a sharp pain in his side which broke his hold on the lieutenant. He grabbed at his waist as it registered that someone used a Taser gun to subdue him. He thought for a moment that his flesh was burning as Sanders dragged him out of the room. His partner assumed that he was finished with Harris, but he wasn't. Kane charged back at the door, punching it several times.

"Michael Kane," a voice said sternly behind him.

Kane knew that the voice belonged to the chief of police. He didn't respond as he already knew that he was in more trouble than he could handle. The chief called his name again and this time he turned to face him.

"I guess I chose the right meeting to come to," the chief stated, nastily. "From what Harris has told me, this isn't your first violent outburst. There won't be another, though. I never thought I would say this, but Mr. Kane, you're fired. I suggest you leave discretely."

Kane could hear Sanders behind him as he tried to coerce the chief to change his mind. Kane knew there was no need. The chief would never give him his job back. He was officially unemployed and Sanders now had the lead on the Santiago case. His face now wearing a scowl, Kane walked up to the chief and yelled an expletive in his face. His positive outlook for the day had officially been lost.

In the meantime, things were looking up for Carmen who had received a set of samples from the *Fresh Prince* collection. Now that the items had arrived, Carmen was preparing to meet with her staff to discuss the line's marketing plan. Upon reaching the conference room with a dolly, she opened the door to find Tiara inside with a slew of papers in front of her. "What cha got?" she asked her, helping an intern with one of the boxes.

"Another proposed budget for the *Fresh Prince* campaign," Tiara replied, holding up a spreadsheet. "You're looking at spending some millions on this thing, you know."

"Well, that's the reason it's a proposed budget. We can probably make some cuts somewhere." Carmen grabbed a pair of scissors, beginning to cut open the box. Pulling back the flaps, she smiled as she saw one of the T-shirts she had designed. "It's like Christmas all over again," she joked, picking up the plastic bag that the shirt was sealed in. "Look at the-"

"Carm, Lieutenant Harris is on the phone. He wants to speak with you."

Carmen grunted loudly at the sound of Cathy's voice. Her receptionist had found the perfect way to ruin her moment. Carmen gave her a mean glare, but Cathy only held up the phone in response. She then gave her an expression that told her the call was more important than the samples on the table. Since Cathy mentioned that it was the lieutenant, Carmen decided to let the interruption slide. She dumped the t-shirt back into the box and grabbed the phone from Cathy's hand. "This is Carmen," she greeted.

"Mrs. Kane," the lieutenant said, as Carmen went into her office. "I know that you are a busy woman, but I needed to speak with you. Since we've known each other for several years, I feel comfortable giving you this news over the phone. I hate to say this, but your son is down here."

Carmen sat down in her office chair and quickly checked her cell phone for messages. Not having any besides a few emails, she brought her attention back to the phone call. "I have three, Harris, is Rakim with you?" she joked. "Let me guess, it has to be King? What did he do?"

The lieutenant started to speak faster like he was pressed for time. "No, Mrs. Kane, it's your other son, Malachi. He has been booked. Apparently, he got into another fight with the same kid from yesterday. He was back in West Brookstone. I guess the fight wasn't over when we first arrested him. This time, he did a whole lot more damage. The kid's parents are definitely pressing charges. I need you to come down here and see about him."

Carmen slumped down in her seat, covering her face. "Excuse my language, but are you fuckin' serious? Obviously, I didn't get through to him yesterday. Get Kane to check on him. He should be at the precinct. Have him make sure that a bail hearing has been scheduled."

It wasn't in the lieutenant's plans to tell Carmen that her husband had been fired. Yet, he knew the deed had to be done. It was the only way he could explain why Kane couldn't check up on Malachi. "Since you don't know, I guess I have to be the one to tell you. Your husband was fired this morning by the chief. He is no longer with us."

Carmen almost threw the phone halfway across the room. Able to control her temper, she quickly told the lieutenant that she would be at the station in five minutes and hung up the phone. While she had only planned on dealing with Jay, she now had two other men to tear into. First, she would deal with Malachi then she would hunt down Kane.

Once she had reached the police department, she ran inside, dropping her Hermès Birkin bag onto the counter. "Where is he?" she asked, staring an officer in the face. He gave her a questionable look, which only triggered her temper. "You know who the fuck I am, don't be looking at me like I'm some deranged bitch. Where's Malachi?" Both of her hands were firmly on her hips as she waited for the officer to respond. When he stood up from his seat, she knew she had his attention.

"Um, Lieutenant Harris actually wanted to see you. He wanted to speak to you, personally," the officer said, coming around the counter. He directed Carmen down a long corridor before leading her into an interrogation room.

Carmen expected to see her son, but her eyes landed on Sanders and Lieutenant Harris. She huffed at the sight of them, knowing that something was up. "Where's Malachi?" she asked, pulling out a chair. She dropped her purse down onto the table, gazing back and forth between the two men. "Say something! Where is my son? Isn't this what you called me down here for?"

Harris cleared his throat as he started in on what they needed to discuss. Though Malachi was a factor, the situation with Jay was more important. "Mrs. Kane, the Brookstone Police Department has reason to believe that Jay Santiago is still running his drug cartel. Now, we got information that he has broken out of the biz, but only a short time ago. We also have confiscated evidence against him."

Carmen folded her arms across her chest, realizing that she had been deceived. The day was getting worse and it was only lunchtime. "Not this bullshit, Harris. Is this why I'm here? Is this some sort of trick? I will tell you now; I don't know shit about Jay being a drug dealer. All I know is that he owns three businesses, Sapphire, Blue Magic, and Iceland. All of that other shit you're talking is just that, shit."

From what Harris could see, Jay still had Carmen wrapped around his finger. The woman seemed to be better allies with him than her own husband. "You know, Mrs. Kane, there is still a part of your case that is unsolved. Wasn't Enosis the name of the man found dead on that ship? We still don't know who killed him. You probably do, though. You were there, right?"

Carmen could tell that Harris wanted to see her sweat. If he didn't, he wouldn't have said Enosis' name. "I don't know what you're talking about," she told him. "I also don't know anything about Jay selling drugs. What I do know is that he has already served his time for that. You had him for seventeen years. Now, tell me this, is my son here, or was this a grimy scheme to get me to be an informant against Jay? Believe me, Harris; you have a better chance at fuckin' me than getting me to be an informant."

Harris stood up, wanting to give Sanders a chance to try and coax her. "Tell your baby daddy that we're on to him. If he isn't coming correct now then he better start. You also better watch your back. If we take him down, we take you down, too. Maybe now you'll stop jumping in the bed with him."

"Go to hell, Harris."

Carmen watched as the lieutenant snickered at her before leaving the room. Once he was out of her sight, she looked at Sanders who was still at the table. He didn't ask her any questions, but simply said that he was going to go get Malachi. Leaving her by herself, Carmen covered her face as her worst fears came to light. She started praying aloud until Sanders' voice sounded once again in the room. When she turned around to face him, she saw Malachi.

Her son's wrists were handcuffed in front of him and he was still in his regular clothes. She told Sanders to give them a minute before saying a quick prayer to God for guidance. By the time she was done, Malachi had sat down in a chair next to her. "I am telling you right now that my nerves are on edge. Tell me exactly what happened. I even want to know how you got in West Brookstone. We're not going to play with straws on this one. Before I pay this bail, we need to have a serious conversation. Now, I realized that the anniversary of your mother's death is coming up. I know that losing her was a hard thing for you to go through. However, the pain that you're feeling has to be expressed in a different way other than fighting. You need to get it out, but in a positive way. There are so many things you can do, art, sports, the list goes on."

Malachi shook his head in disagreement. "Is that all you could come up with? You're like the rest of 'em. None of y'all have any fuckin' time for me. You pop out baby after baby, King is worried about his businesses, and all Akaila thinks about is Georgia. No one pays me any attention. I'm like the fuckin' black sheep of this family."

Carmen mouthed a silent oh, seeing what the problem was. She had first attributed the fighting to his mother, but her son was giving her the same argument that King had when he was in his thug life days. "So that's why you're fighting?" She neared her head closer to his. "You want attention? Well, Malachi, I'm going to give you exactly what you want. Best believe that I will be riding your ass until you're twenty-one. Do you understand that?"

"Whatever, you're not my fuckin' mama," he snapped.

Carmen couldn't stop herself before she snatched him up. The chair turned over behind him as she pushed him up against the wall. He had grown to be about an inch or two taller than her, but Carmen still had the upper hand partly because he was still in handcuffs. Malachi tried, to no avail, to maneuver himself out of her grasp.

"After everything I've done for you, you say that to me? Say it again, I dare you to," she yelled at him, breaking her hold.

Malachi's tone became even fiercer as he said, "You're not my fuckin' mama, bitch!"

Carmen had to take a few seconds to process what he had said and her own reaction. She blinked, but she knew she saw right. Blood was slowly trickling from Malachi's nose. She stared at him in disbelief until she felt the sharp pain that was shooting up through her right hand. It was then that she remembered punching him. Unable to fathom how quickly she had flipped, Carmen sat back down at the table. "I'm sorry," she slowly muttered. "I'm so sorry."

Malachi stood there in silence as the warm liquid found its way inside of his mouth. He couldn't help but to taste it as it fell from his nostrils. "Everyone is busy with their own thing," he whispered. "Akaila and Kristian are all about college; Daddy isn't dependable because he's dealing with his own issues. King spends most of his time working on his businesses. Then, you keep dropping a baby every year. I feel left out."

Carmen rubbed her lips together as she tried to come up with a solution for the problem. She knew she needed to be spending more time with all of her kids, but sometimes it seemed as if there wasn't enough time in the day. Most of the time, she would catch up with them over dinner, but lately she hadn't been in attendance. "What would you like to see happen?"

Malachi shrugged his shoulders. "I don't know."

Carmen knew that the obvious resolution was to simply spend more time with Malachi. She also knew that he didn't want to spend all of his extra time with a forty-one year old woman. He needed someone who was close to his age. "Hmm," she mumbled, "would you like to move in with King?"

A squeal of excitement escaped Malachi's lips before he asked, "Live with him, for real?"

Carmen smiled at how excited Malachi had become. "I'll have to talk to him about it, but I know it won't be a problem. Now, that doesn't mean that you'll be partying over there. There will be rules. I want that to be clear."

Malachi nodded his head as Sanders and another officer returned to the room. The detective informed her that he needed to place Malachi back in his cell until his bail hearing. Carmen wasn't finished with the conversation, but she knew she didn't have a say in the matter. Hopefully, the bail hearing would be scheduled soon. She grabbed her purse and gave Malachi a quick kiss on the cheek. She apologized once again before the officer escorted her back into the lobby.

Chapter Twenty-Seven

Once Carmen had gotten everything squared away with Malachi, she called Kane to schedule a late lunch at Old Town Bistro. She didn't mention anything about Malachi, Jay, or his termination so it was of no surprise when she sensed her husband's excitement through the phone. She knew that he thought they were going to reconcile, but she was going to have to let him down. When she got to the restaurant, she sat for several minutes waiting on her husband to show. *If he thought we were reconciling, he sure isn't showing it*, she thought, *he's ten minutes late.*

"I'm sorry," a voice said, coming up behind her. "I got stuck in traffic."

Carmen watched her husband as he sat down at the table. A bottle of Alice White was already there though Carmen hadn't touched it. She needed the drink, but had decided against it at the last moment. Kane, on the other hand, grabbed it off of the table and poured himself a glass. "You should know how to manage your time," she told him, opening her menu.

Kane looked at Carmen questioningly in response to her tone. When she called him, he thought for a moment that she wanted to resolve their issues. Now that he could hear her attitude, he knew that wasn't the case. Instead of responding to her, he scanned the list of entrees, trying to decide on what he wanted to eat. "Steak, fish, chicken, I don't even kn—"

"Why did they fire you?" Carmen barked, interrupting him and grabbing his menu. "Did you think I wasn't going to find out? What are you going to do about money? You're buying a fuckin' condo!"

Kane swallowed. "Give me the menu back, Carm."

Carmen glared at him harshly before throwing the menu back at him. He opened it back up, scanning the pages as he started to speak again.

"Harris and I had some disagreements. Things got heated and physical, so the chief let me go. That's the truth of the matter. You wanted it. You got it. As far as my place is concerned I still plan on moving out. I have money in my savings account, which will hold me until I can find something else. If things work in my favor, I might be able to go back to the Triad. I'll have to see."

Carmen thought that since they were talking about his job; it was the best time to bring up the investigation. "Well, you obviously can't arrest anybody if you're unemployed." Kane didn't reply, but from his expression, she knew he didn't like her joke. "I guess we'll move on to other news," she continued. "Malachi got arrested again today. I had to go to the station to get him. Harris and Sanders also thought it was a good time to interrogate me. So, were you trying to send Jay to prison, too?"

"I would send him to hell if I could."

Carmen sat her menu down on the table. With the way the conversation was going, she was certain that the bottle of chardonnay would be the only thing on her bill. "I shouldn't be shocked at that response. Knowing you, you'll probably plant false evidence for them to find. You don't like to fail. As long as he's locked up, you're happy."

"No one wants to fail," Kane replied, closing his menu. He set it down on the table, preparing to leave. "Whoever catches Jay first will get the most money out the pot." Kane threw his cloth napkin down onto the table. It was a sign to Carmen that he was leaving. "If you want me to be honest, I don't give a fuck about the money. It's miniscule. What I care about is sitting right in front of me."

Carmen narrowed her eyes at him, as she grabbed her wallet. She took out her debit card, setting it on the table, before saying, "Maybe, one day you'll learn how to prove it." She signaled for the waiter as Kane took a step away from the table. With him leaving, she no longer had a reason to stay for lunch. Jay was next on her list so she pulled out her phone to text him.

"Stop fuckin' Jay and you can prove it, too," Kane unexpectedly shot back.

Carmen didn't get a chance to reply because Kane had walked away too quickly. Given the chance, her response would have been laced with curse words and then she would have thrown a drink in his face. Instead, she cursed him in her head and sat in her seat until the check was paid for. By the time she got her receipt, Jay had texted her back. He was in the basement of Flame, which would be her next destination.

***

With the amount of noise that was in the room, Jay found it hard to hear the contractor. The man was pointing at a large square that had been drawn in the middle of one of the walls where he had started designing a vault. Although the basement was only accessible by using a secret combination on the elevator's control panel, Jay wanted his jewels secured. Currently, he was keeping the diamonds in small safes in the back of the room. He also had plans for an alternative exit, which he wanted the contractor to build.

"My men are going to create something like a tunnel," the contractor was saying, now pointing at the location of the alternative exit. "We're planning on starting tonight."

Jay nodded his head in agreement as he walked over to the space. In the event that he needed to make a quick move, the exit would be there. Though he wasn't necessarily running a diamond cartel, he had to take every precaution when it came to his diamonds. "Make sure the tiles are the same. If someone gets down here, I don't want them to suspect this area. The tunnel should stop in an inconspicuous place. The last thing I want is people coming out of the ground in the middle of downtown."

"I most certainly will, sir. I'm glad you're pleased with everything. I'm going to let you be while I go check up on the materials," the contractor said, holding out his hand. "I'll be back tonight. No worries, Mr. Santiago, everything will be taken care of. Trust me."

He shook his hand before the contractor headed for the elevators. Once he was aboard, Jay's phone started vibrating in his left pants' pocket. When he saw it was Carmen, he quickly answered, knowing she had made it to Flame. She sounded heated on the phone, so he figured King had gotten in her ear. His notion was confirmed when they were finally face to face. She looked disgruntled, which told him that the rest of the afternoon wasn't going to be good. Although it was pointless, he tried to prep himself. He even gave her a quick tour of the room.

Men and women were everywhere, all different races, working on the product line for Iceland. The first place he took her was to the desk of a man who was drawing out the shape of a ring. He let her watch him for a few seconds before he brought her over to a young woman who was sawing off a piece of carving wax. "That is another step of the process," he told her. "She's constructing the band for a ring." He could tell that Carmen was intrigued, but he wanted to show her something else. He led her to another table, picking up a solitaire diamond necklace. "This little baby is a winner. I've got several of these being made. It's one of the more affordable pieces."

Jay was smiling, but it was dampened when Carmen took the necklace from his hands. She set it back on the table before folding her arms across her chest. Her actions told him that he couldn't stall anymore. Ready to take his beating, he led her into a small room. He then closed the door behind him, leaning his back up against it. "Go ahead and give it to me."

"You killed Rico?" she asked him, plainly. Her tone was calm, but Jay knew it was the calm before the storm. "I've known Rico since he was like this," Carmen yelled, using her hand to illustrate the height of a preschooler. "He was twenty years old. He had his whole life ahead of him. Now, you've fucked up your relationship with King. Fix it. I don't know how, but you better do it. Number two, Malachi was arrested again today. I went to get him and Lieutenant Harris nicely informed me that they are investigating you. He even told me that he has evidence."

Jay displayed a sinister smile as he realized that his belief was true. The Brookstone PD had stolen his drugs. It was the only evidence they could have against him. "I knew those motherfuckers were watching me. I even know what evidence they have. Let's see what they do with it." Jay learned quickly that his nonchalant attitude didn't help the conversation. Carmen walked up to him until they were chest to chest.

"This may be a joke to you," she whispered, harshly, "but it's not to me. Whatever bullshit you got going on, I suggest you clean it up quick. I'm not going to go back to prison for you or no one else. You said you were out, you better be out. Don't test me."

Jay parted his lips to reply as Carmen pushed him out the way, opening the door. He could tell she was finished with the conversation because she ignored him completely when he called her name. When he saw her disappear onto the elevator, he made the decision to make up with her later. For now, he would let her have her tantrum.

Meanwhile, Carmen struggled to control her anger. She had enough aggression in her to punch Jay in his face yet she didn't do it. Her entire basement was filled with strangers who didn't need to witness a tirade. In addition, she was at her place of employment. Since it wasn't good for her to blow off steam in the building, she made the decision to return home.

Upon reaching her limousine, she directed Donnie to take her back to her estate. Traffic had picked up so she advised him to take a shortcut so she could get there quicker. *Please make this ride as smooth as possible,* she prayed, closing her eyes. *I have enough on my plate to deal with and I don't need traffic to be one of them.* As she laid her head back, Carmen started to meditate. She spent several minutes talking to God until she felt the car being hit from behind. Her eyes opened in astonishment as the car came to a complete stop in the middle of an alleyway. "Are you—" the question wasn't even out before the front passenger side door opened. A man rushed into the car and Donnie jammed his foot back onto the accelerator. Carmen watched in slow motion as the man shot Donnie at point-blank range in the head.

As the car swerved back and forth, Carmen's adrenaline level increased dramatically. With little time to think, she grabbed the pink Cobra pistol, which she had stashed in between the seat cushions. She quickly fired three shots into the man's chest in front of her. His gun had been pointed directly at her as if she was next on his list. Scared out of her mind, Carmen started to climb over the seat. Her left hand grabbed the steering wheel while the right pushed Donnie's killer into the passenger seat. As she tried to gain control of the car, she could feel her legs being pulled from behind. *Where is my gun? Where is my fuckin' gun?* Carmen's eyes traveled over the vehicle until she spotted the weapon on top of her attacker's body. Still halfway over the seat, she snatched the weapon up before firing a single shot into the face of a masked man. He had come through the back door of the limousine, allowing her to see that she was being trailed.

When his grip loosened, she climbed into the front seat. Both hands gripped the steering wheel as she tried to gain control of the car once again. She even caught a glimpse of Donnie's face. It was drenched in blood and she could see smoke seeping through his dark brown hair. Not wanting to study the gruesome sight for too long, she forced her eyes back on the road. She screamed in shock as she saw the trash dumpster straight ahead. Knowing she couldn't swerve in time, she braced herself for the impact. The next thing she knew, there were a pair of hands pulling her from the vehicle. Fighting for her life, Carmen struggled up against a set of heavy arms as the limo crashed behind her.

As she struggled, a man's hand clamped down over her mouth. She attempted to bite it, but he managed to remove it in time. He pulled her into another vehicle, which sent Carmen into a fighting fit. She kicked, punched, and scratched at him until he used his body weight to overthrow her.

"Shh," he whispered as the car began to move.

Tears streamed down Carmen's face as she realized she was being kidnapped. Instantly, her body went numb but a voice in her head told her not to give up. She attempted to fight back again, struggling against the man until she heard him yell her name. Frozen in place, she looked through her tears to see the face of a Hispanic man that she did not recognize. When he moved away from her, she sat up and realized she was in another limousine. She spotted her purse and cell phone in the car as well.

"I got her, Mr. Santiago," the man said, holding in an earpiece. "She killed two men, though. I'll get Valdez to take care of all the bodies. We'll discard of the limo and the pistol. Right now, I'm making sure she gets home. After that, I'm going to locate that Benz. I didn't see Blu, but I think he's behind this. Hopefully, we can find out."

Carmen listened to him, feeling as if she had stepped into a nightmare. Even when the limousine drove down her street, she didn't feel any better. Adrenaline was still pumping through her veins, causing her heart rate to increase. She tried to remain still, but even that was hard to do. As she stared at the man across from her, she told herself to use him to her advantage. So far, the only thing she knew was that he worked for Jay. "Who are you?" she asked. He wasn't quick to answer, but he did after a few seconds.

"Linx," he replied, looking out the window.

The limousine was coming to a halt as it pulled up in front of her house. Carmen didn't budge. Instead, she studied the man's face. She assumed that he was either Cuban or Puerto Rican. His dark black hair had been cut into a Caesar and he had deep dimples in both cheeks. He looked to be about three hundred pounds and she put him to be at least six feet tall. "Did he tell you why I needed a bodyguard?" she asked, smartly.

Linx didn't reply as he unbuckled his seatbelt. He picked up her purse and cell phone, handing it to her. "Mr. Santiago doesn't pay me to answer questions. He pays me to keep you alive." Without another word, he opened up the door to the limousine. He motioned for her to get out, following behind her once she had.

"You mentioned something about a Benz on the phone. Tell me about it."

Linx rolled his eyes in agitation. "Mrs. Davenport, whatever you want to know should be directed at Mr. Santiago. He doesn't pay me to answer questions."

Carmen's anger escalated to a point of no return. "I almost lost my fuckin' life today. Do you understand that? I don't give a fuck what he pays you to do. If I ask you a question, give me a fuckin' answer. That's what I'm asking for." Carmen tried to hit him with her purse, but he caught it in his hand. He pushed it back towards her, raising his voice as well.

"Say thanks and take ya ass into the house. There is more I have to handle today than you. I have a schedule to abide by."

Carmen stuck her middle finger up at Linx, but he only narrowed his eyes. She realized that he was sticking to his job description whether she liked it or not. As she headed into the house, she realized that everything she knew came from what Linx had said in the car. He was responsible for taking care of her limousine and pistol as well as the men she had killed. She didn't know what he was going to do about Donnie.

Considering the circumstances, Carmen felt as if she was obligated to pretend like his murder never happened. She was already underneath the microscope and going to the police would increase her chances of being arrested. Harris had already warned her and she knew he was a man of his word. Still, she wanted to see justice for Donnie's murder.

Carmen stretched out across her bed, drowning herself in her tears. Her voice came out in whispers as she prayed to God for the safety of her and her family. Two minutes in, her prayer was interrupted by the sound of the doorbell. Certain that Fiona would answer it; she continued praying. However, a minute went by and the noise hadn't ceased. Carmen sat up straight in her bed, realizing that Fiona wasn't there. She tried to pull herself together as she headed down the steps. By the time she was in the foyer, she believed she had done her best to address her appearance. Not bothering to look through the peephole, she quickly undid all of the locks. The second she opened the door, she nearly screamed when her parents yelled, surprise.

Chapter Twenty-Eight

Carmen was less than thrilled to see her parents on her doorstep. She wasn't prepared to deal with them, but like everything else, she didn't have any control. Her mother hadn't even warned her that they were coming so soon. She decided to make the best of the situation for the time being. When Fiona returned with Rakim and Nyla, she placed the kids in the living room with their grandparents to try and keep them occupied. So far, it seemed to be working.

"Get him, Rakim, get him!" Patricia exclaimed. She bowled over laughing as Rakim jumped on top of her husband. He threw a stuffed gorilla down onto his grandfather's chest, pretending that it was biting him. In return, Lotus picked him up, holding him in the air.

"You'll never win!" Lotus yelled in an alien-like voice. "Never," he shouted.

With her parents busy with Rakim and Nyla, Carmen left the living room to steal away for a bit. Fiona had taken a trip to the deli so Carmen knew she would have a second or two to herself. She figured she would make a salad so she opened the fridge and took out a head of lettuce and tomatoes.

"Can we have another shot at a conversation?"

Carmen dropped the items onto the floor, hearing a deep voice. She looked to the right of her, seeing Kane in the far right corner of the room. "How long have you been there?"

"Since you walked in; I guess ignoring me is like second nature."

Carmen didn't feed into his statement, bending down to pick up the food. She placed it in one of the sinks quickly turning on the faucet. She then washed her hands in another.

"Everything is settled on my condo. I'm going to start moving today. Before I do, I want to ask you something." Kane stared at his wife, noticing that she wasn't even looking in his direction. "Do you really want it to be over?"

Carmen shook the excess water off her hands as she opened up one of the cabinets. She took out a bowl, which she set on the counter. "Those words are six months too late," she told him. "It's too late for, 'I love you,' or, 'I'm sorry.' I don't want to hear it. The man I loved left a long time ago. I won't ever make this mistake again. I want the divorce."

Kane's body became inanimately still as he debated in his mind what to say. For the moment, it seemed that silence was the best option. Certain of it, he left the kitchen so he could pack his things. He could hear her parents in the living room and he told himself not to entertain them. If he was lucky, he would make it out the house before they even saw him.

When he returned to his room, he packed quicker than he had intended. He felt that if he gave his wife some distance that maybe she would see what life was like without him. Once she realized that she needed him, she would beg him to come back.

"Going somewhere?" a voice asked, interrupting Kane's thoughts.

Kane looked behind him only to see Lotus in the doorway. He didn't answer his question, continuing to throw clothes into his suitcase. Kane thought his lack of words would prompt Lotus to leave, but it didn't. It only encouraged him to keep talking.

"I see Malachi isn't the only one moving out. I wonder who'll be next. Maybe Nyla will get her own place." Lotus let out a small chuckle. "Well, Michael, what have you been up to? Well, besides the packing, you know. Did you get another job? Carmen told us about you being fired. Mortgages aren't cheap. Take it from a realtor. What do you have lined up?"

Kane made a weird noise with his mouth to let Lotus know that he didn't want to talk. He knew his father-in-law had taken the hint, but he still didn't leave the room.

"Why did you get fired, Kane? I know why the Triad let you go, but what happened with Harris? I mean, you close on a house and then you lose your job. What's going on?"

Kane's temper instantly flared, causing him to raise his voice. "If you must know, Harris and I didn't agree on an issue. However, the last thing I need is you prying into my affairs. I got enough shit to deal with around here. Do us both a favor, mind your fuckin' business. Why don't you go play with your grandkids?"

Lotus stood in silence as he realized that Kane had forgotten who he was talking to. If he was in his younger days, his son-in-law would have been picking himself up off the floor. Since he was a changed man, Lotus kept his hands at his side. "You know, Michael, you would be a better agent if you didn't let your personal life interfere with your work. Carmen told me that the Brookstone PD is investigating Jay again. Why don't y'all go after someone else? There are tons of men out there that are feeding the streets crack. Forget about Jay."

Lotus remained silent for a few seconds, allowing his words to marinate in Kane's mind. "You can't fault the man because he got your wife pregnant. You and Carmen were broken up. You had moved on with Tricia. God rest her soul. I don't want to upset you, but I want you to think about the decisions you're making. How long are you going to fight this battle? Is sending Jay back to prison really going to make Carmen want you?"

Kane dropped his suitcase on the floor. The loud noise was enough to make Lotus shut up. "I don't need any fuckin' reminders," Kane yelled. "I know what I did. I also know what Carmen did to me. She fuckin' cheated on me and got pregnant. That's where the shit started. Do you remember that? Shit, you're doing a lot of talk for someone who isn't Jay's biggest fan. Where did this change of heart come from? Was it when you were helping Jay out with his cartel? Giving him warehouses and shit?"

Lotus made a stern face. "I've been legit for many years. As for my relationship with Jay, if you were really doing some digging then you would know that I'm his godfather. I signed the paperwork forty-seven years ago. Maybe now, you'll understand my position."

Kane looked at his father-in-law, nastily. He wasn't quick to reply, opting first to pick up two of his suitcases. He had packed enough to start making the move. "Excuse me while I excuse myself," he finally said. Kane could hear Lotus starting to mouth off again, but he didn't stick around to hear what his father-in-law had to say. He simply made his way out the room, and headed down the steps. He passed Carmen in the process, but didn't look her way. All he wanted now was to get far away from anything involving her household.

As for Carmen, her attention was focused on the top of the stairwell. Her father was standing there with a grim expression on his face. It was enough evidence for her to know that he and Kane had a battle of words. About to approach him, she was sidetracked when Fiona came back into the house. She quickly told her that she had a chef salad in the refrigerator before running up the steps. Unsure of which room her parents had chosen, she checked the guestroom at the far end of the hall. Luckily, her father was inside, lying down on the bed. His eyes were closed, but Carmen wasn't going to let his act fool her. She knew he was wide awake.

"What was that about?" she asked him, sitting down on the bed. She touched his hand in case he was going to pretend that he didn't hear her. "What did you say to him?"

"Something that needed to be said," Lotus replied. "That is all."

"Details, Daddy," Carmen urged. "You don't have to turn against Kane, too, because we're not on the best of terms."

Lotus opened his eyes so that Carmen could see his full expression. "Your issues are your issues and my issues are my issues. That is all I'm going to say about that. Now, if you don't mind, this old man needs his rest. Rakim is a handful."

"Yeah, yeah, yeah," Carmen muttered. "I'll let it slide for now." She gave her father's hand another squeeze before leaving him to himself. As she headed down the steps, she could hear her mother still in the den with Rakim and Nyla. Fiona, on the other hand, was in the dining room, setting the table. Carmen watched her as she tried to decide on whether or not she was going to join her parents for dinner. While she knew that she should, she also needed to see Jay. With her parents arriving so suddenly, she never got the chance to talk to him about her attack. Since things had calmed down, Carmen knew that she needed to use her time wisely. Quickly telling Fiona not to set a spot for her, Carmen grabbed her keys from her home office. Ten minutes later, she was boarding an elevator in Jay's apartment complex.

The doors were about to close when she noticed the reflection of a familiar face. She could see Linx walking in her direction from looking at one of the mirrors in the lobby. Not bothering to wait on him, she allowed the doors to close before he could board. When the doors opened again, she stepped out, almost running into him. She gave him an odd expression, but didn't comment. Hoping he wasn't coming inside as well, she knocked on Jay's door.

He opened the door, shirtless and barefoot, wearing only a pair of dark denim jeans. It was rare that she saw him like that, but she knew why when he held up the glass of Red Berry Ciroc. His nerves were as bad as hers. She went inside without Linx and asked Jay to pour her a glass as well. Once it was in her hands, she drunk it straight before asking for another one. After he gave it to her, Carmen started to talk. "I want to know what's going on," she told him, sternly. "I have blood on my hands and my driver was killed. I can't even begin to explain how I feel about that. How do I tell his family that he's not coming home?"

Jay let out a loud sigh though he already expected the discussion. After her attack, he had spent most of his time trying to locate Blu and the Benz personally. Even as he stood there, he had two groups of men on the hunt. "You can't tell them. You can't go to the police; you can't do anything. Give me some time and I promise you, I will personally butcher the guy who ordered the hit."

Carmen threw her glass at the wall, allowing it to shatter. "Fuck you," she yelled. "You're worried about saving your own ass. Who's going to cover mine, Jay? I got two fuckin' bodies to my name. How do I know that no one saw me pull the trigger on those men? I was in the middle of fuckin' downtown in a damn alley where the homeless sleep."

Jay narrowed his eyes as he stared at his wall. It was stained with alcohol while the floor was now covered in broken glass. "If he isn't home by now, his wife has probably already put up her red flags. When he doesn't show, she's going to call him. Then, she's going to call the limo service he worked for. If they don't know anything, she's going straight to the police. Next, they are coming to you. You will be the first person they interrogate. Now, if you go over to her house all apologetic, she's going to suspect you. For one, you look guilty. Two, you are guilty."

Carmen grabbed the glass that was in his hand, finishing it off. She then gave it back to him as a sign that she needed more. When he gave it to her, she threw it at the wall as well. It was the only way she could deal with her rage. Nevertheless, she knew that he wasn't going to give her another one. Instead, he gave her an expression that suggested he was becoming annoyed.

"You know the cops are on my ass. If you give them a reason to investigate Donnie, they will try and find a way to connect it to me. We both will be arrested. What I need you to do is this. If the police come at you, tell them that you fired him. Make up a reason why. You don't have to worry about the limo because it will fall on his hands. Also, start driving yourself to work. Whatever else that may come up, I can probably cover. Money solves a lot of problems."

"Money isn't going to bring back Donnie."

Jay took a deep breath seeing that he wasn't going to get Carmen to budge from the issue. He didn't know what to say to her other than what had already been said. It was at that moment that he wished Carmen was as nonchalant about death as he was. Her conscience could ruin things for both of them. "Telling the truth isn't going to bring him back either. It's not going to get my keys back or stop the Brookstone PD from coming at me. I have to keep going until I get out of this bullshit. You have to trust me. I know what I'm doing."

Carmen sat down on the couch, putting her head in her hands. Jay joined her there as well, pulling her into his arms. He was trying his best to comfort her, but Carmen didn't want to be touched. "I love you," he said, solemnly. "Everything I do is for us. It's the reason I hired Linx. I have to protect my family. You, King, Rakim, and Nyla, I would be eight feet under if it wasn't for y'all. I need you to ride with me on this one. Can you do that?"

Carmen heard the sincerity in his voice, but she didn't know what to say. She didn't want to go down for Donnie's murder and at the same time, she wanted justice. Whatever route she took, the outcome could be a no-win. It's what made the decision to side with Jay even harder. Even when they got into his bed, Carmen hadn't answered his question. Jay wasn't going to let up either. When he asked her a second time, Carmen knew she had to answer. This time, she knew the three words to give him: Death before dishonor. He showed his acceptance by planting a single kiss on her forehead. Seconds later, he curled up against her falling into a deep sleep. As much as Carmen hoped to do the same, she couldn't. She stayed awake for most of the night before her eyes were able to close.

Chapter Twenty-Nine

Jay was aware of the immense amount of pressure he had placed on Carmen's shoulder. He wasn't proud of it yet he couldn't come up with a different solution. The following morning, he called Malik and asked him to meet him in the third floor conference room of Blue Magic. He had spoken to him recently regarding Carmen's attack, but he never told him about his issue with King. He hoped that Malik could give him some advice on how to mend the relationship.

When Malik arrived, he came dressed in a white-striped button-up which had been paired with black slacks and Christian Louboutins. Considering the occasion, Jay didn't expect him to be dressed in his finest. Instead of questioning his attire, Jay kept mum as their waiter entered the room. He brought in a pitcher of orange juice and water, placing both items on the table. When he left the room again, he remerged with two large platters. He set them both on the table before disappearing for a second time. At that time, Jay pulled a sheet of notebook paper out of his pocket and an ink pen.

He wrote three letters on the paper, B, L, and U, before passing it over to Malik. "I hired Linx in the nick of time," Jay began. "If it wasn't for him, Carmen would be dead. I suggest you get someone for Tiara. Blu has done his homework too well. We need to show him that we've done ours. That means going into his territory. I want to send some of our men into Georgia tonight. Let's shoot up all of his spots. We need to send him a message since we can't physically touch him." Jay picked up the ink pen again, writing the word, King, on the paper.

"I told him about Rico. I don't regret what I did, but I regret the way I told him. I could've verbalized it differently. Instead of consoling him, I lost my cool. Carmen has always stressed to me that I need to be more of a father than a boss. I get it now. I need to make it right with him, but I don't know how. That's why I'm coming to you."

Malik stared down at the paper where Jay had written his son's name. He knew what he was feeling, but he was unsure on what advice to give him. If anything, all he could tell him was to talk to him. "You know where to find him. It's not going to be easy for you to do, but you have to apologize. Once y'all clear that up then we can get those men in Georgia. I'm down for hitting all of Blu's spots. You want a message; I say we give him a fuckin' billboard. Remember, when we strike, he's going to strike harder. He came at Carmen first, but next time, he'll go for someone else."

Jay listened to Malik's words, knowing they had a battle on their hands. The last time he had gone up against another drug dealer was with Pierre. He had killed him when he attempted to rape Carmen, but then he had to deal with Pierre's right-hand, Shakeem. Carlos took care of him, which killed the whole beef. With Blu, he didn't know who his allies were.

Nevertheless, he chose to follow Malik's advice. Once he took care of King, he could work on putting his hands on Blu.

***

King turned on the faucet, sliding his hand underneath the cold water. He quickly splashed his face so he wouldn't look like he had been crying. Finally visiting Ms. Rosetta, he had broken down when he told her about Rico. She had bawled in his arms for over an hour and he had done the same. Once they were both under control, he had asked her for an update on Jerome. She didn't have one, which didn't sit too well with him. She couldn't even tell him which state Jerome had moved to. She only said that he was in the South. It sounded odd, but he didn't pressure her. He simply accepted her answer and headed over to Sapphire.

Starting to dry his face, he saw a figure walk past the door. He hadn't heard anyone come in and assumed that he was the only one at the club. Automatically, his hand went to the pistol in his waistband. He stepped back into his office as his eyes focused in on his father. Surprised to see him, he watched as Jay sat down in one of the office chairs. "What are you doing here?"

King's voice was as cold as ice, which told Jay that he was still heated from their last conversation. While he needed to tell King about the hit that had been put on his mother, he decided to deal with his son's anger first. "Right now, we need to put all the bullshit aside."

"Is that what you did with Rico?" King stuck his pistol back into his waistband, walking further into the room. "Did you put the bullshit aside? Get the fuck out of here."

Jay could tell from King's response that he had to go headfirst into Malik's approach. "I don't want to argue with you anymore," he began. "I don't believe I was wrong for what I did, but I regret the way I told you. Rico was your best friend and I should have been more sympathetic. I apologize. Right now, we both need to be on the same page. Blu is out there building an army against us while we're in here tearing ours down."

King looked at his father hard, trying to figure out if his apology was sincere. A large part of him didn't believe that it was. He figured that his father was simply trying to save face.

"This shit is real, King. No one told you, but Blu ordered a hit on your mother yesterday. He tried to kill her. She's fine, but there were three bodies that we had to deal with. One of them was her driver, Donnie. That's another track we have to cover up, and more attention that we hope we don't get from the police. Right now, we need each other. We need to be on the same page. We can't let this bullshit tear us apart. We're blood."

King's jaw tightened as he learned what Blu had done. Retaliation now had to take place. Without a doubt, he knew that he couldn't get close to Blu without his father. If anything, pretending to mend things would be more beneficial than detrimental. He could get Blu and bow out at the same time. It would be a trick, but his father deserved it. It would be his own personal payback for what he had done to Rico. With a plan in motion, King held out his hand as a sign that he was calling a truce. Jay shook it, but it didn't mean anything to King. His mind was made up. Once they took down Blu, he was breaking his ties to his father.

Chapter Thirty

Simultaneously, there were two armies preparing for battle. On one side, there was Jay, who was building an army against Blu while on another, there was Kane. He had spent the first part of his day in a meeting with Captain Roberts of the Triad, trying to get re-enlisted. For two hours, he had laid out everything he had learned about Jay's operation. He told Roberts about the drugs and how the Brookstone PD had wiretapped all of Jay's phones. That information, however; wasn't enough. The captain quickly denied him any kind of employment and informed him that he had spoken with Lieutenant Harris and the chief of police. Roberts explained that he was well aware of the circumstances surrounding his termination and feared that Kane would bring that same temper to the Triad. In addition, he didn't want to compete with the police department as it seemed to be that they had a leg up on the case. Kane refused to give up and spent another two hours begging and pleading until Roberts gave him an answer that he could work with.

"Do what you do, Kane," Roberts said. "Bring me a solid lead. I mean a good one. If we can work with it, you're back in. I will cover everything on my part."

Although the man wasn't giving him a job, Kane had received permission to move forward with his own investigation. He knew he could bring more to the plate than what he had. After promising Roberts that he wouldn't let him down, he sped over to the Brookstone Police Department. He and Sanders had officially been pit against each other, which Kane wanted to use to his advantage. It didn't sit too well with him that his old partner had interrogated Carmen; thus giving him reason to tear into his ass. He was parked outside of the station for fifteen minutes before Sanders arrived.

"I heard about you interrogating, Carmen," he yelled, approaching Sanders before he could get out of his car. "What kind of plans do y'all have going on? Are you going to raid Flame?" Kane blocked the man from getting out of his vehicle. Sanders hadn't answered him and Kane knew he was stalling. "Don't get tongue-tied now, talk to me. I know you got time."

Sanders tried to push his way past him, which led to a brief scuffle. When he saw that he was going to be forced to hold the conversation, he sat back down in his car. "I would never give you information. You are no longer a part of this operation. The last thing Harris wants is an unemployed detective snooping in on our investigation. If you knew what was good for you, you would stay away. You are so busy concentrating on Carmen that you're missing the biggest part of the case. Instead of focusing on the drugs, think about the murder. Where is Jarrod Luis?"

"Our fuckin' specialty is narcotics," Kane snapped, "not homicide. We can't even find a fuckin' piece of that boy. What is a murder case without a weapon or a body? Give up on Jarrod. Nobody will ever find him."

Sanders got ready to give his own fiery response, but his attention was diverted as he looked past Kane, noticing a familiar face approaching them. He couldn't think of the man's name, but he pointed in his direction so that he could get Kane's attention. "Um," he began, "isn't he...," the name wouldn't come to mind.

Kane waited impatiently as Sanders started to stutter. When he turned to look behind him, he saw Lotus walking toward them. Once again, his father-in-law had found a way to get into his business. Kane immediately walked away from Sanders' car, knowing he had to deal with Lotus one-on-one. As Kane ventured over to him he watched as his father-in-law fell to the ground in almost slow motion. Automatically, Kane broke into a sprint. He reached Lotus in a matter of seconds and started to assess his breathing as he called 911. While he waited for help to arrive, Kane kept his eyes planted on Lotus. He knew his father-in-law was coming to the precinct to convince Harris to drop the investigation. Before he could even say a word, his deteriorating health had overtaken him.

Though Kane hated that Lotus was against the case, he hated having to break the news of his ailing to Carmen even more. He made the phone call; quickly telling her that her father was passed out in front of the Brookstone PD. She responded with the sound of so much pain in her voice that it was almost unbearable for him to hear. Somehow, he managed to keep himself composed even after the phone call as he waited for the ambulance to arrive.

***

Carmen was driving nearly seventy miles per hour despite the traffic. To make matters worse, her cell phone was to her ear as she tried to call Kristian. Her daughter didn't answer, forcing her to leave a quick message on her voicemail about her grandfather before calling Akaila. "Pick up, please pick up," she mumbled, repeatedly. Carmen was frantically crying as she tried to navigate through traffic. She looked in her rearview mirror, hoping she could get over, anticipating the turn for the hospital. She began to cry harder as Akaila said hello.

"Akaila, you gotta come now. Your grandfather passed out a few minutes ago. Kane found him outside of the police department. I'm about two seconds from the hospital. Is Kristian with you?"

"Mama, we're in New York City. We went there for the day to celebrate the *Seventeen* cover. There's a party up here to celebrate the issue's release. Kristian has to make an appearance. It's like a paid gig. I thought you knew about it."

Carmen turned into the hospital parking lot as she screamed the word, no. She didn't mean to take her anger out on Akaila, but the last thing she wanted to know was that they were in NYC. With Kristian having a paid gig, she knew the girls wouldn't be back until the following morning. "I know y'all are going to be there for the night," Carmen said, as she found a parking spot. "I guess you won't be able to come." Carmen listened as Akaila asked to remain updated on her grandfather's condition. She agreed to it and hung up the phone, nearly jumping out of the car. She knew that she must've looked like a track star as she ran the whole way to her father's room.

When she finally got there, she saw that her father was wide awake. "Don't you ever scare me like that again," she yelled, grabbing his hand. She kissed his forehead right before she asked him what the doctor had said.

"Ahh, he wants to keep me for a day or so for monitoring. It's no biggie. The nurses gave me some insulin. They put me on a stricter diet. All I really want is for them to stop sticking me. Look at what I'm wearing, Peaches. I hope you can design a better gown than this. My whole ass is out!"

Carmen laughed at her father's humor. Glad that he was taking everything in stride, she took a step away from his bed. She scanned the room and noticed that they weren't alone. Her mother was seated in a recliner near the window while Kane was standing in the far right corner of the room. Instead of speaking to them, she focused her attention back on her father. "We're not having any more of these scares," she told him. "You're going to do exactly what the doctor says. To make sure that you do, I'm spending the night. Let me get a few things in order. Do we have a deal?"

Lotus mumbled a few choice words under his breath. "If it means I can get out of this dress than I'll do anything. Give me some pants to put on."

Carmen smiled as she planted another kiss on his forehead. "I'm glad to see that you're in a pleasant mood. Hopefully, some of that will rub off on me." She squeezed his hand before heading for the door. "I'll probably be gone for an hour or so," she said, turning the doorknob. "If you need me, call me." Carmen gave her father a small smile before walking out of the room. As she made her way back to the elevator, she sent a quick text to Jay and Tiara so that they were aware of her father's condition. If she had of been paying attention, she would have seen Kane joining her in the elevator. She wanted to thank him for finding her father, but he got off the elevator without speaking to her.

Kane had ignored his wife on purpose, giving her the same treatment she had given him when she walked into the room. In his opinion, she should've thanked him for saving her father's life right then and there. Since she hadn't, he chose to leave the hospital altogether.

Headed nowhere in particular; he returned to his car and drove to downtown Brookstone. When he had reached the area, he spotted Malik heading inside of Mancini's. It had been awhile since they had last spoken and Kane knew it was because of the investigation. His friendship with Malik had gone down the drain like his marriage. He hated the distance that was now between them so he followed him into the restaurant. "May I join you?" he asked him once he had found where Malik was sitting. Kane didn't wait for an answer before he sat down in the booth. He could tell that Malik was suspicious of him and wasn't surprised when his friend started in with his questions.

"How did you find me?" Malik asked. He pulled his cell phone from his pocket, setting it on the table. "You've been trailing me, too? Tapping my phones? What you wanna know? You want to see some financial reports? You want to look around the building? The owner lets us store our keys in the freezer."

Kane didn't let Malik's sarcasm get to him. Instead, he turned what Malik said into what he needed to talk about. "I wasn't trailing you. I got lucky. Since you mentioned the keys, I thought I should let you know that the Brookstone PD has 'em. Get out now and you won't have any prison time. Roberts is giving me a chance to get my job back at the Triad. If I bring him a good lead then it's a go."

Malik didn't lose his cool despite the pressure that Kane had put onto his shoulders. Earlier that evening, he, and Jay had been contacting several men that used to be a part of their cartel. They had chosen the most aggressive ones, knowing they had no problem pulling a trigger. If everything went according to plan, all of Blu's businesses would be shot up by eight o'clock that evening. Blood would be on his hands and now, so was the threat of a prison sentence. As much as he wanted to comment on the latter, Tiara and Robin were approaching the booth. The conversation was officially over, which Kane knew when he excused himself. He greeted Tiara briefly before exiting the restaurant. Still, the weight and seriousness of what he'd brought to the table remained after his departure.

"What was that about?" Tiara asked, sitting down in the booth. "Was he telling you about Lotus? You know he rushed him to the hospital."

Malik shook his head, not wanting to divulge any details. He expected Tiara to ask more questions, but Robin quickly took her attention. With the focus off of him, Malik had the chance to gather his thoughts. Every second that the cartel's product rested in the hands of the Brookstone PD, he was one step closer to a jail cell. He now had the pleasure of informing Jay since they were in this thing together. Malik knew not to do it at that exact moment. Jay's mind was too focused on retaliating against Blu that he wouldn't even concentrate on the keys. A better time would be once the situation with Blu had settled down. Until then, it would remain a secret.

***

Malik didn't have to tell Jay that the Brookstone PD had his bricks. Carmen had practically done the job for him. Jay would have considered it old news though it wouldn't necessarily be put on the backburner. It would take a backseat to the main issues at hand: the raid in Georgia and Lotus.

When Jay arrived at his godfather's hospital room, he received the text message that he had been waiting on since eight o'clock that evening. The words, it is finished, spoke volumes. The message eased his mind for the time being and he slid his phone back into his pocket before going inside of Lotus' room. Despite there being two large Louis Vuitton suitcases near the recliner, his godfather was inside alone. He headed for the chair next to Lotus' bed as his godfather's eyes fluttered open. "Well, well, well," he greeted. "Navy blue and white suits you well. Not a Flame original, but it'll work," he joked.

Lotus looked down at himself and grunted. He hated what he was wearing, but it was minimal compared to how he was feeling. Certain that Jay might be awhile, he tried his best to get comfortable. "There's a lot going on. You want to talk about it? We have plenty of opportunity; Patricia has stepped out for a snack. Carmen went to check up on the kids."

Jay wasn't quite sure what Lotus knew or was getting at. Personally, he felt that his godfather needed to be focused on his own problems instead of his. "Why don't you tell me what happened with you? How did you end up in this plain-looking dress?" He chuckled as Lotus scrunched up his face once again. Even in the hospital, his godfather was able to take a joke. Jay assumed that he was in good spirits until the vibe in the room changed dramatically. While they both had been wearing smiles, Lotus' face was now sullen.

"It looks," Lotus said with a sigh, "like I might be here for a while." Lotus looked over at his godson as he expressed to him how he felt. "Sometimes I sit and think about everything I've done. I tell you, Jay, my life was like the best of times and the worst of times. Running the streets is like that, eh?"

Jay could hear the sentiment loud and clear in Lotus' voice. He knew there was a lot that his godfather wanted to say, he only needed someone to listen. "It is," he replied. "I remember what it was like when I lived it full-time. Guns, money, sex, that's all it was. Day in and day out, you do the same thing repeatedly. It's the reason I went legit. I got too old for that bullshit. King is grown, but I got two small kids to look after. I have to be around for them. They need me more than I could ever imagine. Shit, I need them."

Lotus ran his fingers alongside his bedrail as he had a flashback of his time in the cartel. "You know what they say. More money means more problems. It was like that, too. The United States government put out rewards for anyone who could give them a lead on Hector. People started snitching left and right. The death toll went up like that." Lotus snapped his fingers as the memory appeared in his mind. "I knew I had to break out then. I made the decision for Carmen. I wished that your father..." Lotus' voice trailed off. "I loved that man, Jay. You know I did. I prayed for him so many nights. He kept saying that he couldn't leave. He had so many men on payroll; so many men were eating off of him. His dream was to have every Hispanic person in the world living a life of luxury. He instilled that in you. That is why you have so many freakin' esés on your team! I swear, Jay, you're more like Hector than I ever imagined."

Jay closed his eyes at the thought of his father. Hector had been taken from him at a time when he needed him the most. Then, not long after, his mother had taken her own life. She had left him alone, which put him in an emotionally dark place where he stayed until he laid eyes on Carmen. It was then that he felt he had a chance of having a family. "My mom," he said, slightly stuttering. "Tell me about her. Like what did you think when you first met her?"

Lotus chuckled as he thought of Lady. "Man, I tell you. Your mother was always the topic of conversation. When people saw her with Hector, they didn't know what to think. You got this man going around, preaching Hispanic this and Hispanic that, but he marries a woman who looked black. She was Puerto Rican, but people didn't know by looking at her. I was living in the Bahamas when he met her. I remember him calling me and saying, 'I found her, Lotus. I met my wife today.' He married her in no time. Several years later, you came along. This big 'ol, high yellow baby," Lotus said, laughing. "I remember when I signed the papers to be your godfather. I was so proud. I was waiting to find the right woman for myself so that I could have my first child. You know, it's a coincidence that you and Carmen are together. I know what's going on with you two is not public, but I have a feeling that it's coming. You two love each other."

Jay tried to hold in a smile as he thought of Carmen. Lotus had given him his blessing despite the fact that his daughter was still legally married. She had started working on divorce papers, but nothing had been filed. "You know more about our love than anyone. You said it yourself. I've been in love with her since I was six. I…I want it to be real. I want to get married. Our relationship is nothing without an official claim." Jay started to say more until the sound of voices outside the door stopped him. With someone about to come in, he knew they would be losing their privacy. "I appreciate you, Lotus," he said, standing up. "We've had our days, but I can honestly say that I love you. It took me awhile to understand your ways, but I get it now."

Lotus grinned as he watched Jay leave. He studied him for a few seconds as Jay placed his hand on the doorknob. "I agree. It took me awhile to understand you as well. I love you, though. Take care of yourself." Lotus watched as a smile formed on Jay's face. He thought he was going to say something else, but he didn't. Jay simply opened the door and walked out of the room. As he left, Lotus continued to stare in his godson's direction. All it took was a few encounters for Jay to fill the void that Lotus had been missing for several years. The more time that he spent with him; the closer he felt to Hector.

***

Carmen paused when she saw Jay walking to the stairwell. From the direction he was coming, she knew he had visited her father. Her thoughts were clouded by suspicion as she wondered what they had discussed. Thinking that Jay had told him about her attack, she rushed to her father's room. Upon entering, she found her father already asleep. She stared at him for a bit to see if he would stir before curling up in the recliner. Her mother returned shortly after, but they didn't speak out of fear that they would wake him. With her mother in the room, Carmen felt at ease to go to sleep. Before she did, she gave her father a final glance. When she saw that he was resting well, she closed her eyes.

Part Four:
The Tipping Point

Chapter Thirty-One

Copperton City, Georgia
August

Carmen shielded her eyes from the sun as she rested her back on the mini-van. For the past two hours, she had been on the campus of Copperfield University, moving both of her daughters into Buchanan Hall. Even with the help of three men, the task was tiresome. In addition, it was emotional. For the past month and a half, she had hardly spent any time with Kristian or Akaila. She had been busy with work and her father while they were wrapped up in their own thing. The bad part about it was that she didn't feel any regret up until that very moment. The sight of them coming out of the residence hall made her realize that they would be away from her for months on end.

She tried to control her tears, but lost the battle when Kristian approached her. "I told myself I wasn't going to do this," she cried. Carmen took a few seconds to try and pull it together, but it didn't work. The tears kept coming as her daughter stood quietly in front of her. "I know that things haven't been the same, Kris. Even though you'll be here, I know we can get our bond back." Carmen took a step forward, grabbing her daughter into a hug. "I don't want you to worry about anything. Concentrate on school. I know you want to work more on your acting and you should. *Peaches* will be fine. We had a great run during the summer and we'll have an even better fall."

"We'll do what we can," Kristian replied, nastily.

Carmen separated from her daughter when she caught her tone. She gave her a questionable look as Kristian walked away from her. She watched her as she headed over to Kane, giving him a hug as well. Their embrace made Carmen a little envious because she sensed the favoritism. She would never voice it, but she knew Kristian's actions were a result of her constantly being put on the backburner. Her daughter was probably even expecting for things to get worse. In an attempt to lift her own spirits Carmen vowed that she wouldn't let it happen.

Despite her self-talk, Carmen didn't feel any better. She watched in silence as Kristian said her goodbyes before Akaila came over to her. It was a welcome distraction from Kristian's affection towards her father. She and Akaila chatted until it was time for them to depart. Once Kristian and Akaila were both back inside of their dormitory, Carmen got inside the mini-van, preparing for the long drive back home. Kane was already in the driver's seat looking as if he was eager to get back on the road.

"Are you stopping in Atlanta?" a voice asked.

King and Malachi both were standing at the driver's side door as if they were plotting their next move.

"Nah, we need to get back," Kane replied. "What about you two?"

King mumbled a low no. "Coco leaves for DC tomorrow. If I get back in time, I want to ride down with her. You know, make sure she is settled in and everything."

"That'll be good," Kane agreed, starting up the car. "This trip to DC will be good for you and Maya. Y'all need some bonding time," he joked.

Carmen didn't bother to involve herself in the conversation. Still upset over Kristian's behavior, she fastened her seatbelt, feeling the car as it slowly moved forward. Now that they were on their way back home, she remembered that she needed to text Jay. He had wanted to accompany her on the trip, but she knew it would be too uncomfortable. It was best that he stayed in Brookstone rather than being in a van with her and Kane. Quickly messaging him, she dropped her phone back into her purse as they exited the university. King was directly behind them, allowing her to see Malachi's face from the side view mirror. His frown hadn't disappeared, which told her that King would have his hands full. Now that Akaila was gone, Malachi was going to need him more than ever.

***

King gripped the steering wheel tightly as he made his way onto the interstate. He was worried about his little brother though they hadn't spoken a word since they had gotten in the car. He knew it would take some time before Malachi would open up about how he was feeling. He hoped that his brother didn't act out. He had gotten himself together, completing mandatory counseling sessions and anger management classes in place of a sentence to juvenile detention. If Malachi had learned his lesson, he would show it by how well he dealt with Akaila being gone.

"Do you want your phone?" Malachi asked, interrupting his thoughts.

King looked over at his brother not even knowing that it had rung. He told him yes and took the phone from Malachi's hand. When he looked down at the screen, he saw that Phase was calling him. He hadn't heard from him in a while since things appeared to be looking up for them. Blu had disappeared from New York and they were making progress on Iceland.

"What's good?" he answered. "It's been a minute. What have you been up to?"

"Man, I thought everything *was* good after we put that lick on Blu. I came up here to Connecticut to visit some family and heard that dude has been talking reckless. My cousin told me he came to him and his boys trying to put together a little crew. He said he was talking real salty about what your father did to his spots. I don't know if he's still here, but I'm going to keep my eyes and ears open. If I catch him slipping, I'm bringing him home to y'all. No doubt about it."

King's body jerked at Phase's words. He quickly put on his right signal light, sliding into the emergency lane. He heard Malachi as he asked him what he was doing, but he ignored him. He put the car into park before replying back to Phase. "What the fuck are you talking about?" he yelled at him. "What lick did my father put on him? I haven't heard shit about a hit."

"Damn, King, weren't you right there with him? You know he wasn't going to let that shit slide with your moms. You were at that meeting we had at Blue Magic. Shit, now that I think about it, you weren't there. Jay sent three cars to Copperton City to shoot up Blu's spots. We had AKs and everything. We did a number on those clubs. I know Blu had to pull out some major paper to fix that shit back up."

King looked over at Malachi as he realized that his father had outsmarted him. Jay had never told him about a hit on Blu. He also had never told him that Blu was from Copperton City, the very same place that his sisters went to school. "Look, man, keep your eyes and ears open. Let me know if you find out anything else." King put the car back into drive as Phase mumbled that he would. He got back onto the interstate as his temper flared. As much as he wanted to go back to Copperton City, he knew it was pointless. If Blu was in Connecticut, he couldn't get close to his sisters. Nevertheless, when the man stepped foot in Georgia, it would be a different story.

***

The majority of the evening, Kristian and Akaila had spent unpacking. Now that they were settled, Akaila could see that Kristian had other plans for the night. Her sister's Lexus had been shipped from New York to Georgia almost a week ago, which gave her the opportunity to freely roam Copperton City. When Kristian pulled out her favorite pair of purple Jimmy Choo heels and a black mini-dress, Akaila knew that Kristian had plans to go clubbing. "So, which hot spot did you discover?" she asked her with a smile.

Kristian turned to face her before pointing to two flyers that were sitting on her dresser. "There's a freshman party at the Sphinx Club. It's like opening night for the club or something. I wanna go. You know, learn the city; meet new people."

Akaila narrowed her eyes as she was unsure about exploring Copperton City. She knew that if Kristian had her heart set on going out then she needed to go with her. Their parents would have a fit if they learned that Kristian had gone to a club by herself. Akaila agreed to go only because she knew she didn't have a choice. While her sister went to shower, she searched for a dress to wear. Two hours later, they were walking up to the Sphinx Club.

A number of people were outside the club's doors, which made the line look ten times longer. To Akaila, the club looked like Sapphire on a Saturday night. The only difference was that she had to wait in line. With King being part owner of Sapphire, she always got in without a wait. However, neither she nor Kristian would get that same treatment in Georgia. It was obvious when they found themselves still standing in line after fifteen minutes. "Maybe, we should go somewhere else," she suggested.

Kristian continued to stare at the line, all while shaking her head. "Let's wait it out," she mumbled. The line was barely moving, but people were still waiting outside like they knew they had a shot of getting in. Kristian wanted to be one of them since it was the first college party of the school year. It would be the talk of the university and she wanted to be a part of it.

"Hey," a female voice said, distracting her. "You're Kristian Kane, right?"

Kristian stared at the girl in front of her, giving her shoes and clothes the once-over. She was dressed in a black pencil skirt and white tank while her dark brown hair hung freely past her shoulders. There was a girl standing next to her who was just as jazzy as her friend. Finally saying, "Yes," Kristian was about to say more until she was interrupted by a guy who came up to them out of nowhere. He didn't appear to be a bouncer and looked like he had stepped out of the pages of a Ralph Lauren catalog.

"I talked to him, Angi, he says he's on his way out," he said, talking to the girl in front of her. "He can still get us in. The holdup is on some electrical problem. You know they're still trying to work shit out after the shooting."

Kristian narrowed her eyes at the guy's words. She glanced over at Akaila who was wearing a similar expression. After hearing about a shooting at the club, Kristian wasn't so sure if she wanted to go inside. Though the girls in front of her had a way in, she was starting to like that she didn't.

When her sister nudged her, Kristian thought she knew what she was thinking. Yet, when Akaila persisted with another nudge, Kristian looked up to see the hint that Akaila was trying to throw. Steadily approaching them was no one other than Jerome McFadden. He was one of King's best friends and the last person she thought she would ever see in Copperton City.

"How many do you need?" Jerome asked, pulling several wristbands out of his pocket.

Kristian listened as the guy said three until one of the girls interrupted him. She told Jerome that there was a star at the club who deserved VIP treatment. It was then that Jerome recognized her. A flash of surprise even appeared on his face. It was like he really didn't believe that it was her. Red flags went up in Kristian's mind as she stared at Jerome. He didn't look too happy to see her although he offered her a wristband. She told him, thank you, which didn't garner a response. It was enough for Kristian to know that he wasn't pleased. However, she felt that if anyone should've been upset, it should've been her and Akaila. They couldn't go anywhere without King sending one of his friends to spy on them.

Jerome pulled them from the line, sending them directly to the VIP room. Before Kristian could even ask him a single question, he left without another look in her direction. She thought to follow him until she felt her phone vibrating in her purse. While Akaila was starting to mingle with the new people they had met, Kristian took a step outside of the room. She quickly checked her phone, seeing that she had a message from Coco.

I haven't told King yet, the message read, *but I decided not to go to DC. With this being my first time away from home, I felt like I needed to be with some familiar faces. I'm coming to Copperfield. My parents and I are on our way now.*

Kristian's eyes grew big as she read about Coco's abrupt decision. She didn't even know that she had applied to Copperfield. In a way, the news was bittersweet. It was a plus that Coco would be joining them in Georgia, but she knew King would be furious. Certain that he was still on the road, he would return to Brookstone only to learn that Coco was no longer there. Aware of what her brother's reaction would be, she quickly replied via text that Coco needed to tell him as soon as possible.

The news of Coco coming to Georgia excited her, but she still had some reservations. *If King has Jerome here to watch us, I wonder who he had lined up for Coco*, she thought. Her first answer was Rico, but she hadn't seen him in months. Then, she started to think that Jerome wasn't in Georgia to keep a watchful eye. In fact, she believed that he was there without King's knowledge. She wanted to question him, but she ended up leaving the Sphinx Club without ever laying an eye on him again.

Brookstone, New York

While Kristian's text message to Coco had been received, her friend hadn't yet informed King of her decision to attend Copperfield University. At this point, the only thing on King's mind was getting information on the hit his father had orchestrated. After dropping Malachi back off at home, he had headed over to Malik's house. He knew it was probably too early for a visit when Malik came to the door half asleep.

"This couldn't wait until eight o'clock?" Malik opened the door, allowing King to come inside. Once he had locked the door back, he sat down at the kitchen table, trying to figure out why King was at his house at three o'clock in the morning.

"Did you know about the hit on Blu's businesses?"

Malik looked at King sideways. "Yeah, I knew about it, didn't you? That was like, almost two months ago. I thought Jay told you. Didn't he meet with you before we put the shit together?" Malik was somewhat confused. Jay and King seemed to be getting along better so he was certain that he had told him about the hit.

"No one said shit to me about it. You didn't even tell me that Blu was from Copperton City. You know Akaila and Kris are going to school there. Why didn't you say anything?"

Malik stood up from the table as he felt a sense of guilt. "Some things are better left unsaid," he told him. "I'm not talking about you not knowing about Blu. I'm talking about your sisters. They don't have anything to do with this mess. They're innocent. Telling them about Blu would ruin their college experience. Instead of them worrying about school, they'd be looking over their shoulders. As for not telling you, we've talked about Blu lots of times. I thought you knew. We had to have said it at one point."

"No, you didn't," King snapped. "You never said it. You and Jay were always like, 'Blu's businesses are in the South', or 'we're going to send him back home'. You never said it. Phase was the one who told me. He knows more about what's going on than I do. I don't like that shit, Malik." King stood up from the table as his anger was now on full display. "You shoot up his businesses, cool, but let me know. This is the same dude who put a hit on my mama."

Malik was at a loss for words. He understood King's anger, but he honestly thought that he knew about the hit. It wasn't something that he intentionally kept a secret. "King, it'll be best for both of us if we have a talk with Jay. We can lay everything out. Right now is not the time. After church, we'll meet up and squash this."

"Phase isn't here. He's in Connecticut visiting his family. Since he's been there, he got word that Blu is around that way. He's trying to get some men together so he can sell up North. It'll be us and Jay. Shit, maybe that's all we need. Make sure you tell Jay about this meeting. I don't want him running from any questions."

Malik nodded his head yes as King stood up, heading for the door. About to let him out, he watched as King paused. When he saw him take out his phone, he hoped that it wasn't any more bad news. Unfortunately, he could tell from King's face that it was.

"This shit keeps getting worse," King muttered. He looked over at Malik whose face was as concerned as his own. "Can you believe that she told me this shit in a fuckin' text? Coco isn't going to Howard. She left for Georgia a few hours ago. Now her ass is about to be in Copperton City, too."

Malik started to comment, but King was already halfway out of the house. He didn't follow him, choosing to let him be. In due time, everything would be worked out. For now, he needed to get back to sleep.

In the meantime, King got inside of his car and slapped the dashboard. Though he hated to admit it to himself, he knew that Coco told him at the last minute on purpose. She didn't want him to stop her from going. If he didn't know about Blu being from Copperton City then he wouldn't have. Since he did, he felt that it was his responsibility to protect her. He didn't know what Blu's intentions were and he had to stay on guard at all times. That thought alone prompted him to dial Coco's number. He didn't get her right off, but when he called her the third time, she answered.

"So you're going to spring this on me?" he yelled. "Who the fuck do you think I am, Coco? You're on some different shit right now. How do you just pick up and leave?" King paused when he heard a loud sigh come from Coco's mouth. Once it was out, he picked back up where he had left off. "You can't do that shit, Coco. You know what I got on my plate right now. You're piling more shit onto it."

She sighed again, but this time King didn't speak. He wanted to give Coco a chance to explain herself and admit that she was wrong. He felt that if she did, he could potentially try to move past the issue.

"You need to calm down," she told him. "Once you do, we'll talk."

The phone immediately went dead as Coco hung up the phone. King was shocked yet he wasn't about to call her for a fourth time. If he did, the conversation would get more heated. He could see himself saying something hurtful that he knew he didn't mean. As for now, the best option was to follow Coco's advice. She was on her way to Georgia whether he wanted her to be or not. All he could do now was wait on her phone call. By then, she would physically be in Copperton City.

Chapter Thirty-Two

Copperton City, Georgia

For the past thirty minutes or so, Kristian and Akaila had been helping to move Coco's belongings into her dorm room. Kristian hadn't yet voiced her concerns, planning to do it once Coco's parents left. At the moment, her best friend was busy saying her goodbyes.

"Alright, that's it," Mrs. Masterson was saying. "If I don't get in this car, I will never leave this place." She gave them a quick wave before blowing them each a kiss. "You girls better be good. Bring home those A's!"

Kristian chuckled at the woman's antics as she waved goodbye. She waved to Coco's father as well who was already sitting in the car. She could tell he was ready to get back home because of his nonchalant attitude. While Mrs. Masterson had drawn out her goodbyes, he was calmer than silence itself. Even Coco had a tear or two sliding down her face. Kristian knew she was upset, but she wasn't ready to see a bunch of waterfalls. "Hey, big girls don't cry," she said, sliding her arm around her friend's shoulders. "Besides, you're not here by yourself. You got me and Akaila! We've already met two new girls, Angi, and Chantel. They live on our hall."

Coco nodded her head as she wiped her face. "I know, but I've never been away from home like this. I've always been with them. What are they going to do without me?"

Kristian and Akaila both glanced at each other before yelling, "The nasty," in unison. The joke seemed to put a smile on Coco's face as they headed towards the front entrance of Buchanan Hall. Almost to the door, Kristian paused as she thought about Jerome. She knew it was the perfect time to bring him up now that Coco's parents had left.

"Guess who we saw last night?" She put both of her hands on her hips as she waited for Coco's answer. When her friend gave her a questionable look, she knew that she didn't have a clue. She tried to get Akaila to help with a hint, but Coco still couldn't figure it out. Finally, she told her. "Jerome McFadden. Can you believe it?" Kristian watched as the smile that Coco was wearing turned into a frown. In return, Kristian grimaced, suspecting that something was wrong.

"Jerome is here?" Coco questioned. "King hasn't spoken to him since he was locked up. He doesn't even know that he's in Georgia. From what he tells me, Jerome fell off the face of the earth. He doesn't even know what happened."

"Are they beefing or something?" Kristian wrinkled her face as she became confused. She hadn't heard anything about King not being able to get in touch with his friends. It was now obvious that something had happened, and she was curious to know what. "Okay, this is the deal," she told them. "If I see Jerome again, I'll ask him what's up. Since you know more than we do, Coco, you can't say a word to King. Let me find out what is going on first. Whatever happens in Copperton City stays in Copperton City. Do we agree?"

Coco and Akaila exchanged glances that said they didn't know what Kristian was up to. They shook on the agreement only because they wanted to know the dirt on Jerome as well. If he was in Georgia without King's knowledge then there was obviously tension between the two. Since they were curious to know why, they took it upon themselves to find out.

***

Brookstone, New York

Tension wasn't necessarily the best word to describe the strain between King and Jerome. It was more suited to describe the relationship that King had with his father. So far, he had spent over an hour waiting for him to show at Blue Magic. Even Malik hadn't strolled through the restaurant's doors. Unsure of why they hadn't showed up yet, he was starting to get anxious.

Aside from the issue at hand, King was still heated with his girlfriend. He had tried to call her again that morning, but she didn't answer. With his rage building, it worked in Coco's favor that they hadn't spoken. His emotions were growing more intense and it only got worse when his father walked into the third floor conference room.

Jay didn't speak to him, simply taking his seat at the head of the table. Malik came in right behind him, along with Cesar, a man his father had brought from Puerto Rico. He served mostly as his father's right-hand, taking over Costa's duties.

As soon as they all were seated, King started in with his questions. "Do you want to tell me what happened in Copperton City?" He stared directly into his father's eyes, wanting him to be the first one to respond.

"I took care of business," Jay replied, plainly. "Is that what we're here to talk about? That shit was like two months ago. Why are we discussing it now?" Jay looked over at Malik and then back at King. "You didn't think I was going to let Blu slide, did you?"

"Hell no," King yelled, "I would've been down for it with you. My problem is that everyone knew about the hit, but me. What's up with that shit? I would still be in the dark if it wasn't for Phase. Then, he got the nerve to tell me that Blu is from Copperton City. You knew that and you still let my sisters go down there. Shit, you let me and Mama go down there. What the fuck were you thinking?"

At this point, King was standing up out of his seat and his words were coming out forcefully. He heard Malik when he told him to calm down, but he couldn't. There was too much rage in him. Regardless of the answer that Jay gave, he knew it wouldn't be good enough. His father had put their whole family in danger; the very same family that he claimed to love.

"I let them go because I knew Blu was in Connecticut," Jay admitted. "The grounds were safe. Phase called me, too. I got the word long before you did. As for me not telling you, I decided that I needed to keep you away from the drama. You're still on probation and you don't need to get caught up. I need your nose to stay clean."

"All I'm saying is that you could've been open with me," King fired back. "My sisters are in this fuckin' city. Not only that, my girlfriend is there, too. What are we going to do if Blu goes at one of them? How are we going to protect them now?"

Jay rubbed the sides of his face as King's voice grew louder. He was tired of going back and forth with him, but it didn't look like anything was going to be settled. "What do you want me to do, King? You want me to tell them to leave? Who's going to be the one to tell them why? Do you even know if they can transfer? How about this, what if they refuse? I can't make them leave college. My name is not Cornel Masterson and it for damn sure isn't Michael Kane. You want this shit handled, you deal with it." Jay stood up, preparing to leave the room. About to head out, he heard Malik as he told him not to go.

"You can't leave until we come to some sort of agreement," Malik told him. "If you do, nothing will be solved. We'll be back where we started." Malik pointed at Jay's chair, letting him know he was serious. "No one is leaving until we have a plan in motion."

"What is the consensus?" Jay asked, remaining in the doorway. He looked over at King, giving him the chance to speak first. His son didn't say anything so he voiced his own thoughts. "If you ask me, I say we leave 'em there. If you're that concerned, King, I'll hire another guy. I'll put him in Georgia. Cesar can probably recommend someone for us. Can't you?" Jay looked at his right-hand, realizing that he had been quiet throughout the whole discussion. When he gave a simple head nod, Jay looked back at King. "Can we all agree on that?"

King would have preferred for the girls not to be there, but he knew he had to compromise. He told his father yes while Malik did the same. He thought the discussion was over until Malik started to speak.

"I never said anything, but I know what happened to the keys. The Brookstone PD has them. You were right, Jay. The hood knows not to fuck with us. However, the police will. They've had the drugs since June so I don't know what they're waiting on. If they want you now, they can take you. Shit, they could take all of us."

Jay didn't show any emotion regarding Malik's spiel. Carmen had told him before her attack that the police had evidence against him. He had assumed then that it was his drugs. "So I've heard," he told them. "They haven't come yet so they're waiting on something. We'll deal with it when it comes."

"If you ask me," King voiced. "It's time for you and Kane to have a conversation."

Jay questioned the suggestion. "What are we going to talk about? He doesn't even have a fuckin' job. His ass isn't knocking on anybody's door." Jay looked at King strangely, but his son didn't let up. King was adamant about him contacting Kane. For some strange reason, King believed that if he made amends with his stepfather that he could get the drugs back. Jay begged to differ, but he agreed to do it to prove him wrong. He headed out to find Kane and told Malik and King to be looking for a text. Whether he was able to get the drugs or not, he wanted to meet with them later that evening at Iceland.

***

On a Sunday afternoon, Jay was the last person on Kane's mind. Right now he was thinking about Sanders. Considering the rift that had formed between them, Kane didn't expect to ever hear from his partner again. However, Sanders had called him out of the blue to inform him that Donnie McClain had officially been declared missing. He also told him that he had learned that the driver was last seen with Carmen. His wife was now the top suspect. Even if she didn't kill him, Carmen was next in line to be interrogated. Kane knew that he had to get to her before the Brookstone PD. He didn't know their intentions, but he knew things weren't looking good. Carmen's name was already being dragged through the mud because of Jay. Now this situation with Donnie would only make the hole that the Brookstone PD was digging that much deeper for her.

Since it was nearing four o'clock, Kane expected for her to be at the hospital. Currently headed in that direction, he thought twice about going there when he noticed a white limousine to the right of him. He knew the car belonged to Jay, which made him think that his wife could potentially be inside. In the midst of turning away, he noticed that the driver was rolling down his window. The man ordered him to pull over as they approached a stoplight. When it turned back green, the limousine lurched forward so he could see into the backseat. "Just my luck," he said aloud, seeing Jay. Kane put his foot onto the gas, following behind the limousine until he was in a nearby alley. Minutes later, he and Jay were both stepping out of their vehicles.

"Beautiful day," Jay said to him, closing the door to his limo. "How is everything?"

Kane knew there was a reason that Jay wanted to meet with him. Something in the pit of his stomach told him that either Carmen or Malik had gotten into his ear. Both of them were well aware of the pending investigation and knew about the evidence. If anything, they had given him a heads up. "Leave the small talk alone, Santiago. What do you want?" he replied.

Jay smiled at the agitation in Kane's voice. It almost matched the agitation he had that he had been forced to talk to him. "The Brookstone PD has had my coke for a while now. Are they going to do something with it?"

Kane responded with a blank expression. Since he was unemployed, he didn't know what the plans were with the keys. Harris had formed a tactical team to take Jay down, but as of yet, nothing had happened. Jay was walking around freely and his coke was still in the Brookstone PD's vault. "We both know I don't have that knowledge," he told him. "I will say this, though. I'm very grateful that Harris has 'em. Maybe, he can put 'em to good use."

Jay felt his face tighten in response to Kane's antagonizing comment. "Twenty years later and you are still heartless and bitter," he muttered. "What happened to you, Kane? I mean, let's go back to the beginning. You did your job. You took me down. What you didn't have to do was take my girl. Why didn't you take Tricia? I mean, eventually, you did, but back then, you didn't try anything with her. You had to have Carmen, though. You couldn't take me down and leave my girl alone? When did it become more about her than the drugs?"

Kane held up his keys as a sign that the discussion was over. "I'm not about to stand here and dig into the past with you. If you came to talk about the drugs, fine, but believe this. Whatever it is you want, please know I'm not going to give it to you. We should dead this whole thing. We don't like each other, we will never like each other, and that's the end of it."

Jay walked up to him until he was practically breathing down his neck. "Tell me, Kane, why do you hate me so much? What is it about me that made you want to take me down? Did one of your family members die from an overdose? What happened that made you want to sign your name onto my case? It had to be something. Was it the paycheck?"

Kane stared into Jay's light eyes, gritting his teeth before answering his questions. "You don't represent any kind of struggle. Everything you have has been handed to you. You make your money by stripping people of their pride and dignity. They lose everything while you gain the world. Like they say, no one man should have all that power. When you get to the top, you have no choice, but to come back down. Sometimes you need someone to pull you. It might as well have been me."

"I didn't struggle?" Jay snapped. "I grew up in a fuckin' madhouse. I was right there at my father's side after Domino shot him in his fuckin' head. I heard my mother commit suicide. I was the one who found her. So what, you think everything was golden for me because my father owned shit? After he died, almost everything was taken away. The only thing I have that was his is Sapphire. Don't talk to me about a fuckin' struggle. Not after seventeen years in fuckin' confinement."

"Well, Jay, you deserved it," Kane replied. "Let's add on another seventeen more."

Jay balled up his fist tightly as he tried to control the fury inside of him. He took a few steps backwards out of fear that he would strike Kane. As he gained his composure, he saw by the look in Kane's eyes that he was never going to give up. He would keep coming at him until he had him locked up for the rest of his life. It made him wonder why King thought that holding a conversation with him would help them get the keys back. The plan hadn't worked.

All he could do was mumble a low, fuck you, before going back to his limousine. Once inside, he quickly instructed Gus to take him to Iceland. When the car started to move, he noticed that Kane was leaving as well. The distance between them was much needed as Jay felt his aggressive urges growing again. When he finally reached Iceland, it was almost full throttle. As he walked into the barely lit store, he tried to combat it. While he had promised King and Malik that they would receive a text from him, he hadn't yet sent it. Part of the reason why was because he needed time to calm down from his conversation with Kane. He was more bothered by his view of him than his refusal to give back the drugs.

What life is he looking at? Jay asked himself. *I know for damn sure it ain't mine. He sees a limousine, a luxury home and thinks I have it made. Shit, fuck him. I didn't ask for this life. It was given to me. I was born into this shit. Men like me are bred.*

Kane's words continuously flowed through Jay's head. He knew he was wasting time as he tried to figure him out. He had even wasted his breath trying to talk to him. Kane was right when he told him that they should dead the whole thing. Regardless of the situation, they would never be cordial to each other. Too much had occurred between them.

Finally deciding to leave well enough alone, he sent a message to King and Malik that they needed to get to Iceland. When they arrived, the first thing out of King's mouth was a question about what Kane had said. Without hesitation, Jay gave him a flat no. "Why would he give it back to me? Shit, that question is rhetorical, what you should be asking is how. If the drugs are already in police custody then it—" Jay stopped talking when King raised his phone to his ear. He felt disrespected as he started to listen in on King's conversation. From what he was hearing, Blu had struck again. As he tried to hear the person on the other end, he moved closer to where King was standing. Malik did the same, but the volume was too low for either of them. It wasn't until King hung up the phone that they knew they would get answers.

"Phase got a lead on Blu in Pittsburgh. He went up that way and somehow ran into the wrong hood. Some dudes started popping off at the mouth and Phase got a little beside himself. Right now, we have two bodies on our hands."

"What the fuck!" Malik yelled. "Whose air supply got cut off?"

King shrugged his shoulders. "He doesn't know who they are. All he knows is that they work for Blu. They sell for him." King turned to look at his father, knowing that his next set of words was aimed at him. "He did say that one of the guys mentioned that Blu is after something of yours. The guy said its worth millions. If you ask me, he's talking about this FedEx thing. Isn't that what Blu wanted in on? I think it's time that you gave us some details."

Jay gave King an expression to let him know that his question wouldn't be answered. It wasn't even beneficial for them to discuss. They needed to be talking about the murders. Since he was not directly involved, Jay knew he had to be especially careful with how he dealt with the situation. Though he was innocent in the matter, Phase was on his payroll. The Triad and Brookstone PD would be quick to add the casualties to his body count. If anything, Jay knew that the first thing they needed to do was get rid of the evidence. "Pennsylvania?" he asked, changing the subject.

When King nodded his head yes, Jay began to scratch his chin. "Knowing Phase, he probably hid the bodies. Our main concern right now is getting rid of them. Before that, though, I need to see who they are. They could be some street cats or they could be somebody that we need to know." Jay dropped his hand back to his side as a plan formulated in his mind. "Go ahead and get Phase on the line. This is where we're going with this. Since he knows where the bodies are, tell him to call Jimenez Funeral Home. He needs to ask for Valdez and Medina. They are both on our payroll. They'll get a van out there to help him with the bodies. It'll take them awhile to make the trip so they probably won't reach him until midnight."

King put his phone back to his ear as he dialed Phase's number. As soon as Phase picked up, he gave him Jay's instructions. He could tell that Phase was relieved now that a plan was in place. After he hung up, he told them that Phase was going to contact the funeral home immediately. "Since that's settled, what do we do now?"

Jay held up his keys as he replied, "We go home, and wait it out. If Valdez reaches Phase by midnight then we won't see 'em until probably late tomorrow morning. I suggest that you both get a good night's sleep. Not only have we shot up his businesses, but we've killed his men, too. Once the news hits Blu's ears, he's going to strike again."

Judging from the way King was looking at him, Jay could tell that his son didn't like his answer. He knew King believed that they should've been doing more to prepare for Blu's retaliation. Instead of addressing the concerns that he knew were there, he chose to ignore them. He led the way out of Iceland, but didn't go back to his limousine.

As a church bell rung in the distance, Jay contemplated his next move. King and Malik were both getting into their cars while he was unsure of where to head next. When they drove past him, he still hadn't decided where he wanted to go. Certain that Carmen had headed to the hospital after church, he assumed that she would be spending the rest of the day with her parents. More than likely, Rakim and Nyla were with her. A large part of him wanted to be with his family, but he didn't want them to see him stressed. Carmen already had enough to deal with that his personal drama would only be another burden. Deciding his apartment would be the most suitable place, Jay got inside of his limousine.

Chapter Thirty-Three

At nine o'clock, the following morning, Jay was in one of the back rooms of Jimenez Funeral Home. He didn't know what to think when Valdez and Medina wheeled in two stretchers. The victims were fully dressed while their clothing was covered in dried blood. From what he could see, they both had been shot in the chest area. Phase was there with him along with Malik and King and he motioned for him to come closer. "This is them?" he asked. Phase nodded his head before mumbling incoherently under his breath. "Chill out," Jay told him. "I'm not mad at you." He turned his attention back to the bodies in front of him. "If it wasn't for you, we wouldn't know anything about Blu's whereabouts. At least we know he went to Connecticut and Pennsylvania. It's more information than any of us have gotten."

Jay reached down into one of the guy's pockets, retrieving his wallet. He opened it, looked at the ID, and read the name, "Robert Sampson." He handed the ID to King, saying, "Keep that." He then checked the guy's billfold, taking out a wad of bills, which he handed over to Phase. "Consider this as payment for your services." Once Phase had taken the money, Jay reached back into the guy's left pocket. He felt around for a bit until he realized that it was empty. "Judging from that ID, he's from Philly. Both of them might be. This one right here," he said, pointing at Robert, "actually had an ID on him so we can place him. I call this shit a dud. These were some haters. They were linked up with Blu and started talking shit. They didn't have a problem with any of us, at least not personal."

Phase paused from where he had been counting the money. "They said a lot of shit before I told 'em I worked for you. From what they told me, Blu is over what happened with the cartel. He wants in on this FedEx thing. He told them that was where the money was. He said he got the news from an associate of his on the coast. Supposedly, that associate works with the ship that brings your product to the states. Word is that you got something big coming from Africa."

Jay didn't reply to Phase's statement. Instead, he signaled for Valdez and Medina. As soon as they were by his side, he gave them quick instructions on what to do with the bodies. Once he was finished, he waited until they were wheeling the stretchers away before he spoke to Phase. "Is that what he's telling people? He wants something that he doesn't even know about." Jay shook his head as he walked towards the exit. He waited until everyone was out of the room before he took another step.

"With all due respect," Malik began, "You need to tell us about this FedEx thing. If this is what Blu wants, he's going to keep coming until he gets it."

"Then let him keep coming," Jay responded. Based on his comment, he hoped that Malik could see that there wasn't any fear inside of him. If Blu kept coming after his diamonds, he would eventually attract attention that he wouldn't want. The cat and mouse game that they were playing would be put to rest in a matter of seconds. His friend in Africa had an army much bigger than his and fiercer.

As they headed into the main foyer of the funeral home, Jay felt a slight vibration in his pants' pocket. He knew it was his phone, which he quickly answered when he saw it was Carmen. He just didn't expect to hear her sounding frantic.

"My mother called me," she cried. "My father had a stroke."

Jay blinked his eyes, and silently reminded himself to keep it together. Carmen sounded like an emotional wreck and he knew he had to be strong for the both of them. He assured her that he would be on his way, which seemed to settle her nerves. Once she had hung up the phone, he made the startling announcement. While he was certain that Phase would go his separate way, Malik and King decided to join him at the hospital.

***

Carmen felt a trembling of fear in her spirit as she stared down at her father. The doctor had noted his condition as stable, which was evident in how he looked. He was sleeping peacefully and had a sort of calm about him. Nevertheless, she remained emotional and tears spilled down her face faster than she could wipe them. Even when she heard the door opening behind her, she couldn't get herself under control. If it wasn't for Jay draping his arms around her, she would've fallen to the floor.

They stood in the same position for several minutes until she started to feel claustrophobic. She separated from him and took a few steps over to the door. She walked out of the room without saying a single word to anyone. She could hear Jay behind her, but she told him to let her be. He mumbled under his breath that he didn't want to, but eventually he complied. By the time she reached the elevator, she was completely alone. A sense of peace was already coming over her until she saw the doors open. About to walk inside, she paused when her eyes met with Kane's. For a quick second, she didn't know which way to turn. One voice told her to run while another told her to get on the elevator. She decided to listen to the latter.

"Is he okay?" Kane asked as the elevator started to move.

Carmen didn't look at him, but replied by only saying, "Stable." Certain that she hadn't made her father's stroke public, she turned to face him as a tear fell down her face. "Who called you?" The question came out negative-sounding though it wasn't her intention. Her concern wasn't necessarily in the fact that he knew, but more so in the press that would be coming. When she saw his expression, she wished that she could have retracted her statement.

"No one," Kane replied. "I wanted to talk to Lotus about something. Your face actually gave you away. You got mascara all here and there," he said, pointing at her. "You look a mess."

Carmen rolled her eyes as she turned away from him. She felt the elevator as it came to a halt and she waited for the doors to open. It would have been the perfect time for Kane to walk away yet something told her that he was going to stay on her heels. She realized he was when he followed her into the hospital's garden. The moment she noticed that he was about to speak, she held up her hand to stop him and blurted, "This isn't the time, I need to be by myself."

"Donnie is missing."

Carmen sucked her teeth. She knew it was only a matter of time before her driver's disappearance was going to catch up to her. It took longer than she'd expected. She stared Kane in the face, wanting him to see that she didn't have any fear. At the same time, she was trying to conceal her guilt. "I fired him a while ago. I haven't seen him since. Did you come to interrogate me?"

Kane overlooked her jab; knowing her statement was a reminder that he had been terminated. "I can't, but the Brookstone PD can. See, Donnie was last seen with you. One of the security guards at Flame confirmed that. He came to pick you up and you got in the car. You want to tell me why you fired him?"

Carmen remained quick and on her toes with her answers. "He was smoking dope on the job. I smelled it on him a couple of times. I told him to stop and he wouldn't. One phone call and he was gone. I liked him, but I can't have that shit around my kids."

"What's the problem with that?" Kane shot back. "Your boyfriend sells dope."

Carmen kept her composure although she wanted to send her fist flying across Kane's face. "Unless you're fuckin' blind, I got enough shit to deal with. You asked me a question, I answered it. You could've left the commentary in the elevator. Now, if you will excuse me."

"I won't," Kane said, grabbing her arm. He tightened his grip so she could see that he were serious. "I got a lot of heat on my fuckin' back because of you. Do you know how I feel when I get calls like that? I've been covering up your bullshit for years, Carmen. Every time I turn around, you're giving the cops a reason to lock your ass up. Maybe I should let 'em. Six months in prison wasn't enough for you."

Carmen jerked her arm from his grasp. "I never asked you to plant a fake diamond in Jay's house. You did that on your own. Maybe you should worry about covering up your own shit." While her words were disapproving, Carmen did appreciate what Kane had done for her. She didn't want to be held accountable for the decisions he had made.

"Keep your nose clean," he advised. "You should get rid of your boyfriend, too."

Kane walked past her, heading out of the garden. Unsure if he was returning to her father's room, Carmen decided not to follow him. Instead, she sat down on one of the stone benches, allowing her eyes to face upward. For the day to be as trying as it was, the sky wasn't a direct reflection. The sun was in full glow without a single cloud in existence. The mere sight of it lessened the weight of her burdens until she thought of her daughters in Georgia. It was their first official day of college and they were clueless about what was going on. Knowing she had to get word to them, she tried Kristian first. When she didn't answer, she tried Akaila next. When her phone rang incessantly she decided to call her again later. At the moment she needed some time for herself. Before she could talk to anyone, she had to clear her own head.

Chapter Thirty-Four

Copperton City, Georgia

Mom was the single word that read on the screen of Kristian's Blackberry. As she neared Potter Hall, her mind went back and forth over the idea of answering. With it being the first official day of classes, she knew her mother was calling with a word of encouragement. Still, she couldn't bring herself to answer. Georgia had become her getaway. It was the only place where she could seclude herself from her mother's infidelity. She used the distance as a Band-Aid to cover her pain. In due time, she knew she would have to come clean about seeing her mother and Jay kissing, but today was not the day.

It was the reason she slipped her phone down into her tote bag and cleared her mind of the call. She stood a few feet from the building that housed her first class and stared up at the structure with her eyes focused on the entrance. Several people were crowded around the doors while others were walking inside. Quick to join them, she continued walking until one of the boys on the steps caught her eye. Shocked that she hadn't noticed Jerome earlier, she knew it was his clothes that had thrown her off. Dressed down in a pair of dark denim jeans and a short-sleeved black shirt, his style was reminiscent of his early high school days. Certain that he wasn't there for class, Kristian decided to approach him. "Welcome to Copperfield," she greeted.

Jerome's feet shifted and he fidgeted as Kristian approached him. He wasn't surprised to see her since he had spotted her at the club, but she still made him nervous. He reasoned that if Kristian was in Copperton City, King probably wasn't too far behind. "What do you want?" he asked her, nastily. "Don't you have somewhere to be?"

Kristian shrugged her shoulders. "You tell me," she snapped. "What are you doing here, Jerome? Georgia is very far from Brookstone. Are you trying to go to school here, too?"

Jerome looked past her as he noticed a black Bentley slowly creeping past the building. The sight of the luxury vehicle made him remember the real reason he was in Georgia. It was a story that Kristian didn't even know the half of. After Rico's death, he had broken his ties with Jay. He couldn't fathom the idea of continuing business with him when he had murdered his cousin. He wanted to retaliate, but he knew he couldn't do it by himself. When he got word that Jay had shut down the cartel, he found someone else who was just as thirsty as he was for revenge: Shawn Blumington. The man had talked proudly about all he had done for the cartel only to get the boot. They both shared the same hate for Jay, which resulted in Jerome accepting Blu's offer to work for him. His status had dropped down to almost that of a corner boy, but it was a small price for what Blu had promised. His new boss had the means to ruin all of Jay's operations. So far, things weren't necessarily working in their favor, but the future was still bright.

"Um, are you going to answer me?" Kristian asked. She folded her arms across her chest as she stared in Jerome's face. She could see his attention was focused elsewhere so she followed his gaze. A Bentley had pulled up and was parked directly in front of them. "Jerome," she whispered as she realized what was going on. "Are you selling drugs on our campus?" He didn't answer her as he started to walk down the steps. When she called his name a second time, he turned to face her like he was hearing her voice for the first time. "Are you?" she asked him.

"Stay there," he ordered as he sprinted towards the car.

"Jerome, I have class!" He pointed back at her like he had given a direct order. Kristian didn't want to be late, but she complied.

Meanwhile, a chill encircled Jerome as he closed the door to the Bentley, after getting inside. If it wasn't for the driver rolling down the window upon his approach, he wouldn't have known that Blu had made his way back to Georgia. From what he had heard on the streets, Blu had been busy trying to put together a group of men who could help him take down Jay. Now, he had made his way back to Copperton City. When he looked over at him, he didn't know what to expect when he saw him flipping through a magazine. He couldn't see the cover, but from what the pages looked like, it wasn't one that he expected Blu to be reading.

"How long has she been here?" Blu asked.

Jerome turned to look out the window. "Are you talking about Kristian?" he probed. He looked back at Blu as he held up the magazine. Kristian was on the front cover. "It's the first day of school," he replied. "She popped up out of nowhere." Jerome swallowed as he saw the calm expression on Blu's face. It didn't match the tone of his voice, which caused him some concern. "Are you worried that she told King about me?"

"I don't give a fuck what she told her brother," Blu shot back. "If you ask me, she's going to tell him. What I care about is how she got here without me knowing. I met her at Mancini's last year. We had a few run-ins, but nothing close to what I really wanted."

"Oh," was all that Jerome could mouth. He looked back up at Kristian until Blu's voice caught his attention once again. This time, the man was talking about Jay.

"I know you're wondering about when we're going to touch down on him. I got something already lined up for today. I've been letting him sleep well for the last two months. I'm not doing it anymore. I got a call on the way back here that Phase took out two of my new cats. Playtime is over, Jerome. I'm going hard on this next one. I'm going straight for him."

Jerome didn't respond as he looked down at the magazine in Blu's lap. He might have been discussing Jay, but his eyes were focused in on one of Kristian's spreads. His hands were rubbing the page like he was actually touching her.

"I tried to get Carmen, but the shit didn't work. The bitch was locked and loaded like she knew I was coming. My plan was to get her then get the diamonds. Shit changed, though. Now, I figured I would get Jay. I'll go at him. He needs to know that anyone in this world can touch him. He thinks he's sitting all high and mighty in the fuckin' clouds. Well, I'm going to make it hail."

"What do you need for me to do? You know I'm ready." Jerome was amped for the challenge that Blu had conjured up. He wanted in on all parts of it so that Jay could know who it was that had brought him down.

Blu held up the issue of *Seventeen* so that Jerome could see it. "I want you to watch her. Matter of fact, you need to tell her why you're here. Make sure you mention me. If we're lucky, she'll get word to King. If he finds out you're in Georgia and that we got our sights on his father, he'll make sure that his mother talks. We'll have the diamonds in no time."

Jerome turned to look back at Potter Hall. Kristian was still standing there like he had asked her to. He understood what Blu wanted him to do, but he had no intentions of hurting Kristian. His problem wasn't with her. It wasn't even with King. He only wanted to get back at Jay for what he had done to Rico.

"Go ahead and handle that. I got shit to do," Blu said, shooing him out of the car.

Jerome opened the door and stepped out of the vehicle. He headed back to Potter Hall as the car took off behind him. In terms of watching Kristian, he was unsure of what Blu actually wanted him to do. He would have preferred to leave her out of it, but Blu had a sick obsession with her. He could see it from the way he was rubbing her photos.

"Do you want to explain that?" Kristian yelled. She pointed to the space where the Bentley had been parked. "I'm already late for my first class!"

Jerome grabbed her arm, pulling her into him. "You're not going," he told her, sternly. "We need to talk." He headed away from the steps, but

Kristian didn't follow. She loosened his grip until her arm was free. "Come on, Kris, you know your brother isn't slinging anymore. I have to do what I have to do. Business is popping right now in the South."

Kristian's mouth dropped wide open. "Does King know about this?"

Jerome scrunched up his face in disgust. "Man, you know your brother and I aren't cool anymore. He dropped us like we weren't shit. He and Jay are only looking out for self."

Kristian took a long hard look at Jerome. From the way he was speaking to her, she knew that he had some built up anger. She didn't want to get into the middle, but she knew that he and King needed to talk. They had been friends for too long for them to let the issue of money get in between them. "You're out here alone, Jerome. Georgia isn't like New York."

"Yeah, yeah, I know," Jerome muttered. "I got this, though."

"You say you do. I guess we'll see." Kristian gave him a crooked smile before she turned away to continue on to class. Given his explanation she felt a little more comfortable about him being there, but she wasn't going to leave the issue alone. The moment she got out of class, she was going to call her brother. He needed to know what Jerome was doing. If he did, there was a possibility that he could get Jerome out of the situation. King may have left the drug game, but she was certain that there was room for Jerome somewhere. She thought it even more when she heard her phone ring from her tote. She hoped it was her brother, but when she looked at the caller ID she saw that it was her mom. An eerie feeling came upon her, but she chose to ignore it like the phone call.

Chapter Thirty-Five

Brookstone, New York

Carmen hung up the phone when Kristian's voicemail sounded once again. Either she was calling at the wrong time or Kristian was dodging her phone calls. Whichever reason it was, the outcome was still the same. Too disappointed to try Akaila, Carmen tossed her phone into the bottom of her purse as Jay joined her in the garden.

"Your husband went upstairs," Jay announced. "Did you know he was here?"

Carmen nodded her head. It was her way of prepping him for the news that Kane had delivered. She had warned Jay that Donnie's murder would catch up to them and it had. Now, they both had to put their heads together to figure out what they were going to do. "Donnie's wife filed a missing persons' report on him." Carmen looked at him only to see that his face didn't show much concern. In fact, he looked to be at ease. "I guess one of the detectives got in touch with Kane about it. I told him that I fired Donnie, but he doesn't believe me. He knows something's up."

Jay didn't speak right off as he wanted to be careful with his choice of words. He knew Carmen was feeling threatened, but he didn't want her to worry. She was safer than she believed herself to be. "I know you hated lying about it, Carm, but you did the right thing. There is nothing out there for the police to find that will tie you to his murder. In due time, there will be justice for his death."

Carmen stood up with a slight attitude when she realized she was hearing the same story as before. She knew she had agreed to keep the secret, but it was killing her to do so. The police were starting to move in on both of them. Before long, they both would have a set of handcuffs around their wrists. "I'm scared, Jay." Carmen let out a small sigh as she admitted her true feelings. "Kane isn't with the police department anymore. They contacted him for a reason. It's like they were warning him that they're going to interrogate me."

"They might, but they don't have anything to go on," Jay responded. "There's no case without a body or a murder weapon. Even if they find one, your prints won't be on it." Jay picked up her left hand, and held it in his. "You need to clear your head. Let's go on home, get something to eat; chill out for a minute." Jay remained silent for a few seconds to let his suggestion marinate in Carmen's mind. She wasn't quick to say yes, but eventually she gave in. They headed back into the hospital and to her father's room. Malik and King were still inside along with Patricia while Lotus remained asleep. After telling them goodbye, Jay followed Carmen into the parking lot. Since they had ridden separately, she chose to drive her car home and he followed behind in his limousine.

By the time they had gotten out the parking lot, Linx's vehicle had slid in between them. As for Cesar, he was trailing Jay's limousine from behind. Glad that his right-hand men were nearby, the drive home was more comfortable than he expected. He wished that it was the same for Carmen. When he saw her face again, he realized that all of the stress that she'd been dealing with was displayed on it. Her actions said it, as well. Upon entering the house, Carmen had retreated upstairs without a single word. Instead of following her, he headed into the kitchen where he found Fiona and Nyla. The maid was quick to tell him that Rakim was in the den asleep before handing Nyla over to him.

"She woke up a few minutes ago so she's full of energy," Fiona said with a chuckle. "I wasn't expecting you all to be here this early. Carmen must have worked a half day."

"She did," Jay replied. He knew that he should've told her about Lotus, but it would only prompt another conversation. He was in a rush to get back to Carmen since he knew she was feeling down. He excused himself from the room, and headed to Carmen's bedroom. When he opened the door, he found her inside, lying on the bed with her back to him. She was barefoot, which Jay decided to use to his advantage. "Do you want to have lunch with me? I can get the chef at Blue Magic to whip up your favorite," Jay said, tickling the bottom of Carmen's feet. He did it as a ploy to get her to talk to him. Her only response was a quick head shake. It wasn't what he wanted to see so he tickled her feet some more as he continued to try and coax her. When she moved her leg away from him, he knew to stop. "Okay, Peaches, you need some me time. Since Nyla is up, I'm going to take her with me. She can be my date. Is that cool?"

Carmen muttered, "Yes." Her utterance was so barely audible that if Jay hadn't been watching her lips, he might not have known that she replied. He rose from the bed, and gave her a quick kiss before walking out the room. It didn't take him long to get Nyla ready and in no time they were sitting in a booth at Blue Magic.

Lunchtime was always the busiest because of all of the businesses that surrounded the restaurant. Due to the large crowd, Jay had chosen to sit near the back. A few people looked his way, but he assumed that it was because he had his daughter with him. Nyla was making a lot of loud noises, which he knew was a major distraction. He didn't mind the extra attention until he saw a figure sliding into his booth. The man stated his name to be Stephen Franklin, the CEO of Continental. Tall, medium build, with dark brown hair and an olive skin complexion, it was the first time that Jay had officially seen him in person. They had only spoken on the phone since Malik and Costa had settled their deal.

Before either of them spoke a single word, Jay noticed that Franklin appeared to be upset about something. Jay was also disturbed; he felt like the man had shown him the upmost disrespect by seeking him out. Franklin knew the proper channels to go through if he wanted to speak with him. It enraged Jay when surprise visits were made.

"Mr. Santiago," Franklin began. "It's been awhile since we've spoke." Franklin set his cell phone down onto the table before peeking over at Nyla. He gave the baby a smile before focusing back on Jay. It was then that his grin straightened. "I wanted to inform you that the Brookstone PD has visited my firm three times in the past couple of months. They even brought a search warrant. They haven't found anything, but they keep coming."

Jay picked up his used steak knife, sliding it back and forth over one of the cloth napkins on the table. He held it up once it was clean. "Believe me when I say this," Jay stressed. "You never have the right to come here, in my face, and bring this business to me. If you needed to talk to me, I gave you the people to contact. I suggest you leave."

Franklin loosened his tie as a direct reflection of his growing nervousness. He was having second thoughts about the visit, but he wanted to get all of his concerns out. "Mr. Santiago, with all due respect, I allowed you to place your product in my basement. You made the decision to move it out, but for some reason, I'm under investigation. The cops that are coming after you are now coming after me."

"The basement is clean. It's been clean for months. There is nothing in your building that can be linked back to me. If you're worried about the cops then you need to tighten up. Shit, let's remember how this deal came to be. How do your arms look?"

Franklin swallowed as Jay brought up his past. He was a changed man, which he hoped he saw. "I've been clean for two months now. I'm regaining the trust of my family. I'm doing well for myself. It's the reason why I don't need some cop trying to put cuffs on me."

"I wish you the best," Jay replied, slipping the knife into his left pocket. "I suggest you stay that way. You won't ever get another key from me. No one in this fuckin' world will."

Franklin hated the fact that Jay was being so nonchalant. His whole career was on the line, but Jay couldn't see that. As a man who was starting to regain his life back, Franklin was looking for some sort of compassion. So far, the only empathy he saw was when Jay interacted with his daughter. "Please understand, Mr. Santiago. My career is on the line. I have a family. Detectives are interrogating me left and right."

Jay stood up from the table, showing him that he was finished with the conversation. He started to prepare Nyla for the ride back home, but Franklin wouldn't let up. Jay let him talk, but after a few seconds, he interrupted him. "None of this bullshit is about you," he told him, plainly. "I know the detective on the case. He used to be partners with the Triad agent who took me down years ago. They're trying to do it again. The drugs, Continental, it's not shit to them. It's about me. You should be sleeping peacefully."

Franklin stood up so that they were at eye level. "Mr. Santiago, you need to give me some assurance that my name is not going to be attached with yours."

"Or what?" Jay questioned, picking Nyla up. "The last thing you want to do is threaten me. Murder is the game I play. If you want to play, too, let me know."

Franklin swallowed. The last thing he wanted was to be on Jay's hit list. Without even knowing it, he could've potentially already placed himself there. Hoping for the best, he held out his hand to him. Jay didn't shake it so he dropped it back at his side. With a final glimpse into Jay's eyes, he parted his lips once again. "I bid you good day."

In response, Jay gave Franklin a single head nod. He watched him carefully as he exited the restaurant. Though he would never verbalize it, he had to give it to Franklin, the man had balls. He had never known anyone to come to one of his establishments on a whim. Franklin was extremely adamant about upholding his image. *If only he thought the same way when it comes to his life*, Jay thought with a smile.

Deciding to put the visit behind him, he quickly exited the restaurant. Cesar was standing at his limousine as if he knew he was on his way out. When he looked at him, Cesar gave him an expression to let him know that he was suspicious of something.

"Stephen Franklin came out a few seconds ago," Cesar voiced. "Is he a problem?"

Jay shrugged his shoulders as he sat Nyla down into her car seat. "He's not a problem, only a man who needs to be sent a reminder. Don't physically touch him, but let him know who he's dealing with. Hopefully, he'll learn his lesson." Jay slid into the limousine, grabbing for his seatbelt. He buckled it as Cesar told him that he would be following from a distance.

Once his right-hand had retreated to his vehicle, he closed the door. "Go ahead, Gus," he said to his driver, "The sooner we get home, the better."

Jay waited for Gus to respond before he closed his eyes. When he heard nothing, he felt a sinking feeling in his stomach. He looked at his driver who was sitting upright with a pair of shades covering his face. Jay couldn't see his eyes so he gave the man a quick shake. "Come on, Gus, I know you're an old man, but we were only inside for like forty-five minutes. You can take a nap after we get home." Letting out a slight chuckle, Jay watched in shocked horror as Gus' head fell down onto the steering wheel. It was then that he noticed the several coils of razor wire that were hanging from his neck.

"What the—" Jay felt the sudden impact before he could finish his statement. He turned to look behind him only to see a black car resting on the limo's bumper. Before he could react, two more cars appeared. Both of them were jet black and in mint condition. Not one to have the emotion of fear, Jay felt his adrenaline level increase by the second as he grabbed a pistol out of his waistband. He then pulled out another one which had been stashed in between the limo's seats. The second he cocked them, a bullet blasted through the front passenger side window.

Not wasting any time, Jay grabbed Nyla's car seat, placing it in the middle of the limousine. He covered her with his body while his fingers pulled both triggers simultaneously. The shattering glass from the windows fell around him like raindrops. Ignoring the pricks, Jay continued firing until his eyes could focus on everything around him. His head shook frantically back and forth at the armament of weapons pointed at him and Nyla. With the way he was positioned any of the bullets could reach them. He reasoned that any shot he took would have to be a kill shot to the forehead. Even with three men down, after the first round of gunfire, there were still three more men coming toward him.

Jay fired at them, but they were halfway to the ground before his bullets even reached them. It was then that he noticed Cesar. Trusting that his right-hand man had him covered, Jay grabbed Nyla's car seat, climbing to the front of the limousine. His next plan was to get away while Cesar handled Blu's goons. He moved speedily, opening the front driver's side door. One hand shoved Gus' remains from the vehicle while the other reached for the ignition switch. To his surprise, his fingers touched nothing, but cold metal. Jay mouthed the word fuck as he searched the front seat for the keys. Coming up empty, he cursed under his breath as he opened up the car door. He quickly searched Gus' body, finding the keys inside of the man's hands. In a split second, he was back in the car, listening as the engine came to life.

As he put the car into reverse, he saw a figure move out of the corner of his right eye. When the passenger side door opened, Jay waited for the man to lean inside. The second he did, he fed his face with a slew of bullets. Blood splattered as the man's body dropped onto the seat. Even with the door wide open, Jay continued to press on the gas, backing out of the parking space. The black car moved behind him as he pushed it out of his way.

Naturally, Jay's eyes scanned the rearview mirror as he sped off. Cesar was struggling up against one of Blu's men while a black Benz was starting to trail him. *These motherfuckers want war!* Jay slammed down onto the brakes before grabbing one of the pistols in his hand. His sudden stop forced the Benz to crash into the back of the limousine. He put the car into park and opened the driver's side door, firing as he stepped out. At this point, he wanted retaliation. The Benz's driver gave him the opportunity to get it when he stepped out as well. The man only took one footstep before his body became riddled with bullets. Though the man was where he wanted him, Jay wasn't finished with him. He grabbed him by the collar, dragging him towards the limousine.

He took the steak knife from his pocket and plunged it into the man's chest. The next five minutes of his life started to play out like a movie in his mind. He could hear Cesar yelling at him in his subconscious, but his adrenaline level was at an all-time high. *You fucked with the wrong person! Die, motherfucker, die!* Jay continued thrusting the knife in and out of the man's chest, ignoring the salty red liquid that was being sprayed into his mouth. Even when he thought he'd done enough, he started gauging the man's eyes out. He didn't stop until a new sound began to emerge in his ears. Pausing, Jay listened to the loud cries of his baby girl. He looked in horror at his daughter who was drenched in blood.

"Get in the fuckin' car!"

Jay felt the hard shove from Cesar as he pushed him into the backseat of the limousine. The back door was open, which was where Jay found himself as Cesar started up the vehicle. No longer stunned, he reached over the seat, grabbing Nyla into his arms. He searched her body frantically for any sign of a bullet hole as sirens wailed into his eardrums. Jay could hear Cesar yelling directives, but he chose to ignore him. Ensuring the safety of his daughter was more important than the ten bodies that were left behind. Even when Cesar had let him into his apartment, he headed straight for the bathroom. Cesar yelled that he was going to go handle things, but Jay didn't respond. He merely stripped Nyla of her clothes, placing her underneath the faucet.

The water was only lukewarm, but from the sound of Nyla's cries, anyone would have believed that it was scalding. As he scrubbed the blood from her skin and hair, he checked the temperature of the water to make sure it had not changed. In fact, the water was starting to become cool. Jay turned it off, picked her up from the sink, and tried to use a soothing voice to calm her. He bounced her up and down in his arms, planting kisses on her cheeks and forehead, but nothing seemed to ease her tantrum. With the way she was carrying on, Jay decided to check her one more time. Though he hadn't seen any signs of a graze or a cut, there was always a possibility that there was an area he overlooked.

Ding! Ding!

Fuck no," Jay mumbled, hearing his doorbell. He stared out into the hallway before pulling up the drain stopper. He allowed the water to run out of the sink before sitting Nyla back inside. When the doorbell sounded again, he grabbed a rag, using it to dry his hands. "Shit, I'm coming," he yelled, trying to speed walk to the door. "Motherfuckers can't leave me alone for one got damn minute," he muttered. Jay pulled out his pistol before checking the peephole. He cringed seeing Cesar, but he knew that he shouldn't have. The man had done the work of an army in a short amount of time. He put the pistol back into his waistband and quickly opened the door. As soon as Cesar was by his side, he closed it back, putting on all the locks. "You hear that shit?" he asked him, making mention of Nyla. "She hasn't stopped since."

"That's the least of your concerns," Cesar replied, pulling out a sheet of paper. He handed it over to his boss already having an idea of how he was going to react. "You made two Most Wanted lists, the Brookstone PD and the Triad. By the time I made it back to Blue Magic, the whole scene was flashing red and blue. All they needed was one person to say that you were there to issue a warrant for your arrest. I know what we're up against, but we need to buy ourselves some time. I got the plane ready. I suggest you start packing for Puerto Rico."

Jay let out a vicious growl as he stared down at an old mug shot of himself. He tore the paper in half before dropping it down at his feet. He knew that he needed to get out of the country, but running didn't seem to be the best option.

"Now that we both are aware that the clock is ticking, let's move." Cesar ran to the back of the apartment where Jay's room was. He rushed inside, going into his boss's walk-in closet. Once there, he grabbed the large duffle bag that was packed for special occasions like the one Jay was in. He retreated into the living room where he dropped it at Jay's feet. "Let's go," he said, sternly, "do you want me to get the baby?"

Jay looked towards the bathroom where Nyla was. He knew he needed to be leaving, but he couldn't take Nyla unless he said something to Carmen. "I need a few hours, Cesar. The Triad isn't coming right now, anyway. I know how they roll. They need a chance to plan. Give me an hour or two to get some shit in order."

Cesar grabbed his head in frustration as he listened to Jay's words. "They are offering a fuckin' reward for your ass. The Triad is offering up to a million dollars for you. You don't remember what happened in that fuckin' parking lot? Ten bodies, Jay. All of them including Gus are under a white blanket right now. Every cop in this city is looking for you."

"And so is Shawn Blumington."

Cesar tried to calm himself so his speech wouldn't be as slurred as it was becoming. "I saw everything that happened, Jay. Only one of Blu's men fired at you. He didn't even shoot in your direction, but in Gus'. Blu wants you, but he doesn't want you dead. There is obviously something else that he wants. Whatever it is, he knows that in order to get it, he has to keep you alive. The same goes for Carmen. We both know that she didn't kill two men out of pure luck. Those men let her kill them because they knew they couldn't kill her. Think about it."

Jay opened his mouth to speak, but he was silenced at the sound of the doorbell. Upon hearing it, Cesar pulled out his glock. "I got it," Jay told him, "if it was the Triad, they would've knocked the door down." He headed for the door, stepping away from Cesar. Quickly looking through the peephole, he saw Carmen on the other side with Rakim. He needed to talk to her, but not in his current state. Since she had showed up to his apartment unannounced, he assumed that the shootout at Blue Magic had reached her ears.

Unsure of what to do, Jay didn't make up his mind until he realized that Nyla's cries could be heard throughout the apartment. He knew then that he couldn't run from his girlfriend. He had to let her know what was going on. "She's going to find out eventually," he mumbled as he reached for the doorknob.

Cesar pulled his hand away from the door in an attempt to change Jay's mind. "Do you know how many fuckin' DNAs you have on your clothes right now? If that's Carmen, let her go. Once she realizes you're not at home, she'll leave. Shit, I'll drop the baby off at her house."

Jay reached for the doorknob again as he ignored Cesar's words. He quickly opened the door, allowing Carmen to see him as he was. He knew his appearance disturbed her when she let Rakim slide out of her arms. Thankfully, their son landed on his feet before running into the apartment.

Carmen stared in disbelief at the sight in front of her. She blinked her eyes, trying to make sure she saw right. Torn and drenched in what appeared to be blood, she couldn't even make out the color of Jay's clothes. If it wasn't for them being together earlier, she wouldn't have known what he was wearing. "Wh-wh," but the word, what, wouldn't come out. She scrunched up her face as she realized what had happened. Before she could react, she heard the loud cry that was slowly starting to echo in her ears. She pushed her way into the apartment, heading straight for the bathroom, which was where Nyla's cries seem to be coming from. Finding her daughter naked, Carmen grabbed her out of the sink as she searched around for her clothes. Not seeing her dress, she realized that the bathroom counter was filled with nothing but bloody washcloths and rags.

"Her dress," she yelled, "where are her fuckin' clothes?"

Carmen ran back into the living room, clutching her daughter close to her chest. She stared at Jay, asking him with her eyes to tell her what happened. She looked him up and down until her eyes landed on what was in his right hand. "Is that her dress?" Carmen stared at Jay until it hit her that they weren't alone. She looked to the left of him, meeting eyes with a man whose complexion nearly matched Jay's. Judging from his looks, he appeared to be a mix of black and Latino. However, she didn't let his looks distract her for long, as she looked back to Jay waiting for his response.

Jay's eyes were locked in on his right hand. He thought he had used a rag to dry his hands off, but inside of his palm was his daughter's green petal sash dress. "I can explain," he began, making sure to speak calmly. "She's fine, she's not hurt. I promise." Jay picked Rakim up into his arms as he walked closer to Carmen. "Give me a chance to explain."

"Explain? How the fuck can you explain that?" Carmen yelled, pointing at his clothes. "What the fuck did you do? Put Rakim down. Look at you, Jay. You're covered in fuckin' blood. My phone has been ringing like crazy. What happened at Blue Magic?"

"Blu struck again," Cesar announced. "He attacked Jay and Nyla this afternoon."

Carmen closed her eyes, but for only a split second as the tears began to fall. Not caring to know anymore, she sat Nyla down onto the couch while she took off her jacket. Sliding it around her daughter, she picked her back up before holding out her hand for Rakim. "Blu, huh?" she asked. "Should I even ask who he is?"

Cesar stepped in between the two, knowing that the tension in the room was rising. "Jay, she needs to take the boy. We have to get out of here. We can work this out later."

Jay stared at Cesar before glancing back at Carmen. He didn't want to give either of his kids up. He also didn't want them to witness him being arrested so he knew what he had to do. He set Rakim back on his feet, but his son didn't move an inch. If it wasn't for Carmen grabbing his hand, Rakim would've stayed by his side. Without another word to him or Cesar, Carmen walked out of the apartment. He didn't know where she was headed, but Cesar promised him that he would stay in contact with Linx who would be trailing her.

"Get cleaned up," Cesar ordered, locking the door back. "I'm going to turn on the news to see what's going on with the investigation. Hopefully, I'll have something for you by the time you're done."

Cursing under his breath, Jay headed into the bathroom to shower. About an hour later, he was dressed and getting inside of Cesar's Jaguar. It was then that his right-hand man informed him that the Triad and Brookstone PD were still scouring the area. He was still the only suspect in the murder of ten men. The news in itself was enough for Jay to form a plan in his mind. "Get in contact with Linx. Tell him to get Carmen and the kids. I want them to come to Puerto Rico with me. We'll stay in San Juan for the night and I'll call Gomez first thing in the morning. He can meet me at the police station tomorrow when I turn myself in."

Cesar gave a single head nod as he started up the car. "It'll be taken care of," he told him.

Jay rested his head back on the seat. He closed his eyes, but only for a brief second. His nerves wouldn't allow him to relax. Thereafter, his eyes remained open as Cesar drove out of the parking lot.

Meanwhile, Carmen wrapped her jacket tighter around Nyla as she placed her inside of her car seat. Her daughter had calmed down since they had left Jay's apartment, but it wasn't the same for her. When she had received the phone call from one of the waiters that someone was shooting at Blue Magic, everything around her seemed to crumble. She knew that Jay and Nyla were there, and she instantly thought the worse. Yet, when she had arrived at the restaurant, all she saw was blue lights and Triad agents. Not wanting to be questioned, she left before she could be seen. She drove straight to Jay's apartment, and there she found more than she had bargained for. She knew that Jay was involved in the shootout and so was a man named Blu. A man who she assumed was really Shawn Blumington. She didn't know why he wanted to kill Jay, but she knew she would find out in due time.

As she left the complex, her phone started to ring. She wanted to ignore it, but something told her that she needed to answer. When she saw that it was Tiara, she knew the news had hit her friend's ears. She answered the call only to learn that her friend wanted to meet up to discuss the incident. Carmen's main concern was getting her kids back at home and settled, but Tiara remained adamant. After a few minutes of coaxing, Carmen agreed to meet with her in an hour. Still, she wouldn't forget the task at hand. After she met with Tiara, she had to find Jay. She knew he had plans to leave, but she couldn't let him. He needed to stick around and face whatever was coming at them. At this point, none of them could run.

Chapter Thirty-Six

Tiara took off her shades as she started the search for Carmen. Her friend said she was already at a table outside of Old Town Bistro, but Tiara hadn't yet spotted her. On pins and needles because of the drama, Tiara knew that her nerves weren't as bad as Carmen's. When she finally spotted her friend, she saw that she was makeup-less and that her hair had been gelled back into a bun. She was also not dressed in her usual pantsuit; instead she was clothed in a yellow t-shirt and jeans. She even had a pair of Nike tennis shoes on her feet. A small sigh escaped her lips as she saw the depression on Carmen's face up close.

The first question out of Carmen's mouth was, "What are they saying?" She hadn't yet watched the news and was certain that Tiara had heard the report. "Fiona tried to tell me some things, but I didn't want to hear it. I simply told her to take care of the kids."

Tiara grabbed her friend's hand as she saw a tear sliding down her face. She hated to be the bearer of bad news, but Carmen deserved to know what the media was saying. "Right now, Channel Five is reporting that Jay may have killed about ten men in broad daylight. They have photos of three Benzes in the parking lot with nothing, but bullet holes in them. They showed a few of the victims, but they were in body bags. The thing is; witnesses aren't saying that they saw Jay shoot anyone. They're merely saying that he was there. One of them even said that he left a minute or two before the shooting started."

Carmen pushed her drink away from her as the tears fell more heavily. "I sit here and think, Tee, about how my daughter was in the middle of all that. What if I had lost her? Shit, fuck Jay, what about my child?" Carmen screamed. "She's barely one. This is not the life I want for her. I don't want this for any of my kids."

"None of us do, Carm," Tiara interjected. "All we can do right now is thank God that she wasn't harmed. She's fine, Carm." Tiara continued holding her friend's hand, hoping that she was saying the right words to her. "Have you spoken to Jay?"

Carmen nodded her head. "I…" she paused again, sniffling. "I don't know what he's about to do. I know he left, but I don't…" Carmen's voice trailed off. "I'm mad at him, but I still love him, you know? I want to strangle him right now, but I…I'm scared, Tee. He is at the top of the Most Wanted list. I don't know how long Jay thinks he can run, but they're going to find him. They found him seventeen years ago and they can find him again."

"Malik doesn't even know yet where he's headed. He knows that he's leaving the country. Right now, Malik is trying to get the paperwork straight for their businesses."

"I've been thinking and praying on things, Tee. I have to get my stuff together, too. This isn't about me anymore. This is about my kids. They have no reason to be in situations like this." Carmen's face now wore a stern expression. She hoped that Tiara was ready for the bomb she was going to drop, but it didn't look like she was. "I'm thinking about filing for sole custody of Rakim and Nyla."

"Y-y-you're taking Jay to court?" Tiara stammered.

"I'm thinking about it. I want full custody and I think I'm going to request that he have supervised visits. That way, I'll know that my kids are protected." Carmen grabbed her straw, digging it in and out of her drink. "I mean, if Jay is on the run, will it really matter?"

"I know you're upset," Tiara began, speaking quickly, "but you know what that judge is going to say when you come with that. You know Jay's background. That judge isn't going to allow him to see his kids. Look at the news. He's a known murderer, Carm. Do you know what this will do to Jay?" Tiara's fist hit the table hard. "You are letting your anger fuel this decision. Take a step back and look at everything for what it is. Jay was attacked. It didn't matter that Nyla was in the car. Matter of fact, Blu ordered a hit on you."

Carmen wore a shocked expression as Tiara spoke. She had no idea that she knew of her attack. It made her wonder how much stuff Tiara really knew.

"Yeah, Carm, I wasn't oblivious like you thought I was."

"Then you should understand why I'm thinking about this."

"I understand your anger," Tiara replied. "But I'm not agreeing with you on this custody thing. Not one bit. Jay loves his kids. He was fighting to protect his daughter. He was one man against ten, Carm. I will always ride for you, but not on this one. You should work something out with Jay, but don't take him to court. If you do that, he will never see those kids again."

Carmen pushed her chair back, deciding that the conversation was over. "It's not set in stone. It's something that I'm thinking about. I haven't made up my mind."

"Carmen," Tiara continued as her friend rose to her feet. "Please don't do this. Let the situation die down for a few days. Then, give it another thought."

"I—" Carmen's words were cut off as a hand clamped down over her mouth.

"I have a strict order from Mr. Santiago that I intend on carrying out. I dare you to try some dumb shit with me," the man whispered in her ear. "Jay wants his kids. It is my job to bring them to him, safe and sound. Do you understand?"

Carmen nodded her head. Her anxiety decreased as she realized that the voice belonged to Linx.

"He also wants you. When we leave here, we're going straight to your house. We have exactly thirty minutes to pack before the plane leaves. We're going to San Juan."

Carmen closed her eyes after hearing Linx's instructions. When she reopened them, Tiara was standing in front of her. Linx removed his hand from her mouth and draped it on her arm. He gave it a slight tug, letting her know that they needed to get a move on. Mouthing goodbye to Tiara, she grabbed her purse as Linx led her to a white limousine. She sat down in the backseat while Linx took the driver's. She didn't ask him about her car, because she knew that he had everything covered. As far as she knew, another one of Jay's men was probably driving it back to her house. For now, it needed to be the least of her worries. The greatest of them was learning what Jay had prepared.

***

Jay's plans might have concerned Carmen, but it was hers that had Malik stressing. Sweating profusely, he wiped his forehead with a handkerchief as he reread the text message that Tiara had sent him. She had divulged the news that Carmen had plans to take Jay to court for a custody battle. As if that wasn't enough, Tiara was demanding that he tell Jay. Malik knew for a fact that Carmen was accompanying Jay to San Juan. If he didn't tell him now, Carmen could potentially make the announcement in the next ten minutes.

"I'm going to clear my head, Malik," Jay told him, looking out the window of the Jaguar. "I'm not running. I need to get out of the United States for a day or two to figure this shit out. If I'm locked up again, I gotta make sure that Sapphire is straight, Blue Magic, Iceland, all my shit. My money has to be straight. My family..." Jay struggled to finish his words. "You better not let that motherfucker touch my family."

"I got you covered, Jay. You know that. Gomez is waiting for the word. He'll be right by your side whenever you turn yourself in."

Jay looked back at Malik. "I never thought I'd see a day like this again. Seventeen years in fuckin' prison and I might have to go back. I keep telling myself that the time is worth it. I protected mines, Malik. I didn't let

Blu kill my daughter. We walked away from all that without a scratch. I did that shit!"

Malik glanced down at his phone for a second time as it vibrated in his hand. He wanted to respond to Jay's comment, but Tiara wasn't giving him the chance. *You have to persuade Carmen not to go through with this. She should be on her way to the airport now*, her message read. Malik wiped his face again at the reminder. "You have a lot on your shoulders right now."

"No shit," Jay mumbled.

"And I'm about to add to it."

Jay didn't comment, feeling something in his spirit as a pearl white limousine pulled up next to his own. Not getting his hopes up, he waited until the doors opened before he spoke. "There they are," he whispered, spotting Carmen.

Malik sat up in his seat, wishing that Carmen's timing wasn't so off. "Give me one more minute, Jay. I have to tell you something." He took a deep breath when Jay looked back at him. "Carmen wants full custody of Rakim and Nyla. Tiara says that she plans on giving you supervised v—" Malik lurched forward as he tried to catch Jay. He was halfway out of the limousine before Malik could even finish his sentence. As the door slammed in his face, Malik was forced to watch as Jay reached for Carmen's throat. In a split second, Linx appeared, separating the two before Jay could do any damage. It was enough time for Malik to get out of the limousine. By the time he reached them, Cesar was pulling Jay in the opposite direction. Curse words were steadily coming out of Jay's mouth while a look of shock was on Carmen's face.

There was no question in Malik's mind about what move he needed to make. The clock was still ticking so he headed straight to Carmen to help with the kids. Meanwhile, Linx gathered their luggage in his hands, transporting the bags to the airplane. Once inside, he expected for Jay to have calmed down, but he could tell that he hadn't. Not only was his face tense, but he was staring directly at Carmen without ever blinking his eyes. Even when the pilot announced over the intercom that the Triad had noticed their plane, Jay didn't order the aircraft to move.

"Look, we got to get this bad boy in the air," Cesar voiced. "Let's handle this on the way to Puerto Rico."

"After I decide whether or not I want this bitch to come," Jay shot back.

Carmen sat straight up before rising to her feet. "What did you say?" She knew she heard right, but she walked closer, wanting Jay to repeat himself.

"Hold up, Carm." Malik stopped Carmen in her footsteps when he saw Jay rise to his feet as well. Though Linx was stepping in between the two, Malik knew Jay's strength. He also knew that Linx would only go so far out of fear for his own life. Linx couldn't put too much pressure on him or Jay would forget who his true target was.

"No, he is not about to sit up here and disrespect me in front of my kids. Who are you calling a bitch, Jay?"

"Carm," Malik began, grabbing her arms. "Look, let's go in the cockpit or something. We can talk there."

"I don't want to talk to you, Malik. I want to talk to that motherfucker right there," Carmen yelled, pointing her finger at Jay. She watched as Jay came forward, but she didn't break her stance. She couldn't have cared less about him putting his hands on her. She wasn't the same weak Carmen as before when he had tried to kill her. Now, she was stronger, and had three men already on her body count. If Jay pushed her enough, she would add one more.

"Get this plane in the air," Cesar bellowed. He grabbed Jay's arms, assisting Linx, but ended up struggling as well. "Take it up."

"Not with me on it," Malik yelled. "I'm not leaving." He looked back at Carmen, knowing he had to break the news to her quick. "Tiara told me about the custody suit," he whispered. "I told Jay. That is the reason why he's so angry with you."

Carmen pushed Malik hard before raising her fist to him. As much as she wanted to punch him, she didn't. Instead, she gave him a deadly expression. "You fuckin' son of a bitch."

"He had to know, Carm. He's planning on turning himself in."

"What?" The word escaped Carmen's lips as she dropped her fists. She turned to look at Jay as she realized what he was up against. If Jay turned himself in, the Triad would make sure that he was found guilty and he would be locked up for the rest of his life.

"Look y'all, we gotta go," the pilot shouted. "The Triad has picked up on the plane. They're ordering a slew of agents over here. I heard it on the airwaves. We gotta move!"

Carmen sat back down, and covered her face with her hands. She listened as Jay ordered the plane to take off. By the time the plane began moving, Jay was sitting across from her with Cesar and Linx at his side.

"You don't think that's a low blow?" he asked her. "I got all this shit coming at me, and you want to take my kids away from me, too?"

Carmen disagreed. The last thing she wanted was to take the kids away from him. If anything, she wanted them protected. Their lives didn't need to be in danger because of the shortcomings of their parents. "Nyla could have been killed."

"I didn't let that happen."

"I don't give a fuck about what *you* let happen. You let this whole situation happen. I don't even know what's going on. If you're going to let something happen, it needs to be your mouth. I'm sure that Blu is Shawn Blumington. What I want to know is this. What did you do to him and why is he trying to kill you?"

Jay swallowed as he continued to stare Carmen in the face. He knew she deserved an explanation. He had kept her in the dark for far too long. With all that was coming at him, he needed Carmen in his corner. "Shawn Blumington," he began, "was moving major weight in the South. Some of my men felt like he could be a potential threat to what we were trying to do. Somewhere along the line, he got involved in my operation. He started thinking that he was running things. I let him know differently and he's been salty with me ever since. He also wants in on this FedEx thing."

Carmen sat on her hands to keep from hitting him. Jay didn't have to say that the 'FedEx thing,' was directly related to the diamonds in her basement. She knew that it was. Still, she decided to ask him about it so everything would be clear. "The FedEx thing is the "thing" in my basement, right? The "thing," that only me and you are supposed to know about."

"Correct," Jay replied, "According to Phase, a guy who—"

Jay felt a stream of blood rush into his mouth before his brain even registered that he had been punched. Shocked at Carmen's strength, he couldn't find it in himself to retaliate. Instead of striking her, he simply wiped his mouth. "Damn, Peaches."

"You deserved it," she fired back. "You promised me that it was between us."

"Sometimes, the brightest of minds can slip up. Since he knows, all I can do is deal with it. Before I can, I have to fight these charges. I have to make sure that my money and businesses are straight. When the Triad comes this time, they are going to pull out all the stops. They're going to try and use everything against me."

"You're right, they will. They have ten good *dead* reasons to do so."

Carmen wrapped her arms around herself. Blu was putting extra strain on their relationship and even more drama in their lives. "Well, this shit gets worse before it gets better," she whispered. From her father's health to the warrant for Jay's arrest, each problem was like a festering wound. She was so unsure of what was going to happen that she couldn't do anything but simply sit there quietly until the plane landed in San Juan.

Chapter Thirty-Seven

San Juan, Puerto Rico

Silvas set a mug of steaming hot green tea onto the table. As Jay picked up the cup, he pulled out a chair so that they could talk one on one. He had been Jay's personal butler since he was around five years old and he knew when Jay needed him. When the news hit San Juan that there was a warrant for Jay's arrest, Silvas prepared himself for what was to come. "You've been here for a few hours. Carmen and the kids are resting well, but you haven't slept any."

Jay sipped his tea for a few seconds, before he responded. "How did my father do this shit all his life?" he asked as he sat the mug back on the table. "He died in this shit. He wasn't like me, trying to break out."

"Jay, your father was a different type of man. Y'all have the same qualities and persona, but he was a little more hardheaded. He thought more about the people working for him than his family. That is where y'all differ. You gave up this life to protect yours. Your father, he made the decision to stay in it so that he could keep taking care of his people."

Jay touched his mug, but didn't pick it back up. Images of his father were flooding back into his mind quicker than he wanted them to. "Am I supposed to hate him for that? Do I blame him for me being this way?"

Silvas shrugged his shoulders. "I've worked for your family for many years, Jay. I sit here and listen to you and your problems just like I did with your father. With the business that your father was in, there were things he had to do. He had to protect his family. Did he want you to see it? No. However, you did. He constantly prayed that he would never see you become like him. He didn't want you to be a murderer. God answered his prayer, too. He never saw you like this. The last memory he has of you is an innocent one. Do you remember that night?"

Jay picked up his mug, taking another sip. He didn't want to recall the events, but he knew that Silvas was going somewhere with his inquiry. "I don't know, my father was in my room, we were talking." Jay didn't think he remembered, but he thought long and hard. "Fight for what you love. Those weren't his exact words, but that was the gist of what he was telling me."

"You're worried about possibly going back to prison and missing out on your kids' lives. However, what you did downtown is what your father told you to do. He told you to fight for what you love. You have nothing to be worried about if you go into that courtroom and tell the truth. You were attacked and you acted out of self-defense."

"True, but what about Carmen, she's threatening to take me to court, too."

Silvas took a deep breath as he thought the issue over. "People say and do things when they are hurt," he told him. "They make all kinds of plans. The only thing that matters is whether they carry through with 'em. If she follows through with this custody suit then you know where your relationship with her is headed. I know you don't want it to be over."

Jay stared down at his mug as he thought about Silvas' words. He knew his butler was right though he didn't want him to be. If Carmen took him to court and won, he knew that he wouldn't look at her the same. He could never forgive her if she succeeded in taking his kids away from him.

Upset, he excused himself from the table and headed up the steps, passing the room that Carmen was sleeping in. Instead of looking in on her, he went straight to the room where Nyla and Rakim were.

In the meantime, Carmen's eyes fluttered open. She didn't feel completely rested so she concluded that she hadn't been sleeping long enough. When she looked at the alarm clock on the bedside dresser, she saw that it read seven o'clock. The house was dead silent which only told her two things. The kids were still asleep and Jay was probably in the living room tying up the loose ends of his businesses. With him being occupied, she knew she needed to check up on the kids.

She got up, wandered into the bathroom, and washed the sleep from her face. She brushed her teeth and then headed to the room where Rakim and Nyla were. Their door was wide open, displaying how dark it had become. She stood in the doorway for a few seconds as she gazed around the room. It wasn't until her eyes reached the far left corner that she noticed Jay. She stared at him for a bit, noticing that he was sitting in the dark.

"Are you hungry?" he asked.

Carmen nodded her head. When he stood up from the chair he was sitting in, she followed him downstairs. "Are you going to cook?" she asked him as they entered the kitchen. "Or did Silvas whip up one of your favorites?"

"I got a little something in mind," Jay replied. He headed straight to the bread box, opening it. He took out a loaf, which he sat on the island before opening up one of the cabinets. He then took out a large plastic bowl, which he sat on the island as well. "Want to take a guess?"

Carmen sat on one of the bar stools already knowing Jay's plans. It was a nice little trip down memory lane, but it didn't distract her from their current issues. "French toast," she answered. "The first meal you ever made for me."

"On the morning I took your virginity."

Carmen cracked a smile. She stepped down off the stool, walking over to where he was. She opened the refrigerator, taking out a carton of eggs, and a gallon of milk. As she did so, she reminisced about that morning. "You obviously did something right. I kept sleeping with you," she joked.

"Yeah, but now you've stopped. I've been celibate for almost a year. Can I get that?"

Carmen looked over at Jay, giving him a look that had the word no written all over it. Jay might have been turning himself in, but that wasn't enough to make her drop her panties. Although it was something that she wanted to do, she knew that she didn't need to. Things were already complicated between them and sex would only cause confusion. Instead of responding, she moved past him to a row of cabinets. She took down a bottle of maple syrup and cinnamon, setting the items on the counter. "Where's King?" she asked, changing the subject. "Why isn't he here?"

Jay sprayed a frying pan with Pam, not turning the stove on. He thought carefully about his words, knowing that his reply could upset her. While he was attempting to mend their relationship, something told him that the evening could go in a different route. "There was a lot of paperwork that needed to be handled. King was the best person for the job. He's in Brookstone, taking care of business."

"You're his father, not his boss."

The stern tone that sounded out of Carmen's mouth was not a surprise to Jay. She had made the comment before, which she knew disturbed him. "I'm not going to argue with you, Peaches. I want us to have a nice dinner. Who knows when we will do this again?"

"Fine," Carmen replied, nastily. "We don't have to talk about it. I was saying—"

"Don't say," Jay shot back. "I don't want to hear it." Jay grabbed one of the eggs, cracking it into the bowl. He took out another and cracked it as well. For some reason, Carmen kept poking the bear that he was trying his best to tame. A small part of him was slowly starting to give in. "We each have a role, Peaches. Your role is to sign your name. My role is to give the orders. King's role is to make sure the order is carried out. Stay in your lane and mind your business."

Carmen jerked the bowl from his hands. She was more than a name on a piece of paper. At the end of the day, she would be affected by the shootout like Malik and King. "You love to downplay what I did for Blue

Magic. If it wasn't for me and my father, you wouldn't even have that spot. I was the one who helped you get back on top. You won over Brookstone because of me and some good food. Fuck your little drugs."

Jay grabbed the bowl back, smiling evilly. "Damn, Bonnie, you've gotten tough on me. You really think you're something because you've killed two men. You're not on my level, but it's a start. Shit, as long as Blu is out there, you'll probably get plenty of practice."

"I've killed more than two," Carmen fired back. "I didn't always get caught."

Jay's smile quickly faded. He stared into Carmen's eyes, not seeing one hint that she was joking. He tried to picture what she was talking about, but he couldn't quite catch it. It wasn't until he pictured a cruise ship that he became suspicious. "You killed Enosis, didn't you?"

"I had to get the pink diamond somehow."

Jay chuckled out of disbelief. "I knew it. In the back of my mind, I knew it. I didn't want to believe it. You sold *my* drugs, killed *my* worker, and stole *my* diamond. Shit, Peaches, what else have you done? Oh, besides fuckin' *my* best friend."

"I had *your* kids."

Jay picked up the gallon of milk, popping off the top. Not bothering to measure anything, he poured the milk into the bowl until he was satisfied. He then added the cinnamon before searching around for a whisk. "Speaking of kids," he said, turning on the stove, "when is the process server coming?" He started to beat the ingredients together as he waited for a response. When she didn't answer right off, he knew he had hit a nerve.

"You're asking me that like I made up my mind. I haven't. I don't know what I'm going to do. All I know is that I'm going to protect my kids. What happened downtown will never happen again. If Blu wants to kill someone, let him kill you, not my child."

"So killing those men wasn't protecting my child? You know what; let's back up for a minute. Blu attacked you, too. What if Rakim was in the car? You would think it was dirty of me if I announced I was taking you to court over something you had no control over."

Carmen pointed her right index finger at Jay as she began to illustrate how he was to blame for their latest fiasco. "You tend to forget that my attack was a direct effect of your bullshit. It had nothing to do with me. It all goes back to you."

Jay's temper rose more steadily leading him to drop the whisk down into the bowl. "Everything is my fault, huh? I'm the one to blame. I apologize for ruining your life. I'll make you happy from now on. Whatever you want, you got. You want full custody, take me to court, and get it. When Nyla and Rakim grow up and wonder why Daddy isn't around, I'll point the finger at you. You'll be the one to blame."

"I want you in their lives, Jay, but I want them protected."

Jay pushed the bowl away from him out of anger. "What do you think I pay these motherfuckers for, Carmen? I'm trying to protect my family. I can't be with you twenty-four seven. I know that. These men have families, too, Carm. They work around the clock sometimes just to look at you shop, eat, and work. Their job is to keep you and the kids alive even if they have to get killed in the process."

"Thank you. I appreciate it."

Jay narrowed his eyes as his anger reached another level. "Sometimes I look at you and all I can think about is how much I love you. Then, I look at you and wonder how I could have fallen in love with a woman like you. It all goes back to the things that you say to me. Has money made you so got damn unappreciative? Do you feel like you can't be touched? When you step out with me, Peaches, you automatically become a target. Did you think about that? Or did you just want my sperm and decided to deal with the bullshit that came with it later?"

"I'm not unappreciative. I'm also not with you for your sperm. I've made it very clear to you over these last couple of months that I love you. I hate your ways. You will never change. I've realized that. You're forty-seven and you still want to run the streets."

"Run the streets? I'm not a fuckin' drug dealer, Carmen. I'm not the head of a cartel. I broke out of that shit for my family. I'm a businessman. I left that and as a result of me leaving that life behind, I got a motherfuckin' maniac on my back. I would kill for a life like yours. I dream of the day I can work an eight to five and come home to a home cooked meal."

"Okay, so you say you're not a drug dealer. Fine, I believe you. What about your diamonds, though? I mean, this is what Blu wants. Isn't this why he wants to kill you? He wants the stones. The ones you take from other people."

"My diamonds are not stolen. The stones were purchased from a diamond mine in Africa. Once I can get my hands on one of my own, I can cut out the middleman. As for Blu, Cesar doesn't believe he wants me dead. He thinks he wants me in a vulnerable situation so I can give up the goods. It's the same for you. He wanted you for ransom."

"And the murders," Carmen asked, folding her arms across her chest.

"I'm a natural born killer. I was created by a killer, I became a killer, and I'm going to die a killer. If anybody in this fuckin' world threatens mine,

I will handle it. Death is death, I don't give a fuck about your age, or how you get there. I dare anybody to test me. I have no problem ending a life if it saves mine."

"See," Carmen said, pointing her finger at him again. "You're not going to change. That part of you is not going to change and you don't even want to change it. I can't live the rest of my life wondering if you're going to kill again. Everything has to be your way. You love walking around like you're a fuckin' king."

"Why should I be a king when I can be an ace?"

Carmen huffed, "That attitude right there is what I can't live with. You try to hide it, but it still manages to come out. It makes me feel like I can never marry you. You won't change. You always have to be on top. You have to have the final say."

Jay could feel his true emotions about to show. Trying to contain himself, he stared into the bowl, knowing that the French toast wouldn't be eaten. Too much had been said for them to even share a meal. "We tried, didn't we?" he asked her. A single tear formed itself in the corner of his left eye. "We tried," he repeated. "We did. We tried to make it work, but we couldn't. It's over, right? We flew out here for that to be the consensus?"

Carmen rubbed her lips together, beginning to agree with him. "I love you, but I can't be with you. I can't live like this, Jay. I don't want to. So, you're right," she said, starting to cry herself. "It is over. We tried and failed."

Jay wiped his face with one hand while he picked up the bowl of batter. He put it inside the fridge before turning back around. "The funny thing about all of this is that you're the only diamond I've ever wanted. I have more money than I can spend, but I could never buy you. You're priceless. It's settled, though. You've made your decision."

Carmen bit her lip as she watched Jay leave the kitchen. A part of her felt that she'd made a mistake by breaking up. Still, she couldn't take back her words or her emotions. Living a life where she had to constantly look over her shoulder was not what she wanted. She didn't want it for herself, her kids, or Jay. Staying with him would mean that she would continue to fall victim to whatever he was involved in. It was too large of a price to pay for love.

Weeping bitterly, Carmen left the kitchen as well. About to head up the steps, she paused in her tracks when she heard Jay's voice from the parlor. She didn't want to intrude on his conversation, but she knew she had heard him say King's name. Curious as to how her son was taking the news, she decided to listen in.

"I haven't spoken with Lotus," Jay was saying. "I don't know if he's awake or what his condition is. I need you to go see him, though. I don't want to upset him, but he needs to know what I'm up against. See how he's doing first, he might be able to handle it."

Carmen stepped away from the door, hearing her father's name. Since she had left Brookstone so abruptly, she wasn't able to get an update on his condition. If King went to visit him, he could possibly report back to Jay before the night was over. She hoped that Jay was willing to talk to her despite their breakup. Hoping that he would, Carmen returned to her room.

Chapter Thirty-Eight

Brookstone, New York

From what King could see, there were two empty chairs on the opposite side of his grandfather's bed. His grandmother wasn't there, which made him feel like his timing was perfect. King was apprehensive about striking up a conversation with his grandfather because he was unsure of how his speech was. When Lotus started talking first, it shocked King as he sat down in one of the empty chairs. Lotus spoke above a whisper, which forced King to move his chair closer to the bed.

"The-they can't keep us down," Lotus told him. "No ma-matter what, we come back stronger than ever, you k-know. The-they try, thou-though. The-they do."

King knew that grandfather's words fell in line with their current situation. The Triad was hours away from tearing down everything they had worked for. Once his father turned himself in, King believed that he would be forced to witness the slow demise of their fortune. He had already helped his father bounce back one time but he was unsure if he could do it again. A part of him hoped that his grandfather could lead him in the right direction.

To start the conversation, King reached over the railing of his grandfather's bed and turned on the television. He changed the channel to CNN so that Lotus could see the story for himself. While the shootout had occurred hours earlier, Blue Magic was still the topic of the city. "Jay is planning on turning himself in. Right now, he's in Puerto Rico. My mom went with him and she took Rakim and Nyla. They're supposed to be coming back in the morning."

After a few minutes of watching the footage, Lotus turned his head away from the television screen. With the effects of the stroke still upon him, he didn't need his blood pressure going up. "The Tri-Triad stopped by here," he admitted. "The-they wanted in-information on Jay. Patricia and I didn't know anything at the time. We told them that." Lotus looked directly in King's face so he could see his grandson's expression. King would never admit it verbally, but Lotus could see his grandson was stressed. He had been given a lot of responsibility in a short amount of time. He also could see another problem hidden in King's eyes. "What are you th-thinking?"

King let out a nervous chuckle. "I can never deal with one issue. I try to focus on one thing, but another one always comes along. Right now, I don't have any respect for my father. I'm out here working my ass off for him, but I don't want to be. I'm doing it because I have to protect myself. I have ties to everything that Jay has. He's not even giving me time to concentrate on the things that I'm dealing with. Rico is dead and Jerome is down South somewhere. I can't find him because I'm dealing with Jay's shit. He runs off to Puerto Rico and leaves me here with assignments. I have to make sure the paperwork is straight, make sure the money adds up, so he and Gomez can argue against money laundering charges. I can't do this much longer, Grandpa. I need to break out."

Lotus didn't favor the idea of King breaking away from his father although he understood his concern. He knew their relationship was scarred, but neither of them was to blame. Jay was being forced to play catch up with a son who had already been raised. They both needed to be patient with each other. "He needs you right no-now," he finally replied. "He loves you. He doesn't know how to show it yet. Trust me."

King refused to believe his grandfather's words because it didn't match up with his father's actions. For one, Jay had never asked him about his feelings regarding the shootout. He had simply called him with a list of tasks. It was like Jay had forgotten that he had almost lost his life.

As he was about to express that to his grandfather, he noticed that Lotus was pointing at the television screen. King focused his eyes in that direction to see a familiar face standing behind a reporter. Since his stepfather had been fired from both of his jobs, he didn't expect to see him at Blue Magic. However, Kane was there amongst the onlookers.

"Everything is on you," Lotus said, turning off the television. "You might not want it to be, but it is. Yo-your parents need you right no-now."

King looked away from the blank screen, allowing his eyes to fall back onto his grandfather. "I know," he admitted. "I know I have to come through for them. I got to find a way to deal with my own shit." King rose to his feet, taking another look at the television screen. He wasn't quite sure where he was headed, but something told him to stop by Blue Magic. The news broadcast was live, which meant that his stepfather was still at the restaurant. If he was able to catch up with him, he could potentially find out the status of the case. In return, he would know what they were up against. He didn't expect Kane to tell him much, but he would accept any information he would give.

***

For the first time in more than twenty years, Kane was on the opposite side of the yellow tape. It hurt him to watch his former colleagues surveying the area while he had to stand alongside the media and residents of Brookstone. He hadn't learned much aside from what the news was reporting. Apparently, shortly after Jay had walked out of the restaurant, a slew of gunshots were fired. Ten bodies later, Jay was nowhere to be found, which made him top the Triad's Most Wanted list. Kane was confident that the situation had finally given him the lead that he had been looking for. The bad part was that the Triad now knew more than he did. The yellow tape in front of him was his main barrier from gathering evidence.

When he noticed Sanders walking behind a body bag, they made eye contact. With Donnie missing and a slew of bodies outside of his wife's restaurant, Kane knew that his presence wouldn't be ignored. He was valuable to Sanders and his old partner knew it, which was why he lifted up the yellow tape. Kane gladly crossed over to the other side now that he had permission to join him. He knew Sanders wasn't going to tell him much, but he was desperate for any information.

"Where should I start?" Sanders asked. "Here," he said, pointing, "we have three lovely Benzes. Over here," he continued, "are ten dead bodies. All of the men are African-American except one. Some had IDs on them, which showed that they are all from different parts of the United States. A few are from Connecticut, a couple from Georgia, and one is from right here in New York. That one was identified as Gus Lopez. He's supposedly Jay's limo driver and the only non-black that was murdered."

Kane didn't move an inch as he looked the scene over. He knew Jay was involved because his driver was found dead, but he couldn't quite put a finger on who could have been attacking him. With three Benzes involved, he knew the person coming after Jay was in a high tax bracket. Whether the money was legal or illegal, it was there.

"I'm telling you all this because the lieutenant saw you over there. You've been watching this thing for a minute. Not to mention, the Commissioner of the Philadelphia Police Department sent over two missing persons' reports the other day. Two boys from Philly are missing. According to a friend of theirs who could be a potential witness, they were last seen arguing with one of Jay's workers. Did you know Jay had business dealings in Philly?"

Kane shook his head as he studied one of the Benzes. Aside from a few bullet holes in the driver's side door, there wasn't much damage.

Sanders walked alongside the Benz, scoping it out as well. "Right now, Jay has thirteen bodies on his hands. I personally, don't think he killed his driver so let's say twelve. The nine bodies found here, Jarrod Luis who's still missing, and those two guys from Philly. We don't know if he fired the gun, but we're adding them to his body count."

Kane took his eyes off the Benz so that he could study Sanders' face. He thought he knew where the man was leading the conversation, but he wasn't so sure. He had told him a lot for someone who wasn't on the force. "What are you saying exactly?"

"The Brookstone PD needs you. The lieutenant wants to get you reinstated so you can help us get Jay. We also need you to get one of these witnesses to talk. You made Jarrod snitch; we know you can do the same with them. Right now, they are admitting to hearing a lot of gunfire. A few said that Jay was eating inside with Stephen Franklin before the shooting. That statement alone is proof that the two are connected. If we put these murders with the coke, Jay won't see the light of day. So, do you want in?"

Kane felt the question was rhetorical. Sanders should have known that he wanted in. He knew he had to go through some hurdles before he could officially become reinstated, but he was ready. "Tell me what you need me to do," he replied.

"Do you think you can find Malik Washington? Maybe he has some insight on what happened here."

Kane shrugged his shoulders. "It's worth a shot. He can't be too far from this city. More than likely, he's at Sapphire." Kane retrieved his keys from his pocket, deciding to go ahead and start the search. "Get the lieutenant started on the paperwork. As soon as it's official then I can tell Roberts that I'm not coming back to the Triad. The last thing I need them thinking is that I'm working on this investigation for them."

"He'll handle all that," Sanders assured him. "Go find Malik."

Kane told him he would and headed back to his car. His old partner had given him a lot of information that he could work with. As he started up his car, Kane began to wonder if he could get Malik to talk. Their relationship had been rocky for the past couple of months, but he believed that a friendship was still there. He might not tell him as much as he wanted to know, but he knew he could get Malik to say something.

When he drove away from the restaurant, he couldn't help but to notice King's car passing him. He was shocked to see him, but he didn't bother to stop. For now, it was in his best interest to continue on to Sapphire. If Malik wasn't there then he would go to his house. It meant getting Tiara involved, but that was a small concern in relation to the situation at hand. Lucky for him, Malik was emerging from Sapphire's doors when he pulled up. "Get in," he told him after rolling down the passenger side window. "We need to talk."

"Fuck that shit," Malik shot back. He quickly locked the doors to the club before heading to his car. When he saw Kane step outside of his vehicle, he knew he wasn't getting away so easy. "Go on with this bullshit, Kane," he told him, unlocking his car doors.

"What did I tell you?" Kane asked him, blocking Malik from getting inside. "I told you to clean up your shit, didn't I? Now you got the Brookstone PD about to put an APB on your ass. What happened at Blue Magic, Malik? Who's gunning after Jay?"

Malik pushed Kane away from his car, opening up the driver's side door. "I don't have shit to do with that. I wasn't even downtown when it happened. I'm in the dark like you are." Malik tried to slide inside, but Kane pushed him away before he could.

"How long are you going to keep protecting him, Malik? There are thirteen bodies attached to Jay's name right now. Someone has to take the fall. If it's not him, it's going to be you."

"Are you threatening me?" Malik took a step away from his car so he had more room to maneuver. He walked closer to Kane so that they were standing toe to toe. "You did this same shit twenty-something years ago, Kane. I gave you what you wanted then. You don't remember? We made a deal. I gave you everything you wanted to know about Jay. I led you right to him. You got what you wanted. You took him down, I kept my freedom. Now, you want me to do this shit again? It's not happening. I'm not putting another skeleton in my closet. Jay is legit right now. We all are. He doesn't have anything to go down for."

"Failing is not an option," Kane responded, sternly. "I'm pulling out all of the stops. I got a job on the line and a marriage. Whatever I have to do, whoever I have to take down, I will do it. I can easily put those men on your body count. Shit, how do you think Jay will feel when he learns that you're to blame for the seventeen he spent in prison? He put you in this shit and you spit on his name."

Malik shoved Kane away from his car. He pulled his glock out of his waistband, aiming it at Kane's head. "I will splatter your fuckin' brains right here for the world to see. Don't test me, Kane. If you open your mouth, I swear on my brother's grave, I will kill you."

"Then tell me where Jay is."

Malik fumed with anger. "You don't get it, do you?" Kane didn't respond to him, but it didn't matter. He slid his gun back into his waistband, covering it with his shirt-tail. "Jay knows you're looking for him. You won't have to look for long. He's turning himself in. You and the fuckin' Brookstone PD will have him in less than twenty-four hours. You're so worried about catching him; you should be worried about your wife whose still fuckin' him."

Malik had said a mouthful, but he still wasn't quite finished with the conversation. He got in, started up the car, and pressed his foot softly on the accelerator. He allowed the car to inch forward as he rolled down the driver's side window. "Jay doesn't even want to give y'all the pleasure of arresting him. Call off your Girl Scouts; he'll be on his way to the station soon."

Kane watched in anger as Malik sped off. Well aware that his wife was sleeping with Jay, he didn't appreciate Malik throwing it up in his face. Kane wanted more than anything to make amends with his wife. He would apologize a thousand times but he couldn't even get her to hear him out.

Kane looked down at the ground as his focus changed. He was supposed to be getting more information on Jay, but now his mind was centered on Carmen. He wanted to talk to her and he figured the hospital would be a good place to start.

By the time he was outside of Lotus' room, he realized that he had made a mistake. The door to his father-in-law's room was wide open, allowing him to see that Carmen wasn't there. Only Patricia was inside, her eyes firmly planted on the news. It took a few seconds for her to notice him in the doorway, but once she did, her whole persona changed.

"Well, well, well, if it isn't our son-in-law," Patricia voiced, standing up from the recliner. "I thought we had seen enough Triad agents, but we had to get a visit from one more. Did you come to question us, too? Knowing you, you're probably on the hunt for your wife." Patricia took a few steps forward, deciding to let her husband handle him. "I'll be in the lobby. Let me know when y'all are finished."

Kane stared at his mother-in-law as she left the room. Instead of cursing her, he headed to the recliner where she had been sitting. Lotus was still watching the television, but that didn't stop Kane from talking. "I don't want to upset you. I know this is a difficult time."

Lotus turned off the TV, putting an end to the extra noise. "Wh-wh-what do you want?"

"I came by this morning, but you were still asleep. I wanted to talk to you about Carmen. You've been watching the news so you know what she's up against. I want to help her, but she won't let me. I figured that you could help me. I know that what I did with Rakim was wrong and I've apologized. I want to put it behind us."

Lotus shifted his body at Kane's request. He believed wholeheartedly that his son-in-law's time with Carmen was only for a season. He didn't feel comfortable saying it. Kane was already suffering enough and a straightforward comment would dampen his spirits more than aid. On the other hand, Lotus didn't want to feed him empty hope. "Carmen is a grown woman. She will make her decision in due time."

"So you know about her and Jay?" Kane asked him. "She told you about them? Or are you on his side?"

In Lotus' opinion, he wasn't taking sides. He was trying to speak the truth. When he looked at his daughter, he could see for himself that she was torn between two men. Each of them gave her what the other one didn't. Carmen longed for the traditional household, which Kane gave her while Jay fed her desire of a quick thrill. Since Nyla's birth, he could tell that Carmen was trying to shape Jay into the man that she needed. His godson had done very well, breaking away from the cartel and becoming more family-oriented. Moreover, his past wouldn't change with him, which resulted in the shootout at Blue Magic. Carmen had chosen Jay, but with the recent events, her decision may have become void.

"I want my wife back, Lotus. At this point, I don't know what to do. She won't talk to me. She looks at me like I'm nothing. When she looks at him, though…sometimes I wonder; what does he have that I don't? Is it the money? Is it the power? Is it the fact that he can walk into a room and people bow down to him? Maybe, it's the obvious. He can make a baby."

Lotus had hoped that Kane had read between the lines, but he hadn't. It was making the conversation difficult for him because he was running off of a little bit of energy. "Everything that you are saying is being told to the wrong person. You need to ask her these things. Be-be-sides, y-y-your own mist-mistakes cost you your wife. It wasn't anything that Jay did. All you have to do is tell her how you feel. If she truly wants you, she'll let you know. If she doesn't, then you need to move on."

Kane knew that Lotus spoke from the heart. It hurt him to hear the words, but it was the truth of the matter. The only part where he and Lotus disagreed was in terms of him moving on. No matter how many times he had to try, he refused to be with someone else. He was certain that Carmen was the one for him; he simply had to convince her of it. Once he did, everything in his life would fall into place. Certain of it, he quickly thanked Lotus for his time before walking out the room.

***

Kane wasn't the only one who sought out Lotus' wisdom. Two hours ago, Jay had departed from San Juan on a flight back to New York. When he made the announcement to Carmen, he expected for her to fly back with him. However, to his surprise, she told him that she wasn't. He pretended to be nonchalant about her decision, but it had hurt him to the core. She knew what he was up against, but refused to stick by his side. She was the main reason he went to the hospital. He had sent King there earlier to deliver a message for him, but now he needed Lotus for himself.

Since he was still a wanted man, he opted to take the steps instead of the elevator. When he reached Lotus' floor, he stared through the door's glass window to see if anyone was in the hall. With visiting hours being over, the hallway was fairly empty. Hoping he could sneak pass the nurses' station, he twisted the doorknob, preparing to walk inside. Unfortunately, his plans were halted when he saw Kane turn the corner. "Shit," he muttered, heading back into the stairwell. He knew that Kane hadn't seen him, but there was still a chance that he would take the steps instead of the elevator. He watched him carefully and when he passed by the door, Jay let out a sigh of relief. He quickly moved to the other side, watching as Kane pressed the button for the elevator. When he got on, Jay opened the door, walking quickly to Lotus' room.

Naturally, his heart rate increased as he drew closer to his destination. Since he couldn't see Lotus' room from the stairwell, he didn't know if there was a Triad agent nearby. At this point, Jay believed they would be exhausting all options to get him behind bars. Obviously, that wasn't their plan because Lotus' door was wide open with no agent in sight. Jay walked inside without hesitation, closing the door behind him.

"Vi-Vi-Visiting hours are over," Lotus announced with a yawn. "Come back tomorrow."

Jay stood by his godfather's bedside, listening to the sound of the television. "You see that?" he asked, looking up at the screen. "Tomorrow isn't an option," he told him as his mug-shot was displayed. "I only have right now." Jay looked down at the controls on the side of Lotus' bed. He found the one for the television and turned it off.

"Do you want to tell me wh-wh-what happened?"

If Jay answered honestly, his reply would've been no. He didn't come to discuss the charges he was facing. However, if he didn't tell Lotus now, he might not get the chance. "Long story short, I brought a guy up from Georgia who somehow got schooled on my operation. He wants revenge because I shut down the cartel without giving him a spot. He came at Carmen and then he came at me. He put his men on my ass and I left a bloodbath at Blue Magic. Now, the police want me in cuffs."

"Y-Y-You acted out of self-defense?"

"Of course, but you know how the Triad rolls. They are going to put anything they can on my name. If anything, I hope the judge will give me bail. At least, I can still see my kids. I have a good defense team lined up so I'm sure I can get out of this one."

Lotus raised his arm, pointing to an empty seat on the other side of the bed. "Sit down, son. I need you to get a sheet of paper. An ink pen should be behind that pitcher. I want you to write something down."

Jay didn't plan to have a long visit, but he complied with Lotus' wishes. He grabbed the paper and pen, taking a seat in the recliner. With the tone that his godfather used, Jay knew that he wanted to discuss something serious.

"There are three words that I need you to pay attention to, three very important words."

Jay nodded his head, indicating to Lotus that he was ready. When he said the name, Carmen Denise Davenport, Jay set the pen and paper back on the meal counter. Those were three words that he didn't want to write. Now that their relationship was over, Jay knew that he had to move on. He had given her more than twenty years of his life, but she had left him when he needed her the most. Jay told himself that he couldn't wait on her any longer.

"I gave you a direct or-order."

"We're done," he told him. "We broke up a few hours ago. As far as I'm concerned, Carmen and I don't have anything else to discuss unless it's about our kids and Blue Magic."

Lotus used most of the strength he had to sit up. He pointed towards the meal counter once again. "Get the pen and paper." He gave Jay a deadly expression to let his godson know that he was serious. It took Jay a second or two to comply, but when he did, Lotus watched as the man scribbled down his daughter's name. "I need you to use every piece of defense that you have in that courtroom. I also need you to make me a pr-pr-promise."

"What's the promise?" Jay questioned. "It has something to do with Carmen?"

"I want you to take care of her. I'm begging you."

Jay could see that there was a hidden agenda behind Lotus' request. Regardless of his current situation with Carmen, he would always be set on protecting his family. Nothing could change that, not even a prison cell. As he agreed to the task, Jay noticed the stream of tears on his godfather's face. "I promise you," he assured him. "I swear on my life. I will always take care of her. No worries, okay?" Lotus nodded, but Jay didn't feel at ease to leave his side. He waited until he had calmed down before he made his exit.

While the police station was supposed to be his next destination, he wasn't quite ready to turn himself in. For the time being, he needed to clear his head. When he stepped back into his limousine, Cesar seemed to sense that he didn't want to talk so he started up the car without saying a single word to him. For most of the night, Cesar drove him around Brookstone in complete silence. They passed the police station multiple times, but Jay never told Cesar to stop. However, he knew he had to say something when Cesar parked the limousine in front of King's house. Originally owned by Carmen's parents and Kane, it wasn't the ideal place that he wanted to be. Yet, Cesar had brought him there for a reason.

"While you were at the hospital, King called me. He said he had talked to you earlier, but he didn't get a chance to talk to you about what happened at Blue Magic. He said you rushed him off the phone after telling him to go see Lotus."

Jay stared at the back of Cesar's head as he felt offended at how he was talking to him. He hadn't rushed King off the phone like he was implying. He had merely said what he needed to say and the conversation had ended.

"He's in this with you, too, Jay. There's more that y'all need to discuss then how to cover up this drug shit. He's your son and right now, I feel like he wants to talk to you as one. In his mind, he could've lost his father yesterday. Did you think about that?"

"Mind your fuckin' business." The response silenced Cesar right before he and Jay met eyes in the rearview mirror. The look that Jay gave him was enough for Cesar to know that he didn't want to be at King's house.

"Carmen is still planning on returning in the morning," Cesar responded, backing out of the driveway, "Maybe, you can see her and the kids before you turn yourself in since you don't want to see King."

Jay mumbled, "Fuck you," under his breath. He couldn't have cared less about what Cesar thought. All he wanted him to do was drive around the city. He didn't care for how long either. He wanted to stretch out his freedom for as long as he could.

Chapter Thirty-Nine

The following morning, Carmen did return to Brookstone. When she approached her house, she expected for Jay's limo to be parked out front, but it wasn't there. She regretted the way they had ended things since he was at a point where almost everyone was ready to put him at the stake. Carmen didn't want him to think that she was one of them. Somehow, she had to find a way to change his mind about her. It wasn't something that was going to be easily done if he had already turned himself in.

As Linx parked the car, she unbuckled her seat belt so she could get Nyla and Rakim out. They both had been rather quiet during the commute, which made her believe that they could feel the tension. Hoping that being at home could change their moods, she picked Nyla up before grabbing Rakim's hand. She headed to the front door while Linx gathered their bags. As she was about to open it, she paused when she heard the sound of a motor. Carmen turned to look behind her, and saw Kane's Jeep pulling up behind the limousine.

"Can we talk for a minute?" he yelled as he got out of the car.

Carmen told him yes before unlocking the door. She told Linx to put the bags on the floor before handing Nyla and Rakim over to him. He seemed a little hesitant in taking the kids, but eventually he grabbed both of them before disappearing into the dining room. By that time, Kane was standing in the foyer with her.

"You didn't have to send them away," he said with a smile. Kane closed the front door, putting on all the locks. "I wanted to come by and let you know that Harris is working on getting me reinstated. After the shootout, they realized they needed me so I'm waiting for the paperwork to be finalized. Once it's a go, I'm back in."

Carmen could feel the word, congratulations, on the tip of her tongue. She didn't say it because she realized why Harris had re-enlisted Kane. He had taken down Jay before and Harris was set on having him do it again. The hurtful part was that she knew Kane wanted the job. He would do anything to get Jay back in prison.

"You don't seem so excited about that, but I knew you wouldn't be," Kane continued. "At least I got my job back. I don't have to keep using my savings to pay on my place. Now I have some steady income." Kane walked towards the stairwell, taking a seat on the second step. "What I really came over here to talk about is us. I know there is a lot going on right now, but I want us to get back together."

Carmen's eyes blinked at Kane's words. Before she could stop herself, her honest thoughts were spoken. "You're kidding me, right? Like, are you seriously asking me this?" Carmen walked over and stood directly over him. "Kane, I know I haven't filed the papers, but I still want a divorce."

"Look, I know the timing is off with what's going on at Blue Magic, but it was like now or never. I talked to your father—" Kane wasn't allowed to finish.

"You talked to my father," Carmen interrupted. "Do my parents have to know every little thing that goes in my life? Damn, Kane, did you talk to the minister, too? He's known about our marital problems for years."

"Carm, I'm trying. All I'm asking is that you try, too. Give us another chance."

Carmen took a deep breath, seeing how serious Kane was about the situation. She knew in her heart that she didn't want to get back with him. Still, she had to give him an answer. "I love you, Kane, I do. I will never lie about that. However, I'm not in love with you. I also don't want to be in a relationship with you. There are other things I want."

"It's Jay, isn't it?"

Carmen wrapped her arms across her chest unsure if she wanted to admit that Jay was the reason. She knew it was the truth, but saying it to a man who was begging for her heart wasn't an easy thing to do. "Jay and I are not together. Were we? Yes, but we're not together anymore. I am in love with him, but there are some differences between us. Some things have been said that I can't take back. Yet, I hope that things can work out between us. I love him." Kane stood up off the step, forcing Carmen to take a few steps back. She could see it in his eyes that he was hurt that she had rejected him. More so because she had told him that she wanted to be with Jay. It hurt her to say the words, but she couldn't force herself into a relationship she didn't want to be in. It would only create misery and tension.

"I can't let you go," Kane replied. "I can't."

Carmen bit her lip. She didn't know what words needed to be said to get Kane to understand that their relationship was over. He wanted to hang on while she had already given up. Sighing at the thought, she felt some relief when Linx returned to the foyer with Nyla and Rakim. It was the interruption she needed to take away the awkward moment. Kane even made his way to the door when Linx had appeared. He left moments later, ending the conversation altogether. Carmen couldn't utter a word, choosing to look over at Linx. His face seemed to read, *what now?* Carmen wished she had an answer for him, but she didn't. All she could do was take the kids from his arms as she tried to figure out her next move.

"I talked to Cesar," Linx announced. "Jay hasn't turned himself in."

Carmen exhaled as she looked down at her kids. "I don't want him to hold out for too long," she admitted. "Shoot, to be honest, I don't even know what I want right now." Carmen closed her eyes, reopening them when she realized what it was that she truly needed. "Look, Fiona will be here soon. I really need to see my father to clear my head of some things. She can take care of the kids while I'm gone. Why don't you go catch up with Jay? I know there's something that he needs for you to do."

"Mrs. Davenport, we both know that even if I'm not standing where you can see me, I will be around. Jay pays me to do that. If you want to go see your father, fine, but I will be going with you. You can even drive yourself if you want. I'll follow."

"Done," Carmen responded. "You can hang out in the lounge until Fiona gets here. Once she arrives, I'll be on my way out." Carmen headed up the steps to her bedroom, leaving Linx in the foyer. She hoped he made himself comfortable because there was about an hour to go before Fiona was set to arrive. When her maid did enter the house, Carmen left Nyla and Rakim with her while she headed over to the hospital. Only a short drive, she made it there in less than ten minutes. Her father was asleep when she walked into the room, but it took only a few seconds for him to sense her presence.

"I th-thought you were your mother," he mumbled, yawning. "Where's Patricia?"

Carmen's face broke into a smile as she sat down in one of the recliners. "Considering the time, I'm guessing she's in the cafeteria. When was the last time you saw her?"

Lotus shrugged his shoulders. "She was here this morning. I don't remember her leaving. Maybe she did go get a bite to eat. Who knows? Shoot, we need the privacy. How are you? A lot is going on, I see."

Carmen let out a deep breath unsure of how to answer the question. "You know how I am, Daddy. My children's father is about to turn himself in. My husband wants me back, and I haven't spoken to Kristian or Akaila. They don't know anything about what's going on. They don't even know that you had a stroke. Add that to the fact that I have a million dollar business to look after and two babies; I'm a nervous wreck." Carmen looked down at her father, seeing his eyes slowly starting to close back. She knew he was tired, but she still craved his attention. Touching his hand, she watched as his eyes fluttered back open. "You do know that Nyla was in the car with Jay?"

"He mentioned it."

"I was considering getting full custody of the kids. Right now, I'm trying to figure out if it's the right thing. Jay thinks I'm doing this to hurt him. I only want to protect them. I want him to be in their lives, but he's not going to change. He told me that out of his own mouth. I can't risk losing my kids because their father wants to be a killer. I refuse to."

Lotus was shocked at Carmen's words, but even more shocked that Jay hadn't told him about Carmen's plans. He now knew the reason why their relationship was over. Jay would do anything for his kids including laying down his life. With Carmen threatening to take them away, he could see Jay forming a deep hatred for her. "You can't do this to him, Pea-Pea-Peaches. This is wrong. Jay was doing real well, yo-you kn-kn-know?"

Carmen didn't hesitate in her reply. "Jay and I have already talked about it. He knows I'm thinking about it. He doesn't like it, but he's not willing to change either. You—" Carmen didn't finish her statement. She could tell she was upsetting her father from the way his chest was moving. "Are you okay?"

"Yo-Yo-You're going to make me cr-cr-croak!"

Carmen grinned in response to her father's humor. "I haven't filed anything yet, Daddy. I wish that you and Jay could see that this could be for the best."

"The best for whom? You didn't need a cu-cu-custody agr-agreement before. Why do you need one n-now? Jay has been a kill-killer since the day you met him. Y-Y-You didn't have a pr-problem with it when he kill-killed that guy who tried to rap-rap-rape you. Y-You're doing this out of anger. That's not the way to go, Peaches. It's not."

Carmen grunted not wanting to hear her father's words. Without a doubt, she knew that she was angry at Jay for what happened at Blue Magic. Saying that her anger was the underlying reason for the custody suit was something she didn't want to admit. So she chose to say she wanted to protect her kids. "What do you want me to do, Daddy?" Carmen waited for a response, but she knew she wasn't going to get one. Her father's eyes were slowly closing again, meaning that his medicine was making him sleepy. "I guess that's the answer," she muttered. Carmen looked down at the floor, spotted her purse, and picked it up. Knowing she needed to head back home, she leaned over her father's bedside, and kissed his forehead. "I love you," she whispered. Carmen smiled, seeing his eyes reopen. "I knew you were faking it."

Carmen sat down on her father's bed, grabbing his hand. The hurt in her father's face made her wish that she had never said anything about the custody suit. The last thing she wanted to do was disappoint him.

Meanwhile, Lotus stared at his daughter, as a million and one questions came into his mind. The questions were combined with shame. He had always blamed himself for his daughter's downfall. A part of him still wanted to know why his daughter had followed in his footsteps. He had protected her from his past for so long that he never thought she would turn out the way that she did. Even though she had changed for the better, he knew that Carmen still had her ways about her. It was obvious when she mentioned the custody suit. He prayed that he could talk her out of it. "Promise me, Peaches."

Carmen looked down at her father, realizing that he was squeezing her hand. "I promise you that I'll think about it. Who knows where Jay will be next week? I might get full custody by default."

Lotus appreciated her answer, but he had another promise he wanted her to make. "Promise me, Peaches," he repeated, giving her hand another squeeze. "Pr-Pr-Promise me that you'll take care of Jay; I beg you."

Carmen was confused by his request. It didn't help that he was squeezing the hell out of her hand either. It was like he wanted her to know that he was serious. "Daddy, what are you talking about? You know I'm going to stay in contact with him. We have kids together."

"I want you to take care of Jay. He's all I have left of Hector."

"Oh, I see," Carmen replied, "I understand, perfectly." She gave her father's hand a squeeze of its own before planting another kiss on his forehead. "I will take care of him," she told him, "and I also want you to know that I love you." Carmen stood up, but she didn't leave the room. She stayed there for another ten minutes until her father fell asleep. Although she was surprised that her mother hadn't returned, Carmen didn't bother to look for her. Instead, she decided to start the search for Jay. She had seen firsthand how the mention of a lawsuit affected her father. If she mended things with Jay, she could change her father's attitude. She knew he loved her regardless, but she wanted to make him proud. As she walked to the door, she hoped that she could get her father to see her in a positive light.

Chapter Forty

Carmen stopped in her tracks as a black limousine approached her at the front entrance of the hospital. When the passenger side window rolled down, Carmen tried her best to peek inside. She could only see half of the driver's face, but it was enough to let her know that it was Linx. "So, you weren't behind me?" she asked him.

"Things got switched around. Cesar is behind you. Jay made me your new driver."

Carmen hesitated. The sudden change made her believe that Jay was up to another trick. "What's going on, Linx? My car is parked over there," she told him, holding up her keys. "You know I drove."

"No problems, Mrs. Davenport, get in, okay?"

Carmen looked out into the parking lot, but she knew to follow his order. Opening up the back door, she caught a small glimpse of Cesar as he walked behind the limousine. She was curious about where she was headed, but she didn't voice it. More than likely, Linx wouldn't tell her, even if she did ask. Since the first day she had met him, he had always been secretive. As she got in the car, Carmen couldn't stop her mind from wandering. She reasoned that if Cesar was behind her then she had to believe that Jay had turned himself in. Her stomach dropped with guilt as she remembered the promise she had made to her father.

"You're not looking too good back there," Linx voiced, looking at the rearview mirror. "You want to talk about the waterfalls?"

Carmen wiped her face in an attempt to hide her tears. "I…," she couldn't get the words out. Part of the reason was because Linx wasn't a person that she felt she could talk to. Jay had put her in a position where she had to trust him with her life, but not with her deepest thoughts. Still, there was one question that Carmen desperately needed to ask. "Do you know where Jay is?"

"Mrs. Davenport, you're testing me."

"Look, if you can't tell me, I understand. I only want to talk to him."

Carmen looked into the rearview mirror, so she could look at him directly. He didn't respond to her request, but she knew he was going to oblige. He quickly changed lanes, sliding into the median. It was followed by a quick left turn, going back the way they had come. When he took another turn, Carmen knew for sure that they were headed to Jay's apartment complex.

"You know the risks associated with you going up there, don't you?" Linx looked back up in the rearview mirror so he could see Carmen's face. "Word already came through that the Triad has the place watched like a hawk. They haven't made a move because they think Jay's got men locked and loaded. You go up there; you might be leading them to him."

"I don't care, I need to see him," Carmen replied as he pulled up in front of the building.

"It's your call. I'll be down here waiting."

Carmen tried to ease out a small smile, but it came out rather lopsided. She simply told him thanks and headed out of the limo. She walked quickly, bypassing the security guard. Normally he opened the door for her, but this time he didn't even acknowledge her presence. She didn't let it disturb her, hurrying to Jay's apartment. Once she was in front of his door, she knocked multiple times until it flew open. "I'm sorry, I'm sorry," she said, repeatedly, grabbing him into her arms.

"Carmen, I'm about to le—" Jay didn't finish his sentence as he closed the door behind her. He locked it with his one free hand while she held on to the other one.

Carmen raised her hands to his face, pulling him towards her, but she felt his resistance. "Jay, please, I was wrong. I'll admit it."

"Carmen, calm down, what happened?"

"I'm sorry," she told him. Carmen looked at Jay strangely, wondering why he didn't understand her apology. "I'm sorry about the custody suit. I don't want it. I was mad at you and I messed up. I'm sorry. I don't want to break up."

Jay took a step back, trying to get his thoughts together. He was on his way to the Brookstone PD and Carmen's visit had taken him by surprise. Now, he didn't know which way to turn. He wanted to stand there and make up with her while he knew he had to get out of the apartment. At any moment, he could be arrested. "I guess this was a now or never thing, huh? Your timing was definitely on point," he told her, moving onto the couch. "Dang, Peaches, I don't even know what to think. You pull this on me right before I'm about to turn myself in?"

Carmen shrugged her shoulders. "I took a chance," she told him. She stood over him, seeing the concern in his face. "I'll go with you if you want me, too." She rubbed the sides of his face where his temple was starting to throb. She could tell that his nerves were starting to get to him. "Calm down," she told him, "we're going to fight this. Death before dishonor, remember?"

Jay did remember. Closing his eyes, he tried to relax, but it was hard to do. It was like a ticking time bomb was sounding off in his ears. He was waiting for the room to erupt. Eventually, the sound faded as he placed his concentration on Carmen's hands. Her technique was doing the trick as he found his blood pressure decreasing. He concentrated on clearing his mind, but Carmen was making the task difficult. When he felt her legs sliding on top of his, his mind went straight to the gutter. He opened his eyes and stared at her, moving his hands down to her legs as he pulled the bottom of her white chiffon dress up towards her waist. His eyes asked her for permission, but something told him that he didn't need it. When she neared her face closer to his, Jay knew she had given in. Their lips became intertwined as he ran his hands in between her inner thighs.

"Carm, wait," he said, breaking away. Jay watched her as she moved off his lap, pulling her dress back down. "This might not be the best time."

Carmen took a step back, knowing that she had rushed things a bit. She didn't expect things to get as steamy as they did, but now she was in the mood. At this point, losing the moment wasn't an option. Despite Jay's concern, Carmen only had one thing on her mind. Proving it to him, she slid her arms around his neck. "I love you," she whispered as she kissed his lips. "More than I ever have."

It was Jay's intention to repeat the words to her, but he didn't get the chance. Carmen's legs became tightly wrapped around his waist as he lifted her off her feet. He carried her to his bedroom, unzipping her dress at the same time. It fell at her waist, revealing a violet embroidered bra. He was pleased with the visual so he pulled the rest of the dress down to her ankles until her matching panties became visible. His eyes zoomed in on the crown of her head before outlining the rest of her body like it was a map. It was evident that he was sexually long overdue as he began to feel his dick throbbing inside of his pants. Quickly undressing, he climbed on top of her until he was centered in between her legs.

For Carmen, the whole world seemed to stop as Jay took one of his fingers, and slid it down her mid-section. Although she had spent countless nights in his arms, there was something different about this particular moment. It was like she knew she was connecting with her soul mate. She cupped his face in her hands as she brought him closer to her. Kissing his lips, she moaned softly as he entered her. In an instant, her thoughts became incoherent as he thrusted inside of her repeatedly. Initially, his pace was slow, but as the excitement grew, Carmen could feel his thrusts getting deeper and rougher. As much as Carmen enjoyed it, she pushed him up and off of her. She felt the need to take charge, so she climbed on top of him.

Feeling his hands on her hips, Carmen used the headboard for leverage to increase her momentum as he guided her back and forth over his manhood. As hard as they were going, Carmen wasn't surprised to feel the vibrations of the bed as it rocked underneath them. Even the headboard was knocking up against the bedroom wall. Seconds later, the sound was accompanied by what sounded like a fist pounding on a door. Carmen could have sworn that Jay heard it too when he slowed her pace. As the banging persisted in getting louder, Carmen mumbled, "Shit." She overlooked the sound coming from the other side of the wall as she felt herself lose control; she then moaned loudly and climaxed.

"Put your motherfucking hands up!"

Carmen jerked the flat sheet over her nude body as she stared at the police officers who flooded the room. Mortified, she tumbled off of Jay before falling onto the floor. Tightening the sheet around her, she watched as one of the officers took off his black hooded mask. Carmen recognized him as Sanders. The sight of the man told her that she was up against more than she could handle. Nervous, Carmen stood up while simultaneously trying to ensure that she was fully covered. Meanwhile, Jay was still fully exposed on the bed.

"I dare you to fuckin' move!" Sanders yelled. "Toss them some clothes."

Carmen's chest heaved up and down, watching as one of the officers collected Jay's clothes from the floor. Another officer came toward her holding her white dress. Carmen grabbed it, quickly sliding it on. She knew why the officers were there, but the last thing she expected was for the whole department to witness her infidelity. Now, they all had firsthand knowledge of her sin.

Sanders looked at Carmen, but remained silent. Although he suspected that she was cheating, he didn't know it to actually be true. However, at the moment he couldn't focus on the affair. Seeing that Jay was now fully dressed, he began the process of arresting him, "Jay Santiago, you are under arrest."

"I figured," Jay replied. "I was going to turn myself in."

"You didn't move as quickly as you should have," Sanders shot back. "Your charges are as follows: racketeering, money laundering, and the distribution of narcotics. In addition, we have a witness who was able to place you downtown at the time ten murders were committed. You're our number one suspect." Sanders watched as Jay placed his hands behind his back. Not wasting another second, he fastened the steel cuffs around his wrists. "You have the right to remain silent. Anything you say can and will be used against you in the court of law," Sanders began. When he was done reading Jay his rights, he checked the cuffs one more time before heading towards Carmen.

"Mrs. Kane, please do not take this personal, but you are under arrest, too. The Brookstone Police Department has reason to believe that you have been allowing Jay Santiago to house his drugs in your establishment, ahem, Flame, Inc. Not only that, Santiago has been using monies from his various illegal operations to fund his soul food restaurant. This is the same restaurant in which you are listed as being his sole partner on. We have reason to believe that you were aware of his actions, so you are being charged with conspiracy." Sanders held out his hand for another pair of cuffs. Once the cold steel was in his hands, he ignored her tears as he cuffed her. "You have the right to remain silent…"

Carmen shivered as she felt the coldness from the metal on her hands. She silently thought, *Lord, this isn't happening. Tell me, this isn't happening. It can't be.* Carmen wished she could wipe her face as the tears burned her eyes. She stared over at Jay, who wore a nonchalant facial expression. *How can he be so fuckin' calm? We're both going to prison.*

"Don't tell me you're pregnant this time," he joked.

His comment made a wave of déjà vu come over her. This was the second time they found themselves being arrested together. If at any time Carmen felt like his Bonnie it was now. While it upset her that she was being arrested, Carmen still briefly smiled at his words. When the police officers escorted them out of the apartment, the grin disappeared. Neither one of them was wearing a smile as they were led outside of the apartment complex and into the littering of reporters, police officers, and Triad agents. Cameras snapped their photos left and right as they were put into the back of separate squad cars.

Now that her future was uncertain, Carmen started praying harder than before, as they were transported to the Brookstone Police Department.

Part Five:
The Aftermath

Chapter Forty-One

The first thing that Jay noticed about the interrogation room was that it was bare. Since the lieutenant wasn't in the room, he assumed that Sanders would be doing the questioning. So far, the detective had been involved with all aspects of his arrest, from booking him to placing him in a holding cell. Now, he had him sitting at an empty table.

"You have a lot of prison time ahead of you," Sanders began, sitting down. "It's a shame you had to drag Carmen down with you. You know she's being interrogated, right? Let's see if your stories match up."

Jay stared at the man blankly without giving him a response. He and Carmen had never discussed how they were going to handle the interrogations. He had to believe that Carmen wouldn't say anything that would dig a deeper grave than what they were already in. She might not have known it, but she had the power to get them both out of this predicament.

"You have a very nonchalant expression on your face," Sanders continued. "Why? All we needed is for one person to place you at the scene. Charging you for ten murders will be easy after that."

"A lot of people can place me at the scene. I own Blue Magic," Jay retorted. "I visit the restaurant on a daily basis, multiple times a day. They can say I was there all day long, but they will never say that they saw me shoot someone. Those are two different accusations."

"We are all aware that you shot somebody, Mr. Santiago. We don't even have to discuss that. In fact, let's talk about your drug business. Word is that you broke out. Somehow, we still managed to confiscate a million dollars' worth of cocaine. It was on its way to Cali; do you still have business out there?"

Jay sat back in his seat, wishing he could rest his arms in his lap. Holding his hands behind him was more uncomfortable than when he was in a strait jacket. "I want my lawyer."

"I got your drugs off an exterminator's van," Sanders responded, overlooking his request.

Jay cracked a smile. "An exterminator's van, are you serious?"

Sanders sat up straight as he could tell that Jay wasn't taking the situation serious. "You find this funny, Santiago, but you are looking at a lot of time in prison. You could get life."

Jay straightened his face, deciding to change his stance. "It isn't funny. In fact, it's a very serious matter. The thing is; I've already spent seventeen years in prison for everything y'all are accusing me of. Do I want to go back? No. I also don't want my girlfriend to go back."

"Carmen, you're speaking of Carmen?"

Jay nodded his head. "Did you like the show?"

Sanders' eyes bulged as the image of Jay and Carmen came back into his mind. It was something he had tried to forget until the man brought it up. If it wasn't for Kane's paperwork not being final, his old partner would've seen the fiasco as well. "No one expected to see that. We saw Carmen go into the building and we knew you had to be inside. It was a chance we took. As far as Kane goes, I don't intend on telling him. However, as soon as he's reinstated, he will have a chance to look at all of the documentation from the bust. I—" Sanders realized he was discussing an issue that had nothing to do with the charges against Jay. "This isn't important. What you choose to do in the privacy of your home is your business. What is important, are these drug and murder charges. Ten men were found dead outside of your restaurant. How did that happen?"

Jay leaned into the table. He found the position was more comfortable than any other since he was still handcuffed. "I'm not going to speak on anything until I've met with my lawyer. Can I get my phone call? It is my right."

Sanders looked at Jay questionably. "That's another stall tactic, Mr. Santiago. I'll let you get your phone call, but we're still going to have this conversation. Tell me what happened at Blue Magic yesterday."

Jay shifted his feet. He tried to make himself comfortable not knowing how long Sanders was going to interrogate him. "No contest," Jay replied. "You can ask me all you want. Until Gomez gets here, I'm going to keep dancing around the issue. Regardless of what I say, y'all are going to charge me and I'm going to have to fight it."

Sanders moved his chair closer to Jay and stared him in the eye. "Why are you fuckin' with me? We both know what happened at your restaurant. What I want to know is why it happened. Tell me that."

Jay chuckled at how persistent Sanders continued to be. "The Triad and the Brookstone PD both have an obsession with my family. It started with my father and carried over to me. I paid my price, and now y'all want me again. All I want right now is to take care of my family and run my businesses. There are hundreds of other drug dealers out there, but you want the man who used to sell drugs. How much money do you really think the government is going to give y'all for me? Is it millions? Will you even get a cut of it?"

Sanders scratched his forehead, knowing that Jay was fucking with him on purpose. He didn't want to admit to his crimes, but Sanders didn't need him to. With the right district attorney and the evidence he did have, he could make all the charges stick. "You have a brilliant mind, Santiago. I'll give you your props. Hopefully, you can put it to work in court." Sanders stood up, motioning for Jay to do the same. He wasn't getting anywhere with him, which was why he decided to give Jay his phone call. He hoped that after he talked with his lawyer that he could get more out of him.

He led Jay down a long corridor to a phone near the booking area of the department. He allowed him to make his phone call while he stood a few feet away out of earshot. As much as he wanted to listen in, he was distracted when an officer approached him. The officer informed him that the lieutenant wanted him in the interrogation room with Carmen. In the meantime, he would keep watch over Jay until his phone call was over. The switch wasn't something that Sanders wanted to do, but he followed Harris' order. When he entered the room where Harris was, he found him face to face with Carmen who, like Jay, was still handcuffed. Without even knowing what had been said, he could tell the two had been having an intense argument.

"Your little empire is going to go down if you don't start talking."

Carmen's face remained tight as Harris continued to coax her. He was trying to use everything he knew about her to get her to turn against Jay. He even threatened to tell Kane that they had found them in bed. Carmen had merely shrugged her shoulders when he said it although she knew that there would be repercussions if he did. Most of it would come in the form of spousal support.

"I can see the headline now," the lieutenant was saying. "The whole world is going to know about you and your little fuck partner."

A quick smile shot across Carmen's face. Her relationship with Jay wasn't something she wanted to hide anymore. She needed to be open about it. Regardless of what happened to them, she wanted the world to know that they were together.

"You're smiling, but all that money you have," Harris yelled. "It could be gone like that," he said, snapping his fingers.

Carmen rolled her eyes before looking over at Sanders. The detective hadn't said a word since coming into the room. In fact, he looked as if he didn't want to be there. When he noticed that she was looking at him, he averted his eyes to the floor. Carmen figured that the situation had become uncomfortable for him. He was Kane's partner yet he had witnessed her infidelity firsthand and then had arrested her. She didn't take his actions to heart because she knew he was simply doing his job. At the end of the day, he had to bring home a paycheck like everyone else.

"See if you can get this one to talk," Harris ordered, speaking to Sanders. "She seems to be a little tightlipped, but I know you can get something out of her. We can use anything at this point."

Not quick to speak, Sanders sat down at the table as he tried to come up with a plan. Since discovering her sexual relationship with Jay, he was even more convinced that she was aware of Jay's illegal activities. A part of him believed if he used a little compassion and wit that he could get her to talk about the incident at Blue Magic. "I know this isn't easy for any of us," he told her, softly. "You're here away from your family while I have to try and find out who's responsible for the ten murders that occurred yesterday. Let's make this a better situation, Carmen. What's going on? What happened downtown?"

"I wasn't there," Carmen replied, quickly. "All I know is what the news is reporting."

Sanders leaned onto the table after she responded. She was being tightlipped with him as well, but he wasn't going to give up. "Okay, well, let's talk about what the news is reporting. Eye witnesses say that Jay was at the restaurant when the gunshots started. He is known to have an enemy or two so obviously someone was shooting at him. They failed to make him a casualty, but that doesn't mean they won't try again. Even if we can't gather enough evidence to say that Jay shot someone, we've got enough to stick some drug charges on him."

"Whose vault did you get that from?"

"I'm not a dirty cop, Carmen," Sanders snapped. "I didn't take the drugs from the Triad's stash to get an indictment. I'm trying to clean up the streets. Unlike Kane, this isn't personal."

"We can make it personal." Carmen moved her arms as she tried to alleviate some of the pain that the handcuffs were causing. It worked, but only for a short amount of time. "Tell me something, Sanders. I know you and Kane have spent a lot of time together trying to build this case against Jay. How much did he really tell you? I mean, knowledge is power."

"I don't know what you're getting at." Sanders tried his best to read between the lines. For a brief moment, he felt as if Carmen was about to start interrogating him.

"The Triad put up a million dollar reward for Jay that no one is going to get. The Brookstone PD arrested him before a civilian could turn him in. If Jay is found guilty, the local police department will get a large sum of money versus the agency that controls most of the government's top affairs.

We both know that Kane's heart is truly with the Triad. The only reason he took a job at the Brookstone PD was because of me. He will do anything to protect the Triad like you will do anything to protect him."

"Kane and I talked about a lot of things. He never gave me a reason to believe that he might need protection from anything. He's supposed to be clean as a whistle."

"He's not," Carmen admitted. "If you want me to talk, I'll talk."

Sanders laughed as he realized the game that Carmen was trying to play. She wanted to give him a little bit of dirt, but it would only make him an accessory. "What do you want, Carmen? You're willing to give up some information for something? What is it?"

"I want you to release me and Jay."

"Of course, the obvious," Sanders replied. "Not going to happen. You both have a chance at making bail, but Jay's chances are slimmer than yours. The judge will probably set his at something in the millions to ensure he doesn't get out. Then again, Jay has millions so who knows? He might be able to pay it. This information, though? Is it worth your freedom?"

"I don't think my freedom will be threatened," she told him, playing on a hunch. "I've already paid a little debt to society."

Sanders stood on his feet as Carmen's revelation suddenly became of more interest to him. "Tell me," he ordered, "What do you know?"

"More than twenty years ago, two Triad agents planted a fake pink diamond in the house of Jay Santiago. That same pink diamond got me out of my sentence. They did this knowing that I had stolen the real Pink Sunrise."

"The two agents were..."

"My husband and another guy, I never knew his name."

Sanders paced the floor as he tried to connect her secret with Jay's case. To him, the connection wasn't very solid, but Carmen had told him for a reason. She probably knew that Harris was working on getting her husband reinstated. If the lieutenant knew about Kane's involvement with the Pink Sunrise than that plan would be halted. To Sanders, it didn't matter if Kane got his job back or not, he could get a guilty verdict without him. About to voice his thoughts, an idea entered into his mind; one which promised a more solid lead. "The Triad," he muttered. "Although it was your husband, you can say that it was the Triad. The Triad covered up your crime, thus committing one their damn self. If that other agent still works there then he knows where the Pink Sunrise is. You know where it is. It's like...," Sanders' paused. "You have the whole agency in your hands. If you open your mouth in court, you will put the Triad under a microscope. Every single investigation will be halted."

Carmen displayed a large smile on her face as Sanders caught on to her scheme. About to agree with him, she was interrupted when another officer stepped into the room. He kindly informed Sanders that Kane was in the lobby. It wasn't exactly good news to Carmen's ears, but she knew that Sanders now had the chance to question Kane. She knew he was going to when he told the officer to escort Kane into the interrogation room.

"You might want to take a seat," Sanders said once Kane was in the room. "We're both going to be here for a while." An odd expression fell upon Kane's face, which Sanders noticed. "Do you know where the Pink Sunrise is?" he asked him. Kane's eyes narrowed, but he didn't answer. It led Sanders to ask the question again, this time with more force. "Do you know where the Pink Sunrise is? Apparently, your wife does. She claims that you and another agent hid a fake pink diamond in Jay's house. Whereas this has nothing to do with the charges against her or Jay, she can use this information in court. It would take the focus off of Jay and put it onto the Triad."

Kane's eyes grew large. All he could focus on was Carmen. The last thing he expected her to do was to tell Sanders or any detective about the Pink Sunrise. Not to mention, it didn't help that he was wearing his wedding ring. The Pink Sunrise was inside of it, which was all the proof that Carmen needed.

"To protect this information, she wants her freedom and Jay's. If we can't give that to her then she's going to talk. Now, this could be a big takedown for the Brookstone PD. I could use this to advance my career. The problem is; the Triad controls too much shit for us to let it fall. Now that I know this information, this shit is on my plate. I'm about to put it back on yours. What are you going to do?"

Kane wiped his face as he started sweating. Sanders wanted to know what he was going to do, but the only logical answer was nothing. He hadn't yet been reinstated at the Brookstone PD and he no longer worked for the Triad. He didn't have any power in his hands. Carmen had taken that from him when she opened her mouth. "I know my wife's motive in doing what she did, but telling you about the Pink Sunrise isn't going to get her or Jay out of a charge. This whole thing still has to play out in court. Maybe—" Kane was interrupted when the door opened up. The same officer who had escorted him into the room had returned.

"Harris wants you to sit back in with Jay," the officer announced to Sanders.

Kane looked at Carmen preparing to tear into her ass the minute that they were alone. He was days away from getting his position back at the Brookstone PD and she could potentially halt it. In addition, she probably was assuring him his own cell next to hers. When Sanders walked out the door, he immediately ran to her side of the table, grabbing her shoulders. "What did you do that shit for?"

Carmen used her legs to back her chair away from Kane, but he kept his grip on her. "I did what I had to do," she told him, "If I go down then the Triad goes down, too."

"Don't you know this can backfire on your ass? They can throw you back in jail for theft. Did you think about that? You're trying to get out of cuffs, but you could be putting yourself in 'em. Shit, you're putting me in 'em, too."

Carmen shot Kane an evil look before jerking herself away from him. "We both know that the Triad and the Brookstone PD are going to keep coming after Jay. It doesn't matter what he does, they want him locked up. If I tell them what I know then I feel like I've given them a reason to keep their hands off of him. If the Triad wants to stay intact then they'll do what I want. That is, leave Jay alone. I can fight my charges on my own."

Kane narrowed his eyes as he looked back at the door. He didn't know when Sanders was coming back, but he knew he needed to think fast. Either he let Carmen share the news in court or he found a way to get Jay out of serving time. Neither option was one he wanted to take.

In a split second, Carmen's revelation had set off a grenade. She was forcing him to make a decision that wouldn't affect a season, but an entire lifetime.

Chapter Forty-Two

Less than ten minutes after Sanders had initially left Jay's side, Gomez had shown up at the precinct. Upon entering the station, both he and Jay were led back to the interrogation room. Left alone for only a few minutes, Harris quickly joined them in the room. The lieutenant quickly relayed all of the charges they were looking to bring upon Jay. Gomez didn't respond to the allegations, saving his breath for his conversation with Jay. Once Harris was out of the room, he gave Jay an earful. Certain that the lieutenant was still listening in, he spoke in a whisper.

"We knew this was going to happen," Gomez began. "We prepared for this, remember? There are financial records, contracts, and a lot of paperwork that can take away some of these charges. As far as the murders go, we're going to have to plead self-defense. That means, telling the courts the truth about Blu. It was a business deal gone wrong. He got upset, he retaliated and you retaliated back to protect your family. In order to win this, we have to paint a picture of you as a family man. You're going to have to step out of your comfort zone."

Jay eyed Gomez suspiciously. He already felt like he was out of his comfort zone. He had handcuffs around his wrists and had spent the last hour or so at the police station.

"Years have gone by and you've said nothing. We need to get the world on your side. It's time that you open up. You have Carmen in your corner, three kids, and the world needs to know that. They need to see that you deserve your freedom. As long as the world is scared of you, the courts will be, too. If the people love you, they'll ride with you. They'll force the courts to let you go."

Jay outstretched his eyes as he realized what Gomez wanted him to do. Talking to the public had never been his intention. When he was first arrested, he had numerous requests for interviews, but he turned them down. He felt like people would only be interested in having him talk about his father.

"I see your face, Jay. It has no written all over it because you're still not hearing me out. We want the world to see you as someone who is safe. Right now, these people view you as a monster. However, to your family and your girlfriend, you're a gentle giant. That is what we need the world to see. If we don't get them this round, you will be locked up for the rest of your life. Believe me."

Jay shook his head. "I'm not about to open up to any of these motherfuckers. I acted in self-defense so we'll roll with that. I'll take my chances."

Gomez opened up his briefcase as if Jay hadn't said a word. He slid out a folder filled with images that had been collected from various news media. Most of it pertained to the shooting at Blue Magic while the rest were photos taken when Jay's warehouse was raided almost twenty years ago. "You see this?" he asked him, showing him the photos. "This is what they are going to show. They are going to use these photos to convince the jury that you're nothing short of a monster. However," Gomez reached back inside of his briefcase. "This is what we want them to see." He pulled out a single picture of Jay and Nyla that had been sent to him when the baby was first born. "Do you understand now?"

Jay's body shifted a bit in his chair. He was about to speak until the door of the interrogation room opened and Sanders walked in. No longer alone, Jay quickly told his lawyer that he would think it over. He then directed his attention to Sanders.

"What do you know about the Pink Sunrise?" Sanders asked.

Jay looked at him in confusion, and said, "What does that have to do with anything? I don't have it." Jay glanced over at his attorney who was wearing a look of confusion, too.

"Carmen is demanding to tell anyone who'll listen that she knows where it is. She is willing to put the entire Triad under investigation in exchange for your freedom."

"I can't convince her not to talk. You see where I'm at. Shit, it's not like I want to talk her out of it either. She's looking out for me."

Sanders peered down at the floor before wiping his hand over his face. He couldn't put the two in the same room, but he needed a way to keep Carmen mum. Ideas were coming few and far between only making him more frustrated. "Give me a sec," he mumbled. He turned away from them, going out the door. Seeing a detective to the left of him in the hallway, he motioned for him to watch the room while he headed back to Carmen and Kane. Certain that his old partner was still in the room, he needed his help in coming up with a scheme.

Upon walking inside, he wasn't surprised to find Kane next to his wife. They both looked rather flushed like he did. Sanders didn't know whether to yell or punch a wall. In fact, he wanted to do a little bit of both. Instead, he paced the floor. He knew that his future in law enforcement was resting on that very moment. Taking a deep breath, he asked Kane to step outside of the room.

Carmen was still handcuffed, which meant that there wasn't much she could do while they talked. "I'm not about to worry myself over this shit," he told him once they were in the hallway. "Choosing between the two is too hard. Right now, the only evidence we have that can indict Jay is the drugs. As far as the murders, we don't have a solid witness that says they saw him shoot someone. They're not even saying he had a gun. If we charge him anyway, he can easily get off with a self-defense plea. We need something we can use to get Carmen to shut up, save the Triad and save Jay's ass as well. Then again, I know you want that guilty..." Sanders paused as a new thought suddenly entered into his mind. He thought it over for only a few seconds before a smile emerged on his face. "The drugs," he whispered. He turned and looked directly at Kane who had been rather quiet. "We can get him to take the drugs."

Kane looked at Sanders sideways, wondering if he heard right. "Wait a minute; you want Jay to steal the drugs?"

Sanders begin whispering a mile a minute as the idea turned golden. "I can get a floor plan of this building. The drugs are locked in the vault. I'm sure that Jay has some connections to some construction workers. I say, we let him get out of this crime with another crime. You want Jay in prison, get him there. Make him think that you're on his side and trying to help. Let him win his case. When that blows over, indict him on this new charge: stealing police evidence. That way, we shut Carmen up, but get Jay in prison at the same time."

Kane's face tightened as he thought about all the risks they would be taking. Not to mention, they would have to express the idea to Carmen and Jay. Unless they were in on it then it wouldn't work. Convincing them would be the hard part while the execution of the plan would be the easy part. Still, it was better than nothing. In the end, the Triad would be protected and Jay would end up in prison. He wouldn't be there as quickly as Kane wanted him to be, but nonetheless, he would be there. "It sounds perfect."

Sanders held out his hand to Kane. When they shook on it, Sanders suggested that they part ways. Kane would return to the interrogation room to share the idea with Carmen while he would tell Jay. Prior to meeting with him, he had to get the blueprint of the building. It took him about an hour, but it was worth the wait.

"There's a lot to be discussed," he announced when he finally returned to the room. Gomez was nowhere to be seen and Jay was sitting alone.

"This has to be about the diamond," Jay replied. His eyes glanced down at the manila folder that Sanders had placed on the table. There weren't many papers inside, but Jay knew that quantity didn't matter. All it took was a few words to send him right back into a prison cell.

"It is about the diamond," Sanders replied. "It's also about protecting you and the Triad. Right now, we have a million dollars' worth of coke, which we can use to indict you. It was the Brookstone PD's decision to use that evidence against you in court. Nevertheless, as you know, a problem arose. Mrs. Kane has threatened to reveal a secret involving one of the Triad's cases. If she does, the whole agency will be under investigation. Now, a feat like that is one we'd like to have. Still, you have to look at the bigger picture. If the Triad goes down, a lot of criminal investigations will be halted. America can't take that loss."

"So, what are you saying?" Jay interrupted. "Y'all don't want to take them down?"

"I'm saying that we can't take them down. We can't let Carmen talk. The only thing we can do to keep her quiet is to promise her that you'll be a free man. If you want me to be honest, we can't even promise that. The only thing we can do is help you with the evidence. Getting rid of the drugs can clear you of a drug charge. Self-defense clears the murders."

Jay listened attentively. Although he heard Sanders' words, a part of him didn't want to believe what he was saying. Nonetheless, he encouraged him to continue speaking.

"Right here," Sanders said, opening the manila folder, "is a floor plan of the building. X marks the spot." Sanders slid the paper across the table to Jay. "That X signifies where the vault is. The vault is where a million dollars' worth of your drugs is stored. You want your freedom; you need to make that disappear."

Jay didn't bother to look at the papers. "Tell Kane to make it disappear."

Sanders cleared his throat as he continued to coax Jay into stealing the drugs. "We are already taking a large risk. Now, you have two options; you can either steal the evidence or we can use it against you. It's your freedom, Mr. Santiago. Pick what you want."

"What's in this for you?"

"Nothing," Sanders answered, honestly. "This is about the Triad."

Jay looked over at the door, unsure about the offer in front of him. His instinct told him that there was a catch, but he wasn't quite sure what it was. Clenching his jaw, he took a look at the floor plan. He already had a plan of how to get the drugs, which was the easy part. What he deemed as the hard part was getting the job done in less than forty-eight hours. "So say I decide to work with y'all on this, what about bail?"

"You have a lot attached to your name right now. Bail may be an option, but you won't be able to see a judge until tomorrow. I suggest you get comfortable because you'll be spending the night here. In order for this to play out right in the media, this thing has to go to court. I suggest you look at a jury trial. Without evidence, no one can find you guilty. For the murders, you had better plead self-defense. We can cover up the drugs, but the murders are on you and Gomez."

Jay nodded his head becoming more comfortable with the idea. It seemed feasible, but he had to make sure all of his bases were covered. The feat could easily come back and bite him in the ass. "What if the jury still finds me guilty?"

Sanders shrugged his shoulders as he stood up from the table. "I don't have anything to do with that. To be honest, we're not doing this for you. We're doing it to protect the Triad."

"Of course," Jay responded. "I never got that twisted. You're doing this to protect yourselves. Tell me, though. How does this protect Carmen?"

Sanders didn't have a quick answer to the question. He hadn't thought about how they were going to protect Carmen. He was also certain that she hadn't thought about it. Still, he knew that if there weren't any drugs to indict Jay then a charge against Carmen wouldn't be able to happen either. "Insufficient evidence," he replied. "She was arrested because we believed that she was conspiring with you to use illegal funds to run Blue Magic. If we can't prove that you're a drug dealer than we can't prove that she knew about it." Sanders grabbed the floor plan back from Jay. "You don't need this right now. See me about it after you post bail. If the judge denies it then we'll work something else out." Sanders placed the blueprint back into the manila folder.

"I'm going to think this over," Jay replied. "As for right now, I'm denying the offer. If I get bail, things may change."

Sanders nodded his head in agreement. Not saying much else, he escorted Jay back to his cell. He then returned to the interrogation room where Carmen and Kane had been. Surprised to find neither of them there, he was informed by an officer that Carmen was returned to her holding cell. Kane was nowhere to be found, but he hoped that he had done his job. If he hadn't, Sanders would find out in the morning.

Chapter Forty-Three

Even as she stood in front of the judge, Carmen had a multitude of thoughts running through her head. For one, she was more nervous about the outcome of Jay's hearing than her own. If he wasn't granted bail, she didn't know how he would be able to steal his drugs back from the Brookstone PD. She knew he could use his connections to do it, but the plan would work better if he wasn't behind bars.

Then, there was her concern for her kids. She hadn't spoken to Fiona since she had left the house yesterday afternoon. A part of her hoped that her maid had stayed to watch them, but she couldn't be so sure. Once the fiasco was over, Carmen knew she would have to call home. In addition, she needed to telephone her parents. She knew they were worried about her since her mug shot had been displayed everywhere, thanks to TMZ. If it wasn't for her father's health, she knew they both would've been at her bail hearing. For now, the only person with her was Clement.

It bothered her some until the judge granted bail. From then on, all she felt was anxiety. It started when she was transported to the precinct to pay it and only worsened when she was picked up by Linx. His lack of nervousness didn't ease hers though she hoped it would. In fact, her anxiety grew when she ended up back at the courthouse for Jay's hearing. She took a seat in the back of the room and noticed that Kane was in the audience along with King and Malik.

From what she was hearing so far, the judge wasn't too thrilled about giving Jay bail. The charges were too serious and he viewed Jay as being a flight risk since he had ties around the world. Carmen listened as Gomez tried his best to paint a better picture of Jay. He did a good job and eventually the judge agreed to set a larger bail. Jay would pay anything for his freedom, which he proved when he bailed himself out.

Carmen tried her best to keep her composure as she and Jay emerged from the police station only to be met with a media circus. Casually, she used one hand to slide on her Gucci shades while she entwined the other with Jay's. Reporters and camera crews had them completely surrounded, firing question after question.

Carmen ignored them as Linx led them out of the station and into a black limousine. The moment the doors were closed, she took off the shades, throwing them on the seat opposite of her. "They're like fuckin' vultures," she yelled. Angrily, she stuck up her middle finger although she knew they couldn't see.

"We gotta deal with it," Jay told her, sliding his hand onto her right leg. "It's going to get worse before it gets better. We can handle it, though." He gave her thigh a slight squeeze, trying to calm her down. "Let's focus on getting home to the kids. We can worry about everything else later. Right now, we need to focus on Nyla and Rakim."

Carmen tried to take his advice, but it was hard to do with all of the yells and screams outside of the limousine. It wasn't until the car started moving that she felt some form of relief. "You know," she began. She failed to finish her statement as she remembered that her phone was still off. She pulled it from her coat pocket and turned it back on, allowing several voicemail alerts to come through. Most of them were from her mother while one was from Kane. "Funny, I was thinking that I needed to call my parents," she said.

Carmen started to dial her father's room number as Kane beeped in. She knew why he was calling, but she didn't necessarily want to speak to him. Still, she needed to be cordial. As long as she was having a public affair, he could always sue her for adultery. "Good morning," she greeted, answering his call. "I see it was an early rise for you, too."

"I was trying to catch up with you," Kane stated. "I was hoping to speak with you at the courthouse, but you left before I could get to you. Did you leave the station already?"

Kane's voice sounded frantic, which made Carmen fear that he was going to drop a bomb on her. "I did. I'm on my way home. What's wrong?"

"I thought that…" Kane paused. "I figured that this was a good morning for us to talk, you know? Maybe, you could come back to my condo and we can discuss things."

Carmen looked over at Jay, knowing he was listening to her conversation. He may have pretended that he wasn't, but she knew he was hanging on to every word. She also knew that he wanted her to tell Kane that they were officially together. "We don't need to do that," Carmen began. "Jay and I made up before we got arrested. We're back together."

"You need to think things through, Carm. Right now, a decision like that isn't one you should be making. You need some more time to think. Look, I'm still at the station, but we can meet somewhere. If you don't feel comfortable coming to my condo then we can go somewhere else. Name the place."

"Kane, you're not listening to me. What I'm telling you is that I'm going to move forward with the filing. I want to be with Jay. I'm divorcing you."

Carmen knew she had to tell him the truth despite what he wanted to hear. She couldn't lead him on only to break his heart. Carmen listened as the phone hung up. She let out a huge sigh, and told herself that she would deal with the issue later. At this point, she needed to be calling her parents. Quickly dialing her father's room number again, she listened as her mother picked up. She could tell her mother was upset by the way she answered the phone, but Carmen didn't let her speak. "Mama, please believe me when I say that I've been through hell," she told her. "So have you? Tell me about it." Carmen glanced over at Jay to see his expression. He looked rather content though he was facing the window.

Jay held in his true emotions as he replayed Carmen's words in his head. *I want to be with Jay.* Those were the words that he wanted Carmen to say. Now that he heard her say them to her husband, he knew he was on the right track to getting what he wanted. The only thing left was to get her a new engagement ring. While one thing had been accomplished, he had much more to achieve. He reached into his suit jacket for his cell phone, but his fingers never touched it. The second he heard Carmen's piercing scream, everything stopped.

Jay grabbed Carmen into his arms as Linx slammed onto the brakes. Carmen was crying hysterically, but he wasn't sure why. All he knew was that the word, hospital, was being muttered continuously out of her mouth. He ordered Linx to drive them there as he tried to question Carmen about what was going on. She was in a state of shock and she wouldn't answer. He picked up her phone to talk to her mother, but Patricia had already hung up. He looked down at Carmen as she sobbed in his arms. "Talk to me, Peaches," he coaxed. "What happened?"

Carmen didn't speak, as she found it harder to breathe. She broke away from Jay as the limo came to a sudden halt in front of the hospital. As she realized where they were, she began to have what she believed to be an out of body experience. She felt like she had merely floated to her father's room. Once there, she nestled against his chest as she tried to come to grips with what her mother had told her. Her father couldn't be dead. It wasn't possible. *I saw him yesterday. He was fine*, Carmen thought. She told herself that her eyes were playing tricks on her. Her father was simply sleeping. He was going to wake up at any time and tell her that he was ready to eat. He might even ask her to change the channel so he could watch golf. Carmen was certain of it. His medicine had made him sleep longer than usual, which was why she wasn't able to wake him. As soon as it wore off, he would stir. Then, she would show her mother and the doctors that they were wrong.

The thought made Carmen smile inside. She felt herself calming down, but the feeling went away when she heard a door open. Not at all fazed on who had entered, she listened as two voices started whispering. From what she could hear, one was male and the other was female. She couldn't quite make out their words, but she knew they were talking about something serious by their tones. Seconds later, she felt a firm hand caressing her back.

"Baby, we have to go," Jay whispered in her ear. "He'll be fine, Peaches, I promise."

Carmen ignored his words, knowing that Jay was in denial as well. Her mother had fooled him, too. Carmen knew that the longer she lay there, the more time she had to show them that they were wrong.

"Baby," Jay began once again. "The undertaker is here. They have to take him."

Carmen didn't respond. She told herself that she didn't need to. In a few more minutes, Jay would see for himself. Her father would wake up with either a yawn or a cough, proving that he was still alive. He would then make a joke that they were crying waterfalls for nothing. "Damn, can't a man get some rest?" she imagined him saying. The whole room would erupt into laughter as they realized they were bamboozled. Then, Carmen would point her finger and say, "I told you so."

"I don't have a choice," Jay said. "He's been out all morning."

Carmen heard Jay's words, but she didn't know his plan. She found out quickly when he pulled her from her father. He had a firm grip on her, but Carmen still managed to grab the bed's handrail. She held on, crying for him to put her down. He wouldn't, which only made her hold on tighter. Out of the corner of her eye, she watched as her mother neared her. Patricia grabbed her fingers, loosening her grip on the handrail. That was enough to send Carmen over the top. The moment her hands were freed, she turned on her mother, striking her. "You're lying!" she screamed, lunging at her. "He didn't have a stroke! Tell them the truth!"

Carmen's arms were brought back behind her. She felt Jay's hands as he lifted her off her feet, carrying her away from her mother. She tried to get out of his grasp, but to no avail. Her anger wasn't directed at him, but he was blocking her from being with her father. Naturally, she fought against him until she realized that her father's bed was empty. A stretcher was leaving the room with a covered body on it. It was all Carmen needed to see to know that she had failed. The image alone made her face reality. As she collapsed into Jay's arms, tears poured from her eyes heavier than before. For several minutes, she couldn't even move. It wasn't until the tears started to dry that she was able to break away from Jay.

"Let's go on home," Jay whispered into her ear. "I'll call King and Malachi so that they can come over. I'll tell them everything when they get to the house."

Carmen nodded her head as she looked at her mother. She wasn't quite sure what to say to her, but she knew that she needed to say something. An apology seemed to be the best place to start. "I'm sorry," she told her, "for everything." Carmen paused for a brief second as another tear fell down her face. "It hurts," she continued.

Patricia rose from her seat, making her way over to her daughter. She gave her a warm embrace, whispering in her ear that she was sorry as well. She hated that her husband had passed without giving Carmen a final goodbye. "I know, Peaches. We're going to get through this, though." Patricia pulled away so she could see Carmen's face. While her daughter had her father's dark mocha skin, she had her features. She saw so much of herself in her daughter that she sometimes envied it. "Let's head back to the house so we can deal with all of this."

"Okay," Carmen agreed, wiping her face. "I need to call Tiara." She looked around the room for her purse, which she spotted on the floor near the recliner. She picked it up and followed her mother and Jay outside of the room. She could hear the nurses giving their condolences, which she left her mother to respond to. Hearing their words only reminded her of what they were currently facing. While she had come to grips with it, she wasn't ready to talk about it with anyone beyond her family. By the time they were back in the limousine, her mother had already telephoned the publicist for Davenport Realty. In less than fifteen minutes, a statement would be released on their behalf.

Once the news hit, Carmen knew the phones at Flame would be ringing off the hook. More than likely, the phones already were since her arrest was breaking news. She knew she couldn't deal with it all so she called her best friend. Carmen hated to break the news to Tiara over the phone, but it would be worse if she heard about it from the news media.

When Tiara answered, she hardly let Carmen get a word in. She immediately rattled off a list of questions in regards to her arrest, which then led to questions about bail and court dates. It wasn't until Tiara realized she was the only one talking that Carmen told her about her father. "He had another stroke. This one was full blown. He passed this morning, Tee." Carmen listened as a large gasp sounded on the phone followed by the sound of crying.

"I'm so sorry, Carmen. Whatever you need me to do, let me know," Tiara cried. "I have Robin with me, but I was going to stop by the office right quick to check up on some things. I'll send out an email blast and once things are settled, I'll be over. I know you need me right now."

"I do, Tee. Don't rush, though, take your time." Carmen listened as Tiara mumbled, "I will," before hanging up the phone. She knew her friend wasn't okay, but neither was she. Still very much distraught, Carmen pulled her Gucci shades from her purse. She covered her face as the tears started to fall once again. Jay grabbed her hand, but the comfort wasn't enough. Deep down, something told her that it never would be.

Chapter Forty-Four

Tiara told herself to keep it together. When Carmen had first told her the news, she tried to get all of her emotions out right then and there. Apparently, she hadn't because she spent another hour crying on the phone to her husband. Tiara knew it was because she felt like she was losing her own father. Ever since she had met Carmen back in middle school, Lotus had always treated her like she was his blood. The news of his death caused her nerves to go haywire and she even found it hard to drive. With her daughter in the backseat, an accident was the last thing she needed. Thankfully, she had finally reached Flame.

The local radio station was already broadcasting about Lotus' death, so Tiara was certain that Cathy had caught wind of it. She was always one step ahead, therefore, Tiara expected to walk in with her having already done the hard part. It wasn't always easy to assign tasks to the other executives when everyone's plate was already heavy. Still, whether the President was there or not, business still had to be taken care of.

Tiara was pleased to see the whole building was in full swing as she walked through the door. Everyone was so busy that Robin wasn't even a distraction. Any other time, everyone would have been vying for a chance to hold her. Considering the circumstances that brought her to Flame, Tiara didn't want to be bothered so it worked to her advantage. Unfortunately, she didn't go unnoticed for long.

Tiara wasn't in the elevator for one second before Blu boarded. Though she had never met him in person, Malik had shown her a photo of him. He wanted her to be prepared in case a situation like this happened. Clutching her daughter close to her, Tiara stared at him as he joined her. She didn't know what he wanted with her, but she figured he was going to tell her. A slew of his men had been murdered and she knew he was heated. Retaliation had to be next on his agenda.

"Good morning," he greeted.

Tiara didn't bother to return the greeting. The only thing she did was move further into the far right hand corner of the elevator. She kept her eyes planted on him, suspicious of any movement that he made.

"Shawn Blumington," he said to her, holding out his right hand. "I don't think we've met. I used to do some work for Jay Santiago. You know him, right? Owner of Blue Magic, Sapphire; he's about to open a jewelry store downtown called Iceland. Does that name ring a bell?"

Tiara stared down at his hand, knowing not to touch him. She allowed her expression to speak for itself. She wanted him to know that she knew who he was. He took the hint when he dropped his arm back down at his side.

"So I see that we're not strangers. Well, that makes three of us. You know, Carmen and I met one day here. It was a quick convo, somewhat pleasant. I have a relative who works in the mailroom, too. I think she's like my father's second cousin or some shit. Whenever I visit her, I get a badge with full access. Bitch doesn't even know I'm using her."

"Get the fuck out of my building."

"Your building?" Blu asked with a smile. "When did Flame become yours? I thought Carmen Davenport was still running things. Don't get it twisted, Tiara. You may put in over sixty hours a week for this company, but it's not yours. You're no different than your bitch-ass husband. Both of you have the ability to strike it big, but you won't out of fear. Do you like being Carmen's sidekick?"

Tiara glared at him as she tried not to feed into his words. Flame was as much hers as it was Carmen's. Flame wouldn't be where it was if it wasn't for her. Blu could talk all day, but Tiara knew she wasn't anyone's sidekick. If anything, she was loyal. Loyal to the point that she had put in over twenty years of work and helped her friend create a multi-million dollar brand.

Blu didn't speak, noticing that the elevator wasn't moving. He walked closer to Tiara, pushing the button for her floor. He really didn't have any business with her, but he wanted to speak to her because she was Malik's wife. Blu knew she couldn't help him because the woman couldn't even help herself. As long as Carmen was breathing, Tiara would always be in the same spot, second place. "Are you scared?" he asked her, turning to look at her. He could see fear on her face, which made him laugh. "I'm not going to touch you, Tiara. Believe me; going after you is a waste of time, money, and men. You're worthless. Oh," he said as the doors opened onto her floor, "one more thing."

Tiara didn't bother to wait as she ran past him. He caught her by the arm, which threw her off guard. She tried to break his hold, but he only tightened his grip.

"I'm speaking to you, bitch," he whispered, harshly.

"Let me go!"

Blu quickly broke his hold because he didn't want any extra attention. He had said enough, but he still wanted to get into Tiara's head. "I learned a lot working with your husband. He might not have said things to me directly, but I heard a lot of dirt. Before you go running off to Carmen, you need to check him."

Tiara looked at Blu inquisitively, as she asked, "What is that supposed to mean?" When she saw an evil smile emerge on his face, she knew that he was trying to imply that her husband had been unfaithful. It was very easy for her to believe him once he said, "A powerful woman is every man's weakness. Remember that." He then stepped back into the elevator right before the doors closed.

Tiara parted her lips as she felt herself on the verge of tears. She knew that Blu had a devilish spirit, which he was putting to good use. Hinting at infidelity on her husband's part was a perfect example. It was a tough issue for her because Carmen was always the one who men were fighting over. Her friend was always the one that was wanted. It wouldn't be a complete shock if her own husband had vied for Carmen's attention. Tiara would never tell Malik about her encounter with Blu. She would question Carmen, though. She had to know if she had slept with her husband. Whether it was in the past or recently, Tiara didn't care. She had to know.

Without wasting any more time, she quickly walked to her office. She didn't speak to anyone, but wrote a lengthy email regarding Lotus' death. She assigned the major tasks for the day to Jerry while instructing him to use his best judgment. Five minutes later, she was hitting send and walking back out the door with Robin. No longer crying, her next destination was Carmen's house for a heart to heart discussion.

***

Despite the water's cooling temperature, Carmen didn't attempt to get out of the tub. She had been in the water for nearly two hours and she felt like staying for two more. It seemed to be the only thing that brought her relief as she was coming to grips with her father's death. She was flip-flopping between forcing herself to accept reality and believing his passing was a hoax. Life without him wouldn't be easy, but her father had always taught her to lean on her faith. It had brought her out of many storms and it would do the same for her this time.

Staring into space over the edge of the tub, Carmen heard the bathroom door opening. She was surprised to see Jay come in, dressed in a pair of sweats. After they had arrived home, she had gone upstairs to bathe while she assumed he had remained downstairs. It was obvious by his attire that he had gone back to his apartment to change. It puzzled her that he wasn't wearing a suit or a button-up and slacks.

"How are you feeling?" he asked her, sitting down on the edge of the tub. "Have your nerves calmed down some?" He reached his hand into the water, placing it on her upper thigh.

"Some," Carmen answered, honestly. "I've been thinking about things."

"Me, too," Jay replied. "I've been thinking about a lot of things. You know we have to move quickly with this whole vault situation. I called Sanders to let him know I'm going to do it. I got the blueprint, which I went ahead and handed over to King. It wasn't easy because at the same time, I had to tell him about his grandfather. He's real emotional right now, but he knows we have to take care of business."

Carmen adjusted her position in the tub, making sure she was sitting up straight. "You know he needs to be here, Jay. Can't we leave the vault alone until my father is in the ground?"

Jay wished that he could, but he knew the longer he held out, the greater the risk. "As long as the Brookstone PD has my keys, they will always have a leg up on everything. To be honest, it's not only them. Blu is out there, too. We can be in the middle of the funeral procession and he can pop off if he wants to. I gotta handle this. I got King getting these contractors together so we can get in there and get the drugs. Once we get rid of the evidence, I can focus on finding Blu. Shit, I didn't even tell you about the phone call I got from Cesar. All of the bodies that were left at Blue Magic ended up at Jimenez Funeral Home. You know what that means? I get another chance to show Blu who he's fuckin' with. I shipped two of those corpses to his restaurant in a fuckin' box. I gift-wrapped it; put a bow on it and all."

Carmen gasped after Jay's spiel. His mindset was still the same as it had been when they were in Puerto Rico. She knew he wasn't going to change overnight, but she did hope that her father's death would have some kind of effect on him. From what he was demonstrating, his mind was solely focused on getting his drugs back and killing Blu. Hers on the other hand was focused on her family.

"Your face says everything, but your mouth says nothing."

"It's the same shit that was said in San Juan," Carmen said as she stared him square in the eye. "King doesn't need to be running around trying to get together contractors. That shit can wait. Preliminary hearings aren't going to start for another two months or so. What we need to be dealing with right now is our family. Did you even see Nyla or Rakim? I haven't even called Kristian or Akaila. I've been too busy dealing with the fact that my father is dead to even look after my kids. That's not good."

"I saw Nyla and Rakim. Matter of fact, Akaila is here. She flew in when she heard about us being arrested. The kids are in her room."

Carmen stood up in the tub as she realized that Jay had overlooked the true meaning of what she was trying to say. *He doesn't get it. He really doesn't get it. He's talking to make me feel better instead of addressing the issue.* She stepped out, grabbing a towel to cover herself with. As she pulled it around her, she felt Jay's arms slide around her waist. She knew an apology was coming since he realized he had upset her.

"Look, we're both real sensitive right now. I don't want you to think that I'm putting your father on the backburner. I'm not. I'm dealing with this shit in my own way. I've been through this before with both my parents. I'm putting all my pain into my work right now."

Carmen wiped her face as she started to cry again. Not wanting to, she quickly took a deep breath to calm herself as Jay pressed his lips down on hers. They shared a short kiss before she pulled away.

"We're going to get through this, Peaches. It's ride or die, right?"

Carmen nodded her head as a knock sounded at the door. She secured the towel around her before she told Jay to see who it was. She breathed a sigh of relief when he told her it was Tiara. She quickly told her friend that she would be down in a minute and to wait for her in her home office. Her conversation with Jay wasn't quite over, so she followed him into the bedroom as she started to get dress.

"Since we are for real with this thing and its ride or die," he said, sitting down on her bed. "Why don't I move in? Let's make a home."

Carmen dropped the bottle of lotion she was holding. He caught her off guard, but not in a negative way. She wanted him to move in. She just didn't think that it would be this soon. She figured that down the line they would get engaged and he would move in then. "How soon?" she asked him, picking the bottle of lotion up from the floor. "Like now?"

"It's a good time, don't cha think? I got a couple of months left on my lease, but that's not a problem."

Carmen had to agree that Jay was right. It was a good time for him to move in. She had already broken the news to Kane that their marriage was indeed over and she needed Jay's support. Having him nearby would be beneficial to her and the kids as well. "Then let's do it," she told him, "starting tonight." Carmen watched as a smile emerged on Jay's face. He didn't say much else, allowing her to continue to dress in silence. Once she was finished, he gave her another hug before they parted ways. He went to Akaila's room to check up on the kids while she headed into her home office. Upon entering, she noticed the angry expression on Tiara's face. She hadn't expected to see a smile, but neither did she expect to see an evil scowl. She didn't address it right off, taking a seat at her desk. After a minute or so of silence, Carmen parted her lips to speak only for Tiara to beat her to the punch.

"Jay, Carlos, and Kane are the only men you've been with, right?"

Carmen's head tilted slightly to the side as she digested the question. "Where the fuck did that come from?" Carmen watched as Tiara stood up from the sofa she had been sitting on.

"Someone made a comment to me today about you and Malik. Therefore, as your friend, I'm asking you to tell me the truth. Were those the only men you've been with?"

"Are you asking me if I slept with your husband?"

"Did you?" Tiara shot back.

Carmen pushed her chair away from her desk, as she stood up. She glared hard at Tiara not believing that her friend was questioning her loyalty. "Hell fucking no," she yelled. "I would slit my damn wrists before I touched your husband. You know me better than that, Tee. Yeah, I've done some fucked up shit, but I wouldn't sleep with your husband. Did you bring this up to Malik, too?"

Tiara told her no. "I wasn't sure if I was going to," she replied. *Actually, I'm not going to,* she said in her head, *I can't ask him about this.*

"Who said something to you, Tee? I know you went to Flame before you came here. Was it someone there? No one knows shit about my personal life aside from Cathy. That's only because she acts more like a personal assistant than a receptionist."

Tiara rubbed her lips together because she was hesitant to say it was Blu. If she told Carmen that was who it was then her friend would immediately argue that it wasn't a credible source. If she was honest with herself then Tiara had to admit that she knew he wasn't. Her own insecurity had led her to believe that her friend had betrayed her. "I rather not say," she replied.

"Then I suggest you get the fuck out."

Tiara's feet shifted. "Names aren't important," she argued. "The accusation is. The idea of you and Malik together is not that farfetched. You say you didn't do it, though. Maybe, you didn't. Who knows?"

"Get out," were still the only words to leave Carmen's mouth. The order was firm and made Tiara walk out of the home office. Carmen listened as Tiara collected her daughter from Fiona. When she was certain that Tiara's car was pulling out of her driveway, she slammed the door to her office. In the process, she was able to catch a quick glimpse of Akaila coming down the steps. It was a simple reminder that Kristian was still in Copperton City. She knew she needed to call her daughter, but the argument she had with Tiara now had her not wanting to talk to anyone. Scared that she would take her anger out on Kristian, she decided to take a quick fifteen to cool down. Her plan was to draw for a bit until her nerves were under control. Once she was back to her normal self, she would make the phone call to her daughter that her grandfather had passed.

Chapter Forty-Five

With the house being relatively quiet, the sound of a door slamming was noticeable. Jay had made it downstairs in enough time to see Tiara storming out of the house. A part of him wanted to go after her, but he changed his mind when he realized that it was Carmen who slammed the door. He figured it would be in his best interest to check on her first. However, he changed his mind again when he remembered how Carmen was whenever she was upset; she would take her anger out on him until she calmed down. The best option was to let her be and act like he hadn't heard a thing. Therefore, he headed towards the den were he knew Patricia was. He hadn't seen her since they had returned to the house and he wanted to check up on her before he left.

When he went inside, he saw her seated on one of the couches with several pillows around her. Barefoot and clad in a cream dress, she looked more distraught then Jay had imagined. It was because of the way she looked that he didn't say anything. He simply sat beside her, allowing the silence to linger. They met eyes through the television screen until Patricia turned away and looked directly at him. He did the same, turning to face her. "I figured I would check on you before I left."

"It's probably good that you're leaving. I got off the phone with Kane a minute ago. He's on his way over. No one even bothered to call him. He had to hear about Lotus on the news."

Jay became tickled. Patricia was advising him to leave not knowing that he was there to stay. "Carmen and I decided to move in together. He can come over, but I'm still going to be here. I'm only leaving so I can handle some things. Once I come back, I'll be in for the night."

Patricia's eyes widened as she realized what her daughter had done. She hadn't even divorced Kane and was already moving another man into the house. Then, instead of Jay asking her to get her paperwork in order, he was going to move his stuff in. "Could you at least show some kind of respect? You're already doing the man's wife, but you're going to flaunt your dick in his house, too?"

Jay was seeing a side of Patricia he had never seen. She was naturally feisty, but vulgarity wasn't in her nature. Lotus' death was bringing the worst out of her, too.

"We are in mourning," she continued. "The last thing we need is Kane coming over here riled up. He and Carmen moved into this house together. It was a fresh start for them. Now, he has to come in and learn that it's a fresh start for you, too."

Jay started getting defensive when Patricia's attitude didn't change. He wasn't trying to cause drama, but Kane was well aware that he and Carmen were together. If Kane had read the police report then he would've known that they were arrested after being caught in the act. "Look, Patricia, I didn't mean any harm. Since you live here, I thought it would be best if I told you that I was moving in. As far as Kane goes, we will always be enemies. I'll be cordial, but I don't care about his feelings. I know everyone is sensitive right now because of Lotus's death. I am, too. Now that he's gone, it's like I'm losing my dad all over again."

"How dare you compare my husband to that son of a bitch?"

Jay immediately stood up as he tried to figure out how he had gotten on Patricia's bad side. He knew that he was wrong for being with her daughter, but he didn't expect the woman to flip on him like she was. It made him question if something else had happened that he wasn't aware of. "They were best friends," he explained. "Birds of a feather flock together."

"Is that what Hector taught you?" Patricia let out an evil chuckle. "Birds of a feather may flock together, but you can't fly with the eagles if you're hanging with the chickens. The best thing that Lotus ever did was breaking his ties. Hector ate himself alive. Lotus would have done the same if he had of stayed with him. Praise God, he didn't."

Jay folded his arms across his chest as a way to control his anger. If Patricia was offended that he had compared the two then he knew that choking her would really enrage her. In fact, he knew that it would be viewed as premeditated murder. It was a crime that he never hesitated in committing. "I see now that we're not as cool as I thought we were. It shocks me because we've always gotten along. Even when I first met you, we had a cordial relationship. Lotus was the one who didn't like me. Now, he loves me."

"Loves you?" Patricia straightened her posture as she found her anger intensifying. "Do you really believe that my husband loved you? Damn, Jay, you're more fucked up in the head than I thought. Lotus merely tolerated you."

"He told me that he did. He said it before he passed. You were never there when I would come visit him in the hospital. If you were then you would know that he did."

Patricia huffed. "Please, Lotus could never love you. Who could? You're the product of the devil. You're some sort of maniac who feeds off the innocent to get power. You destroy everything you touch."

Jay took a step back from Patricia for her own safety. He didn't want to add fuel to the fire, which was why he chose his words carefully. "I'm going to pretend that this is your mourning talking. So we can cool the air, I'm going to leave. I'll be back later tonight, but if there's anything you need, let me know."

"Please, like I would call you for something," Patricia yelled, standing up. "Everything that I have has already been taken away from me. There is nothing you can give me. You took it away a long time ago."

"I haven't taken shit from you," Jay yelled back. "Let's get that straight. I haven't done shit to you and I haven't taken shit. If you knew what was good for you, you would check yourself before you get dealt with."

"Dealt with, is that a threat, Mr. Santiago? I'm not one of those little men downtown that you can pop one of your little bullets into. See, I fight back. I don't stand there while some deranged killer walks up on me with a gun."

"Were you there, Patricia? Did you see what happened? From the way that you're talking, I could have sworn that you were in that limo with me and Nyla. Let me know if you're working with Blu, too. I already put two dudes in a box to be delivered to him." Jay waited for a response, but Patricia didn't give him one. The silence prompted him to head for the door.

"I hate you," Patricia said, finally speaking. "Not only you, but all things Santiago."

"Does that include your grandkids?" Jay didn't bother to turn around. "Answer the question," he yelled. "Does that include your grandkids? They have my blood in their veins, Patricia. When was the last time you looked at King? He looks like his great-grandfather, Vincent. Rakim has my eyes. Nyla is the female version of me. She looks nothing like Carmen. Do you hate them?" Jay turned around, staring her in the face.

"You can't hate the innocent. They are mere products of sin."

Jay narrowed his eyes as his hand balled into a fist. He kept his feet planted, but he didn't know how long he could keep them there. The only thing that helped him maintain control was that he noticed Patricia was crying. It made him start to understand that she was simply taking her anger out on him. She was hurt beyond imagination because her husband was dead and she didn't know how to deal with it. Instead of taking her time to grieve, she chose to degrade him.

"You know why I hate you, Jay? It's not because you tried to kill my daughter years ago or because you ruined her marriage. Every single time I see you, I remind myself that it was your little drugs that took my company away from me. Carmen may have been schooled by Carlos, but she worked for you. You supplied her with what she needed to turn Flame into a multi-million dollar business. I had the pleasure of sitting back and watching."

Jay's face scrunched up as he took in Patricia's words. Never in a million years did he think that she would admit to being jealous of her own daughter. Now that she had, he understood why she gave Carmen so much grief. She envied her. Patricia was an old woman who had already lived her life. The dreams she had, she had to watch Carmen fulfill.

"I spent almost my whole life trying to do what she did in a year. I still haven't made it."

"Get over it," Jay growled.

"You get over it, motherfucker. You get over it. You didn't have to sit back and watch. You didn't have to read the headlines. She took everything away from me. She should have died. I lost the only thing I had left. Lotus was all I had. Like my company wasn't enough, she had to take my store in Texas, too. Yeah, did you know that? She bought me out."

Jay reached into his pocket, pulling out his wallet. He opened it quickly until he found what he was looking for. "You need her more than me," he told her, handing over the business card. "Her name is Dr. Stuart, she's an excellent psychiatrist. Give her a call."

"I don't need a fuckin' psychiatrist. What I need is a break. I've worked all my life, building Flame and what do I have to show for it? Not a damn thing, I have nothing."

"So you blame the world?"

"Oh, there are people to blame, Jay. Believe me. Everyone had their hand in the pot to ensure that I never succeeded. One of those people was your mother. Yeah, Jay, I knew her. I knew her very well. Lady and I, we...we were friends at one point. Then, I guess she didn't like my success since she was nothing but a housewife. It wasn't like Hector allowed her to do much else. Once Flame got good and rolling, she turned into another person. She became the devil."

Jay shifted his feet but his conscience told him not to strike her. She had disrespected his father, her daughter, and now had moved on to his mother. He was used to people talking about Carmen and Hector, but not the latter. His mother was an angel. She was the exact opposite of anything evil. To Jay, his mother had been pure.

"Lady tried to ruin my life because she was miserable in hers. I hated her for that. God knows I did and still do. Like your father, she's burning in hell."

Jay couldn't hold himself. He snatched Patricia up by her neck, pushing her down onto the couch. He grabbed a pillow into his hands and stuffed it on top of her face. He held it there until he heard his subconscious yelling inside of his head, telling him that she wasn't worth it. Jay knew that she wasn't so he removed the pillow, and marveled as Carmen's mother laughed in his face. "This is your final warning," he told her through gritted teeth. "Next time, I may not be able to catch myself." Jay backed away from Patricia as she continued to laugh. He made his way to the door just as Carmen came in. Her facial expression told him that she suspected something had happened. The last thing he wanted to admit was that he had attacked her mother.

"What happened?" Carmen asked, looking at both of them. "Someone say something."

Jay failed to reply, before walking past her. He hoped that Patricia would opt not to answer, too. Bringing Carmen into their argument would only start another war of words. Patricia would argue that he had attacked her while he in return would tell Carmen that her mother hated her. It was a no win situation for them both. "I'll be back later tonight," he told Carmen, placing his hand on the doorknob. "I'm going to my apartment for a little while." He gave Patricia a final glance before going out the door.

Carmen stood there waiting for her mother to answer. Instead of doing so, her mother simply turned on the television. Already annoyed, Carmen decided to let her be. She returned to the office, knowing that it was time to make the phone call to Kristian. She hated having to tell her when the news was everywhere, but it needed to be done. She picked up the phone and proceeded to dial her daughter's number. As usual, she didn't answer. Carmen left her a voicemail message, telling her to catch a flight home as soon as possible and that she loved her. She then hung up as she sat back down at her desk. A sketch of her father was still in front of her, which she decided to return to. For now, it seemed to be the only thing to keep her sane until Kristian came home.

Chapter Forty-Six

Copperton City, Georgia

The first thing that Kristian expected to see when she walked into her room was her sister. It was only a little after four, meaning that Akaila should have been back from her afternoon class. When she saw she wasn't there, Kristian assumed that she might have been in the library. Akaila was known to go there on occasion to study. *She probably went with Angi or Chantel,* Kristian thought, *they all have similar schedules.*

She placed her tote bag on her desk and headed over to Akaila's bed where a sheet of paper was lying. Kristian picked up what appeared to be a note, and was slightly surprised when she saw that it was addressed to her. *I hate to tell you like this, but Mama and Jay were arrested last night. Right now, they're out on bail. Don't be mad, but I went ahead and left for New York because there was a flight heading out at one o'clock. I'll call you once I get back in Brookstone. Love you, Akaila.*

Kristian pulled out her cell phone, which had been on silent for most of the day. There were five missed phone calls including two from Akaila and one from her mother. She quickly exhaled before sticking the phone back into her jeans' pocket. She folded the note in half as she started to contemplate her next move. She knew she needed to head home, but it wasn't an easy step to make. At this point, Kristian knew that her mother was well aware of the tension between them. The ignored phone calls were enough proof that there was bad blood. By returning to Brookstone, she would be forced to finally hold a conversation with her.

Still, Kristian knew she had to go home. She made a spur of the moment decision and emailed her professors to let them know that she would be out for the rest of the week. Once the message was sent, she started to search for a flight to New York that evening. Lucky for her, the next flight out was in less than two hours. If things worked in her favor, she would be in Brookstone no later than eight. Pleased with the plan, she purchased a one-way ticket to Brookstone. Thirty minutes later, she had a bag packed and was on her way to the airport.

Before the plane was set to take off, she received a text message from Coco. Her best friend was looking for her, but Kristian was far from campus. She texted her back that she was on her way to Brookstone right before the flight attendant instructed everyone to turn off all electronic devices.

Kristian didn't turn her phone back on until the plane landed in Brookstone. Coco hadn't responded to her, but Kristian was certain that she would speak to her that night. If things were serious enough, King would send for Coco to come home. Judging from what she was seeing when her taxi reached the gates of the Kane Estate; Kristian knew the situation was serious. A slew of reporters were at the gates, taking photos and filming footage of their house. No one was outside, but it didn't matter to the paparazzi. They were waiting for any shot that they could get. The commotion continued until she was inside of the house.

Expecting to hear mayhem, all she heard was silence. She dropped her bag onto the floor before racing up the steps. "Hello!" she called out, "I'm home!" She continued up the steps two at a time until she heard sounds coming from Akaila's room. She headed that way and gave the door a single knock before she opened it. Dressed in a pair of black leggings and a large pink T-shirt, Akaila was on her bed, writing in her journal and crying. "Did I miss something?" Kristian inquired, coming into the room.

Akaila gave her a simple head nod as she wiped her face. "You got my note?"

"Yeah," Kristian replied. "Three hours later than when you wrote it. What's wrong?"

"Grandpa passed this morning, Kris. He had another stroke. This one was far worse than the one before. Grandma says that he died almost instantly. The doctors tried to revive him, but they couldn't. It actually happened early this morning. Grandma didn't say anything right off because she wanted to spend some time with him by herself. Not to mention, Mama and Jay were in police custody until they made bail."

Kristian shook her head in disbelief. She knew she hadn't been keeping up with her grandfather like she should have. Her modeling career and school had taken most of her attention. Now, she had inadvertently come home to attend a funeral. "Where's Grandma now? Shit, where's Mama? King isn't here? Where's Malachi? Did Daddy come by?"

"Grandma is in the den. She called Daddy and he's supposed to be on his way over. He heard about it on the news. Malachi is at King's house. Supposedly, King is out handling some business for Jay so he doesn't have a way over here. Mama has been moping around so I couldn't get her to go get him. I figured I would wait until you came home. Your old Lexus is still here so I figured we could drive that."

Kristian felt overwhelmed by all that she had heard. Tears were staining her face from the news of her grandfather, while she wanted to find out more about why her mother was arrested. She didn't even know which one to deal with first. "No wonder Coco was looking for me. Our entire family has made headline news. Where's Mama now?"

"She was downstairs in the office the last time I checked. Jay was here earlier, but he's gone now. Tiara came by, too. The only people I haven't had contact with are Daddy and King."

Kristian mumbled, "Okay," before leaving the room. She knew she needed to find her mother, but she wasn't quite sure what to expect. Either her mother would be glad to see her or she would be distant. Kristian knew she deserved the latter from how she had treated her since the graduation party. As she opened the door to her mother's office she held her breath because she was uncertain how her mother would receive her. It wasn't until she saw that the room was empty that she exhaled. The relief was short-lived when the sound of cabinets being opened took her attention. Following the noise, Kristian headed into the kitchen where she found her mother. She was pulling a large bowl from the refrigerator, which she placed on the island.

"I didn't know all of this was going on," Kristian admitted. "I came home and got more than I bargained for." Kristian sat on one of the bar stools, hoping to break the ice. It was a big step for her to take since she was still hurting from her mother's affair. However, she needed to reveal that hurt to her mother. "I know it's been awhile since we've talked," she continued. "I'm ready now."

Carmen's nerves were already on edge and from the way Kristian spoke, there seemed to be another issue that was about to reel its head. "It sounds to me like you've been holding something in."

"I know about you and Jay," Kristian revealed. "I saw you two at the graduation party."

Carmen was glad that the elephant in the room had been identified. She always knew in the back of her mind that Kristian was angry with her, but she didn't know why. Now, the cards were face up on the table. "We did have an affair," Carmen admitted. "Now, we're together. We made it public today. It's not a secret anymore. I wish you would've told me instead of holding it in. I never wanted any of y'all to see that. To be honest, I didn't want anyone to know until I was certain that Jay and I were going to be serious. This doesn't surprise me, though. I knew something was wrong when we were in Georgia. You didn't even want to look at me."

"Mama, you and Daddy remarried. You made a vow before God. I know that things were rocky because of what happened with Rakim, but you could have worked through it. I don't want to go through another divorce. It's like making us pick sides."

"No one is making you pick sides, Kris," Carmen shot back. "I remarried your father out of love. I swore that he was it for me. To this day, I still love him, but our relationship isn't going to work. I'm in love with someone else. People fall in love all the time and it takes years before they see that they didn't marry their soul mate."

"I'm not talking about people, Mama. I'm talking about you."

Kristian became outraged as her mother tried to brush off her sin. She wanted her to believe that it was nothing, but Kristian couldn't. She had faith in her mother up until she saw her in a lip lock with Jay. It was then that Kristian lost all hope. Her mother still hadn't learned. If her father made one mistake than her mother wanted to use it as an excuse to go sleep with another man. She would never deal with the issue and forgive.

"Look, Kris," Carmen began. "Things are—" she stopped talking when she heard the kitchen door swing open. Glancing back, she rolled her eyes when she saw Kane. The doorbell hadn't rung, which meant that he had used his key. It was a clear reminder that she had to change the locks. Once Jay moved in, she didn't need Kane making surprise visits to their home. Though Kane was interrupting the conversation, she let him be. He went straight for Kristian, hugging and kissing her cheeks.

"I've missed you, baby," he was saying. "How were your first few days of school?"

"Interesting," Kristian replied.

Kane broke his hold, looking back at Carmen. He knew that she was shocked to see him because it read on her face. "I wanted to come over and see everyone," he explained. "No one called me. I had to find out about Lotus from a damn news story. Did I come at a bad time?"

"We were talking," Kristian interjected, "but we all belong in this conversation."

Carmen glanced back down at the fruit salad in front of her. She didn't know what Kristian's intentions were, but she knew she was about to find out.

"It looks like there is some tension," Kane mumbled, looking between the two. "Looks like I came at the right time. Does someone want to tell me what's going on?"

Carmen sighed out of frustration. She opened one of the cabinets, grabbing a small bowl before going back to the fruit salad. A spoon was already on the counter, which she used to put some of the salad into a bowl. As she did it, Kristian continued the discussion.

"Is the divorce official?"

Kane looked over at Carmen although he knew the honest answer to the question. In a way, he hoped that she had changed her mind. "Not yet," he answered. "She hasn't filed the papers. I don't want it, but what choice do I have? I keep praying that she'll see how bad I want my family back."

"I don't want to talk about this anymore," Carmen interrupted. "This whole thing is a done deal. Kane, we've been separated for seven months now. You know our relationship has run its course. I'm filing the papers as soon as I can. Hopefully, I can do it after the funeral."

Carmen's words set off a spark in Kristian that turned into an angry outburst. "Here he is, pouring out his heart to you and you don't even care," Kristian yelled, jumping off the stool. "You don't care about anybody but yourself. You want what you want, which is to keep fuckin' up our lives."

Carmen immediately started to feel guilty. She hadn't necessarily showed any of her kids a healthy relationship in the past couple of years. There had been nothing in their house but mayhem since Jay had come back into their lives. "You have every right to feel the way you do. I haven't been the best role model lately."

Kristian stood with her arms at her sides as she thought about what she had said to her mother. Her spiel was a result of an impulsive word vomit and she hadn't even realized the curse word that had slipped from her lips. "That is how I feel. I probably would've kept in touch if I had of said all of this earlier. For the past few months, I kept everything bottled up."

"You shouldn't have," Carmen replied. "Now that you've said everything you needed to say, let me say something to you. You can't help who you fall in love with. You can try to control your heart all you want, but it does what it wants to do. You also can't help falling out of love. It's a part of life. Last, but not least; you have every right to be upset, but you will respect me. I'm not your friend. I'm your mother."

"Sometimes I wish that you weren't."

Carmen threw the fruit bowl in Kristian's direction, but her daughter moved before it hit her. Her temper had instantly flared and now her wall was covered in a variety of colors. "You wouldn't be here if it wasn't for me. Everything you have, I gave you. I can take it away, too. Shit, you weren't even conceived naturally. I made the decision to create you. Maybe, I shouldn't have. Then, I wouldn't have to live with the regret."

Kane immediately stepped in between the two when he saw the look on Kristian's face. He was shocked at Carmen's response as well, almost speechless. Even after Kristian vowed to never speak to her again, Kane couldn't utter a single syllable out of his mouth. Their words to each other were harsh, which made him believe that they were angry about more than the divorce. Unsure of exactly what it was, he knew he wouldn't get the answer when Kristian ran from the room. Although his daughter was crying, Kane didn't run after her. Instead, he felt it was more important to deal with

Carmen. "You know you shouldn't have said that. As the adult, you should have been the bigger person."

"Fuck you!"

Kane stood straight up as Carmen gave him the same treatment. He knew that he needed to turn the other cheek, but he didn't want to. "Both of you took the situation to a whole nutha level. She's mad because you downplay our relationship. We were together for like twenty fuckin' years. That doesn't mean shit to you? I mean, what kind of dick does this dude have that has you so hemmed up?"

"It has nothing to do with sex. Damn! That's the first route that you want to take because of your own insecurities. Accept that I'm not in love with you anymore."

Kane shook his head in disbelief. "You don't get it. Fine, Carmen, have it your way. Do you and I'll continue to do me," he fired back. Kane headed for the door, knowing that it was time for him to leave. "As far as Kristian goes," he continued, "you better fix that shit otherwise you'll be repeating history. I know you don't want to be like Patricia." Kane ducked when he saw one of the toasters flying straight at his head. It hit the door before dropping onto the tiled floor. He stared at it for a second or two before looking back at Carmen. She was leaving the kitchen on the opposite side of the room. He stared at her until he could no longer see her. Fruit was still on the walls while a broken toaster lay on the kitchen floor.

Grunting loudly, Kane made his way out of the kitchen. Not even bothering to speak to Patricia, he left the house immediately. By the time he was outside, he could see Kristian's old Lexus leaving the driveway. He thought to follow her, but he knew she needed her space. He also needed his.

Chapter Forty-Seven

It had been awhile since Kristian had strolled through the Brookstone City Park. After the argument with her mother, she knew she needed to get out of the house. The park had always been her refuge and thankfully, it didn't fail her this time. There weren't many people there, which allowed her to walk around with little interference. She headed towards the lake, taking note of her surroundings. The closest people to her were still far off, which made her think that she had found her safe haven. She took a seat on the grass, trying to make sense of everything that had happened.

I made the decision to create you.

Kristian wiped her face, not wanting to cry. She knew she had said some hurtful things to her mother, but she never expected her mother to retaliate. However, she had and her words hurt her deeply. Kristian knew that she wasn't conceived naturally. She had heard the countless conversations her parents had when they thought she and King were asleep. It always started with her mother asking for another baby while her father would argue that he didn't want in vitro. Then, her mother would remind him of how they'd gotten their second child. The discussions never bothered Kristian, but now it did. *She made the decision? What is that supposed to mean? I thought she wanted me. I thought there wasn't any question in her mind that she wanted another baby.*

"Perhaps our eyes need to be washed by our tears once in a while, so that we can see life with a clearer view again."

Kristian furrowed her brow as she tried to picture who was speaking to her. For a quick second she thought she had caught the voice, but she wasn't sure. Turning around, she stared in amazement at Nicholas. He was the last person she ever thought she would run into in Brookstone. She hadn't even thought about him since Blu had mentioned him at the mall.

"Alex Tan," he said, sitting down beside her, "one of the greatest quotes ever."

Kristian stared at him and gave him a quick once-over. He looked pretty much the same, but she could tell that he had lost a little bit of weight. He wasn't as muscular as he once was. In addition, he was clad in a pair of nicely tailored jeans and a blindingly white button-up.

"You want to tell me why you're crying?"

Kristian shrugged her shoulders. "I really didn't come out here to talk."

"You never do," he replied. "I find a way to make you."

A slight chuckle escaped Kristian's lips as she remembered some of their past discussions. Nicholas always did have that effect on her regardless if she wanted to admit it. She figured that this time wouldn't be any different. "How are you doing?" she asked him.

Nicholas swayed his head from side to side. "Good for the most part. I'm a junior this year. Credits are looking right so I'm going to graduate on time. I'm trying to put my dirty money to good use. I want to start my own business. The music industry is the thing right now." Nicholas gave Kristian a half smile. Since he had her in front of him, he used it as his time to dissect her. The last time he had spoken to her, she was fifteen, naïve, and was physically still growing into a woman. Now, she was eighteen, appeared to be more mature, and had the body of Teairra Mari. As he noticed her growth, he figured that she could see his, too. He had done a complete three-sixty from the guy she had first met. Both of their changes appeared to be for the better. "So," he asked her, "why are you crying?"

"My grandfather passed," Kristian replied. She gave him an honest answer though it wasn't the full story. It only described half of why she was crying. Telling him the truth meant discussing the drama with her mother. "He's the founder of Davenport Realty. I know you've heard of Harold Davenport. No one really knows him as Lotus Pagua."

"I have. I'm sorry to hear that," Nicholas responded. "Damn, I know that was tough. He passed right after that shit went down at Blue Magic. That is fucked up. Your moms got locked up for that shit, right?" Nicholas looked at Kristian, but it was obvious that she didn't know what he was talking about. "How long have you been home, Kris?"

"I got here about an hour ago," she told him.

Nicholas looked behind him as he scoped the park out. There weren't a lot of people out there, which made him believe that he could speak freely. "You don't know what the hell is going on, do you?" When Kristian shook her head, Nicholas knew that it was time to fill her in. "Due to the history that we have, I intentionally kept my distance. That didn't mean that I didn't care or that I wasn't trying to see you. It meant that I was trying to respect the space that you were in. You caught me, though. Remember that day that I was outside of Brookstone High? I was in the parking lot."

"Yeah, but what are you getting at?"

"I'm getting at Shawn Blumington, Kris. I know who he is. I saw him at your school. I haven't been able to find him, but I know what he's about. He's the one who's behind the shit that happened at Blue Magic. Word is that some guys who worked for him attacked Jay in the parking lot. Santiago dropped them all. Shot them up and everything. Cops then put out a warrant for his arrest. They said they had some keys of his, too. They got your mom only by association. They're trying to charge her with conspiracy or some shit."

Kristian shivered, realizing that her mother was in the middle of a war between two drug lords. *Damn, Mama, you're in some deep shit this time. I hope you can get yourself out.*

"I don't know what the beef is between the two, but Blu wants Jay dead. He didn't get him this time so I know he's going to try again. Y'all are going to need around the clock security. Who's been watching you since you've been in school? Where do you go, anyway?"

"Copperfield University, it's an HBCU in Georgia."

"Cop—" Nicholas didn't want to speak too soon. Yet, he was certain that the school was located in Copperton City, the very same place that Blu was from.

"Jerome is down there, too," she told him. "King doesn't know about it. I've been holding the secret."

Nicholas wiped his face trying to make sure he heard right. As soon as Kristian had dropped Jerome's name, he became suspicious. "Hold up, I haven't seen that dude in a hot ass minute. He used to roll with King all the time. It was him and his cousin, Rico. They were stacking mad paper. I felt like they really came up once I got out the biz. Jerome got that bad car, started rocking all them suits. Dude was slinging crazy." Nicholas shook his head as he remembered the most important part of what Kristian had said. "He's in Georgia now?" Nicholas rose to his feet. "Man, Kris, you got to stay away from him. If he's in Georgia, he's only there for one reason."

"What?" Kristian glanced up at Nicholas, noticing the stern expression on his face. "Why?" she asked him, standing too. "I mean, I know Jerome is still hustling, but he's my brother's best friend. Jerome is harmless."

Nicholas grabbed her shoulders, knowing that Jerome was working for Blu. The man had Georgia on lock and if he was still hustling, Jerome didn't have a choice, but to work for him. If he did then that put him and King as enemies. There was no way that Jerome was working for Blu and King was cool with it. "I'm not playing with you on this Jerome shit. Stay away from him."

"You have to give me more than that. I've known Jerome all my life. I..." Kristian paused as she remembered something important. "Do you still have your red Cadillac?"

"Why do you care about that?"

"Do you still have it?" Kristian yelled back.

"Hell yeah, it's a classic."

"Get rid of it. Blu saw you at my school. He put a hit out on you."

Nicholas balled up his fists as he turned towards the parking lot where his car was. The incident at her school had happened a while ago, which meant that he wasn't at the top of Blu's hit list. "Maybe, it isn't safe for either one of us," he told her. "I suggest you get out of here. I need to be doing the same. If he's serious, he's going to take any opportunity like he did with Jay." Nicholas slowly backed away from Kristian, but he knew it wouldn't be the last time they spoke. "Remember what I said about Jerome. Stay away from him."

Kristian nodded her head and started to walk in the opposite direction. She walked at a fast-paced as she headed back to her car. Thanks to Nicholas, she now had a new set of worries. While it had taken her mind off her problems with her mom, it had given her a new set of things to be concerned about. She had always been suspicious of Jerome, and now she knew why.

As she returned home, Kristian thought about warning King. *Maybe it wouldn't be a bad thing to tell King about Jerome being in Georgia. He might need to know.* She thought she would have the answer by the time she made it to the house, but she was wrong. She was instantly reminded of her first set of worries when Jay's limousine pulled in behind her car.

Before she saw him, she saw a large duffle bag being placed on the ground. Is my mom really letting him do this? Is she for real? Kristian watched as Jay got out of the vehicle. She shook her head in disbelief as he walked up to the house. After the argument they had, Kristian was certain that her mother would tell Jay to keep his distance. But from what she could tell, that was not what her mother had done. In fact, it looked as if her mother was expecting him because Fiona let him in without a problem. *First, he's spending the night. Next, he'll be moving in. Thanks Mom, this is the perfect way to teach us how to act when we're married.* Kristian let out a huge sigh before grabbing her purse off the passenger seat.

She told herself to ignore the situation, but it would be harder to do with Jay in the house. With every move she made, he could pop up, giving her another quick reminder. *I guess I have to deal with it. I'll be leaving before he will.* Kristian went into the house, heading straight for her room. When she reached the top of the steps, she could see Jay going inside of her mother's bedroom. She stared in his direction until the door closed behind him. Unable to eavesdrop, she continued on to her room. Judging from the way she was feeling, it was the best place for her to be. She didn't turn on any lights; simply going inside and laying down on her bed. A flood of tears then made its way down her face. Kristian remained in that position until her tears eventually drew her into a deep sleep.

***

Jay sat his duffle bag on the bed when he realized that his presence wasn't going to garner a response from Carmen. Busy sketching, she hadn't even looked in his direction. When he'd last seen her she was concerned about the encounter he had with her mother. Before that, he had witnessed the tail end of an argument between her and Tiara. Either one of those situations could be the reason that she was being withdrawn. Wanting to find the underlying cause, he moved his duffle bag off the bed, sitting down beside her. She didn't stop drawing, which prompted him to move closer to her. She continued to ignore him until he placed his hand on the sketch pad. It was then that she looked his way.

"Long story," she said as if she was reading his mind.

Jay picked up the sketch pad from off her lap to give it a glance. He instantly recognized her father's likeness although the sketch was more of a rough design of a man's suit. He gave it back to her, exhaling. "Talk to me, Peaches."

Carmen moved the sketch pad onto the end table. She had been working on it nonstop since her blow-up with Kristian and Kane, but she knew it was time to actually talk out her problems. It wouldn't be easy, but she had to do it. "I got into like three arguments today," she told him. "The first one was with Tiara." Carmen looked over at Jay as she felt herself getting upset over the memory. "She asked me if I slept with Malik."

Jay narrowed his eyes as he heard the unthinkable. He knew that Malik had put the question in his head months ago, but his friend quickly denied ever touching Carmen. For Tiara to ask the question, someone had to get in her ear. "Why did she ask you that?"

Carmen shrugged her shoulders. "She never said. I told her no, but it's the fact that she asked me. I mean, we had this discussion before. I cleared it up then. I...I shouldn't be dealing with this, Jay. I shouldn't. As if that's not enough, Kristian drops the bomb that she saw us making out at Sapphire. She was mad at me for months and I didn't even know it until today. I sensed it, though. I knew something was wrong. She also doesn't want me to go through with the divorce."

Carmen's last statement made Jay realize that she was fighting an internal dilemma. He knew that she no longer wanted to be with Kane, but that decision was creating a wedge between her and her daughter. "Do you want me to talk to her?" he asked. "Maybe, I can get her to come around. I mean, you're still going to go through with the divorce right?"

"Of course," Carmen replied. "I've made my decision. Now, if you're going to talk to her, be careful with what you say. Kane is her father and you know she's going to take sides. She was siding with him anyway. She wants me with him regardless if I'm happy or not."

"I'm not going to rush into it. I'm going to apologize and let her know that I love you. She might not like it, but at the end of the day, she can't do anything about it. Can she?"

Carmen shook her head. "She can't. It is what it is. What about the Tiara situation?"

"Y'all have been friends your entire lives. She should know you by now to know that you wouldn't touch her husband. You told her you didn't do it, she should believe you. Shit, she should've asked Malik. He would've told her the same thing." Jay curled up next to Carmen so that his lips were touching her neck. He gave her a few kisses before she pulled away from him.

"What happened between you and my mom?"

"Nothing," Jay answered, quickly. "She was upset about Lotus."

"So you—" Carmen was interrupted by the sound of Jay's phone ringing. She didn't want their conversation to be over, but she knew that there were other things that needed to take precedence. From what she could hear, King was the one who had called.

"Forty-eight hours is the deadline," Jay was saying, discussing the vault. "Keep check on everybody. Make sure everything is running smoothly. Take tomorrow off though. Don't work on anything, Iceland, Sapphire, nothing," he continued. "Don't be like me, working through your grief."

Listening to Jay's words, Carmen suddenly remembered that she hadn't seen King all day. She wasn't necessarily worried about him because she knew he was stronger than his other siblings. Based off his conversation with Jay, he seemed to be holding up well. Their talk didn't last long and before she knew it, Jay was off the phone. While their conversation had been interrupted, she didn't want to sway away from it. "My mom," Carmen asked again. "I don't believe that was nothing. I heard y'all." Jay didn't reply, instead he stood up from the bed and began to take off his clothes. After he had gone down to his boxers, he flipped the light switch, leaving the room in complete darkness. "What were y'all arguing about?" Carmen repeated.

"Nothing," he replied. He pulled the covers back, getting in the bed next to her. "I promise. She was upset about Lotus, that's it."

Carmen didn't believe him, but she decided not to probe him any longer. If he didn't want to talk, he didn't have to. Her mother would tell her in due time. For now, Jay could keep his secret. *Daddy always said,* Carmen thought, *whatever is done in darkness will come to light. Jay can keep quiet for now, but soon the wolves will be howling.*

Chapter Forty-Eight

While everyone else was getting comfortable in their beds, King was waiting for his father's private plane to arrive at the airport. He had asked Coco to fly home to be with him and despite her hectic class schedule, she had obliged. Certain that she had told her parents about the trip, he knew that they wouldn't be spending the night together. Coco was the type of girl who always did things decently and in order. For the most part, King liked that about her. In situations like this, he didn't. Tonight, he wanted her all to himself since they had recently made up.

When his father's plane stopped a few yards in front of him, he knew he would soon find out if he would get his wish. A bouquet of roses was in his left hand and a surprise present from Iceland was in the other. A large grin formed on his face when Coco appeared in the doorway. He allowed her to come down the steps, meeting her at the very bottom. "I've missed you," he yelled, grabbing her into his arms. "I've missed these, too," he told her, copping a feel.

"King, we're in public," Coco squealed, backing away. "You can't be grabbing on the twins like that!"

King chuckled before grabbing Coco's bag out of her hands. "These are for you," he told her, handing her the roses. "And this," he said, showing her the box, "is a little gift from Iceland. I had it custom-made."

Coco tried to hold back her excitement, but she knew it was showing through. As she followed King towards their limo, she shook the box, trying to hear what was inside. The box made a loud rattling noise, which made her believe that it was either a bracelet or ring.

"Did you tell your parents you were here?"

Coco shook her head as she sat down in the car. "I was going to call them, but I didn't get the chance. I texted Kristian before I got on the plane, though. She didn't respond so I don't know if she got it. I figured I would stop by tomorrow to give my condolences."

King smiled to himself, knowing that he could put his plan into action. "So, you're spending the night with me? I mean; its ten o'clock. You didn't tell your parents you were coming so you might as well stay at my house. Malachi is there, but he won't be bothering us. I bought him three new video games. He'll be busy with those."

Coco looked out of the corner of her eye as she continued to shake the box. "I didn't say all that," she replied, starting to open it. "We'll see."

Coco pulled the lid off of the box to see an eighteen karat white gold baguette ring inside. "Are you serious?"

King stared down at the ring as he nodded his head "Dead serious," he told her. "Will you marry me?" King eyed Coco carefully as she gazed at the ring. When she hesitated, he knew that she was thinking about her mother. Maya Masterson wasn't his biggest fan and wouldn't be the least bit thrilled that he had proposed. It would be hell on earth when she saw Coco wearing his ring. "Say something," he urged.

"King, there's so much going on. You want to propose right now?"

"Yeah," he said with a chuckle. "Can I get an answer?"

Coco knew her answer was yes, but she was hesitant to say it. She knew her mother was against her being with King and would be furious to know that she had accepted his proposal without discussing it with her. She wanted to marry him yet she didn't want to feel her mother's wrath. Still, she couldn't let her mother stop her from following her heart. If she wanted to be with King forever, accepting his proposal was the first step. "Yes," she finally told him. "I want to marry you."

King's face lit up as he watched her slide the ring onto her left hand. Excitedly, he leaned in, centering his lips on top of hers. They kissed for several minutes until Coco pushed him away. He figured she had grown uncomfortable since his hands had made their way back to her chest.

"Okay, Jayceon," she said, straightening her shirt. "You've gotten your freebies."

"I can't have anymore?" he joked. "What about taking things a step further?"

"Taking things a step further?" Coco questioned. "Is sex really on your mind?"

"Shh, he can hear you," King whispered, pointing to their driver.

Coco narrowed her eyes, lowering her volume. "Are you serious about this? King, your grandfather died. Your parents almost went to prison. I thought you would be stressed and crying. I definitely didn't expect a proposal or a discussion about sex." Coco watched as King's entire disposition changed. He moved away from her, looking out the window. "Uh oh, those words changed your whole mood. Something is bothering you."

"I don't want to discuss it," he replied. "It's the same ol', same ol'."

Coco grabbed King's hand, wanting to comfort him. She wasn't exactly sure what the problem was until King started expressing his thoughts.

"My father isn't going to change. He proves it to me every time he calls with an order. Sometimes I wish I never signed on to his team. Yeah, we're legit now, but helping him cover his tracks is a hassle. He stays on my back like I'm the one that fucked up. He goes and creates a bloodbath and what do I have to do? I have to clean the shit up. I've been the clean-up man since he got back in this game. I'm tired of it, Coco. I'm ready to be out."

Coco moved closer to him, resting herself up against his lithe frame. "It's going to work itself out. I know you hate the way things are going, but your dad is in a tough spot right now. He has so many things on his plate that he doesn't even realize that he's putting so much on you."

"Sounds like you're taking up for him."

"I'm telling you what I see. Jay didn't meet you until you were seventeen years old. He doesn't know anything about being a father. He's been in your life, for what, about three years? All he knows how to do is run a business. Now that he has Rakim and Nyla, he's learning. They don't know right from wrong so he's the perfect father to them. You had Kane growing up. You know what a father is supposed to do. Jay is playing catch up."

King didn't want to admit that Coco was right. He knew he needed to be patient with Jay, but he wished his father learned faster than what he was. With the way things were going, it seemed that their relationship would never get on track.

"Okay, you're getting quiet on me." Coco peered up at him to see his expression. His face wore a scowl, which she desperately wanted to change. Taking him by surprise, she quickly kissed him on the lips. When he smiled at her, she kissed him again. This time, she opened her mouth, allowing their tongues to dance.

"Now we're getting somewhere," King joked. "Are you thinking about it?"

Coco pulled away so she could stare into his eyes. His mind had gone from his problems back to sex in a short amount of time. She knew now that he was serious about the discussion. In fact, a part of her was starting to question his proposal. *Did he ask me to marry him so he can get some? King knows I'm a virgin. We've never talked about sex before. Well, he did tell me that he had slept with two girls. I know about him and Akaila's mom, too.* Coco bit her lip as she thought about giving in to him. Her concern wasn't necessarily in the physical pain that came with losing her virginity, it was the aftermath. She had heard countless stories about girls who had gave it up only to become single again. She didn't want to be one of them.

"Say something. We're almost at the house."

"I don't know," Coco responded. "I really don't."

King backed away because his ears had heard an entirely different answer. She had said, I don't know, but in his mind, he had heard a firm no. "I feel like I took a mature step by proposing to you. If we could get married tomorrow, I would. I gave you the best part of me that I've never given anyone else. I gave you my heart. I'm asking for a part of you that no one else is going to get. It's something that will always be mine. If you're worried about me hurting you, it's not going to happen. I promise."

Coco felt his lips slide over hers once again. This time around, his kiss was short and sweet, because they were pulling up in front of his house. Once the car stopped, he merely grabbed her things before leading the way out of the limousine. She didn't get the chance to respond to him until they were in his bedroom. "Can we talk about it some more?" she asked him. He nodded his head, but didn't say much else. "I feel like you threw this on me. We never had a serious conversation about sex, never. Now, you have one with me, but it's so quick. It's like bam, bam, we talked, now let's do it. What's up with that? Is this the way you're trying to deal with your problems? Do you think sex will make you forget?"

King paused from undoing the buttons on his suit jacket to think about her question. He didn't want to say what it was exactly when he wasn't sure himself. "All I know, Coco, is that I love you and I'm ready," he replied. "I do have a lot on my plate, but to say that I'm using sex to deal with it would be wrong. I'm not pressuring you. I don't want to be the guy that does that. If your answer is no then the answer is no. We'll go to sleep and that'll be it." King pulled off his jacket, throwing it on the lounge chair in his room. Continuing to undress, he tried not to notice that Coco was doing the same.

When they finally got inside the bed, they were both half naked with the exception of their undergarments. Her head rested on his chest while he had one hand running through her silky black hair. It looked like a picture perfect moment yet both of them were overtly nervous.

"Tomorrow we're going to your parents' house, right?"

King nodded. "We'll be there first thing in the morning. I haven't even spoken to my mom. No telling what she's thinking right now. I don't even think that Malachi has been over there."

Coco leaned up off his chest so that she could look into his eyes. "I'm not in a rush to go home. We can spend all day with her," she told him, giving him a kiss on the lips. "Let's take our time." Coco kissed his lips again, this time opening her mouth. She could feel him following her lead as if he knew her words were allegorical.

The longer they kissed, the closer she became to giving in to him. Eventually, his fingers found their way to her strapless bra, which he removed in a matter of seconds. Already shirtless, he slid away from her, pulling his boxers down until his manhood was fully exposed. At that moment, Coco knew that there was no turning back.

As each second passed, King's body seemed to move closer to hers. She put her arms over his shoulders as one of his hands cradled the back of her head. Coco could feel her nerves kicking in though she tried to keep them at bay. It became harder to do as King showered her body in kisses, starting to explore several unseen areas. Her desire was to do the same until she felt his body shift on top of hers. He pulled her into him, allowing his body to become situated in between her thighs. It was then that Coco noticed that King had managed to remove her underwear. They locked eyes as he slid the tip of his penis inside of her.

Coco raised her eyebrow at first because it was painless. A bit confused, her face quickly scrunched up when King pushed himself further inside. The pain seemed to hit all at once. Her grip tightened on his shoulders as he began to thrust repeatedly, but he didn't stop. He continued on and she eventually became numb to the pain. While she could tell that he was enjoying it, it wasn't until he was almost finished that the pain slowly turned into pleasure.

For the first time that night, Coco felt herself enjoying their connection. Yet, as quickly as it had begun, it was over. King's body became complacent on top of hers as he rested. When he did finally move, Coco placed her head back on his chest and he nestled his hand in her hair. Not a single word was spoken and eventually they both fell asleep.

The very next morning, King awoke, expecting to find Coco beside him. When he saw that she wasn't there, he immediately listened for any sign of movement in the house. The first thing he heard was the sound of something hitting the floor. The noise wasn't that loud, but he still climbed out of his bed to check it out. He pulled on a pair of jogging pants and stopped first at Malachi's room where his brother was packing a suitcase. "Going somewhere?" he asked him with a yawn. "What's that for?"

Malachi looked up at him, answering his question as he continued to pack. "Akaila is at home. I figured I would stay at the house for a few days. I want to spend some time with her." Malachi dumped three t-shirts into the suitcase before zipping it up. "Is that okay?"

"It's cool, no problem."

King watched him for a few more seconds before deciding to get a move on. He told Malachi he was going to go look for Coco while at the same time announcing that she was there. Malachi didn't seem to mind as he turned his attention to one of his video games. In the meantime, King left the room, heading for the stairwell. Before he even reached the bottom step, he could hear Coco's voice. He didn't like to eavesdrop, but he knew he needed to because of what had happened between them. Based off what

Coco was saying, she and Kristian were discussing their trip back to Georgia. Funeral arrangements for his grandfather had been made for Saturday, but Kristian wanted to fly back to Georgia on Sunday. The news didn't sit too well with him, which immediately sent up a red flag in his mind. He knew that if he really wanted to know what was going on, he had to hear more. He went into the kitchen right when Coco was rushing Kristian off the phone.

"Morning," she mumbled, setting her phone onto the counter. She smiled, shyly, seeing the suspicious expression on King's face. "I couldn't sleep," she explained. "You know how that goes, being in a new place and everything."

"I see," he responded. King stared at her for a few seconds before looking down at her cell phone. He thought to ask her about Kristian, but he could hear Malachi coming down the steps. Not wanting to prolong them from getting to his mother's house, he told her that he was going back upstairs to get dressed. An hour later, they were in his mother's foyer. Malachi retreated upstairs to his old room while Coco followed behind him to Kristian's. King ended up in his mother's office, finding her at her desk. "Miss me?" he asked.

Carmen looked up, seeing King standing in the doorway. While a part of her wanted to run to him, the stress of planning her father's funeral kept her planted in her seat. "I always do," she told him with a smile. "You need to come around more."

King approached his mother's desk, taking a peek at what she was working on. Her right hand was busy putting the final edits on a design while the paper next to it was a rough outline of his grandfather's homegoing service.

"I'm designing his suit," Carmen told him. "Your grandmother is going to sew it. I've already booked the church and Minister Harrison has agreed to do the eulogy. Everything is coming together except for the fact that we don't know any of my father's family. We decided to do another press release, acknowledging that he was born Lotus Pagua. I don't know how my father would have felt about that, but I want to meet his family. I hate that he had to pass in order for them to finally come around."

King parted his lips to reply, but he was interrupted by the sound of someone coming down the steps. He looked towards the doorway only to see his father with Rakim in his arms.

For the first time since his little brother had been born, King felt a spark of jealousy that he didn't know existed within him. He felt the emotion even more when he made his way into the dining room for breakfast. His grandfather had tried to make him believe that Jay loved him yet his father didn't show any signs of it. He didn't even speak a single word to him during the meal. Jay's attention was solely focused on Rakim, which made King sulk. He believed wholeheartedly that if Lotus was there, he could help him make sense of it all. Since he wasn't, King had to deal with his problems on his own.

For the duration of the visit, he held everything in. Once he was back in his car, he could no longer keep his emotions bottled up. Without any signs or pretense, King cracked. Coco tried her best to comfort him, but she couldn't give him what he wanted. No one could except Jay.

Chapter Forty-Nine

For the most part, King kept his breakdown to himself. Turmoil was ever present in his mother's house and he knew that adding to it wasn't the best option. His grandfather's funeral had been set for Saturday afternoon, which gave him three full days to spend at his mother's estate. In that short length of time, he had learned about his mother's argument with Kristian and discovered that she was planning to file for divorce on Monday morning. On Friday, she made it known to the rest of the family.

As if that wasn't enough, Kristian was adamant about leaving Sunday evening to return to Copperton City. King felt that it was too soon, but Kristian griped that she couldn't live another second in their mother's house. Despite the family's attempts to convince her to stay for another week, Kristian wouldn't give in. In the end, both of his sisters and Coco decided to return to Copperton City at the same time on Sunday.

The only person King felt was acting normal was Malachi. His brother often kept to himself, making only small talk with the rest of the family. Occasionally, he would ask to go shopping and King would take him to get a break from the house. Once they returned, they were again submerged in the tension. It all came to a head when his stepfather visited the house on Friday night. Kane had popped up out of nowhere, anxious to know the details of his father-in-law's homegoing. To make matters worse, he had come right after his mother had announced that she was filing for divorce. No one spoke a word of it to Kane when he arrived, which seemed to be the best route because his stepfather went off about Jay being in the house. That particular argument had ended with his mother cursing him to hell and his stepfather slamming the door as he left.

Even now, at his grandfather's burial ceremony, King could see the hurt on his stepfather's face. Kane's eyes were hidden behind a pair of black shades yet his pain was apparent. His mother had previously stepped out in public with Jay after their bail hearings, but now she had taken it up a notch. She arrived to the funeral hand in hand with him while Kane followed shortly behind her with Kristian. Security could only do so much to control the paparazzi, but the news had already spread that Carmen Davenport and Jay Santiago were officially an item. Though the funeral had made his parents a hot topic, King tried to keep his mind centered on his grandfather.

"We commit his body to the ground," Minister Harrison was saying, "earth to earth, ashes to ashes, dust to dust. The Lord bless him and keep him, the Lord make His face to shine upon him."

King glanced to the right of him to look at his mother. One of her hands was intertwined with Jay's while the other was inside of Grandma Pat's. Her expression hadn't changed since the funeral, which prompted King to turn away from her. He looked back at his grandfather's white casket only to see a familiar face standing afar off. Dressed in a black suit, Lil' Noc was standing alone almost as if he didn't want to be noticed. Unsure of why he was there, King waited until the ceremony was over before he made mention of it to his father and Malik. After both of them persuaded him to talk to him, King headed in Lil' Noc's direction. Before he even reached him, Lil' Noc had started pacing. "You got some real balls coming here. You didn't get enough at the last rundown?"

Nicholas took a step back as he studied King's face. He could tell that he was in defense mode, but he needed time to explain himself before King flipped. "I wanted to pay my respects," he began. "I also needed to talk to you. I've been doing a little digging."

"Digging?" King questioned. "You thought this would be the best time to give me some news? This is a fuckin' funeral."

Nicholas swallowed, but he told himself not to let King's attitude derail what he had come to say. "I know y'all have bad blood with Blu. I know he was behind what happened to your father at Blue Magic. See, the streets on the Westside have been talking. Most people know that we aren't on the best of terms. They've been dropping dimes in my ear."

King put both of his hands into his pocket as he stared Lil' Noc in the face. Certain that he wasn't bluffing; he decided to hear him out. "Speak," he ordered.

"Blu left Brookstone a couple of days ago. He's back in Georgia. He isn't the only one, though. After your father closed up shop, a lot of men were out of work. One of them was your friend, Jerome. Word is that he's in Georgia, too, working for Blu. I can't tell you if he knew about the hit on your parents, but he's there."

King scrunched up his face as his body temperature rose. He could understand Jerome moving away, but to work with Blu was the ultimate no-no. Then again, he didn't know how trustworthy Lil' Noc's information was. "Why are you telling me this shit?"

"Man, I'm trying to look out for y'all. This isn't even on any revenge shit. I heard y'all were legit and so am I. I graduate in a year or so with a degree in Business so I figured that you could help me put my dirty money to good use. I still got a few stacks."

An evil smile spread across King's face. "Are you asking me for a job?" King straightened his face as he started to feel like he was being tricked. "How do I know you aren't working for Blu? You're standing here trying to get on the inside to give him a quicker route to us. Admit it, Lil' Noc, we took a lot of money out of your pocket when we started slinging full-time."

"First thing," Nicholas replied, raising his voice. "Don't call me Lil' Noc. My name is Nicholas Powers. Second, I told you, I'm not on any revenge shit. If you really want to know, I'm telling you this because I care about Kristian. I know she goes to school in Copperton City. The last thing I want is to see her get hurt. So if I have to protect you to protect her then I'm going to do it."

King mumbled incoherently as Nicholas revealed that he still was crushing on his sister. "So you think that saying her name is going to make a difference?" King stared at Lil' Noc, hoping that he realized he didn't get a pass when it came to Kristian. "Yeah, yeah, yeah, you want a job, here it goes. Help us find Blu. Since you claim he's back in Georgia, we're going to take a little trip this week. Get your guns ready."

"King, I'm not trying—" All Nicholas needed was a quick memory of what Kristian had told him at the park. Blu had a hit on him and could strike at any moment. Because of the threat on his life, his Cadillac now wore a forest green shade. "Okay, King, you got me. I'm in."

"Good, meet me Monday morning at seven o'clock on the third floor of Blue Magic. I think Phase will be happy to see who joined the—" King paused when he realized that his mother was beside him. An inquisitive expression was on her face so he gave her a slight smile only to ease her concerns. "We were talking about doing some business," he summed up.

Carmen looked over at King before she looked at Nicholas. The guy gave her a smile as well, which calmed her nerves that he wasn't there on BS. She then looked back at King, holding up the plant that was in her hand. "Akaila and I are going to put flowers on her mother's grave. Mama isn't doing too well so we're going to leave in about thirty minutes."

"Cool, I'll be back over there in a sec," King replied. He turned back to Nicholas, but didn't finish his statement until his mother had walked away.

In the meantime, Carmen walked towards Akaila, holding a lily bouquet. Halfway there, her step was cut off. Carmen wasn't shocked to see Tiara at her father's funeral, but they hadn't spoken since their argument. Still slightly upset over it, Carmen knew that if Tiara tried her, she would jump down her throat.

"Everything was real beautiful," Tiara voiced. "I know your father is—" Carmen stopped her before she could finish.

"Tiara, you know we're not cool like that," Carmen said, keeping her voice above a whisper. "Don't play me. If you're going to say anything to me than it should be an apology. You accuse me of sleeping with your husband and then want to pretend that everything's alright?" Carmen dimmed her eyes as she relived the argument in her head.

"I'm sorry, Carm. I am," Tiara cried. "I let someone get in my head, and I messed up. If I could take it back, I would. Can this just be over? I love you. You're my best friend."

Carmen wanted to hold a grudge, but she knew she couldn't stay mad at Tiara. They had been through too much for her to even let the accusation hurt their friendship. Though she was still bothered by it, she gave in. "I accept your apology," she told her, holding up the lily bouquet. "I have to meet with Akaila to visit Tricia's grave so why don't we talk tomorrow? Is that cool?"

Tiara quickly agreed, prompting Carmen to walk away. She found Akaila at Tricia's grave, setting a peace plant next to the gravestone. Carmen wasn't sure if she needed more time alone with her, but when Akaila noticed her presence, she quickly told her that she was done. Carmen would have preferred for them to give their flowers together, but she knew there was a reason for everything.

She took a deep breath and knelt down in front of Tricia's tombstone. "Well, it's not a secret that we weren't the best of friends," she told her. "I wouldn't exactly say we were enemies, but we had our differences. For some reason, we never confronted each other about them. I don't know if that was a good thing or a bad thing. What I do know is that I'm going to do everything in my power to make sure that your kids grow up to be successful. I know you're proud of them and so am I. Without you, I wouldn't have them. I guess that means I'm indebted to you." Carmen placed the lily bouquet on the right side of the tombstone. "I know that I could never take you or Consuelo's place. I don't want to. I just want to make you proud," she continued.

Carmen stared at the tombstone for a few seconds longer before rising to her feet. She gave her daughter a quick hug before they proceeded to walk back to be with the rest of the family. She could already see her mother getting back into the limo while Jay was in a huddle with Malik and King. In addition, Cesar and Linx were standing with them as well. Their conversation looked serious so Carmen didn't bother to interrupt them. Instead, she made her way to the family car. Once inside, she sat there quietly as she watched Jay interact with the men around him. A rock sat in her stomach as she stared at him, remembering that she had unfinished business. She had never told Jay, but she had plans to visit Donnie's wife.

After they left the cemetery, they returned home, but she didn't stay long. Only about ten minutes had passed before she drove to Jessica McClain's two-story house. As she waited patiently for someone to come to the door, a slew of thoughts bombarded her mind. Donnie was still being declared as a missing person, yet his wife had remained silent throughout the entire investigation. Carmen found it slightly odd, but she assumed that the woman was simply letting the police do their job. If that was the case, they weren't doing a good job of it. They were more concerned about getting Jay in prison than finding a missing limo driver.

Carmen rolled her eyes at the thought as a blonde-haired woman came to the door. When it finally opened, she put a small smile on her face before sticking out her hand. "Hi, I'm Carmen Davenport," she greeted.

"Oh, hi," the woman replied, "I'm Jessica, Jessica McClain." She gave her a shy smile, which quickly disappeared. "I'm sorry to hear about your father. I saw it on the news."

"Yes, I, um," Carmen became tongue-tied. "I, um, I kind of wanted to say the same. I know about Donnie's disappearance and I wanted to know if there was anything I could do. I felt like I owed it to you to say something since he worked for me."

"Well, um, I actually was in the middle of something. Maybe we can catch up later?"

"Oh," Carmen whispered. "That would be fine. I have a—" she paused as she reached inside of her purse. Pulling out her wallet, she opened it up to get a business card. "This has my office phone number on it. Give me a call whenever you want to get together." Carmen handed her the card, but she knew that she couldn't end the conversation that way. She felt the need to apologize to her without looking guilty. "Look, Mrs. McClain," Carmen began. "I know we have never met, but I wanted to know if there was anything I could do. Donnie didn't work for me long, but we became good friends in a short amount of time. I want to help."

Mrs. McClain covered her mouth as if she was going to have an outpouring of tears. Instead of breaking down, she simply frowned. "It's been hard, you know. We had this baby and now this. I haven't started back working so things are tight. I haven't given up hope, though. I still believe that Donnie is coming home."

Carmen folded her arms across her chest as she got a flashback of the gunshot wound in Donnie's head. She didn't want to tell his wife that he wasn't so she remained quiet. She wanted to give her some form of encouragement, but she didn't want to give her false hope. "The best thing to do is pray. Stay strong."

"I keep telling myself that," Mrs. McClain cried. "I've been praying, but sometimes…"

Not wanting to upset her anymore, Carmen took a step back. "Look, if you need anything, whether its money or whatever, give me a call."

Mrs. McClain let out a small smile. "Thank you, Ms. Davenport. I appreciate it."

"Anytime," Carmen replied. "You take care."

With those words, Carmen turned around, walking down the porch steps. She had remained composed when Mrs. McClain was in front of her, but now she no longer could. Tears flooded her face as the guilt stabbed her heart even more than before. As if that wasn't enough, she soon learned that she didn't come to the house alone. Though Linx had driven her, Kane's Jeep was right behind the limousine. His window was rolled down as if he had been watching the entire conversation. She walked in his direction, but he quickly drove away to avoid confrontation. His actions made her curse under her breath, but she told herself to let it go. Things between her and Kane would get worse before they got any better.

Chapter Fifty

Monday morning brought a new set of worries for Kane. For one he had caught Carmen visiting Donnie's wife and two, his daughters had returned to Copperton City. He was more understanding with the latter since he knew of the struggle Kristian was having living with her mom. In regards to Carmen, his wife always found a way to make him suspicious of her. Now, all he saw was the word guilty on her forehead.

Currently sitting outside of Starbucks, Kane took another sip of his Caramel Macchiato as he waited for Sanders to arrive. While he was desperate to tell him about Carmen's visit to the McClain residence, he knew it was best to keep the news at bay. The deal they had struck with Jay was more important. For the most part, he knew that the narcotics were no longer in the vault at the Brookstone PD. While he knew that Jay took them, he wouldn't know how the operation had been staged until Sanders arrived. Lieutenant Harris had promised to have him reinstated, but the paperwork wasn't yet final. It was the one thing that kept him from being in the know.

"Good morning to you, too," Sanders said, dropping a large stack of papers onto the table. "You could have gotten a cup for me."

Kane eased out a small smile before reaching for the stack. "No time for chit-chat, let's cut to the chase. What are we looking at?"

Sanders chuckled a bit as he started to sift through the papers. "Those three days didn't do you any good, did they? You were supposed to be in mourning, but you were itching to get to this meeting. It's understandable." Sanders pulled out a series of photos so that Kane could see the status of the vault. "I took these photos when I first noticed that the drugs were gone. I think it's safe to say that Jay did this overnight. If you look at the vault, you won't see any damage. The only thing gone is his drugs."

Kane picked up several of the photos, examining them. With the exception of the missing coke, it didn't look like anything had been touched. Realizing this, he dropped the photos back down on the table. "What about the prints? I mean, what do we have that says Jay did this?"

"There are none. The cameras were also destroyed so there isn't any footage."

Kane clapped his hands together signifying that they had nothing. "What is this shit, Sanders? You could've called me about this. We don't have shit to go on, but we got a million dollars' worth of missing coke. Where the fuck is that going to lead us?"

Sanders didn't reply. He took out an ink pen, pointing at a shot of the floor. "The flooring is tiled. I have a hunch that if we bring in a contractor we can find out how Santiago got the drugs. Once we learn how he got in then we can learn how he got out."

"All that is, is a hunch," Kane shot back. "It's worth looking into it, but we still don't have shit. Jay can fight his charges and walk away scot clean. Then, you know what's going to happen? The Triad and DEA are going to shut the department down because we lost our biggest bust. Fuck this shit. We should've played a different game with this joker." Kane picked up his beverage, and took a large sip. "Give me some good news if you got any."

Sanders rolled his eyes as he reached into his back pocket. He pulled out Kane's badge, setting it on the table. "It's a done deal. The paperwork is complete."

A grin appeared on Kane's face. He kindly took the badge and put it into his own pocket. "See, that's what I'm talking about. That's good—" all of a sudden a man walked up to their table. He was dressed plainly in a pair of black slacks and a light blue shirt. He didn't look familiar, but Kane knew the man had to be approaching him on business.

"Michael Kane?" the man asked.

Kane got ready to say yes until he noticed the thick envelope in the man's hand. A part of him became nervous, but he knew that he shouldn't have been. He had been in the same situation almost a year ago with Rakim's paternity. Still, a rock sat in his stomach as he realized that he was staring at a process server. The word yes was mouthed from his lips as he watched the man drop the envelope on the table before walking away. Kane tried his best to not let his embarrassment show. He simply opened up the envelope, and started to read the papers. When he saw that Carmen was moving forward with the divorce, he clenched his jaw. As he continued to read, he learned that she didn't want to give him spousal support or visitation rights to Rakim and Nyla. At that point, he lost his cool. Before Sanders could even speak to him, he was out of the chair, headed to his car. One hand held the divorce papers while the other held his phone as he called Carmen. She didn't answer, but Kane didn't need for her to. He knew where to find her.

He immediately drove to her house and parked behind one of two limousines. He could tell that someone was getting ready to leave because he could hear the motor running in one of the cars. He hoped it wasn't his wife because he was ready to tear into her.

He pulled out his house key, attempting to unlock the door, but it no longer fit. *This fuckin' bitch changed the locks. Is she fuckin' serious?* Kane banged on the door several times until Carmen opened it. When he saw her, he had to remind himself not to strike her. "This is some fuckin' BS," he yelled at her as he pushed his way inside.

"Well, that was quick. Clement works fast," Carmen joked. "So you got the papers."

"You changed the fuckin' locks?"

Carmen instantly became confused over what Kane was angry about. She thought it was about the divorce papers, but he seemed to be fired up about the new locks. "Kane, you don't live here anymore. Why would I keep the locks the same?"

Kane paced around the foyer as he tried to control his anger. He wanted to punch everything in sight, but he knew it wasn't for the best. "This is some fucked up shit, Carm." Kane began to spit out all of his thoughts, almost speaking incoherently. "I'm sitting up here, reading this shit, and then I see that you don't want to pay me. You only give me visitation for Malachi? I put twenty years into this bullshit. You don't think I deserve anything."

"Spousal support?" Carmen questioned. "Okay, you're upset over that, fine. As far as Malachi goes, he's the only minor child we have. Rakim and Nyla aren't yours. Why would I grant you visitation for them?"

"Carm, I lived right here with them. I gave you twenty fuckin' years of my life. Then you got the nerve to bring your lover to your father's funeral? You flaunt him in front of the church members when they know you're married to me." Kane marched up to her, but the sound of someone clearing their throat stopped him in his tracks. He looked to the stairwell, seeing Jay at the top step. "I should've known he was here." Kane turned around so Carmen could see the hurt in his eyes. "You said till death do you part to me twice. At what point did you realize it was a lie?" Kane waited for her to respond. When she didn't, he tore the papers up in her face. He left the remains there on the floor as he walked out of the house. Immediately, he called Sanders and quickly apologized.

"I'm sorry about that. Right now, I don't care what we have to do," he told him as he got back into his Jeep. "I'm not taking my foot off his neck. Go ahead and call a contractor. If we have to tear up the basement to get this motherfucker then we have to. I'm all in."

Sanders quickly expressed that he'd been thinking the same. They agreed to have something together in forty-eight hours before Kane informed him that he was on his way to the precinct. He hung up the phone as he passed through the steel gates of Carmen's estate. When the gates closed behind him, Kane felt like it was symbolical of his marriage. After twenty years, the chapter was officially closed.

Jay watched as Carmen began picking up the torn pieces of paper off the floor. He hadn't witnessed the entire argument, but he felt like he had seen enough to say something. As he came down the steps, he thought about the appropriate words to say. "People do a lot of things when they're hurt," he told her as he leaned down to pick up some of the paper, "Say a lot of things, too." He picked up the last few pieces before meeting eyes with Carmen. "He's a wounded dog."

"He has reason to be," Carmen replied. "I don't get why he's acting like this is all a big surprise. I told him a long time ago that I wanted a divorce. Is he mad because I actually went through with it? Maybe, he still has his hopes up for reconciliation."

Jay shrugged his shoulders. "It could be. If you ask me, it has nothing to do with the divorce. It's the fact that you're leaving him for me, that old fashion love triangle."

"More like the Bermuda Triangle," Carmen joked. She held out her hand for Jay to give her the paper he had picked up. Once he gave them to her, she went into her office, and threw them into the trashcan. "Were you headed out?" she called into the foyer.

Jay headed into the office, but she was actually on her way back out. They bumped into each other accidentally in the doorway. He let out a small chuckle before giving her a quick kiss on the lips. "I got a few things to take care of. I want to swing by Blue Magic for a few minutes. You know this past week hasn't been so good with the restaurant being closed. I want to walk around, generate some ideas for when we do open back up. I'm thinking of hiring some security so people can feel safe. You know we got a bad rep for having a shooting. I wonder who's responsible for that." Jay broadened his smile as he wrapped his arms around Carmen's waist. "I won't be gone long. I promise."

"Take your time; you know my mom is here."

Jay glanced back at the stairwell. Patricia had been keeping her distance, proving that she wasn't too keen on having him in the house. Since she was set to receive half of Davenport Realty as well as Lotus' other assets, Jay was certain that she would be moving into a place of her own. "I should," he joked. "I should never come back, huh?" He loosened his embrace as he prepared to leave. "Did Linx come in with you after your meeting with Clement?"

"Yeah, he's probably watching television or something."

Jay placed his hand on the doorknob, slightly turning it. "He'll probably check in with Cesar in a little while. I'm going to go ahead and head out. I'll be back in a few." Jay took a step outside only to hear the limousine running. He closed the door behind him, continuing on to the car until he was seated inside. He started to direct Cesar to Blue Magic when he noticed that the man's arm was raised in mid-air. He was holding a box in the palm of his hand, which Jay had given him earlier that morning. Already knowing what was inside, he told him to hang on to it. "We'll deal with that after Blue Magic," he told him, "one thing at a time." Cesar set the box down in the passenger seat, and put the car in drive as he proceeded to leave the premises.

Less than fifteen minutes later, Jay was walking around the dining hall of Blue Magic. The inside of the restaurant was still very much intact while the parking lot was decorated with yellow tape. It was almost as if a dark cloud had been placed on the restaurant. He wouldn't consider reopening until the tape was removed.

As he surveyed the restaurant, Jay heard loud footsteps coming from the stairwell. He pulled out his pistol and moved toward the steps defensively. Gomez had advised him not to carry a weapon, but Jay hadn't followed his advice. As he got closer to the stairwell, he was relieved when he heard a familiar voice. It belonged to King who was coming down the steps with Lil' Noc. "What are y'all doing here?" he asked them, putting his gun back in his waistband. "I was about to murk both of you."

King was shocked to see his father. He hadn't expected him to be at Blue Magic since his meeting with Nicholas had been private. Given that his father was there, he felt obligated to tell him of his plans. "Talking business," he replied. He pulled out a chair at one of the tables and sat down. "Nicholas is about to join the team. You still got good relations with his pops, right?"

Jay nodded although it had been years since he had spoken to the man. "We're on good terms," he replied. Jay looked at Lil' Noc, deciding to call him by his real name since that's what King had used. "So Nicholas, what are you bringing to the table?"

King beat him to the punch. "He's been doing some research for us. Apparently, Blu made his way back to Georgia and he's supposed to be in Copperton City as we speak. Not to mention, he took another one of our soldiers with him. Jerome is in Copperton City, too. He works for Blu now."

Jay wasn't surprised at what he heard. "Jerome bowed out after I killed Rico. I didn't keep up with him so I figured he was around here somewhere. I guess his paper got a little short so he had to go to the next best thing. Bad choice, but I can handle it. I find Blu then I find him. I'll kill 'em both." Jay scratched his chin until he realized what he had said. He looked at King, but his son didn't look angry. In fact, he looked content.

"I concur," King responded. "My sisters and Coco are there right now and I know one of them got their eyes on 'em. They're probably waiting to pounce. Hopefully, Cesar's guy has been doing his job."

Jay stood up straight as he remembered telling his son that Cesar could refer a bodyguard for the girls. Cesar had given him a few references yet he had never officially hired one. The girls had been living under the watchful eye of no one except God.

"What's that expression for?" King asked, noticing the change in his father's face. "You got nervous real quick about something."

"I forgot about that," Jay revealed.

King stood up out of his seat as a slew of curse words came out his mouth. "You better be fuckin' playing with me right now. Tell me, you're fuckin' playing."

"Damn, King, they were only there for like, what, fuckin' two or three days or some shit? I can get on it in a minute. Cesar is right outside in the limo."

"I ask you for one fuckin' thing and you can't even do it. You're not worth shit," King muttered. He sat back down in his chair, and put his hand over his face. "Man, real talk, I'm not doing this shit anymore. I'm going to Georgia tomorrow, I'm going to take care of Blu, and then we're going to call it quits. I can't work for you anymore."

"Whoa, whoa," Jay yelled, walking up to King. "We got to handle one thing at a time. When did you decide to go to Georgia? You can't go down there in Blu's territory without backup. You got to have some major heat if you're going to deal with him."

"I can get the heat, that's not a problem. I'm going to have boxes of ammo and shit at my house tonight. Nicholas is going to roll with me. You tore up his spot before, well, we're going to do it again. We're going to keep going until we get him."

Jay shook his head in disbelief because King wanted to continue the war without him. "You weren't going to tell me, were you? Wait a minute, wait a minute, how in the world are you going to go down there and regulate when you couldn't pull the trigger before?"

"Things are different now. Don't worry about that, though. Go ahead and call Gomez, I'll get Clement and we can take care of the paperwork with these businesses. I want to be running my own shit."

Jay didn't mean to snatch King up, but somehow he did. He was angry over King's plans for Blu, but it was his threat to quit that made him aggressive. Nicholas quickly intervened and separated them. "You are really fuckin' up, you know that," Jay yelled as Nicholas pushed King in the opposite direction. "You can't do shit without me. I'm the fuckin' machine behind you. You think because I gave you a little knowledge about the game that you can do this shit on your own? Fuck you, King."

King didn't even bother to curse back at his father. It wouldn't mean anything, anyway. There wasn't anything that Jay could say or do to get him to change his mind. King had never asked him for anything except for him to get someone to watch his sisters and Coco. Jay had failed to do so, which told him that he was only looking out for himself. "I told you what the deal is. I'm going to Georgia to get Blu. You can ride out if you want. None of this arguing and cursing is going to change anything about what I'm going to do. I'm going to be good regardless. I made it seventeen years and I can make it seventeen more."

Jay stuck his middle finger up at King and headed out of the restaurant. A rage was forming inside of him that was ready to tear apart everything in his establishment. If he had stayed a second longer, he would have demolished the whole place. The worst part of it all was that Jay knew he had to make a decision. He couldn't let King go after Blu by himself. The problem was not in going, but in the timeframe that King had given him. Tomorrow was coming faster than Jay would've liked. King didn't have anyone to answer to while he had Carmen. Cesar reminded him of it when he held up the box once again, asking if it was time. Jay grabbed it out of Cesar's hand though he was unsure of what he was going to do. He had everything figured out at one point, but King's news had thrown him for a loop. "I'm dealing with some bullshit right now. Drive around the city for an hour or two."

"No problem," Cesar replied, "whatever you want."

Jay rested in his seat, dropping the box into his lap. He closed his eyes, attempting to calm his nerves, but it didn't work. Since there wasn't anything in the car that he could break, he had to deal with the frustration. He prayed that by the time he returned home, he would be back to normal. Once he hit Carmen's house, he had to put the box to work.

***

Carmen walked past the staircase as Jay walked back into the house. Certain that he was coming to their bedroom; she didn't bother to greet him. She continued on into her walk-in closet so she could finish straightening it. With Jay moving in, she needed to make a little bit more room for him. While moving some of her clothes, she heard a sudden burst of noise in the house. Rakim was wide awake and obviously wanted to make sure that everyone else was as well. Thinking that either Fiona or Jay was with him, she was surprised when she felt him latch onto her legs. "What cha doing?" she asked him, looking down. She only took a quick peek at him before placing her eyes back on a collared shirt.

"Wi-ll yy-oo-uu marr-eeey meeee?" he exclaimed.

Carmen immediately looked back down at him. He was holding his hand out to her, which made it easy for her to notice the ring. Her mouth dropped wide open when she realized that her son was holding a diamond, that was over twenty carats in his hand. Unsure of what to say, she grabbed the ring from him before picking him up into her arms. "Where did you get this?"

"Wi-ll yy-oo-uu marr-eeey meeee, Momm-eeey?" he screamed again.

Carmen was in a state of shock, which prevented her from responding. She knew Jay was behind the ring, but he had completely taken her by surprise. There was so much going on that being engaged was the last thing on her mind. As she stared at the ring, she noticed how it differed from the others he'd given her. This one in particular was the most expensive and intricate. In addition, it contained only white diamonds.

"Wi-ll yy-oo-uu?" Rakim asked, touching her face.

Carmen quickly kissed his cheek, as she heard Jay approaching. Not the least bit surprised to see him; she gave him a seductive smile, and asked, "Did you get this from Switzerland, too? Now, I see how you spend your millions."

"Answer me," Jay ordered. "I believe there's a question on the table."

Carmen looked at him sideways, but she could tell that Jay wasn't backing down. His expression was serious as well as his tone. She whispered her answer in Rakim's ear before putting him down. Almost automatically, Rakim ran to Jay while Carmen slid the ring onto her left hand. She then walked over to him, and planted a long kiss on his lips. "Yes," she told him, once they had broken apart. "How long have you been planning this?"

Jay wanted to say, forever, but the truth was that he had decided to propose during his night in jail. After their argument in San Juan, he was more than fearful of their relationship. His feelings didn't turn around until Carmen barged into his apartment, apologizing for threatening to sue him for custody. She had proved to him that she had changed for the better. Moreover, she was still by his side although he hadn't fought all of his charges. He was determined to make their relationship work and he could tell that she wanted to as well.

"A few days," he told her, finally answering. "Getting the ring was the easy part, deciding when to propose and how was the hard part. Thankfully, Rakim can actually speak so we can understand him. I thought he was the best man for the job."

Carmen chuckled as she placed another kiss on his lips. "He was, baby. You both did very well." Carmen glanced back down at her ring before smiling down at Rakim. He was holding onto Jay's legs, resting up against his father quietly. "Once my divorce is final, we can start with the planning."

Jay shook his head, not wanting to put off the wedding plans. He wanted them to start as soon as possible. That way, when the divorce was final, they could get married immediately. "I want us to set a date."

Carmen took a step back, and hugged herself. "The problem with setting a date is that my divorce isn't final. Kane and I haven't even gone to court. How do I know that he isn't going to put up a fight? If he does, this thing could get drawn out."

Jay didn't change his mind because of the complications that could arise. "I don't give a fuck what he wants. I want a date. If it helps, I'll pick, what about March?"

Taken by surprise, Carmen said, "Jay, its August. We both have charges to fight and you want to plan a million dollar event in less than eight months? I need more time. Shit, I need to get divorced first."

Jay blinked his eyes as he realized that he would have to compromise. The issues they each had to address weren't being kind to either one of them. Sighing, he decided to go with December. "Next year, then," he told her. "Let's get married in December. Matter of fact, let's do it December 25th, Christmas Day. We can keep it small, no more than ten people in the wedding party. We can even have it at my house in San Juan. There is plenty of room for a wedding and even our guests can stay there."

Carmen rubbed her lips together as she seemed more comfortable with the idea. "Well, at least I have a year to plan. San Juan, though? I'm going to need a team of event planners for this one. I guess I better start calling the DreamGirlz now. I hope they're not booked up." Carmen draped her arms at her side as she made her way to her bed. She sat down on it, watching as Jay came over to her. She thought his expression would appear more joyful since they had a date, but it actually looked worse than before. "Uh oh, there is something else."

"There is," Jay whispered. He wiped his hand over his face, uncertain of how to share King's plans with her. Their son had put him in a very uncomfortable situation. He knew Carmen wouldn't agree with his decision, but he couldn't let his son fight a battle without him. "I'm going to Georgia in the morning," he stated. "I'm not going to lie to you, it's about Blu. King wants to go after him and I'm not letting him go by himself. We both know that he isn't ready for this. He needs me."

Carmen wore a pained expression on her face as she felt the weight of a boulder on her shoulders. The day that was supposed to be memorable, because of the moment they'd shared, had taken a turn for the worse. "You are looking at spending the rest of your life in prison and you want to give the Triad something else to charge you with? King is on fuckin' probation. If any murder is tied back to y'all then you both are behind bars for life. So what, you make me happy with a ring then tell me you're going on a bounty hunt?" Carmen rose up off the bed, but Jay pushed her back down so she wouldn't leave.

"I was going to do it, but not this soon. Right now, it's not even about Blu. It's about King. You know he can't go by himself. Gun battles aren't his thing, they're mine."

Carmen closed her eyes as she tried to fight back her tears. "I know you want to get back at Blu for what he did, but you have too much to lose. Nothing is working in your favor right now. You can lose everything by chasing him. That includes your life."

"Blu is going to keep coming until he has what he wants. That is our diamonds and me dead. If we don't handle this right now, we might not get another chance."

Carmen cried silently, hating that she was allowing Rakim to see her so emotional. The tears came even faster when she felt her son's arms wrap around her legs as if he was trying to console her. She picked him up as Jay pulled her into an embrace. Although she didn't want to, she slowly was beginning to accept that Jay was leaving. Fearful of the future, every second counted that she had with him. In knowing that, she told him to take the remainder of the day to handle his business. Once the evening came, she wanted him home with her and the kids.

Jay respected her wishes, leaving shortly after their conversation. By seven o'clock that night, he was back in the house. He assured her that everything was a go and not to be worried, but Carmen still was. There was an unsettled feeling in her stomach that wouldn't go away for the remainder of the evening. In addition, memories of the past constantly flashed in her mind. It started with the image of Jay coaxing her into using her basement to her chance encounter with Blu. From there she saw Donnie being shot in the head to her standing in front of a judge at her bail hearing. The flashbacks seem to continue until she had fallen into a deep slumber.

Copperton City, Georgia

Blu glanced periodically out of the window as he was led down the streets of Copperton City. As he tried to relax himself, he lit his Montecristo, briefly taking his eyes off his surroundings. Once the cigar was between his lips, he directed his driver to take him onto the grounds of Copperfield University. For the past year or so, the campus had become his kingdom. Every time he saw the place, emerald-colored lights would flash in his mind like dollar signs. While the money was good, he wanted to get his hands on the black diamonds that he knew Jay possessed. This time around, Blu believed he had found a plan that would garner him a win. He had even found someone to carry it out. "You can stop right here," he told his driver. "Right in front of Potter Hall."

Blu slid his cigar out from between his lips when he saw Jerome. He had caught him in the middle of a sale, which was enticing to Blu's eyes. *More money, more power*, he thought. He rolled down his back window so that his presence could be made known. Jerome didn't see him right off, but once he noticed the Bentley, he hurried over. Once he was inside, Blu directed his driver to cruise the campus. "How are things looking?"

"Better than last night," Jerome replied. "Man, I was struggling out here."

"Keep your head up; you don't have to do this for much longer. Matter of fact, I got a new proposition for you." Blu cleared his throat before noticing that they were passing Buchanan Hall. He quickly instructed his driver to stop when he caught a glimpse of a familiar face. As if on cue, Kristian made herself visible right when he needed to see her. "I want that," he told Jerome, pointing in her direction. "That's what we need."

"Kristian," said Jerome, quizzically. He looked at her, hoping that Blu wasn't thinking what he thought he was. "She got back on Sunday. You know Harold Davenport passed. They had his funeral this weekend."

"I don't give a fuck about that shit," Blu barked. "I want her. We get her, we get those diamonds. If we're lucky, we'll get Jay in Georgia. His bitch isn't going to be too happy when she finds out her daughter is gone. Santiago will do anything to make sure she's pleased. I promise you."

"Man, Kristian is nothing. Let her be." Jerome shook his head as he began to think that Blu was going too far. Kristian didn't have anything to do with their beef with Jay or King. She was only connected to them because of who her mother was. "We can think of—" Jerome was silenced when he felt Blu's cigar burning into his shoulder blade.

"I want her. Get her for me. The sooner the better," Blu told him. "I don't think we need to go into the dynamics of the situation if you don't. Matter of fact, you might want to get started now. Tonight seems like as good a time as any, what do you say?"

"Come on, Blu. She doesn't have anything to do with Jay."

"Do it. Once you have her, meet me downtown by twelve. I'll take her off your hands."

Jerome cursed under his breath as he turned back towards Kristian. She was headed to her car and he knew that he would have to follow her. It was already a little after nine and Blu wanted her that night. He shook his head in disagreement as Blu told him to get out of the car. Jerome didn't want to leave the vehicle, but he didn't want to feel Blu's wrath again either. He tried to weigh his options, and eventually came up short. He ended up getting out of the Bentley right when Kristian's brake lights came on. When he saw her backing out, he could hear Blu's car moving behind him.

I don't even want to do this shit, he griped as he watched Kristian's car turn the corner. *This isn't even my style.* Jerome closed his eyes for a quick instant, but reopened them, knowing he had to stop stalling. He hurried to his own vehicle and followed Kristian out of the campus.

Meanwhile, Kristian headed downtown. She wasn't looking to go anywhere in particular, but she needed a break from being cooped up in her dorm room. Although she had returned to campus, she didn't bother to attend any of her classes. She had spent most of her time depressed over all of her problems. Now, she needed a break.

Downtown seemed to be the best place to drive since there was plenty to stray her attention. Halfway to the area, she realized that she had been riding around in silence. While her thoughts had kept her occupied, Kristian knew she needed a little background noise. Turning on the radio, she listened as a dark bass line filled the car.

"See nothing in the air but green dollar signs/ they say I can't claim it, but from the looks, its mine/ I love the way it shines/ my ski mask, the next in line/ I steal with cats cryin'/ my eye is set on the diamond"

The song was one of many that the DJ would play that night. Since she didn't find the song particularly catchy, Kristian turned the radio back down. Slowly approaching Middleton Avenue, which was a block away from downtown, Kristian saw the street was fairly empty. She increased her speed until she came to another red light.

Out of nowhere, someone slammed a baseball bat down onto her windshield. A loud, crackling noise sounded in her ears as the glass broke into hundreds of pieces. Automatically, Kristian's foot rose off the brake, allowing the car to slightly roll forward. Then, as if the initial damage wasn't enough, the bat knocked out her driver's side window. The glass pricked her skin, forcing Kristian to slam onto her brakes. Suddenly, a figure appeared beside her as the car came to a complete stop. Kristian could tell from the body type that it was a male. He was dressed in all black with a ski mask covering his face.

Screams ascended from the back of her throat as she watched the person clear the remaining glass out of her window. He then grabbed her seatbelt as she attempted to push him away from her car. In the process, her foot came off the brake, allowing the car to roll forward. Still, her attacker didn't let up. Kristian tried to fight him back, but she knew this was a battle she was going to lose. Then, unexpectedly, the bat connected with her head. She felt the car come to an abrupt stop right before she blacked out.